A WRINKLE AND CRIME

A WRINKLE AND CRIME

ZOMBIE COSMETOLOGIST SEASON ONE

J.D. BLACKROSE

Charlotte, NC
FALSTAFF
BOOKS
WWW.FALSTAFFBOOKS.COM

Cover Design by Natania Barron

Editorial by John G. Hartness & Theresa Glover

For Alison, who always laughs at my jokes.

PLUCK & COVER

1

I couldn't find my penis. I'd last seen it on the nightstand next to my walk-in freezer, but when I emerged in the morning, it wasn't there. I didn't need a penis, but I'd had twenty human years with one, and I'd gotten used to it.

"Mrs. Ross? Are you here? Have you seen my penis?"

"You need a new one, Waylon." Mrs. Betsy Ross' specter floated into my room, holding the missing appendage.

"I know, but they have to be fresh and coming upon a juicy, still-warm body is a tricksy thing. Can you please sew this one back on?"

"You don't urinate or have sexual relations."

I sighed. "Mrs. Ross, it is humiliating enough to ask you to connect my male member to my body, please don't make it worse."

"Fine." She sniffed. "Sit on the couch."

I followed her to the living room, placed my rear on the couch, spread my legs, and closed my eyes while one of history's greatest seamstresses made me whole again. If I could have blushed, I would have reddened from my toes to my ears. As it was, I squirmed until she smacked me on the thigh.

"If you want this sewn on properly, you'll stop your fidgeting."

I held still but stared out the sliding back doors at an Evergreen Pear tree, fists clenched. The tree's beauty distracted me, the white flowers still visible, the bees and birds swooping in and out. I was glad it was thriving in the northern exposure. I had worried it was too far west and would need more early morning sun, but it was doing well.

"There," Mrs. Ross said, rubbing her hands together, bringing me back to the situation at hand. "I'm done, but it looks mighty sad."

"What's looking mighty sad?"

I hadn't heard him come in, but Dr. Samuel Early peered over Mrs. Ross' shoulder, extracted his reading glasses from his shirt pocket, and placed them on his nose.

"It's too gray," he said.

"It's not." I pushed them both away and closed my legs.

"No, wait, let me get a good gander," Early said.

He leaned close, only a few inches from my body, and studied my penis, clucking his tongue. I bit my lower lip and wondered if I should plant another Golden Rain tree in the front yard. They were terrific for shade.

Early tsked. "Shriveled and discolored. Why are you holding on to this?"

I shoved him away, glaring. "You want to give me yours?"

Early pulled up short and sauntered back a few feet, raising his chin to meet my eyes. I was six-foot-five, and Early was all of five-foot-eight. With shoes.

"Certainly not! I'm still using mine."

"Yours is only usable because of me," I reminded him.

He wrinkled his nose. "I know, but you don't mind because I'm useful."

"You're *necessary*. I wouldn't be like this if it weren't for you. You owe me," I said.

"Instead, you'd be dead."

"Exactly!" My breath came out in an exasperated huff.

I'd explained it to him and explained it to him but getting Early to understand why I wanted to die after one-hundred and some odd years was impossible, but then, he didn't look like me. He was a living, warm-blooded, average human with an exceptionally long life. Swallowing zombie flesh once a month will do that to you.

It killed me, pun intended, that I needed him.

I harrumphed and turned to Mrs. Ross. "Mrs. Ross, do we have any clients today?"

"Mitzi."

Early cocked his head, and I noticed he had jowls I hadn't seen before. I guess swallowing Waylon bits didn't stop aging altogether, which was something I hadn't considered. Unaware of my scrutiny, Early's face lit up as he said, "Mitzi? From that TV show and the tabloids Mitzi?"

I nodded. "But remember that I have client/cosmetologist confidentiality. You are forbidden to see her or say anything."

"I can't even see her? She's gorgeous!" His eyes narrowed. "Why does Mitzi need you?"

"She swears by my facials."

Early's eyes opened wide. "You're the reason Mitzi is so hot? Whooo, boy! Good on ya."

"Stop talking, Early. It's not doing you any favors."

"Can't I meet her? I'll never tell."

"No. Mrs. Ross, when is she coming?"

"Twenty minutes." Mrs. Ross fanned her face with her hand, a habit she'd maintained since her death. It meant she wanted to say something.

"What is it?" I asked.

"You need to get dressed."

"Of course. Anything else I need to know for today?" I turned and was heading to my bedroom. Her delicate cough made me look back.

"What?"

She pulled a notepad and pen from somewhere I couldn't see and checked a list. "Captain Perkins, from the Los Angeles Sheriff's office, wants to see you. He's the head of the Malibu/Lost Hills station."

I stopped short. "Why?"

"He didn't say."

"Did you ask?"

"What do I look like, your secretary?"

I breathed to a count of five. "Actually, yes, Mrs. Ross. Because, in fact, you are my secretary. Asking why someone wants to see your boss is part of what secretaries do."

She shrugged. "Fine. Then I want to be an executive assistant."

"Oh. My. God." I left the room for my bedroom, pulled on boxers, dark dress slacks, a long-sleeved blue Oxford shirt, and knotted a darker blue tie. I couldn't do anything about my hair, which was a golden blonde and flopped into my eyes, as it always would. Even if I cut it, it grew overnight. No one could explain it, but metaphysics and magic didn't follow predictable rules.

I did my make-up. The scars would never fade, but I found that hiding them made it easier for the living to look at me. The dead didn't seem to mind.

I'd gotten my cosmetology license and studied special effects make-up with some of the top Hollywood artists. I had a long list of clients who didn't believe I was a zombie but did believe that I could hide any imperfection. In California, I wasn't a zombie. I was an eccentric marketing genius. Like the business cards said, "Zombie Cosmetology: No Scar Too Hard. Calabasas, CA." I wondered if the captain needed a peel. It would be a good idea, given how much he was in the sun.

While I covered my skin, I left my eyes alone. They were a normal chocolate brown with blond lashes and looked normal, which was a saving grace because they helped me pass as human.

I pulled on soft tan gloves so thin and flexible that I could still tie my dress shoes. I walked to my procedure room and donned by a white lab coat that hung on the back of the door. As I gathered my instruments, I called out for my secretary, err…executive assistant.

"Mrs. Ross. What time is Captain Perkins coming?"

"An hour after Mitzi," she called back. I caught sight of her floating in the hallway.

"Are you filing your nails?"

She gazed at me, one hip at an angle, pausing mid-air with her emery board. "Yes, what of it?"

"Your nails don't grow."

"Neither does your penis."

The doorbell rang. "Just get the door, please. And make sure your feet touch the ground. Mitzi doesn't believe in ghosts."

Mitzi, one name only, was a celebrity from two successful television shows, the first one a reality show and the second an honest-to-God acting job. Her role called for her to look amazing at all times, which was fine because she was a natural beauty. Or, at least, I made her look that way. She'd had acne as a teenager, and we needed to do touch-ups and treatments now and then. That's what I thought we would be doing today.

Until I saw her and my natural finesse took over. I tripped on my own two feet rushing to get to her and smashed my forehead on the door's upper molding.

I rubbed my forehead, although it didn't hurt, because that's what normal people did. "Mitzi, what's going on? What's with the humongous sunglasses? Are they Prada, by the way?"

Mitzi's lush dark hair swung down to cover her green eyes, and she held her designer glasses on with one hand.

"Mitzi?"

"It's nothing."

"What's nothing?"

"Promise you won't tell?"

"Mitzi, we have a confidentiality agreement."

She took a deep breath and removed her glasses.

My client's face was a mass of bruises, including a real shiner on her left eye.

"Sweetheart, were you in an accident?" I asked while reaching out with both arms to pull her into my examination chair. I settled her in and pulled my light and a magnifying mirror closer to her face.

Her eyes welled with tears, and a tiny snot bubble dripped from her nose, belying the glitz and glamour of Hollywood life. Forget putting our pants on one foot at a time. We all ugly cried when things got rough.

"I annoyed Jason when I didn't make our dinner reservations on time. By the time I met him, he'd consumed a bottle of merlot by himself, canceled our table, shoved me into a car and took me home. I apologized, but he went on and on about how I'd embarrassed him in front of the maître d'. He's right, I should have called, but I was working. Things ran late on set."

I put a cooling mask on her face to bring the swelling down and retrieved cold tea bags I kept in the freezer for her eyes. My hands were steady, but my mind was racing. My voice low and calm, I said, "Jason hit you?"

"Like I said, I was late."

"That is irrelevant. Jason Teague, star of *The Marvelous Five,* the top superhero movie of this past summer, a man so muscled that his muscles have muscles, used that strength to beat you up?"

"I should have called."

"Mitzi," I said, massaging her temples. "He had no right to hit you."

"He lost his temper, it's true, but it was my fault."

"No. It. Wasn't."

A creak at the door told me someone was looking in, and I was betting by the intake of breath that Early was sneaking a peek at the gorgeous TV star despite my warning him off because he was just that kind of asshole.

His breath turned into a controlled exhale and a deep rumble of controlled anger, and my annoyance lessened somewhat. He had a lot of faults, one being that he was a former southern Civil War doctor that experimented on dying men to turn them into zombies, but on the other hand, his southern sensibility meant he had an old-school sense of propriety around women. It may be antiquated today, but for Early, this violence would be an anathema punishable by hanging. Mitzi was so absorbed in her own worries that she didn't hear him.

"No judgments, please, Waylon. I need to be at the studio in an hour. Can you cover this mess?"

"Sure, Mitzi. You'll look great." The bruises required a mixture of yellow, green, and peach concealers to neutralize the florid colors, followed by a full-coverage foundation applied in layers with a special feather-light brush. I gave her a strong winged eyeliner and three coats of mascara to bring attention to her eyes and went with a light lip gloss. She had naturally dramatic eyebrows, so they only required a bit of shaping. Adding a touch of shimmer on the top of her cheekbones finished the look.

By the time I finished, you couldn't see a thing. "Will the make-up artist at the studio be okay with another professional doing your face?" I asked.

"I'll handle her, don't you worry. You're the best, Waylon." She threw her arms around me and gave me a warm hug that made me wish, again, that I could have a girlfriend.

"Don't let him do this to you again, Mitzi. Call for help. Call me if you need me, anytime. Go to the police. This is assault."

"It's just the one time." She gave me a wink, but there was sadness behind her eyes. As she reached for the knob, the door swung open.

"Oh, Waylon, I'm sorry. I didn't know you had a client." Early stared at Mitzi. "Oh, Mitzi! I love your show. You look beautiful as ever." He leaned close, speaking in a conspiratorial whisper. "Did my friend Waylon treat you right?"

"Oh, yes. He's magic."

Early nodded and held out his hand. "That he is. My name is Dr. Samuel Early. I sometimes consult for Waylon."

"Oh, you're a dermatologist?"

"I'm a specialist, yes."

"That's terrific. I've got to go. Nice to meet you, Dr. Early."

"Let me escort you to your car." Early held out his elbow and she took it, giggling.

"Such a gentleman."

Early led her from the room, shooting me a look over his shoulder as he did so. I acknowledged with a sharp nod. Early would keep an eye on her and, if I were a betting man, would locate one Jason Teague.

The thought was a little unsettling.

2

Captain Perkins knows you're a ghost, but it's not nice to rub his face in it. Concentrate and make yourself solid."

Mrs. Ross fluttered her eyelashes. "I'd like it if he rubbed his face in certain places."

"Mrs. Ross! Not appropriate."

"He's a fine-looking man, Waylon Jenkins, and all I have to do is wait another forty years or so to get a crack at him."

"Ugh. Don't say such things. It makes me want to stick my hands in my ears and la, la, la my way out of here. When he's dead, you do you, but for now, keep it clean, please."

"You are the most boring zombie I know."

"You don't know any other zombies!"

"Doesn't make my statement any less true."

"Just get the door."

Mrs. Ross cooed at Captain Jacob Perkins, the leader of the local constabulary and human as they come, but a man aware of the supernatural. I didn't know his history with the paranormal in detail, but we'd met a time or two, and I'd confided what I was. It didn't mean he liked me, and for him to pay a house call portended bad news. I wondered what brought the lawman out to see me.

"Captain. Welcome to my office." I proffered my hand.

The captain's eyes were cold, and he looked at my outstretched arm like it was a dead fish.

"Tell me, Mr. Jenkins," he said, sitting down while taking his hat off his head. "Are you eating well these days? Feeling a little peckish now and then? Going out for a bite?"

I sat, wary. "Captain, what are you talking about?"

"Don't you zombies eat human flesh?"

"No, those are orcs. Zombies eat nothing. Where's this going?"

The captain slapped his hat on his leg. "I've got bodies, Mr. Jenkins. Three of them."

"Homicides?"

"Every damn one."

"I'm sorry to hear that, but why come to me?"

The captain leaned in, his blue eyes sharp and furious. "Because, Mr. Jenkins, every time I get to one, it's missing body parts."

"Animals?"

"No, not animals. Our murderer did it with a sharp instrument, like a--" He hesitated, his lip curled.

"A what?" Now it was my turn to lean in.

"A chef's knife."

"Unlikely," I said, sitting back in my chair and steepling my fingers.

"Sounds paranormal to me."

"I don't know about that. Humans do pretty weird stuff too."

"Waylon, let's put this in a straightforward manner. I'm taking you to the Coroner's office to examine these bodies. This is woo-woo stuff, and you are the only–ah, person–I know who has an eye on the paranormal."

"I'm a cosmetologist! I don't do murders."

"Consider yourself drafted. In the meantime, tell me about your relationship with Jimmy Ricci."

"Jimmy the Duck? Absolutely nothing. He's a scumbag, but I know that from the news, not by personal association."

"You can prove that?"

"Prove that I don't know him? No one can prove a negative, captain."

"But if I look through his bank accounts, follow his cash flow, I won't come to you?"

"If he lets you look through them, you won't find a trail to me."

"He'll let me alright."

"How? Caught him red-handed with a chef's knife?"

"Naw. He's dead. He's the last of the three bodies I was telling you about."

"Somebody whacked Jimmy the Duck?"

"Someone killed him. No one says 'whacked' anymore."

"Still, it takes nerve to do that, right? His dad is probably out for blood."

Perkins waggled his hands in a so-so motion. "His father is shook up. It's his mother that worries me. Rita has a mean streak."

I studied him. "Rita? First name basis? You know her?"

"Went to the same high school. I didn't know she would marry such a putz."

I cringed. "Language, Captain."

"Fuck you. I've got three dead bodies with missing parts, and you're the only guy I know who could use them. I still like you for it, but even if you didn't do it, you are the only one who can shed light on who might have. So giddyap."

I sighed and stood, my frame dwarfing the lawman, even though he was a former football player and not too small.

"Lead on, Captain. Let's go see who carved up the Duck."

3

All manner of things resided in the coroner's office. Random objects rested on shelves, languished in boxes, and teetered on tabletops. Doctor Sorya Sang, who was a tiny Cambodian lady, scooted around her small, cramped office like she didn't see the clutter. In fact, she buzzed like a bee on espresso, and I blinked multiple times to make sure she wasn't winking in and out of existence.

"Sit, sit," she said, sweeping a pile of papers off of two chairs onto the ground and then kicking them to the side to reveal a few inches of carpet for our feet. "You want to see the three slasher victims, right?"

"Slasher?" I asked, lowering myself into a chair and wishing it didn't have armrests. Armrests were tough on large people.

"Cut up, cut off, cut open. Slashed, sliced, and severed. Cleaved, divided, and hacked. Call it what you will, someone took a sharp edge to those bodies and divided them into parts."

"There must have been a lot of blood," I said.

"Some. I'm estimating the butcher did the deed within 24 hours of death but not immediately."

I said, holding up a hand. "Are you saying the severing instrument, whatever it was, wasn't the murder weapon?"

"That's correct. Something else killed them. I'm waiting for toxicology to come back with the report, but I suspect poison."

"You can't tell what kind of poison?"

"No immediate odor or changes in skin color. The only thing I noticed is *rigor mortis* set in sooner than I would have thought, but again, my time estimates on death might be skewed since each body was outside, and no one has come forward to verify time of death."

I mulled this, ignoring how Captain Perkins watched me like a hawk, judging my every word and move. I was about to ask another question when Dr. Sang jumped to her feet.

"Let's go check these chunky monkeys out."

Following her out, I whispered, "Does she always talk this way?"

Captain Perkins wrinkled his nose. "What way?"

"You know, disrespectful of the dead and rapid-fire."

"She's disrespectful?"

I wasn't sure what to say to that. If you were around dead bodies all the time, you might get immune, but being a dead body hadn't done that to me yet.

The cadaver room was as opposite of the doctor's office as could be. Cold and sterile, painted light blue, almost gray, the room contained one wall of stacked stainless-steel boxes with handles. There were also three rolling stainless-steel tables, a stainless-steel countertop with a sink and various plastic-packed instruments, a closet, plus single-use gloves in multiple sizes, some purple, some not.

"I'm not allergic to latex," Dr. Sang said, noticing my inspection of the different colored gloves, "but other people are, and I maintain a stock of various sizes. Here," she said, handing us both protective coverings and masks. "Gown up."

We donned the gear, including face masks, and she opened three drawers, extracting long trays holding bodies. Captain Perkins recoiled at the smell, but it didn't bother me.

She lifted the covering on one of them. "This is Jimmy Ricci. No gunshot wounds, as we might usually see from a member of this family. But if you look below, you'll see something interesting."

She pulled the cover down all the way and it was immediately evident. Jimmy's leg was severed at the thigh. Not gnawed off but cut clean.

"This wasn't a knife," I said, leaning in closer to see the wound. I'd had some experience removing limbs from bodies. A lot of experience, actually, given that I needed new parts regularly, but I was big and strong. Taking a leg off with a knife was hard for any living person. I wasn't sure it was possible.

I continued. "No knife took that leg off, at least not by itself. You'd need a saw."

"Oh, really?" Captain Perkins gave me a look.

"Or so I believe, Captain," I said. "You know my tenant, Dr. Early?"

"Don't know him personally but know of him. He works for that Industries outfit, right? That military organization?"

"They're private but yes, run on military contracts. They research advanced wound treatment and prosthetics. He's taught me a thing or two."

"I'm surprised you are handling this so well, Mr. Jenkins," said Dr. Sang. "You don't seem bothered by the corpses or the odor."

"I just have a terrible sense of smell, Doctor," I replied. "Show me the other two bodies."

"This here is one Hugh O'Connell, a small-time bookie. How he got killed and chopped up, I do not know," said Perkins, as Dr. Sang pulled up the covering so I could get a good look. This one was missing both legs at the knee.

The third was a computer systems hacker of some kind who was missing one whole leg and the other foot.

"All criminals?" I asked.

"All bad guys doing bad things, yes."

"So, our killer has a conscience?"

"I don't know about that. These guys were shady, so maybe they just ran into our murderer through the course of business or whatnot," replied the captain. "Not that it matters. I'm not sad to see these men go, but they shouldn't die at the hands of yet another low-life who gets his jollies taking body parts."

"Not just any body parts, Captain. Our murderer is a leg man."

The captain snorted. "No breasts to be taken."

"Exactly. The victims are all male."

"Right. So, what are we looking at here?"'

Dr. Sang slid the bodies back and motioned for us to strip off our gear. Once finished, we followed her to her office.

She plopped into her chair, curling up crisscross applesauce. "Okay, Zombie, what's up with the bodies? Who wants men's legs? Shapeshifters? Sasquatches? Wendigos?"

I stared at her.

"Did you tell her, Captain?"

"I said nothing."

Sang waved her hand in the air. "I see everything, Mr. Jenkins, and I do mean everything. I've autopsied things that weren't human. You've done a good makeup job, but I'm betting you've got scars underneath, and you're wearing gloves when it's warm out. Besides, who hasn't heard of the Zombie Cosmetologist, The Secret of the Stars?"

I groaned. "I hate that TV show." A year ago, this entertainment program called *Celebrities Tonight,* had cornered me after learning about my A-list clientele. I hadn't given an interview, but they ran a segment anyway.

"Everyone thinks you're unconventional, an oddball, but nothing more. I took one look at you and knew the truth. Now, what gives, Mr. Jenkins? Who's killing our criminals?"

"I don't know."

"Not good enough, Jenkins," said Perkins, giving me a hard cop stare.

"Well, geez, Captain, so sorry, but I'm a cosmetologist, not a detective. I looked at the bodies, and I can tell you only one thing. The weapon that removed those legs wasn't a simple kitchen knife."

"I agree with that assessment, Perkins," said Dr. Sang. "I use a Mopec 5000 autopsy saw. I mean, think about it. It's hard enough to cut through a chicken joint with a chef's knife."

The captain, who'd probably never made anything more complicated than a scrambled egg, stared at her blankly. "Okay, fine. We've got some kind of poison plus a big saw."

I clapped and stood. "Great, glad we had this talk, now, if you'll excuse me, I've got clients to see this afternoon."

"I do not excuse you, Waylon. You're going to be my partner in this investigation until we figure out who or what is poisoning their victims and cutting off their lower limbs."

"Why?"

"Because I'm lonesome, ornery, and mean. Besides, that way I can keep an eye on you, and if nothing else happens while I keep you busy, I'll have a good reason to think you're my perp."

Now I was in the weird spot of hoping something else did happen. What kind of person wishes death on another?

Someone who couldn't die themselves and was looking for a way out.

4

The first thing we're gonna do," said Perkins, holding one finger in the air, "is talk to your friend, Early. You raised a good point about him knowing stuff from his work at The Industries, and having a chat with him might do our investigation a world of good."

"He's a tenant, not a friend. We have a professional relationship."

"You say potato; I say pa-TAH-to."

"I'm not sure he's at work right now, Captain," I said, looking at my feet. *He might be tailing a starlet to identify the residence of her abusive boyfriend.*

"You have a cell phone, don't you?"

"Right. I'll text him."

I didn't like my mobile phone because my thumbs were too big for the touchscreen, and I didn't always catch the typos before hitting send, which led to some embarrassing scenarios.

Me: Hi. Where are you hip?

Me Again: You? Where are you now?

Early: Why?

Me: Captn wants to talk with you.

Early: Captain?

Me: Captain Perlins.

Me: Perkins.

Early: Why does Captain Perkins want to talk to me?

Me: There have been murdoos. Tree of them. Missing purts.

Early: Three murders? Each of them missing parts?

Me: Yes.

Early: I can't talk to him.

Me: Why?

Early: I'm busy.

Me: Wjat you wnat me to tell him?

Early: Make an appointment.

Me: He ill. He's got to do his dilly dally,

Early: What?

Me. Argh! He will, He;s got to due his due diligence.

Early: Understood.

Me: How's MItzi

Early: Fine. I found Jason.

Me: hows he?

Early: talk to you later.

Me: Donut kill him.

Early: Why? I'll just bring him back to life later.

Me: EARLY!

Early: You worry too much.

I turned to Perkins, smiling. "He'll be happy to talk to you. He asked that you make an appointment."

"I hoped to talk to him now."

"Sorry. He says he's busy now, but call the company. I'm sure they can fit you in."

"Doesn't he live with you?" Perkins beeped the car door open, and I slid in. I'd already moved the seat as far back as it could go.

"He rents the cottage house on the back of the property."

"I'll wait for him at your house."

"He has his own entrance and driveway. I do not monitor his comings and goings. Captain, I have clients to attend. Call Early's office like he asked."

"I'll make an appointment for tomorrow. I'll text you. Give me your personal number."

"No."

"Fine, I'll call that lovely Mrs. Ross and let her know when I'll pick you up."

"Why do I have to go?"

Perkins put the car in reverse, backed out, and eased onto the highway. "'Cause you're my ace in the hole, Waylon. Hard to lie in front of a friend."

"He's not my friend, but Early has no reason to lie. Remember, he's an expert in wound treatment and prosthetics, not a mad doctor."

I crossed my finger when I said that.

"Uhm hummm. That he is. Wait for my call, Waylon." The captain dropped me off at my home and sped away.

I texted Early. *What do u know?*

No response.

Mrs. Ross yelled out the door. "Waylon, why are you waiting outside in the sun? You just got another appointment. Come on in and get yourself ready."

She was right about the sun exposure. It made dead skin char like kindling in a campfire. I needed to take my own advice and wear sunscreen and a hat.

My next appointment was a B-movie actress with big plans. She needed a sinus drain massage and a major mustache waxing.

"It's the Italian genes," said my dark-haired beauty as she leaned her head back, making it easier for me to use my fingertips to rub in small circles on the sides of her nose. "I was almost tempted to shave it off the other day."

I gave her my sternest look. "You know better. That's just asking the hair to come back darker and fuller."

She sighed under my touch. "I know, Waylon. That's why I made an emergency appointment. I'm auditioning tomorrow for that new Jason Teague movie." Her eyes sparkled. "I know I'm right for this part. The femme fatale is Greek. That's practically Italian."

"It is, you know. There is a tremendous shared history."

"Really? Whatever. I just meant they are close to each other on the map." She opened her eyes wide. "They are, aren't they? Close together?"

"Yes, they are. You are completely correct," I soothed. I switched topics. "What do you know about Jason Teague?"

"Jason is a big-shot and the 'it' guy right now. Think a younger Tom Cruise without the Ron Hubbard. I've only met him twice."

"Ever seen him with Mitzi?"

"On the red carpet? Of course. They look beautiful together." Her voice was soft and far away, and I knew she was falling asleep under my ministrations.

I had the solution for that. "Wake up, princess, the hot wax is going on."

Five seconds later, believe you me that she was wide awake.

"Don't rub it, darling. It will calm down. Let me put some cream on it."

"What's in that magic cream, Waylon? It's amazing."

"Shhh…secret recipe." It had zombie skin cells in it. When I replaced a body part, I froze the old one and scraped a bit into my cream formula. The rose water made it smell good, but the zombie particles were the key to the regeneration properties.

Not FDA approved.

"You could sell it. I know people if you want me to hook you up with financing."

"No, I'm good, but thanks." I handed her a bottle of water. "Now, stay hydrated and knock 'em dead tomorrow."

She kissed me on the cheek. "Your skin is so cold, Waylon. Maybe you should get out in the sun more."

As she left, a new swing in her sashay, she got me thinking about the magic of zombie regeneration. I needed a fresh body to replace a part, and that had to happen on a semi-regular basis because my parts tended to disintegrate. Once I attached a limb to my body, it would "take" and become a part of my body until I needed a new one.

The funny thing was that once I removed that worn-out part, it retained its zombie nature, so much so that I could use a little in my skin products.

The original procedure used by Early all those years ago in the woods at Shiloh had been archaic but lasting.

I couldn't help but wonder what advances The Industries had made.

5

The lock turned with a clank and a swear word from Early as he dropped whatever he was carrying. I didn't get up to help him.

He flicked on the light and jumped back, his arms so full of groceries that he used his foot to push in his fallen bag. It was a paratrooper's heavy-duty canvas messenger bag, and he loved the thing. It wasn't a yuppie reproduction bought online, either. He'd grabbed this one off a body at some point, but I never asked for details.

"What the hell are you doing here?" he asked. He kept his voice just below a snarl.

"I wanted to have a chat with you before Captain Perkins does."

He walked to the kitchen, open to the main living area, and placed his groceries on the counter, then walked back to the door to get his bag and put that on a side table. He didn't look at me while he grabbed a tumbler and a bottle of whiskey, then poured three fingers. He gulped it down in one go, poured himself another, and finally sat in the rocking chair in front of me. I took up the whole loveseat on my own.

"The Industries had an escapee," he said.

That caught my attention.

"What kind of escapee?"

"The zombie kind."

I clapped my hands together to keep from taking his head off. "They're still making them? New ones, I mean?"

"Yeah."

"I thought they'd stopped. You told me they'd stopped."

Early was quiet and sat there, sipping his drink. I heard the curtains flutter.

He shifted in his seat. "They told me they did, but there was a team I didn't know about that had a secret contract and continued."

"More war-time fodder?"

Early sipped again and nodded, eyes down.

"Early, how could you let this happen?"

Now he did snarl. "I didn't *let* it happen! They did it on the sly. I continued my research into ending zombie lives while they were still making new ones, and I didn't know. I. Didn't. Know."

Ah. Now I knew what was bothering him. I sat back and crossed my arms. "You've lost control of the outfit."

"If I ever had it, but at least at one time I sat at the executive table and knew all the teams."

"Who's running the outfit?"

"New guy, only been there nine months. A Brit named Quint Addington. Could his name be any more pretentious?"

"Probably not."

"My point. He's a prick. A well-connected prick, and I must grudgingly admit he's brought in additional funding and gotten rid of some dead weight—"

"Dead weight? Bodies?"

"No, you dumbass, catch up with modern slang. I meant scientists and doctors who were nonperformers."

"Ah. How does he feel about you? Given that he didn't tell you about the zombie team?"

"It may mean nothing." He tapped his hand on his knee.

"Have you produced any papers lately? Brought in any grants?"

Early jumped to his feet and took the empty glass to the kitchen. "I fail to see what that has to do with anything. I'm working on a singular project."

I kept my voice mild. "Just wondering what Addington's definition of 'dead weight' is."

I knew I'd hit a soft spot when Early turned his back to me.

My needling him was necessary because his research was the only chance I had of dying for real. He couldn't get fired, or my chances were over. He couched his research in terms that made it palatable to funding committees, but basically, he was searching for a way to kill me.

On my request.

"How many active zombies in the military today, Early?"

"I would have said ten, but now I don't know."

"Any of them asked to die?"

He didn't answer.

I stood and faced his back. "Early?"

"I think so."

"So they decided to make more."

Early whirled on me. "They feel that it is better to use zombies than living humans because zombies don't feel pain."

"Yeah, we just get up, get stitched back together, and they throw us out there to do it again. We have personalities, Early. Our minds. Our hearts. It's traumatic to be torn to pieces and remade."

"I *know* that, but they don't care. If they can keep sewing you guys up and sending you out, no blood, no pain, and no family to notify, they're going to keep doing it. The government likes the reduction in casualty numbers since you can't count zombies twice."

"Bastards. Tell me about the escapee."

Early grabbed two slices of bread and a jar of peanut butter and made himself a sandwich.

God, I wished I could eat. I'd almost forgotten how good food tasted, but I could still smell it and, though I know it didn't happen, I imagined my stomach rumbling in response. I wanted to enjoy a glass of wine. Taste fresh corn on the cob. Feed a strawberry to a pretty girl.

I would never, ever have those things.

Early swallowed a bite and retook his seat. "The zombie is about five-foot-eleven with brown hair and eyes. He died in Iraq with no known family, even after an extensive search. He used to have a sister, but she died in a car crash."

"What's his name?"

"Living, his name was Edward Sampson. Went by Eddie. I think they..." He trailed off.

"What?" My voice was more urgent. I knew I wasn't going to like what Early was about to say.

"Zombies are given numbers, not names."

"But they are still feeling, thinking beings!"

"Maybe they found a way to inhibit the personality." Early had the decency to look at least a little bit miserable.

I paced the floor, which only took three steps one way and three back, but I had to burn off my anger.

"Fine, so let's accept that they are creating mindless cannon fodder out of dead soldiers, why did Eddie run for it?"

Betsy Ross popped through the door. Early dropped his sandwich, glared at her, and went to make a new one.

She ignored him. "Maybe they need some to be creative thinkers to lead the other zombies. I mean, what's the point if they can't make decisions on the ground?"

I pointed at her. "You're right. They still need leaders. Early, we need to find Eddie."

"Do you think he has anything to do with the murders?" He slapped jelly on his bread this time.

"He may not have anything to do with them whatsoever. Why would he kill people? Kill criminals? It makes no sense. If I were him, I'd want to get as far away as possible, not make a scene murdering random crooks."

"So, why do you want to find him?"

I stared at Early long enough that he blinked. Mrs. Ross floated beside me, giving him her best ghost glare. "Because he may need help."

"Right. Of course. I just meant that maybe he is better off alone, staying hidden, traveling out of town, and forging his own path."

"With no money and no friends? I don't think so."

Mrs. Ross nodded. "He'll want a place to sleep. You guys still need rest, even if not as much as a living person, and you prefer the cold."

"I agree. He'd want a place that gets him out of the sun, where people aren't likely to stumble on him, but not so far out that he can't get a glimpse of civilization. If I were in his shoes, I'd be lonely. Seeing people, even if he can't interact with them, would make him feel a little less isolated."

"He'll need something new to wear," Mrs. Ross said. "Army clothes will stand out."

It hit me like a hammer. "What if they didn't? What if he chose a place where his strange looks might be assumed to be something else?"

Early snapped his fingers at the same time Mrs. Ross' eyes lit up. They spoke simultaneously.

"Paramount Ranch."

6

The drive to Paramount Ranch was awfully quiet, Early and I each meditating on our thoughts. The park was nestled in the beautiful Santa Monica Mountains, part of the National Park System, and had gorgeous hiking and horse paths. The Ranch was originally leased by Paramount Pictures in 1923 and had since served as a "western town" set for major motion pictures and television shows. It was a popular tourist attraction since visitors could swagger through the cowboy town with its bathhouse, saloon, and old-timey bank. We walked over the rickety bridge to traipse the dirt streets with the tourists and their dogs, kids, and strollers.

Two men stood back-to-back in front of the main building, pretending to have a duel, and a woman posed for a photo in front of the Mud Bug Hotel. You couldn't go in the buildings, but walking around made you feel like you were in the Wild, Wild West, panning for gold or searching for that small piece of land to call your own.

One area was roped off because of a movie currently filming there, although no one was on set today. As luck would have it, the movie was *Zombie Cowboys from Space*, which seemed ideal for Eddie and had motivated our visit. One Stetson, a pair of low hung jeans and a bandana and Eddie could blend easily and make scale while doing it. If he camped in the mountains at night, no one would find him.

Of course, he could be long gone by now. I'd been looking for Jesus everywhere and never found him. I'd searched hard, too, far and wide, because I had questions. I'd even taken out a full-page ad in several newspapers, both in the US and abroad. The headline read, "Come to me, Jesus." I got well-meaning messages from pastors and ministers and church ladies telling me that I had it backward, that Jesus doesn't come to me, that I had to go to Jesus. I told them I would if I knew where, but they just said, "Go to church," and that didn't work. I'd already searched churches of every denomination.

Point being, it was a big world, and one resurrected man could stay hidden if he chose.

Early and I wandered for an hour, taking our time, and then met in the center of town. I was less certain than I had been that this was the right place, but Early seemed confident.

"How do you think we handle this?" I asked.

"We wait here and let him come to us."

I almost told him about Jesus but decided not to.

"How do we attract him?" I asked.

"Do you have make-up remover in the car?"

I drew myself up, offended. "Do *I* have make-up remover in the car? I have my whole kit. You never know."

"You never know when there's going to be a make-up emergency?" His voice couldn't have been drier.

"Hey! It's Los Angeles; stranger things have happened. A month ago, I rescued a bride on her wedding day when it rained. No one plans for rain in L.A., but I happened to be nearby and fixed her face."

"You're a hero." Early picked a long piece of grass from the edge of a trailhead and tucked it between his teeth.

I let him chew on it for a good thirty seconds and then said, "You know, they allow dogs in this park."

He spat it out.

"Maybe we should leave a message," I said. "If I were him, I'd want to know what we want, and to make sure we're not The Industries coming back for him."

"That's precisely what we are going to do. Go take off your face."

I jumped back a few feet. "I beg your pardon?" He couldn't mean that.

"I meant take off your make-up, you twit. Use that makeup remover you're so proud of in your car and show your scars. He'll recognize you as a zombie."

"So? He won't know who I am. He'll think I'm part of a well-laid trap."

"You are part of a well-laid trap. Our trap."

"We aren't trapping him! We want to help him."

"All the same. We want to get in arm's reach."

I marched to the car, relieved to see that most people were leaving the area. I didn't want to scare anyone. I grabbed a bunch of cotton squares and my micellar makeup remover. (I use the drug store brand. The French brand is too expensive for no good reason.) A few minutes of gentle wiping—don't rub, people—and my skin was *au naturale*.

It wasn't pretty. Scars ran vertically from my ears down the entire length of my throat and diagonally from my temple, across my cheeks to my nose. They weren't equally spaced, so one side's stitches were higher than the others, and my skin tone was noticeably green, like a light puce, the color living humans turned when ill with food poisoning. My nose was sewn on by itself, having been replaced several times and repaired with careful stitches from Mrs. Ross. All in all, I looked like a monster.

I sat in the car, staring at my face in the rearview mirror, not enjoying what I was seeing and terrified to open the door and show my face in public. A young family was getting into the car next to me, and I turned my head away, holding a cotton square up like it could shield me.

Tap. Tap.

A little girl peered at me through the window.

"Are you putting on your makeup for the movie?" She bopped up and down like she had to pee.

"I'm so sorry, mister," said her father, grabbing the girl under her arms and swinging her into her car seat in the back. "She's super nosy." He grinned while he said that, clearly charmed by his outgoing child.

"It's not a problem," I said. "Yes, tell her not every monster is a bad one."

"Oh! I know that!" yelled the little girl, leaning forward so far that she strained the belt on her chair. "I watch cartoons! And *Sesame Street*! And my favorite movie is *Monsters, Inc.*"

The dad blushed and closed the door. "I like old movies."

"I do, too. She's sweet. I'm glad the special effects makeup didn't scare her."

"Naw, she's tough. Have a good day."

"You, too."

They drove off, and I felt a bit better. Maybe if I pretended I was an actor, I could do this.

I exited the car, shoulders back, and brought my makeup kit with me.

It rolled along, wobbling on some rocks here and there, but instead of fear, I got swarmed by the remaining families.

"Can I have your autograph?"

"Are you someone I should know?

"I thought they weren't shooting today."

Early strolled over. "Easy, folks, easy. We're just doing some test shots in the late afternoon light. No actual filming today. Thanks for your enthusiasm, though."

A few stragglers stared at me, but Early kept up his prattle and took out his iPhone like he was taking some photos or emailing important people, which set them at ease. Meanwhile, I carried my kit to the edge of the town and looked toward the Coyote Canyon Trail, then slowly made my way up the historic racetrack toward the Hacienda Trail and Marco Polo Hill. I completed the circle by tromping south, walking the Medea Trail, and hiking to the Western Town Overlook. If Eddie was out there, he'd have seen me.

Early followed me on this journey, giving me directions to turn this way and that, holding up his hands like he was checking camera angles. All-in-all we mugged it up for the onlookers who eventually got tired of his act and my face because they all wandered away, leaving us with a darkening sky and no zombie.

We decided to wait at the "Sheriff's Office" and see if Eddie would show up. By this time, I decided we'd wasted our afternoon, but Early was still optimistic.

While we hung around, leaning on a hitching rail, I pondered the possibility of getting a dog, something I'd considered many times, but hadn't done yet out of fear the dog might be scared by my appearance or disturbed by my smell, which wasn't the same as a warm-blooded human's. My skin was cold, and my scent more like a cadaver's. I stayed away from dogs on purpose, but the dream of a constant companion never left. I'd have to stick to trees and plants, though, given the circumstances. They didn't judge. The point being my mind was occupied when a voice rang out.

"Why are you looking for me? I'm not going back."

Early popped to his feet and turned in a slow circle, showing his empty hands. I copied him, my arms outstretched.

"We aren't here to capture you or take you back. We just want to talk to you."

"Why? Who are you?"

"My name is Samuel Early, and I'm a doctor. This is Waylon Jenkins, and as you can see, he's like you, except he isn't part of The Industries. He lives free."

"Jenkins, is this true?" The voice was a little closer.

"It is," I responded, raising my voice so it would carry. "I'm a makeup artist."

"No shit? You can't feel pain or bleed or die, and you spend your time smoothing out women's complexions?"

I crossed my arms now, a little grumpy at this zombie's attitude. "I learned special effects makeup so I could cover my scars and pass as human, and I need to support myself. I have a house and a career, and you're hiding in the mountains, so don't be so condescending."

"I didn't mean it like that," said Eddie, his voice contrite. "I'm probably a little jealous."

"Why don't you come down here, and we'll talk about it?"

"No offense, but I'm not in a trusting mood."

"Understood. Can I ask you another question?" I was taking a chance, but I had to know.

"I guess."

"There've been three dead bodies that have come to the police's attention. Each missing lower limbs. You know anything about that?"

Crickets. Literally.

"Eddie?"

Early tried. "Eddie, we aren't saying you killed the men. We just want to know if you have information."

I pulled a business card from my kit and stuck it into the corner of the Sheriff's Office window. "This is for you, Eddie. If you get access to a phone or something, check me out. You'll see I'm telling the truth. We'll be back tomorrow. Hoping you want to talk then."

Early and I walked back to the car and drove off. I took one last look behind me and saw a flash of light from someone hiking the Medea Trail. Guess our Eddie had stuck around and listened. Maybe he'd show tomorrow, maybe not. We'd have to wait and see.

7

My penis disintegrated in the shower that evening. I loved the feeling of hot water sluicing down my back, but I didn't appreciate the plopping noise the offending member made when it hit the tile, nor the look of it when I picked it up, and it oozed between my fingers.

I needed a new one, but that meant finding a fresh body or getting Early to procure one from The Industries, even if I despised them for the zombie program resurgence. I knew they used cadavers for experiments and training, and that they applied the learnings from prior zombie programs to both dead and living tissue for wound and prosthetic procedures, but making new zombies from scratch? That was something they had supposedly given up.

Eddie was proof they hadn't.

Until I knew more about what they were doing and Early's status there, I didn't want to get anything from The Industries. I was going to have to live without a penis for a while, which made me sad. I was already less of a man than I wanted to be, and now I'd been diminished further. I was a zombie eunuch. How depressing was that?

Mitzi arrived the next morning dressed in an adorable floral sleeveless summer dress with red kitten heel sandals.

"Darling, you look wonderful," I said as I hung her bag on the back of the door and helped her into my chair. "Love the flirty hem."

"Thanks, Waylon," she said, leaning back and taking off her sunglasses. "How am I doing?"

"Much better," I replied. "Your bruises are almost gone. We'll get some foundation and cover-up on there, and you'll be good to go for set in no time."

I placed more cold compresses on her skin while I gathered the base, color Fair in number three, as well as the matching concealer, plus a cream blush, a standard of mine that I used on practically everyone. The color was divine, and the tiny milled gold flecks added a lovely glow to all complexions.

I took a breath and dove into the more pressing questions. "While we have this moment together, Mitzi, have you kicked Jason to the curb?"

"You know, I didn't have to. He was so apologetic the next day and has been so charming and thoughtful ever since. I think he turned a corner. I don't know what changed, but he's been a total gentleman lately."

I knew what did it. Or, who did it. I didn't know how.

"That's nice to hear, but you know abusers don't really change. They tend to repeat their same bad habits. Be careful."

"He's not an abuser, silly!" Mitzi patted my arm. "He's just a strong man who got a little flustered. It's all good now."

I wanted to argue with her, but I knew my pleas would fall on deaf ears. I hemmed and hawed and said benign things as she told me about the script for the day's shoot and how her agent was working on a movie deal with a big-name director. She was happy, and I didn't want to burst that bubble.

"Hold still and look up, dear, and I'll get this mascara on. It's a Korean fiber brand, so you'll need a good waterproof makeup remover to get it off later. Do you have one? If not, I'll give you a little bit of mine."

"Oh, I've got everything at home, Waylon. No worries." She blinked a few times, and I made her wait a moment while I got a cotton swab and dotted away a few mascara streaks.

"There, you're perfect. Go knock 'em dead."

"Waylon, I couldn't do this without you. Thank you. You're a lifesaver."

She traipsed to her car in her cute dress and heels, with a flawless face and a chipper attitude, and I vowed to learn from her. I would face my day with an equally positive attitude, and for a moment, I was actually cheery.

"Waylon?"

"Yes, Mrs. Ross?"

"Captain Perkins will be here in fifteen minutes. He's taking you to The Industries for an interview with some higher-ups there."

And there went the cheer. All of it, in one fell swoop, replaced by extreme anxiety as I realized I would be walking into a pseudo-military, scientific complex that created zombies and lived to study them. If I wasn't careful, I could wind up as their newest lab rat.

I got ready with as much care as I gave to Mitzi. Makeup to cover the scars, blotting to a skin-like finish, glasses with clear lenses to draw attention to my human-looking eyes, a dark gray suit with a pink shirt and a silver tie with delicate ivory polka dots. A black belt and black shoes, smooth Oxfords, not Brogues, completed the look. I certainly qualified for "Best Dressed Ambulatory Non-Living Personhood."

I decided not to wear gloves but used fake skin employed by special effects artists to, ironically enough, create scars and wounds. I used a liquid version that was smooth and flexible.

"How do I look?"

Mrs. Ross gave me a once over and said the sweetest thing.

"You look normal."

I texted Early.

Me: Coming to officially.

Early: What?

Me: Comin to office.

Early: My office? Now?

Me: ? Bee there soon.

Early: Who are you meeting with? He didn't make an appointment with me.

Me: Don't know, perkins st up.

Early: Oh. Dear.

I was well and truly scared to do this, but I couldn't figure out how to refuse the captain. I had no doubts that if Perkins believed I'd killed those men, he'd arrest me and out me. Or, as unlikely as it seemed, he could try to kill me, and that would be worse, because he couldn't. He'd just reduce me to smaller and smaller bits, which meant my consciousness stayed with those bits until Early reassembled me. The reconstruction was trivial when it was a large body part or two, but once the components got smaller, it took tinkering. I had to be reconstituted like a jigsaw puzzle and then left to regenerate the rest of the way. Then, depending on what healed and what didn't, he'd have to find larger parts to piece me back together.

And yes, we knew this by actual trial and error. My body couldn't be destroyed and wouldn't completely decompose. My consciousness stayed tethered to those tiny, remaining parts, and there I lingered, unable to speak, move, or touch, but aware of everything that was happening around me.

It was hell, and it was what was potentially facing me if Perkins thought I was guilty. I'd let him kill me if I believed it would work, but he'd fail.

On the other hand, The Industries would love to have me in its grasp, and that thought gave me the chills.

The captain was the rock and The Industries, the hard place.

Perkins rapped on the door, sharp and quick. Betsy Ross answered, her feet firmly on the ground.

"Captain, good to see you."

"Is he ready?"

"I'll call him."

I walked to the captain, my arm outstretched. "No need, Mrs. Ross. Captain, nice to see you."

The captain turned his back to me, ignoring my hand. "Let's go, Frankenstein."

I refused to move. "Don't call me that."

He turned slightly. "Why? You're like him, aren't you?"

"Maybe, yes, but you meant that in a derogatory way, like if I called you 'cracker,' or 'redneck,' given you're from the south."

"Didn't know you had such delicate feelings."

"You want my help, Captain?"

"Not really, but I don't have enough evidence on you to hold you accountable yet, so keeping you in my sights seems like the right thing to do. Although I'm getting close to nailing you on this, Jenkins, since another body showed up yesterday."

"What? Where?"

"Like you don't know. Paramount Ranch."

I didn't say a word, just stood there blinking.

He pulled out his phone and handed it to me. It was a photo of me walking toward the old west town, rolling my kit along.

"I was there, yes."

Perkins all but spit at me. "That's obvious."

"I didn't kill anyone."

Perkins got close to me, and though he craned his neck to see my eyes, and I gazed downward, his stare made me cringe. "Then. Why. Were. You. There?"

That was a nifty question. I couldn't tell him about Eddie, yet.

"I was there to audition for the movie."

Perkins stepped back, his eyebrows squinched together. "*Zombie Cowboys from Space*?" He took another step back. "I guess I could see why you would want to." He gestured to my body, sweeping a hand up and down. "It certainly suits." He rubbed his eyes. "They weren't shooting yesterday."

"So I discovered. I'm going back today, this afternoon, in fact."

He gestured for me to follow. "Still, awfully coincidental."

"Oh, come on. Someone dropped a body in the Santa Monica Mountains? That can't be too unusual, Captain."

Perkins harrumphed and jerked his head for me to follow. He slid into the driver's seat of the tan unmarked car and belted up. "Let's go," he said.

8

"Who are we meeting?" I belted up too, although I could go right through the window and walk away unscathed.

"Quint Addington, the director. I made an appointment with his assistant."

"I thought you wanted to speak to Early," I said.

"I mentioned Early when I made the appointment."

"What do you know about Mr. Addington?"

The captain pointed to a manila folder shoved in between his seat and the center console. I opened it and read the single sheet of paper it contained.

"British, recently relocated here. Educated at Oxford but with study abroad stints at the Sorbonne and Humboldt University of Berlin. Master's Degree from the London School of Economics."

"Yeah," Perkins said. "A real smarty-pants."

"Spent time in London working for a consulting firm, then moved to New York for a position at Smith, Whyle, and Grimmons, whoever they are. Now at The Industries. Unmarried. No children."

I looked at Perkins. "This man lives for his work."

"And sounds like a spook."

"I'm sorry?"

"That resume sounds like someone who works for a clandestine agency. Secret Intelligence. MI6. Call it what you will, that's what he sounds like to me."

"Why would a spy work for The Industries?"

The look he shot me would have withered my nether regions if I had any.

"Don't be naïve, Jenkins. A top-notch United States military funded think tank? Why wouldn't he want access? The only question is whether he is there with the approval of the CIA or not. I have to think they know about him or even invited him because he's not pretending to be someone he's not. He's not here undercover."

"Maybe it's a cooperative thing, or Mr. Addington left MI6 and went to work in the private sector."

Perkins snorted. "Possibly, but I know the type. They never completely leave."

The building was several floors tall and sprawling. Its gated entrance had two uniformed guards manning the post. Perkins leaned out the window to talk to one of them while the second surveyed our car from the outside and scribbled on a notepad, presumably writing down our license plate number.

"We have an appointment with Mr. Addington," Perkins explained, handing over his identification and gesturing to the star pinned to his chest.

"Yes, sir." The guard took his ID, checked a list, and made a call. The other guard came around to my side and knocked on the glass.

"We'll need your ID, too, sir."

"No problem." I handed over my driver's license, which was real, although the birth certificate I used to get it was fake, and he took it back to his colleague.

Perkins rolled the window up, calm on the exterior, while they checked us out,but he kept fiddling with the radio. Finally, they returned our identification, handed us each a badge to clip to our clothes, and slipped a placard onto the inside dash that indicated we were guests.

"Leave that on the car when you park, Captain. That way, we won't suspect a bomb and blow up your car."

Perkins and I both startled at that.

The guard grinned, or, more accurately, showed us his teeth. "Just kidding."

"Ha." That was all Perkins said. I didn't say anything.

We parked in a guest spot right in front of the door, and I checked my makeup in the mirror. It was a nervous tic, and I shouldn't have done it, given the outside cameras and what the security staff would make of a man powdering his nose.

Perkins didn't seem to care. He was taking in the surroundings, noting the cameras, the K9 patrol on the far end of the campus, the high fences, and he looked up when a helicopter flew overhead.

"What the fuck are they doing here? Wound care?" he whispered to me as we approached the imposing front doors. "Sure as hell isn't bandages, antibiotics, and butterfly clips."

Again, I went with silence.

The armed guards at the front door inspected our badges and waved us through. The man and woman at the desk inside the foyer wore plain clothes, pretending to be receptionists, but I noted the holster bulges under their jackets.

The woman addressed us. "Captain Perkins. Mr. Jenkins. Mr. Addington will see you in his office. Allow me to escort you."

Perkins and I exchanged glances. Like *we* were allowing anything. It was obvious that they were calling the shots.

She used a card key to access the elevator and ushered us in, pressing the top floor, which was indicated by a blank white button. All the other buttons had numbers on them and were black. The C-suites ranked anonymity.

The door opened, and a man in a suit greeted us before we could step out.

"Captain Perkins and Mr. Jenkins, welcome. I'm Peter Shunk, Mr. Addington's executive assistant. Please follow me."

The elevator door closed behind us with a soft hum. Only way to go was forward, but my discomfort was growing by the minute. I was lucky I didn't sweat, or it would be dripping down my face. Perkins kept pulling at his cuffs, a sign that even his cool veneer was cracking. He wore his uniform, a tan, crisp button-down, a dark tie with a silver tie clip, his star over his heart, and dark green khaki pants. His duty belt was fully kitted out with his gun on his right hip, extra mags in the back, handcuffs, pepper spray, and a pouch for gloves, as well as other paraphernalia that made him look dangerous and all business.

Peter slipped across the carpet like a well-oiled dinner cart in a five-star hotel, silent and unobtrusive. His steps didn't even leave footprints in the plush fibers. With his dark slick hair, pointy chin, and mincing walk, he reminded me of a praying mantis waiting for an unsuspecting bug. I comforted myself with the thought that male praying mantises don't live all that long and often met sad, tragic ends.

He knocked on a simple wooden door without a name placard.

"Come in."

Peter opened the door and motioned for us to enter. It was a simple office, basic furniture, southern exposure windows, and a medium-sized man with glasses in an utterly nondescript, tailored gray suit standing to greet us. Peter followed and sat in a chair in the corner of the room.

"Quint Addington, CEO of The Industries, at your service. Pleasure to meet you." His eyes were brown, and his nose was broad with huge nostrils. It was the only thing memorable about his face. Everything else was the taupe of facial features.

Captain Perkins shook his hand, but I fumbled with the back of a guest chair and gave him a weak wave. I didn't want to touch hands with him and take the chance he'd notice the fake skin. He looked at me quizzically for a moment.

"I didn't catch your name," he said to me.

"Waylon Jenkins."

Addington perked up. "Ah, yes. Captain Perkins mentioned you when he made our appointment. You're friends with Dr. Early."

I tipped my chin in acknowledgment. "Early is a tenant on my property."

"How nice for you."

Not really, I thought.

"Peter, would you fetch Dr. Early, please?"

"Of course, sir."

"So, gentlemen, how can I be of service?" Addington sat back in his chair and steepled his fingers.

"We've had some bodies show up, recently," stated Perkins.

"I'm sorry to hear that," Addington said.

"Yes, yes. The thing is, all of them were poisoned and are missing limbs. We know that your facility deals with amputations, and we thought we could pick your brains about how that could happen."

Addington sniffed. "I assure you we have nothing to do with murders."

"We didn't say you did," Perkins said in a bland voice.

Peter re-entered, Early on his heels.

"Ah. Early, please take a seat. I take it you know Mr. Jenkins."

Early gave us a nod and pulled up a chair. "Of course, he's my landlord. Captain, nice to see you again."

Addington continued. "Captain Perkins says that they've had some murders of late, awful that, where the bodies are missing limbs. They'd like to know more about how one would remove a limb."

Early turned to Perkins. "And, you think we would know, because?"

"Waylon told me you had teams specializing in amputation."

Early nodded. "We do, that's true."

"Well, what do I need to know?" Perkins took out a notepad and pen from his front right shirt pocket.

"Did the amputations happen before or after death?"

"After, is my understanding."

"That means the murderer didn't have to deal with screaming or wriggling," said Early, and I had to stop myself from slamming my head to my hand. Could he have been creepier? Addington's smile became strained.

Perkins blanched but wrote that down. "That's one way to put it."

Early gave him a pointed look. "What I mean is that a living person isn't so willing to lose arms and legs. There would be signs of a struggle, binding, and the cut would be messy. Is the cut clean?"

"It is, and the bleeding was post-mortem."

"That settles that then," Early said with satisfaction.

"A bone-saw is best to get through the femur although it could be done with a hand saw or a bow saw, like the ones you would use to take down tree limbs. An ax could do it, but that would leave a different kind of post-mortem wound. The muscles would be ragged, and the bone would be splintered. You'd notice."

"That's what we thought," Perkins said, still writing. Without looking up, he asked, "Can either of you think of any reasons why someone would want to cut off a dead body's leg?"

"Of course not, Captain," said Addington, before Early could respond. "We hope to replace missing arms and legs here and to do so on living people. We aren't murderers or fetishists."

"Again, no one said you were," Perkins responded with a mollifying smile. "Dr. Early, you were about to answer that question?"

Early cast his eyes at Addington and shook his head.

Perkins leaned in. "Are you sure, Dr. Early?"

Early shrugged. "The only reason would be to experiment with necrotic tissue. There are some scientific reasons to do that. Some labs study larval therapy for removal of devitalized tissue."

"What does that mean?"

I heard Addington shift in his seat.

Early continued. “Maggots. They study the use of maggots to remove necrotic tissue.”

“Does this facility do that kind of research?”

“We do not.” Addington’s voice was clipped and definitive. “Captain, Mr. Jenkins, I’m afraid that’s all the time we have for you today. Peter, will you show them out? Dr. Early, please stay with me a moment.”

“One last question, please,” Perkins said, holding up his hand.

“What?” asked Addington.

“The victims were poisoned first and, while we don’t know the poison, it seemed to speed up *rigor mortis*. Can you think of anything that would do that?”

Addington had had enough. “We don’t deal in poison here, Captain Perkins.”

Peter slunk forward. “Please, follow me.”

“Thank you for your time,” Perkins said, his voice pleasant.

9

We exited twice as fast as we came in, as if the building and its occupants couldn't wait to spit us out. We walked to the car and stood there for a moment.

"That was interesting," said Perkins.

"How so?" For me, it was interesting in a "won't you come into my parlor said the spider to the fly" kind of way, but I wanted to know what Perkins thought.

"Their reaction to the questions. I thought there would be more scientific interest, that they would approach it with a detached academic curiosity, but instead, they got ruffled, made it more personal than I expected. Tells me they have things to hide. Definitely more spook than just military and certainly a place with secrets."

"Doesn't mean they have anything to do with the murders though," I said, leaning against the hood of the car.

"Isn't that hot?" Perkins asked me, his face incredulous that I was touching the car without screaming in pain. The sun was out full force.

I jumped up. "Didn't notice until you mentioned it, Perkins. Guess it is."

"Can't you feel heat and cold?"

"Yes, I can," I explained, "but not the way you do. Hey, is that Early?"

"Sure is."

Early was exiting the building and walking toward us. His face was red, and he walked like a man with a purpose.

"What's up, Early?" Perkins asked.

"Mr. Addington wanted me to assure you that if we think of anything else, we'll call, but he asked that you keep in mind that our work here is delicate and not for sharing with the public."

Perkins eyed him. "Y'all keep a low profile."

"That we do."

"You boys stay here for a moment. I want to ask these front door guards a question or two." He sauntered toward them, hands loose by his sides. I had no idea what Perkins wanted, but it gave me a moment with Early. Still, I kept an eye on the Captain, hoping the guards saw his body posture as non-threatening. Something about them made me think they had itchy trigger fingers.

Early watched, too. We stood side-by-side, not saying anything, both tense.

I broke the silence. "Saw Mitzi today."

Early raised an eyebrow. "How is she?"

"Better. Her bruises are fading."

"That's good. She's a delightful young lady."

"What did you do to Jason Teague?"

"Me?" He shrugged. "I just told him that beating up on women was wrong."

"You simply spoke to him?" I crossed my arms and gave him the beady eyeball.

"I might have also mentioned that I had done some research into him."

I eyed him some more. "What kind of research?"

Early blushed. "Let's just say that with company computers, nothing disappears. Even things you tried to erase from the internet stay forever."

Now he had me curious. "Like what?"

Early looked around. I thought I saw some movement from the thicket of trees nearby, but Early didn't seem to notice.

"Jason Teague is Captain Colossal."

I didn't understand. "Who?"

"Captain Colossal was an adult film actor about three years ago. You can guess why." He winked, gesturing at his crotch. I rolled my hand to tell him to get on with it but kept staring at the copse of trees.

"Captain Colossal wore a mask at all times. He never revealed his face. Let's just say that with a few taps on a special search engine, plus a phone call or two, I was able to unearth the truth. He thought he'd hidden the evidence, but there it was. Jason Teague, Hollywood heartthrob and everyone's favorite boyfriend was once the world's *biggest* porn star."

The more I thought about it, the more I liked it. "You threatened to reveal this?"

"More like I mentioned that I knew, and he figured out the rest."

I smiled a wicked grin. "You know, Early, in this case, I approve of your methods."

Early waggled his eyebrows but turned his head when he saw my face. "What is it?"

"There's someone over there." I pointed.

"Behind the trees?"

"Originally, that's where I saw movement, but now, look further away, past the trees, toward the gate in the back."

Early shaded his eyes and peered where I told him, straightening in alarm. "Why is that person skulking?"

I peered at the figure hugging the fence. "Don't you think he'd be tripping some motion sensors or something?"

Early's voice was low. "Unless they want him to come back and are letting him enter."

"Letting!" It hit me. "Is that Eddie?"

Before Early could stop me, I took off toward the fence. "Eddie, if that is you, go back! Go back! They're trying to lure you in!"

"Stop!" The voices behind me rang with command, but I didn't care.

Perkins' voice followed. "Don't shoot him! He's with me!"

I ran straight across the vast expanse of grass, dimly wondering—too late—if they land mined the place. I didn't *think* they could do that, but I had an image in my head of Indiana Jones-like spikes springing from the lawn, impaling my feet.

I ignored my macabre imagination and kept running, calling out. "Eddie, is that you? Turn around, run away! It's a trap."

My Admiral Ackbar warning caught his attention. He froze, his back against the tall fence, and shifted his body to retreat in the direction from which he'd come. Inch-by-inch, taking care with his steps, he moved to his right, toward an outdoor electrical box at least three feet tall and four feet wide. He scooted closer and jumped on top of it.

I didn't see anything more because a man grabbed at my blazer, which I let him have, letting my arms go loose so he pulled the sports coat off of me. He reacted by grasping my shirt, untucking it from my slacks as he ripped it upwards. I dove forward, yanking myself free, trying to see where Eddie had gone. The thought of The Industries recapturing him drove me to a state of near madness. He's just gotten out of there. Why would he come back?

"Mr. Jenkins, stop running! Why won't he slow down? What is he trying to do? Why would he pursue that man? He should have let security do their jobs!" I wasn't paying attention to who spoke, though the voice was familiar.

"Yeah, maybe he should have, but it wouldn't have mattered. Your visitor was gone," puffed Early, straining with the chase. "Waylon. Waylon! Slow down!"

"I want him arrested! We had an intruder, and he let him escape!" said the same snarky voice, not labored at all, as if the speaker ran a daily 5K regimen, rain or shine, and judged you for not doing the same.

"Calm down, Shunk," said Perkins. "Hey! Waylon, get it together. What's got into you?"

Before I knew it, my face was in the dirt as someone tackled me from behind. The two security guards had caught up with us. Without hesitating, one of them shoved a foot in my kidneys, and the other held a hand to the back of my head, grinding my face so I couldn't breathe.

Perkins ordered them to stop, his voice deep and commanding. "There is no need for excessive force! Stand down!"

Early followed with, "Hey, shit-for-brains, get your hands off of him!"

Peter said something unintelligible, but I distinctly heard the word "Taser."

I heard it. I heard all of it, but it was too late. A hum, like rushing water, filled my head, drowning out their voices. My mind buzzed like a swarm of bees had taken up residence, my chest grew tight, and my lips tingled as I tried to find a slice of reality to tether myself to, blinking fast to focus on something, anything, that could be a lifeline. While I struggled, their conversation faded further into the distance. They didn't know I didn't need to breathe, but they also didn't know that being held down triggered my flight or fight response, heavy emphasis on fight.

I surged upwards, grabbed the first guard by his belt, and threw him several feet with a roar. The other guard went for his gun, and I kicked it out of his hand with one size thirteen foot and then shoved that same foot into his stomach. He hit the ground with an oomph.

Though a part of my brain told me that I knew the other men present, that my friends would stop the attack, I couldn't calm down to comply with their requests to stop opposing them. All I knew is that it was happening again. I was being attacked, disabled, broken apart, and I couldn't let that happen. I swung my head around, looking for a way out, and saw the electrical box. I took two giant leaps, landed on top of it, grabbed the fence and vaulted over it, ignoring the electricity sheering down my arms into my body. I mean, seriously? An electric shock? Might as well give me a protein shake.

I landed on the other side and took off at an all-out sprint, not caring where I was going because my only drive was to escape. My blind rage and fear made me fly down the road, unaware that some of the fake skin on my hands was gone, my clothes were askew, and I looked like the ravaging monster I tried so hard not to be.

10

"Jenkins, how did you become a zombie?"

I froze, then, I spoke quietly.

"Captain, have you ever spoken to a rape victim?"

"Yes."

"Remember how reluctant they were to talk about what happened?"

"Yes."

"That's how I feel about that question. Being turned into a zombie is a violent, unnatural, unholy act. It is a violation of the natural order, and I do not speak about it."

Perkins was quiet for a moment, thoughtful even, then he said, "Okay."

I didn't look at Early, and he didn't look at me, but his knee bounced an aggravated foxtrot.

The three of us sat together in Early's cottage, Perkins with a cup of coffee, Early with tea. Me, as usual, with nothing but a soft blanket wrapped around my body like a cocoon. I'd returned to my house filthy and exhausted, made my entrance as quietly as possible, and took a shower. I threw my clothes into the trash, not wanting to see them again, and settled into my freezer for an hour.

When I emerged, I redressed, and Mrs. Ross was waiting for me, her eyes solemn.

"Dr. Early asked if you would join him and Captain Perkins at his home."

"Thank you, Mrs. Ross."

I wanted nothing more than to sit in the freezer forever, but that wasn't going to happen, so I'd knocked on the door.

Perkins took a sip and held the mug Early had given him to the light, studying it with a wry smile. It said, "10-4, Coffee That."

"I'm not going to press, Jenkins, but as a professional observation, you acted like a man with Post-Traumatic Stress Disorder. I'm going to head back to the office now to get my notes in the file and see what other crises are brewing, but I want you to know that I have resources I can recommend to you if you want help with it."

He placed the mug on the kitchen counter and let himself out.

"It's been an interesting day," said Early.

"That's one way to put it," I said.

"Want to make it more interesting?

"How?"

He grinned at me, a little feral. "Let's go back to Paramount Ranch and see if we can find our wayward zombie. Besides, you told Perkins you'd be back this afternoon to audition. Wouldn't want to be a liar."

I slapped my hands to my knees and got to my feet, happy to do anything but brood. "Let's get a move on, Early. I've got questions, and Eddie's got the answers."

Our trip to the ranch was short and silent, me not entirely over my freak out and Early absorbed with his own thoughts.

I reached basecamp, the telltale sign of the film industry, with its fleet of trailers. The first was one for Jason, then one for the Director, another for the Assistant Director and Producers, and a fourth for hair and makeup. Then, several more working trucks holding equipment. The place teemed with people, some hurrying this way and that, others hanging around doing nothing. One woman with a soft measuring tape draped around her neck sat on the half-lowered lift gate of a fifty-four foot wardrobe trailer, swinging her legs in a carefree manner.

"Oi!" she exclaimed when she caught sight of me. "Whatcha doin' with your makeup all done and you not on set? Get your ass up there right now!" She pointed in the direction she wanted me to go. I hadn't hidden my skin, but I did wear a hat, jeans and a short-sleeved shirt with a jacket.

"Yes, ma'am," I replied, "But I do need to ask someone something before..."

She cut me off with a flick of her hand. "They're about to shoot. All the extras need to be there right now." She eyed me. "Your outfit. Was that approved by the on-set costumer?"

Before I could answer, a harried production assistant spied me, flicked her hand in a "go-go" motion, all the while taking to someone on a walkie-talkie. "Found another BG by wardrobe. Flying in with him now." I remembered that "BG" was background. Extras were all background in film. I mentally patted myself on the back for remembering my lingo.

I hustled to the staging area just south of Backdrop Trail, leaving Early behind. Someone barked at me to take off my hat, and I did, handing it to a crewmember who told me I could get it later. He motioned for me to take off my jacket, and I did that too, self-conscious because my elbows were a graveyard of stitches and seams.

I found myself standing next to two women in a crowd of a dozen or so "zombies from space." I scanned the crowd looking for Eddie, but I didn't see him.

"I'm Barb Wolf," said one of the women, holding out her hand. Her face was a crisscross of fake zipper scars, and her hair was mashed down on her head like it was wet. "I hate makeup, usually. Isn't that funny? But, I always wanted to be in a movie, so when they said they were looking for extras, I thought, 'What the hell?' It could be fun. Besides, my kids are grown, and I'm bored, bored, bored. Who are you?"

"Waylon Jenkins."

"Pleased to meet ya, Waylon. This here is my friend, Michelle Duffy. She loves hair and makeup."

Michelle shook my hand like she was pumping water, her makeup blood and guts chic. "But with four kids, I never have time to do anything with myself. Not sure what I'm doing here except Barb dragged me. I even had to get a sitter to meet the children after school."

Barb bumped Michelle's hip. "You're enjoying it."

Michelle nodded, only a little grudgingly, "Yeah, I am. I wasn't prepared for all this waiting around, though."

"It is a lot of hurry up and wait in the movie biz," I said.

"Hey," Michelle said, "Who did your makeup? It's the best there is. So realistic."

"I did it myself."

"Wow. You should be doing the special effects here, not warming a square foot of dirt as an extra."

"I was hoping to meet a friend here. Is there another group of extras somewhere?"

Barb nodded. "I think there are some hiding behind those trees." She jerked her chin to indicate where.

"Yeah," said Michelle. "I think those are the ambush zombies. They've got the whole make-up thing going on too, but some of them are wearing space helmets and have ray guns." She crouched like a gunslinger and stuck out her fingers in a "pew-pew," position, aiming at me, dead center.

I winked and pretended to die, my hand to my heart, staggering backward, the three of us laughing until I saw their eyes open wide and felt a hand on my shoulder.

"Dude. We need you. We'll get you an updated contract later," said a deep, masculine voice.

I turned to see Jason Teague, of all people, and my mouth hit the floor.

"Come on, come on, you're being upgraded. You're a tall, somewhat handsome zombie, and I need a sidekick. Don't be insulted I said that. You know how it is. Can't have you outshining me in the looks department."

I babbled something incoherent, and he kept on talking, dragging me by my arm.

"Your makeup is superb. They didn't do the arms on everyone. I think you were supposed to be up front. What were you doing way in the back?"

"I think there's been a mistake."

"No mistake, just your lucky break. You're an actor, right? You look like an actor. I've seen you before. Don't worry. We'll work with your agent later to get your pay squared up."

A guy I figured was an assistant director or some such position stopped Jason with a hand to his chest. Jason looked down at it until the man removed it.

"Jason, you can't just do this. You don't upgrade an extra by yourself!"

"I can do what I want." Jason puffed out his chest. Such a peacock.

"Jesus! Let me talk to the director."

The AD stalked to the director. Jason followed the AD and after a lot of whispering, arm gestures, and a dash of swearing, I was suddenly a cast member.

Jason approached me, smiling, pointing to the coach. "Hop on up here. You take the reins since I've got to do the stunts. I like to do my own stunt work if I can."

I clambered into the stagecoach and took the reins like Jason said, wondering what the hell was happening and what I was supposed to do next.

A woman with a baseball cap and a huge coffee mug pointed at me. "What's your name?"

"Uh."

"Your name? No name? Fine, you're Chet. From now on, on this set, you're Chet."

"Okay."

"Chet, here's the deal. We're going to hook up the horses and take some shots, then we'll remove the horses, and we'll act out the scenes using this motion machine. Safer that way. It will feel bumpy and real but don't worry; you're not really driving the coach. Just pretend you are. Got it? Good."

She circled her fingers in the air and sat in the director's chair. "Let's roll!"

Jason took his place next to me. "I've got all the speaking parts, Chet, so don't say anything. Your job is to pretend you're driving and when the ride gets rough, to look scared. You can do that, right?"

"Look scared? Yeah, I've got that down."

He slapped my shoulder. "Atta boy."

A crewperson hooked up two beautiful chestnuts to the coach. They danced in place, skittish at the number of people milling about and the lights and noise. I hoped they'd do this part fast.

The first assistant director motioned for everyone to settle down. "Picture's up!" Several production assistants repeated this so everyone would shut up.

Then, "Roll Sound," followed by the boom operator, who was standing on a ladder to be above the coach and horses, announcing "Sound speed." We got through the rest of the routine until the clack of the old-fashioned slate when the director said, "Background." The extras started milling around and the next thing I knew, we were rolling.

The coach jolted up and down like it was really moving, and I hung on to the reins, trying to look like I was controlling the horses. Jason stood and peered over the horizon.

"Cut!" The director had her hands on her hips. "You! Chet!"

"Yes?"

"You look constipated. Relax. You're a stagecoach driver and do this every day. Loosen up."

I gave her a thumbs up. I hadn't been constipated in over a hundred years, so I was amazed I could look that way. Maybe I was a better actor than I knew.

A dolly camera came on our side, focusing on the horses, trying to capture the look and feel of us bouncing along the trail. Jason stood beside me, and I held the reins in a loose grip. This time, the coach kept up a gentle sway, and the horses seemed fine, although they were standing in place.

"Okay, now we're going to let the horses walk a little. Don't worry. Their trainer is standing right there." The director pointed at a man wearing a red bandana tied around his neck. The man waved.

The director continued. "The horses are trained to walk directly to him. That's as far as you're going. Let's do this."

I barely heard the routine start again. "Picture's up. Sound speed. Roll camera." All I heard was Jason rubbing his hands together muttering, "Yeah, let's do this already, bitch."

I startled and turned my face to look at him. "What? Why did you call her that?"

"Patricia thinks she's a big hotshot, and you know how women in power are." Jason rolled his eyes.

I let go of the reins. "No, I don't know." I stood to face him. "That's the most misogynistic, stupid thing you could have said." I could feel my hand curling into a fist.

"Really? You're going to get into it with me here and now?" sneered Jason. "I'm giving you your big break!"

I shook my head. "You're a moron."

Patricia's voice was angry. "Boys! No fighting! Jason, Chet! Calm the hell down, and Jason, stop complaining about me. I can hear you, you know, and I don't care! You're upsetting the horses!"

Jason shoved my shoulder.

I took a half-step back, trying not to fall off the coach.

My foot got tangled in the reins.

I lifted my foot to slip it out of the loop, but it got caught on my heel, and I flicked and stomped my foot to disentangle it.

That slapped the leather against the horses' backs.

In a split second, the animals bolted, taking me, Jason, and the stagecoach with them. A strained mechanical sound followed by a *clank* told me the motion machine had separated from the coach, and before Jason or I could say another word, we were flying down the trail.

11

Mother fuckerrrrrrrr!" screamed Jason as we took off.

We bucked and swerved as the horses ran wherever they wanted to go, their manes flying behind them. To my chagrin, my reins were fake and not connected to the horses' bits, making them as useful as a squirt gun during a highway robbery. We careened to the left, and Jason fell against me with his full weight while I held onto the lip of the seat and the side of the carriage, praying to the zombie gods that we wouldn't fall off. I didn't want to have to replace arms and legs, or my entire torso.

Jason screamed the entire time. "Whatthehellarewegoingtodo?" Followed by, "Stopstopstopstop!"

And then, as a branch whipped by and hit his cheek, "Ohnonottheface!"

The horses kept up full pace, and the encroaching trees created a real and present danger to our heads, so I slammed my hand on top of Jason's skull and shouted, "Duck!" Decapitations of living people are messy and, in my case, it would be hard to explain why I could still talk.

Jason moaned as the horses kept on. I closed my eyes and held one arm over my head, keeping the other one on Jason to keep him low.

Finally, the horses seemed to slow, and I noticed a buzzing above us. I chanced a look up and saw a drone following our every move. At least they knew where we were, I thought. I almost relaxed.

The most maniacal, ear-splitting wail hit my ear, and we flopped forward as the horses shied from a bobcat in the middle of the trail. That damn cat stood its ground singing a song of defiance, and the horses knew who was boss. They bucked, front hooves pawing the air. and came to an abrupt stop. Jason and I flew ass over teakettle into the brush and rocks. By some miracle of physics, I grabbed him mid-air and held him to my body, cushioning his fall by landing on my back.

I fell smack in the middle of a prickly pear patch and lay there with spines stuck to every part of my body. Jason scrambled from my grasp and got on all fours, keeping his torso low.

"Where's the cougar going?" Jason said, his voice a whisper.

"The *bobcat* is sauntering off. His work is done here," I answered, easing to my feet while plucking spines from my arms and hands. "Are you hurt?"

"I'm going to sue that useless cunt Patricia for everything she's got! The studio, too! And the stunt coordinator! I could have died or been disabled! My life and my career ruined. What if I broke my nose or cheekbones? My face would never be the same. Do you know I have an insurance policy on my face alone? It's my money-maker."

I rubbed my eyes and immediately regretted it when I got some tiny little stickers in them from my fingertips. My eyes watered, another sign of their retained humanity, and I heaved in a huge gulp of air, which made me breathe in the strong but normally pleasant scent of pine, and I coughed like I was upchucking a lung.

My companion didn't notice.

"Goddammit! I think I've twisted an ankle. I can't walk out of here! OW!" Jason tripped and landed hard in a patch of Blue Dicks, and all I could think was how morbidly appropriate that was and how I wished he hadn't squashed the purple petals.

"Why do you have to be such an asshole, Jason?" I asked, my voice raw.

"I fight for what's owed me, and to hell with anyone else. You've only just met me, and you're already calling me an asshole?" Jason managed to get to his feet, balanced on his good foot, and stared at me, hands on his hips. The horses grazed happily a dozen or so feet away.

"Calling women cunts makes you an asshole. Calling Patricia a bitch makes you an asshole. Hitting Mitzi makes you a raging, gaping, asshole." My hands hung loose and ready in case he decided to throw down.

I hoped he did.

I was ashamed of that, but it was the truth. I never wanted to hit someone before, not like this, but maybe Early was rubbing off on me.

I leaned forward, jutting my chin, basically begging him to take a shot.

We glared at one another, and then, he obliged.

He hit me with an uppercut to the jaw that would have knocked out a normal man. As it was, I flew in an arc up and back, slamming into the earth flat on my back. I scrambled up and dove at him, using my size to tackle him and bring him to the ground, hard. I heard his bad ankle crack and felt a tiny moment of remorse.

Which was eradicated the second he bit me.

Contrary to popular belief, Jason would not turn into a zombie from biting me or me biting him, but it did reveal to him that not only did I taste bad, I didn't bleed.

"Crap! That fucking hurt!" He spat in my face. "What the hell are you, man? You freak! Freak! Get off me!" He scurried back, cradling his hand and favoring his injured ankle.

He continued his rant. "What kind of monster are you? You some kinda mutant? No wonder you hide out at the movies. I'm going to tell the studio."

My hands shook in rage, and I bit my lip to keep from saying anything more. My carefully curated life was flashing before my eyes as this little putz scrambled away, threatening to out me. He didn't know the full truth, but he'd put enough together to be a concern.

I tried for calm. "Jason, it's nothing. You didn't hit skin, that's all. I have layers of fake skin underneath this shirt. They wanted me ready in case I needed to go bare-chested."

The tiniest rustle was the only sign. A hand clasped around Jason's mouth from behind and a soft, menacing voice said, "Don't say one word more, you piece of shit."

I eyed Eddie. "Amazing. I wouldn't have seen you if I hadn't been looking for you."

Eddie shifted his head to the right so I could see his face. It was better than mine, more human. Still had the odd green tinge, but fewer scars and those were mild, like he'd gotten a facelift. In California, no one would even blink at his appearance. He wore camo and had belly-crawled low and slow, like the drill instructors in San Diego had taught him. Or, maybe it was Parris Island. I caught a whiff of southern in Eddie's speech.

Jason's eyes were wide, body frozen in fear, and he visibly trembled at what Eddie said next, speaking so softly into Jason's ear I almost couldn't make it out.

"Jason, I know where you live and where you drink. I know what car you drive and the restaurants you prefer. I know your dog's name and where your aunt goes to church. You say one word, one goddamn word about this man and you will hear from me. Nod if you understand."

Jason nodded.

"It should go without saying that I am not a nice person, and I am in a permanently pissed-off mood, so don't test me. Nod again."

Jason's head did a minute up and down movement.

Eddied winked at me. "Jason, lay the hell down on the ground now. Yes, on your stomach, and stay there until Waylon tells you to move. No, I don't give a shit that your face is in some prickly phlox, smash it on down there and don't make me put a boot in your ass."

Platoon leader. Absolutely.

It wasn't until Jason was flat on the earth that I noticed the figure in the nearby trees. I snapped my fingers at Eddie and pointed.

"Busted!" Eddie said. "That's Shunk again. He deployed a two-man team to look for me. He knows I'm trying to get to the others. Gotta jet. Remember what I said, Jason."

Eddie took off at a run, relying on speed to get away, not stealth. Peter pointed a rifle and took a shot, rocks flying in the air just in front of my fleeing friend. Eddie zigged and flashed Shunk the finger.

"Shunk! You idiot!" I yelled. "There are human beings out here!"

Peter put his gun down and motioned to someone behind him. They melted into the tree line.

Others. There were other zombies, and Eddie was doing what he trained to do, go after his soldiers, leaving no man behind.

"Oh, thank God!" Patricia's voice carried in the breeze. "We had no idea that could happen."

The director scrambled down the rock to us, a man in a black suit and skinny tie right behind, his toupee askew. Early clambered after him, giving me a small wave.

"Of course," wheezed the man, "If Chet here hadn't stomped his foot, the reins wouldn't have scared the horses and everything would have been fine. The studio is not liable."

I stared at the little weasel in disbelief, then I shrugged and pointed to Jason. "I'm not injured, but your star has a twisted ankle and a busted hand. You're going to have to deal with him."

Patricia stared at Jason. "Why's he on his stomach like that?"

"It's been a bad hour or so."

"Jason," Patricia said. "Get up. Let's take a look at you."

Jason rolled to his seat and stayed there, not looking at me. He decided to take out his ire on Patricia.

"You stark-raving insane bitch. You coulda killed me." Jason hopped up on his one foot and snapped his arm like he was going to backhand Patricia across the mouth. He didn't make it, being off-balance, and all Patricia had to do was side-step, and the jerk went down, crying out as he used his bad hand to catch his fall. Early walked to me and if he happened to step on Jason's injured hand again, who was to tell?

Patricia's stare was cold. "I'll call an ambulance for you." She turned and took a couple of steps, and then spun to look at us.

"By the way, I got footage of the whole thing by drone. No sound, of course, but great visuals."

"The whole thing?" I asked. "What do you mean?"

"The drone ran out of juice right after you guys flew from the coach and landed on the ground. Chet, you played to the camera when you protected Jason with your own body. You'll be everyone's favorite loyal sidekick. It'll be great in theaters! We'll stage the rest."

Early cleared his throat. "I'm Chet's agent, ma'am. I'll need to renegotiate his contract given the unexpected action sequences and larger role."

"Of course." Patricia elbowed the weasel in the side. "Take care of it, will ya?"

The sweaty, uncomfortable man grunted and handed Early a card.

12

My new acting alias now had a bank account with several thousand dollars in it, and a contract with gross points, meaning a percentage of profits. The headlines reported that Chet Manning, new action movie star, was actually reclusive makeup artist to the stars Waylon Jenkins, but, unfortunately, Jenkins wasn't available for comment.

A perky redhead with beautiful blue eyes was reporting from the scene for *Celebrities Tonight*. "Facial recognition software confirms that Chet Manning is a good match for Waylon Jenkins, but that's not all."

The redhead raised her eyebrows and leaned toward the camera, giving everyone an eyeful of...microphone. "None of the makeup artists officially attached to the production did Chet Manning's makeup, which they acknowledge is the best they've ever seen."

The camera cut to a makeup artist I knew in passing. He was a nice guy, and I was glad to see he was getting work.

"I didn't do that special effects work, and I'm head makeup artist here, so I don't know who did that work, but I'd like to meet the artist. First, to say stop fucking with my set, and second, how the hell did you do that? The skin was seamless." They bleeped the expletive, but it was obvious what he said.

"You certain you don't want to make a statement, Waylon?" Mrs. Ross asked, blowing on her nails. "You're famous already. There was a tourist who caught the action on his iPhone. It's blurry, but it's obvious you protected Jason Teague. They're calling you a hero."

I was typing notes about different clients into my computer files. "I should have let him fall on his expensive face."

"Pshah. You'd never let that happen."

"Do we have any appointments today?"

"Well, Mitzi will be here in an hour, and yes, the phone is ringing off the hook with new clients since the story broke about Chet Manning."

"Schedule appointments for those that sound legit, Mrs. Ross. Use your judgment. If they sound like reporters or publicity hounds, get rid of them."

"That's what I'm doing. I like messing with gawkers."

That made me look up. "What do you say to them?"

"I tell them the only openings you have are at midnight during the full moon." Mrs. Ross's smile was a gift from the Devil himself.

Huh. Now that was a thought. I'd never asked her why she was trapped here.

I moved on. "What do they say?"

She laughed. "Some of them are ready to do it! Imbeciles. Then I tell them the up-front fee is half-a-million dollars and a vial of blood."

"Mrs. Ross!"

"I've had two takers. You are about to meet one now." The doorbell rang and Betsy floated away to answer it.

"What? Mrs. Ross!"

My secretary escorted my new client to the office, and not only had she solidified her lower half, so she appeared alive and human, she'd also conjured the sound of heels clicking on the floor as she walked down the hall.

"Dr. Sang! How good to see you." I breathed a sigh of relief.

The tiny woman shook my hand. "Sorya, please."

"What can I do for you, Sorya? And, please don't mind Mrs. Ross. She didn't mean the whole vial of blood thing."

Sorya smiled, and I noticed how white her teeth were.

"I knew that, and I told Betsy that I admired her attempts to protect you from the crazies out there, but honestly, I could have brought a vial if that was needed. I do work in a morgue."

"I'm glad you didn't, and she's not protecting me. That's giving her too much credit."

Sorya shook a finger at me. "Don't be so certain, Waylon."

I sat back in my chair, admiring her perfect smile and big, brown eyes. Her hair looked soft, too, and I wondered what it would feel like to run my hand through it.

Whoa, Waylon. Down, boy.

"Why are you here, Sorya? Your skin is divine. You don't need anything except sunscreen."

Sorya bounced to her feet and paced a few steps away, whirled around, took a deep breath, and said, "Would you go on a date with me?"

I blinked at her a few times. She rocked in place, and I remembered how she'd buzzed like a bee the last time we met.

"Never mind, I shouldn't have asked," she said. "Sorry to have bothered you."

"No. Stop. Please." I bounded out of my chair and caught her arm. "It's just that you know what I am."

She shrugged. "I spend a lot of time with dead people, Waylon. Too much. I don't know many living people, and I have no idea how to talk to them. You're a half-step for me, being living dead."

"I'm your dating training wheels?"

She flapped her arms. "That's not what I'm saying. I like you and hoped we could go to a movie sometime. I know you don't eat, which is fine because I only drink coffee, so no restaurants."

I rubbed the back of my neck. "You know I can't do certain things, right?"

She giggled. "That's presumptuous of you. I asked about a movie, and your mind jumped to sex."

"Guess I'm still a man in that regard." I grinned too.

"We can start as friends and let the rest take care of itself."

"I love this idea. Saturday evening? Pick a flick you'd like to see. I have no preference."

She clapped her hands like a little girl, and her happiness was so catching that my spirits lifted as well. "I was thinking about an action movie with Jason Teague." She winked at me.

I groaned. "Okay, I do have a preference—no Jason Teague."

"Give me your digits, and I'll text you."

I took a step back, alarmed. "My digits?"

She rolled her eyes. "Your phone number, Waylon, not your fingers."

"Oh, right." I typed my phone number into her phone, and she texted me right then and there so I would have her number.

I walked her to the door and kissed her hand. "Thank you for coming today, Sorya. I'm looking forward to Saturday."

"Me, too."

I watched her through the window, Betsy next to me.

"Thanks, Mrs. Ross."

"Don't mention it, Waylon."

13

I knew something terrible happened the second Mitzi walked in the door. Her sunglasses hid her eyes, but it was the downward turn of her chin that scared me the most. Mitzi skipped through life, vibrant and positive. This woman was a stranger.

"Mitzi, what happened?"

She paced my office, her walk stiff and lurching.

I touched her upper arm and swallowed my shock when she jerked away, wincing.

"Don't touch me, yet," she said, her voice thick and low.

"Ooookay." I sat in my chair and observed her body language. She ran one trembling hand through her hair, and the other gripped her purse strap. She wore loose palazzo pants and a long-sleeved, flowy shirt, and my heart jolted as I realized the clothes most likely hid bruises.

Mrs. Ross' head shimmered through the door ,and I mouthed "Early." She retreated before Mitzi saw, but she got the message.

"Tell me, Mitzi, so I can help."

"I don't think you have to help."

"Why?"

"Someone else told me not to worry. A man." Her voice wandered off.

I rubbed my forehead, confused. "Mitzi, you're not making sense. Please, dear, start at the beginning."

She spoke in a shaky, halting voice, and she sounded like she had a cold. "Jason was…angry. The movie shoot didn't go as planned."

She faced me, and while I couldn't see her eyes through the dark lenses, they bore into me. "Were you there? The news reports say that guy, Chet Manning, was you."

"Mitzi, do I seem like the action hero type?" I crossed my legs in my most effeminate, make-up artist manner and spread my arms, holding them palms up. "Would I be out in the middle of the mountains without gallons of sunscreen and a hat? Come on."

"Stranger things have happened." She tapped her foot, analyzing.

"Mitzi, I trip on my shoelaces and bump my head on low doorframes."

"True." She made up her mind and dismissed her suspicions with a wave. "Right. Of course not. Those shows love to speculate and spread rumors."

"Exactly. Now, tell me what happened."

My nervous client's demeanor changed into something new—rage. She'd entered a caged, terrified animal, but as she gathered her thoughts, she gained confidence, and righteous anger took the fear's place.

"The shoot was a disaster, as you've heard. The studio is thrilled with the scene, but Jason injured his ankle and is off his feet for at least a week. Something else happened, too, something that injured his pride, I think. He gets mean if he's teased or ridiculed, even in good sport."

She stopped pacing and removed her glasses. "This is what he did to me."

She had two massive black eyes with extensive swelling, encompassing both cheekbones and her nose. No wonder her voice was different.

I squeezed my eyes shut and counted to ten, then twenty. Early's warning hadn't made a difference, and now I was done. Jason would pay for this.

"Have you seen a doctor?"

"No." She put her sunglasses back on, and her shoulders sagged. Now that she'd shown me, a little tension drained away, and fatigue set in.

"My colleague who you met earlier, Dr. Early, is on the premises. Will you let him examine you? It's important to know if you broke your nose or cheekbones."

She swayed in place. "They do hurt. A lot. Will he tell anyone?"

"No, but medically, you will likely need a specialist."

She collapsed in my chair, spent. "I'll let Dr. Early look at me, and then we can see what he recommends."

"Tell me about the rest of you. He didn't stop at your face, did he?"

"No."

I waited for a beat, and she sighed, then rolled up her left sleeve so I could see the finger-shaped bruises on her forearm.

"He's a bastard, Mitzi. This is criminal behavior. You should report him to the police . I'm friends with the Captain. Let me call him."

"I can't go to work today, you know," she said, ignoring my request. "He may have done permanent damage to my face."

"All the more reason to call the authorities."

"He's a big star and knows people. I might never work again." She murmured this, talking to herself, not to me.

"Let me get Dr. Early." I rose and exited, leaving my battered client to think.

Early patrolled the perimeter of the living room, spinning to look at me. "What happened?" he asked.

"He beat her up, including her face. She won't commit to turning him in, but she's agreed to let you examine her. You'll need to convince her to see a real doctor, Early. She may need a plastic surgeon."

Early's lips were stretched thin. "I'm going to kill him."

"No. You're going to treat your patient with kindness and understanding and persuade her to take the necessary steps."

Early rolled his shoulders and breathed deeply. "Patient first."

"Patient first," I repeated.

Early strolled past me into the hallway and knocked on my office door with a soft tap-tap. "May I come in, Mitzi?" he asked in a gentle voice. "It's Dr. Early. I promise I won't hurt you."

"I trust you, doctor," Mitzi said. "You're Waylon's friend."

That about broke my heart. She thought I was a good guy, but Eddie and I hurt Jason's fragile ego. Mostly Eddie, but that was because of me, and Jason took out his humiliation on Mitzi.

Mrs. Ross drifted through the room, fluffing pillows, straightening picture frames, and opening and closing the drapes, using a lot of energy to manifest and interact with the physical world.

"Mrs. Ross, do you have something to say?"

"He's a rat bastard and should be in jail. I don't care what Mitzi says, that man should be in handcuffs."

"I agree."

"If you agree, do something about it, Waylon! Don't be so passive. In my day, a man grabbed a musket and shot the nuts off an abuser. No questions, no reprisals."

"You lived in a different time, Mrs. Ross."

"So did you, Waylon, or did you lose your guts when you lost your penis?"

"Mrs. Ross!"

"I'm sorry, that was out of line, but someone has to protect that woman and like it or not, you're the one she turns to."

"I'm a lover, not a fighter."

"You're neither, and if it weren't for me, you wouldn't even have a chance at the former. It's up to you on the latter. Stop standing on the fence of life, Waylon. Live in the here and now. Don't wish to die. Wish to live."

"Look at me! Mrs. Ross, really, truly, look at me! I'm a freak in a mutant body."

"At least you have a body, Waylon," said my ghost friend, as she drifted away.

That brought me up short since I'd never considered it from her perspective.

I stared out the sliding glass doors, watching a family of ducks walk through the yard. I had this lovely home, a carriage house, acres of grass and trees, even a small pond that I'd stocked with koi. I'd accumulated wealth through the decades—thank you, compound interest— and I'd used it to create this refuge for me, Early, and Mrs. Ross in one of the most stunning places on Earth. I loved my trees, all of which I'd planted myself, and watched them grow.

Mrs. Ross was right. I lived in a twilight, wishing for death, not appreciating life. It was time to change that.

I rapped on my office door and entered, prepared to tell Mitzi that I had to call the police no matter what, but that was unnecessary because Early was already on the phone speaking to 911.

"We need an ambulance for a woman who's been beaten. Yes, she'll make a statement." Early gave them my address. "They'll be here in a minute. Mitzi, thank you for trusting me."

She sighed, or, tried to sigh. She inhaled and flinched in pain. I reached for her hand, and she gave it to me, tears streaming down her face. "It hurts," she said. "It's hurting more every minute."

"Dr. Early called the police, but I'm calling in my friend. This case needs the highest attention."

I thumbed my cell phone on, found my recent calls, and redialed Perkins.

"Perkins. What is it, Waylon?"

"You know the name Jason Teague?"

"Yeah, big shot actor that you interacted with yesterday, although I'm not supposed to know that, I presume?"

"You presume correctly."

"Stupid of you to be caught on camera." I heard rustling noises in the background. I imagined him moving papers from one pile to the other.

The ambulance pulled up and Early hustled to the front door to meet the EMTs and the cop car that accompanied them.

"Is that a siren?" Perkins asked, his voice suddenly sharp. "What's going on?"

"Jason Teague beat the holy hell out of one of my clients, an actress. She's afraid of him and that she'll be blackballed in the industry if she turns him in, but Dr. Early says she needs medical attention. I'm afraid he might have broken her nose or cheekbones, Captain. She's a mess of bruises."

The captain's voice had a hard edge to it now. "I don't care how famous someone is, if he assaults someone, he's a criminal. He can be a celebrity criminal for all I care, but a criminal, and eventually an inmate, just the same. Who came with the ambulance? Which officers?"

I peeked my head in to see the two EMTs conferring with Mitzi in low voices. Two officers stood nearby, one woman and one man. The woman positioned herself closer to Mitzi while the male office stood back. I could see by the way they interacted without speaking that they'd done this before.

I motioned to the male officer and handed him the phone, mouthing, "Captain Perkins." He snapped to and answered, "Hodges here, sir."

Perkin's voice was audible but not clear. Hodge's side of the conversation was clear and uncomplicated.

"Yes, sir."

"Yes, sir."

"Understood."

"Cooper is with her."

"Yes, sir."

Hodges handed me the phone. "Captain wants the statement sent directly to him. My partner will work with her at the hospital. First priority is to get her looked at by a physician."

The EMTs brought in a stretcher, still talking to Mitzi, using their voices and bodies to communicate safety and understanding. Their postures broadcast competence and certainty, and Cooper's eyes never left Mitzi's, letting the actress know she wasn't alone. I placed my hand in Mitzi's for a brief moment before they wheeled her out.

"I'm here for you."

"I know." Her eyes welled with tears again.

"I'm coming with you, Mitzi. That is, if you want?" Early said.

"That would be great, Dr. Early."

I shifted a curtain an inch and stopped the EMTs from moving forward with an outstretched arm. "Paparazzi outside. Probably saw the ambulance and chased it, the bastards."

"Out the back?" asked Early.

"Yes. If you guys bring the ambulance inside the gate," I said to the EMTs, "we can take her out the back and load her in there."

Hodges exchanged a glance with Cooper and the EMTs, and that became the plan. The driver stepped out the front door, smack into a gaggle of photogs, snapping pictures and yelling questions.

"Who's inside?"

"Is this Waylon Jenkin's house? Did he sustain an injury yesterday?"

"Can you confirm that he was the mysterious Chet Manning?"

The driver kept his head down, flexed his muscles and pushed his way through. He backed the ambulance up, and I hoped he'd run over a few.

14

I canceled my appointments for the afternoon and drove to Paramount Ranch in search of Eddie. I kept my phone in my pocket, waiting to hear about Mitzi's status and Jason Teague's arrest, and the anxiety made me antsy. Better to be active.

Due to yesterday's events, they closed the movie set. I was relieved, happy not to run into anybody I knew who saw me on set. I'd covered my face and hands well, wore a large, floppy, hat, hiking pants, and a long-sleeved, lightweight shirt, but anyone from the movie would recognize me.

I hiked to the spot where I'd last seen Eddie, absorbing the beauty of the place. The smell of flowers, sage, and pine, the twitter of birds, and the glorious sight of a falcon circling on the thermals, reminded me of my promise to live in the present and appreciate what I had.

I stood with my arms outstretched in the exact spot I'd stood yesterday, my face to the sun, enjoying the warmth, sunscreen be damned.

"Eddie? Are you here?" My voice carried in the open space.

I turned in a circle. "Eddie?"

I crossed my fingers that Eddie hadn't returned to The Industries' campus, believing he could sneak in and get to his guys. He needed help, and maybe a different approach. That's what I wanted to discuss with him.

My voice echoed, and I frowned in concern. What if Peter had shot

Eddie after all, or that strike team proved more capable than I'd believed? I wandered toward the tree line to see if I could find any clues.

A pattern of smashed scrub alarmed me, although it was subtle and not something I would have noticed if I hadn't looked for it. I followed the flattened brush, hurrying now, wondering if they knocked Eddie unconscious and dragged him.

Until I saw the dark stains in the packed earth, black but unmistakable. Blood.

That was a stumper. Eddie wouldn't bleed.

My mind flashed to the captain's bodies. Could this be another killing?

More careful now, not wanting to raise an alarm but concerned I'd destroy evidence, I followed the trail.

And ended in a body.

My chest clenched at the sight. A foot at an impossible angle, swollen. The dark jeans were torn at the hem, the back of a weightlifter or athlete, coiffed hair now covered in dust and blood. No shoes. I circled the body, pulling out my phone to call Perkins, noticing all the limbs were attached.

One arm blocked my view of the face, and I didn't want to move it or disturb the body, so I kneeled and twisted my neck to get a look at the man's features.

My mind went blank as I worked through what I saw, then twisted in a burst of static as I plunged my phone into my pocket and scrabbled back.

Jason Teague was dead.

I shuffled back another fifteen feet and considered what to do. Calling Perkins was the right move, but I called Early first.

"Hi Waylon, I'm with Mitzi. She's got a broken nose, but the cheekbones are intact."

"That's good news, I guess. Can you move to somewhere private?"

"Sure?"

The hospital background noises receded as Early relocated.

"What's wrong, Waylon?"

"I know there's no way you could have done this..."

Early's voice was crisp, pointed. "Waylon. What is wrong?"

"I'm at Paramount Ranch. Came here to find Eddie and talk to him about his plans. I've given the situation some thought."

"Okaayyy?"

"Found a dead body."

"Eddie is a dead body."

"An unanimated one."

Early hesitated. "Who is it?"

"Jason Teague."

Early hissed. "Someone got to him before I could. Damn it."

"I think you're missing the point. Someone murdered Jason and dumped his body out here."

"Who would do that?" Early's voice was quiet and thoughtful.

"Mitzi didn't, although she'll be a suspect. Someone from the movie? Patricia?"

"Murder their meal ticket? I don't think so."

"I have to call Perkins."

"Wait a moment. I'm coming."

"Why?"

"I want to see for myself."

"Do you think Eddie did it?" I asked. "He threatened Jason yesterday."

"If Eddie killed him, he'd be buried so deep no one would find the body. Eddie's a professional."

"I'm in the car. Just hold on." A car door slammed, and a motor revved.

"I'm near the same spot from yesterday."

"Gotcha."

Twenty-five minutes later, Early huffed and puffed down the trail, his man-purse bumping his hip, and I waved him over. I'd come to terms with Jason's death in that time, not caring at all that he was dead, but trying to work out who had killed him.

Early examined the body from my position, feet away, not wanting to get closer.

"He wasn't killed here."

I nodded. "Not enough blood. I noticed."

"Why don't you call Perkins and wait in the parking lot to lead him here. I'll hold the fort. We've got to get the police involved."

"He's not going to like this, but okay."

I placed the call while walking to the movie set area. It went as well as I expected.

"How in the absolute hell did you, *you* of all people, just *happen* to stumble over Jason Teague's body?" I held the phone away from my ear and it still sounded like he was right next to me.

"Lucky?"

"Luck? I don't fucking think so! Waylon, you stay there. I'm coming to arrest you, you two-faced lying liar…"

I interrupted him.

"Perkins, listen to me and listen well. I did not kill Jason Teague. I did not kill anyone. I came here for a walk, a private walk. It's beautiful out here, and I didn't get to appreciate it properly yesterday. The movie isn't shooting, and I came to clear my head. Someone put this body here."

"He wasn't killed there?"

"I doubt it."

"Stay there, and don't fucking move."

I stayed there and didn't fucking move. The police arrived, followed by Sorya in her car.

Perkins barreled out of his cruiser, pointing at me. "You better not have touched the body."

"I didn't."

Sorya smiled at me as she gathered supplies, including an expensive-looking camera. "Let's go see what we can see, zombie-boy."

That quip didn't bother me as much as it might have. In fact, it made me grin.

Officers fanned out, looking for clues or whatever it was they did. Mostly, they kept their heads down, eyes on the ground, and avoided Perkins. I wished I could do the same.

"Early! What are you doing here?" Perkins took care with his steps even though he was spitting mad to find the doctor there.

Early shrugged. "Waylon called me at the hospital."

Perkins whirled on me. "Why did you do that?"

"I knew you'd react the way you are now."

He sputtered something unintelligible and motioned for Sorya to do her thing.

"He definitely died somewhere else, and the body's been shuffled around a bit and the clothes disturbed. I'll need to get him to the morgue to do tests," she said. "He's pretty stiff, given that he was alive yesterday." She patted the body and pressed into the legs with her fingers.

"You said that about the bodies we found before, the ones with missing legs.You think this is related? He's got all his pieces and parts."

"No, he doesn't."

"Whatcha mean? I see two legs."

"He's missing his penis."

"What!"

Aghast, I shot Early a look, and he turned from me, patting his bag, just a little tap. I coughed.

"Something to say, Waylon?" asked Perkins.

"No, not at all."

Early strode past me, leaned in and muttered, "Would be a shame to waste the Colossal, don't you think?"

"Can I go, Captain?" I asked, already taking a step to follow Early.

"Yes, but don't leave town. I'll need your statement."

"Wouldn't think of it."

Early and I marched to our respective cars and made it home in record time.

Mrs. Ross did an excellent job.

15

A discrete knock at the back sliding glass doors interrupted the inspection and admiration of my new addition, and I hurriedly zipped my pants. Mrs. Ross disappeared in a blink, and Early snuck a look behind the blinds. He blanched.

"It's Eddie."

"Let him in. I expected him to show up."

Eddie wore black gear now, including black combat boots, a mesh cap, and a matte black watch that looked like it could make dinner. I didn't see a gun, but that meant nothing because he wore a lightweight tactical vest.

"Dressed for war?" I asked.

"Peter Shunk's hunting me for real now."

I decided to be straight. "Did you kill Jason Teague?"

Eddie shook his head. "I think Peter did."

Early and I jerked at that. "Why?" asked Early.

"Peter's trying to make more zombies against protocol. He's testing a new drug that 'fixes' a body immediately so that it can be transported for an extended period before the science wizards must begin the transformation, or risk losing the soldier to true death." Eddie made air quotes around the word "fixes."

Early pursed his lips and stared at his shoes, thinking.

"Early? Will that work?" I asked.

"It's an intriguing thought."

Eddie jumped in. "It's the holy grail of Zombieology. Being able to take soldiers home and change them in controlled conditions rather than makeshift medical tents or zipping them to Ramstein Air Base."

I shuddered at the term "Zombieology," but didn't comment. "Germany?" I asked.

"Central Europe, good air transport access, and understanding allies."

"What about Asia?"

"We get them to an aircraft carrier," said Eddie.

"I didn't know any of this," said Early.

Eddie shrugged. "Top secret. Like, super top secret."

"Where were you changed?" I asked. "If it isn't rude to inquire."

Eddie gave a rueful laugh. "Bagram."

"Afghanistan," said Early.

"Roger that."

"Let's get back to Teague," I said, changing the subject. "Why did Peter target Jason Teague?"

"He's got a weird sense of justice. He's only targeted criminals for his experiments, bad guys he thinks no one will consider a loss. He witnessed Jason's behavior yesterday. Maybe that's what drove him."

I snapped my fingers. "Maybe that's what intrigued him, but I bet he followed Jason home and saw what happened to Mitzi. Mitzi said that when she ran out of the house, a man told her not to worry anymore."

Early's brows furrowed. "She didn't mention that to me, or in her statement to the police."

"She said it in passing. I didn't focus on it."

"Who's Mitzi, and what happened to her?" asked Eddie.

"Mitzi is an actress and was Jason's girlfriend until he beat on her and put her in the hospital."

Eddie punched a fist into an open palm. "My sympathies are with Peter on this one, then. Seems like he did a public service."

My voice was wry. "He still can't go around killing people."

Eddie paced between me and Early, frowning. "I left the compound because I knew Peter was up to something, and I wanted to discover what. Soldier zombies are an important tactical advantage, but we can't make them willy-nilly."

I stared at him, startled. "You support the zombie program?"

"Yeah, it's got its place, but it should be done right, with the right type of soldier. My guys are devoted to their country and want to keep protecting it, but you can't do this to just anyone."

"What about dying?"

"We don't die."

"That's correct. Exactly. Not. Ever."

"Why would I want to?"

I looked Eddie in the eyes. "I don't think you understand. Even if your body is pipe-bombed into smithereens, into particles so small they can't be collected, you don't die. Your consciousness stays with the largest chunks, even if those chunks are small. We could put you in a blender, and you'd still be you. You never leave, move on, or end."

"What happens then?"

"You hover, aware but unable to interact with the world. Eventually, your body might pull together enough for you to occupy it, but it would take a long time."

Eddie stood stock still.

I cocked my head. "Bet they never told you that."

"No, and fuck, that sucks."

"I'm not sure they know," said Early.

"Early, how could they not know? It's in your notes. You've documented this."

Early wrung his hand, a nervous gesture I rarely saw. "My notes are old, Waylon. I've reinvented myself a dozen times. I can't be sure the current administration understands all the ramifications of, uh, Zombieology, especially since they've sidelined me more than I knew."

"Wait," said Eddie, holding up a hand, looking at me. "How old are you?"

"I was born in 1841, turned in 1862, but Early was born in 1832."

"He's not a zombie."

"No. We discovered that if he consumes zombie flesh once a month, he lives a long life, but stays human."

Early explained. "I get sick, bleed, could die in a car crash. I feel pain, get cavities, and eat food."

"Eating flesh sounds distasteful, but if it gives you long life." Eddie trailed off as he thought about it.

"Waylon's keeping me alive so I can discover how to kill him. I turned Waylon at the Battle of Shiloh during the Civil War. It's my job to determine how to free him."

"Holy shit. What do you do at The Industries?"

"I keep to myself, do my science, and no one bothers me. Some money siphons off, and no one seems to notice. It's been a legacy fund for a long time."

"Well, fuck me. We need you. Once we figure out this thing with Peter, I'll speak to Quint about getting you back on the team. If it became general knowledge that eating zombie could keep you alive indefinitely, there'd be a riot. We can't let that information get out."

"I thought you went AWOL."

"Not exactly. Quint knows I'm here. No one else does. He's going to bust a gut when I tell him about eating zombie flesh."

"There are drawbacks to it," said Early, wrinkling his nose.

"Like what?"

"Another time. Right now, we've got to catch Peter. He's out of control."

I was curious, so I lifted a finger. "You like being a zombie, Eddie. Don't you miss eating? Drinking? Sex?"

"I miss eating, but what do you mean, missing sex? That's no problem."

"What? Are you kidding me?" I gaped like a fish on a hook. Early did the same.

Eddie waggled his hand in a so-so manner. "I exaggerate when I say sex isn't a problem. It's not entirely solved, and it doesn't feel like it used to, but you can pleasure a partner. We just need to solve the breakage issue."

"Breakage!"

"Yeah, leaving bits of undead flesh inside a woman isn't healthy. I mean, a lady can get toxic shock syndrome from a tampon. Imagine what a zombie can do..."

"I'd rather not," I said.

Eddie waved me off. "We can talk about this later. Right now, we need to find Peter. He's a murderer several times over, but I can't testify against him, so we need to find evidence and bring it to the authorities."

"Perkins will need something solid, something incontrovertible."

Eddie's smile was wicked. "I know how to do it, and I know how to get him here."

"How?"

"Easy. We use me as bait."

16

That's not a good idea," said Early. "He could shoot you on sight."

"What about 'not able to die' are you forgetting?" said Eddie? "If he shoots me, I keep on walking."

"You might need a new body part," I said.

"Which you will get for me. I trust you. Look, I won't get caught, but the key is that I'm just the bait. You guys need to get a confession."

"Exactly how are we going to do that?" asked Early, shaking his head. "Peter may be a lot of things, but stupid is not one of them."

"I'm just a grunt. You two are the brains of this operation." Eddie stepped outside to knock dirt off his boots, came back inside and asked, "Where's a broom?"

I pointed to the kitchen. "In the long cabinet."

He left his boots outside, gave me a lazy salute, and padded into the kitchen.

"I know how to get Peter talking," I said to Early.

"How?"

"We tell him the truth. We tell him I'm a zombie, and you're more than one hundred years old, and if he lets us in on what he's doing, we'll share with him all we know from the last century of research."

"That might work!" yelled Eddie from the kitchen.

"How did you hear that? Did they give you super hearing?" I asked, turning to watch him enter the room with the broom and dustpan.

"Don't be a knucklehead. I've always had excellent hearing, is all. Good eyesight, too. The Air Force wanted me, but I'm a glutton for punishment, so I became a Marine."

"You don't like to fly?" I asked.

He pointed to his nose. "And I don't like to fly. Like the water just fine and boots in the mud makes me happy."

"Born to be a Marine."

"That's what my momma said."

"Your mother wanted you to enlist?"

"She knew I wasn't college material and didn't want me to waste my life. She knew the Marines would give me purpose and a family, and she was exactly right. That's how the rest of my squad feels as well. It's why we chose the zombie program, so we could keep doing what we're good at."

"When you, ah, *retired*, what was your rank?"

"Never retired. I am officially part of the Corps, Waylon, just serving in a Special Ops. Oh, and to your question, First Lieutenant when I died. Captain now."

"Okay, Captain, how do you propose we lure Peter and where do you want to meet with him? We also need recording equipment, and I don't have that equipment lying around the house."

"Leave the tech to me. We'll meet him here."

17

Early placed the call as dusk settled, his anxiety about our sting operation translating well into convincing phony fear. Peter took the call right away, and I listened since Early left the phone on speaker.

"Early, what's up? Are you sick? You're not at work."

"How did you know that, Peter?"

"I get a report every day that lets me see who clocks in."

I mouthed, "Creepy, much?"

Early nodded but continued.

"Peter, you know where I live, on Waylon Jenkins' property?"

"Yes."

"I know this is crazy, but I think I saw that guy who tried to sneak onto The Industries' campus, you know, the one who ran away?"

Peter's voice rose, high pitched and wary.

"Why would he be there?"

"Waylon has many acres, Peter. It's a good place to hide, maybe? Or..." Early let his voice trail off.

"Or what?"

"Do you think he's here for revenge? You know, Waylon didn't catch him, but he chased the guy and messed up whatever he'd planned. Could Waylon be in danger?" Early put a little quiver into his voice.

"What did he look like?"

"I can't say exactly. He wore black from head-to-toe and, to my eye, not that I'm an expert or anything, moved like a soldier, fast and silent. I saw when the motion sensors near my cottage flashed and made me look outside."

"That could be anyone, Early. If you have an intruder, call the police."

"He turned his face in my direction, and I saw a scar that ran from his ear down his jaw."

Peter was silent.

"Peter?" Early winked at me, knowing Peter was on the hook.

"Doc, that man is armed and dangerous. You need to stay inside and keep Waylon there. I'll get my people out there as soon as possible. I'll text you when we arrive."

"Thanks, Peter. We'll feel better once you check it out."

"Just stay inside, Early, and don't do anything to spook him." Peter hung up.

Early and I high fived, and then I flicked the light on and off to signal Eddie, who was hiding outside somewhere doing the voodoo only he could do.

"Mrs. Ross?" I called. "You ready?"

"Yes, Waylon. I know my part." Her voice came from everywhere and nowhere, and I wondered how she did that and then wondered why I hadn't asked her more questions about her past and origins. She'd always been there, taking care of me, and for the life of me, I couldn't remember how that had happened.

"Mrs. Ross, when did we first meet?"

"Waylon!" Eddie knocked on my back, glass door. "Did he say he was coming immediately?"

"He implied it, yes."

"Someone is here, but I don't think it's him." Eddie ducked, looking right and left. "Something's not right."

And he was gone.

Early and I exchanged glances, and he took a breath, ready to say something, when the sliding glass cracked, shattering inward. Early dove for cover while I stupidly stood there and let a bullet go through me front to back, exiting at kidney level. I watched it pass through and heard it embed itself in the wall.

"Down, Waylon!" A ghostly hand yanked me by the collar and pulled me to the floor. "Don't be foolish. Getting yourself torn up isn't going to help anyone, and I don't want to repair all of those holes."

I crawled behind the couch as the bullets continued to fly. "Thanks, Mrs. Ross. Who's shooting at us?" I yelled.

"I can't tell," said my spectral friend.

"I have no idea!" Early yelled.

"Are those sirens?"

Early hazarded a glance out the window. "Someone must have called the police!"

The phone rang, and I smacked one hand to my head, knowing who it had to be. I didn't even say hello.

"Waylon! What in hell is going on over there? I've got shots fired in a civilian area, and the shots are coming from your house."

"Perkins!" A shot zinged over my head and knocked a painting off the wall. "I can't hear you. Sorry."

I hung up.

"What do we do?" Early asked, army-crawling to my side.

"We get out of here. They may escalate the attack."

"What do you mean, escalate?"

Whoosh! A grenade, a freakin' *grenade*, bounced through the broken back door and landed two feet from us.

"Holy shit!" Early scrambled to his feet, me on his heels. I used both hands to shove him toward the front door, then turned. He'd never get out in time if I didn't do something.

"Run!" I hissed, giving him one last shove on his shoulder.

"Waylon!" He tried to grab my arm, but I was too far, and an arm in law enforcement khaki seized him by the hand and pulled him to safety.

"Mr. Jenkins!" Another voice this time, but I ignored it and launched my body into the living room, covering the grenade with my torso, held it to my chest, grasped the corner of the thick Persian area rug that lay on top of the carpet and rolled myself and the grenade in it.

The explosion still took out the top of the house, flinging chunks of wood, plaster, cotton, and zombie flesh into the early evening sky. I looked down on what was left from mid-air as my top half disintegrated into far-flung bits and saw my waist, legs, and feet laying askew in what remained of the house.

My consciousness floated, and I got a good look at the carnage and the players.

Peter and his team hunkered down in the northeast corner of the property, while Eddie held his post on the northwest corner. I let my consciousness fly closer to Eddie and saw he wasn't alone. He had two men with him. I wanted to see more but my lower body was pulling me back. I had just enough mental energy to check on the police.

They were in the front spanning both east and west along the southern border. Two police officers leaned on Early, using their combined body weight to keep him from running back in the house. Dimly, I heard him screaming my name.

A movement behind the police, encroaching on their position from across the street where my neighbor lived, caught my eye. I peered closer, hoping the police had evacuated that family, and faltered as I saw another military-style unit of a dozen or so men fanning out behind Captain Perkin's team.

Who the hell were they?

That's all I could garner before what remained of my body yanked me down to earth, and there I was anchored to my lower half, unable to talk or walk, locked in the carnage of what used to be my house, unable to warn Perkins to watch his six. My spirit kicked and screamed, railing at my impotence. I scanned my mind, skittering from thought to thought, ping-ponging from idea to idea, a frenzy of mental energy with no outlet. Imagine being in a coma, your family standing over you, talking about when they should pull the plug, and you can hear and understand everything but are powerless to let them know. That was me.

I was no help to anyone like this. I needed to calm down. To think. I focused, suspended above my legs and lower torso, and heard a voice or something—not a voice, per se, but communication.

Waylon, can you hear me?

Mrs. Ross?

Yes. Good. I need you to listen.

You're staticky.

Yes. Listen, you are spirit and body now.

Half body and half spirit, you mean.

More like a combination of both.

In other words, useless to everyone. Mrs. Ross, there is an unknown player in this game. I don't think we've seen the whole picture. Can you reach Early?

No. He's out front, past the boundaries of the house grounds, and with the main house in wreckage ...

What? You're fading, Mrs. Ross. What's happening?

I'm tied to the main house. I'm fractured. That's why I'm hard to hear. I don't have much time. The house continues to collapse. You have to focus and move your lower half. Your spirit can control your lower body.

That's absurd.

You're a half-bodied zombie talking to a broken ghost. Nothing is absurd.

She had a point.

I'll try.

Focus on a small movement first.

I stayed close to my burned body and concentrated on my right big toe.

Come on, toe. Wiggle! Wiggle, dammit.

My left toe jerked.

Okay, my left toe. I'm open to any toe at this moment.

My right toe twitched.

Okay, progress. Did you see that, Mrs. Ross?

Mrs. Ross?

Nothing. No answer.

More bullets tore through the air, coupled with shouts from all sides. Shrieks of pain and confusion from the police in the front caught my attention, and I redoubled my efforts. After what felt like forever, I rolled both ankles, bent my knees, and flipped my lower torso and legs to the front, pushing to my feet. I staggered out of the wreckage, half a human body walking on its own.

And was promptly tackled by a muscular arm and knocked to the ground.

"Waylon? You managed to animate half a body? That's amazing, dude."

My spirit studied this gargantuan, African-American man who looked like he ate boulders for breakfast, except for the fact that he was a zombie and wouldn't eat anything.

"Oh, right. You can't answer me. I'm Everest. Eddie sent me to get you, or what was left of you. I'm psyched there's a whole part. I wasn't looking forward to loading up bone shards and grody tissue into this basket." He patted a picnic basket he had tied to his waist. "Would have done it. Orders and all, but I wouldn't have liked it. I have a sensitive stomach."

He motioned for me to follow and squatted, duck walking away, dropping the basket to the ground. I squatted my lower half, and duck walked too, proud of myself for getting the hang of it.

Until I passed the first body.

"Yeah, watch out for him. We've got one for you already, so we don't need him. Stay low, though," he said, as another bullet zipped over my kidneys.

He dropped and rolled, so I did the same, discovering it was harder to move a body without pectoral muscles or arms, but I managed.

"Coolio, dude. You're the shit."

At least Everest thought I was doing well.

"Everest? You got him?" This voice was higher pitched, and the face that matched it was baby-faced, pale, and wore glasses. I'd have to ask later why a zombie needed spectacles.

"Affirmative, Clipper. Look what he can do."

I sat with my legs out straight and wiggled my ass in the ground.

"Huh."

"Yeah, look at that. Awesome, right? You have the body?"

"Uh-huh."

I got the sense Clipper was a man of few words.

"Where's Eddie?" Everest asked.

"Peter."

"Shit, man. He promised he wouldn't go after him alone!"

I wiggled my butt harder and kicked my feet. Everest lay a hand on my knee. "Don't worry, dude, we'll take care of you."

I was exhausted and flopped on the ground, spent, just in time to see a shadow behind Everest. I pointed my toe, shaking my foot as hard as possible, trying to warn the zombie, but it was no use. A hand clamped over Everest's mouth and nose and pulled him to the ground. The shadow plunged a needle into Everest's arm, and the zombie went still. Clipper's soft grunt told me the same happened to him. I was betting that was fixing solution, and I wondered what it did to a zombie.

The shadow was a medium-sized man, wrapped ninja-style in black cotton. Even his face was covered, with only a small opening for air around his nose and mouth. He jerked his head at the darker shadows pressed against the trees. "It's time to end this. Go get them."

The shadows melted away, and the ninja kicked my leg.

"I knew you were a zombie the first time I saw you, Waylon. The fake skin and makeup didn't fool me, although you're outstanding at it. I have to give you that."

The voice. Familiar.

Nothing peculiar about it, smooth but not distinctive. Then, he sniffed, and I had a mental picture of large nostrils in the most boring face on the most boring body in the most elegant but nondescript room, wearing a tailored but ordinary gray suit.

Quint Addington?

What was he doing out here dressed like an extra in a Jet Li movie?

"Since we can't have a real heart-to-heart, Waylon, given you are missing one right now, I'll let you hover there and watch, and yes, I've read all of Early's writings. I know your spirit is anchored to your body, but I've kept that tidbit quiet. The whole point of the zombie program is to have cannon fodder. If people knew your spirits lived on, suspended on this plane, they'd get itchy about retrieving bodies and the like, and that would ruin everything." He turned to this right. "Oh, look. Here they are."

Two brawny men covered head-to-toe in ninja gear like Quint strong-armed Eddie and Peter to our position. Peter sported a bruise on his face the size and shape of a fist, and Eddie's right sleeve hung loose due to a lack of an arm. I wondered where that was. It takes a lot of strength to rip off a limb, but when I saw the troll bringing up the rear, I guessed that he was the culprit.

He wasn't really a troll. As far as I knew, trolls didn't exist, but this human's bulk made my new buddy Everest look like a grassy knoll. His body's black wrappings stretched to the limit, cotton fibers fraying at the edges, and, with his face bare, I could see his features, including his dull eyes. He was a zombie of unusual size, built for brute strength, robbed of intelligence, the equivalent of a bulldozer or a wrecking ball, and his very existence angered me to my core. This had once been a feeling, thinking, human being, and he'd been transformed into a violent giant to follow his maker's wishes.

I heard an anguished intake of breath, followed by a low purr of suppressed violence.

Quint looked around, wondering where that sound came from. He counted his men, eyed Peter, who was hanging his head, drool and blood dripping from his lips, and sniffed again at Eddie, who stared at him with unrestrained fury.

"Don't huff at me, Eddie. We made you just as we made him. You owe your new life to us. We decide who leads and who follows, who is best for strategy, and who is best for blunt trauma. Mikey here was never much of a thinker."

Eddie didn't say a word, but I knew that Quint was mistaken.

Eddie wasn't the originator of that sound. Early was. Early had somehow figured out where I was and was hiding nearby.

Which raised an important question.

Where was Captain Perkins? Because there was no way Early snuck away from the police without him.

Which meant my two friends were nearby and thick in the middle of freakin' Crazy Town, and all I had was two legs, a derriere, and a colossal penis.

18

Quint cocked his head and held a finger to his ear. Shouts and orders issued through a megaphone told me the cops' reinforcements had arrived, and I surmised that Quint's team was asking for orders. My suspicions were confirmed when Quint said, "Team A, retreat, get back to the meeting point. Team B, second stage."

Even super-soldier zombies might get caught by the police if the authorities stretched their net enough, but Quint seemed awfully sure of himself. I didn't know what he meant by "second stage," but I worried officers would be hurt. I had just enough time to imagine multiple scenarios when an explosion concussed the air, and Quint smiled.

"Not too much damage," he quipped. "Just outside The Commons," he said, noting a popular open-air plaza with shopping and dining. "They'll need to evacuate. That'll keep them occupied."

"That's a busy area," Eddie said, his eyes hard, his voice brittle. "You probably killed some people. You definitely destroyed property. And for what? To catch me?"

Quint kicked Eddie in the balls, the strike lightning fast. Eddie oomphed and bent over, but Quint was unsatisfied.

"That didn't even hurt you, you big actor. Your reaction is a memory. An artifact."

Eddie coughed. "I feel pressure. It's not painful like it would be, but it isn't pleasant."

Quint waved Eddie's objections away. "I eat zombie flesh once a month to stay young, but I don't get the benefits of being a full zombie. I can die and feel pain and all that stuff. You don't know how good you have it."

"Then why don't you kill yourself and come back as a zombie yourself?" Eddie asked.

"Great question, and despite my dislike of time-wasting soliloquies, I'll answer it, because we have an excellent example of why sitting in front of us." Quint toed my leg, and I shook him off.

"This is why. You can't move on. You're stuck, right here, right now. Body is evaporated? You're still here. Body burned beyond recognition? Still here. Body shoved through a wood chipper? Still here."

Eddie spat in the dirt. "Given your recent activities, I don't think you want to find out what comes after this life, Quint. What if Hell is real?" Eddie adjusted his stance a little, and Mikey let him have a little room, proving that Quint was right. Mikey wasn't a thinker.

"This is why we made you a captain, Eddie, because you're smart. Here's the thing, I don't think what I'm doing is wrong. I'm making our military stronger, fighting the good fight. I stand for truth and justice."

"No, you don't."

"I only killed criminals, Eddie. Doesn't that count for something? I figured no one would care about a bunch of small-time criminals, especially if I found the answer to our biggest problem."

"Fixing bodies for longer times? Maintaining a soul's connection?"

"Got it in one, Eddie. Now, you two," he said, pointing at his guards, "Let's get all of these zombies back to the meeting point. Hands on your head, Peter. Eddie, for you, hand on head. Let's get moving."

Peter complied, but Eddie pressured Quint.

"You set Peter and me against each other?"

"Peter figured out someone from the firm was doing experiments, so I told him it was you, gone rogue. Then, I told you it was him, and presto, my problem was solved. You guys went after each other. Then Waylon and Early got involved, and things got complicated, so I decided to shut it down. Genius, don't you think?"

"Again. No."

"Whatever. You have no right to complain. Some of your men got the legs as a side benefit. No use wasting perfectly good extremities. Small thinking, Eddie. Small minds. We need to think out of the box."

"Small mind, one arm, but still a loyal soldier, you sonofabitch." Eddie reared up, head-butted Mikey, who took the blow with a small shake of his head but without orders, didn't know how to react. Peter, who must have been faking the extent of his injuries, pulled a knife out of somewhere and stabbed his guard in the neck, then ripped it out with a hard grunt. The guard managed a look of surprise, clapped his hand to his wound ,and then fell backward when Peter kicked him in the knee.

Everest staggered to his feet, moving stiffly, and Clipper followed, each jerking like marionettes, but they got in there swinging, adding to the mayhem. Quint barked something into his lapel as he ducked a wild punch from Everest.

A hand grabbed me by the pants and pulled me backward as a wave of cops ran through the yard, pointing guns at Quint and his team, Peter, Eddie, Everest, and Clipper, without knowing who was a good guy or a bad guy. A SWAT vehicle clipped my poor Evergreen Pear tree, and the brawl trampled my flowering Jacaranda's purple-blue carpet of petals.

Tiny problems in the scheme of things, but I noticed, and noticing made me realize anew that I wanted to live. I mean, does a person who wants to die care if a tree has the right sunny spot with well-drained soil, or wonder if the pink Crape Myrtle would look good with a purple one beside it?

Decidedly not.

I twisted my legs right and left, searching for an avenue of escape when Early's voice said, "Stop struggling, Waylon. It's me."

Early pulled me toward the koi pond and beyond. He dragged me to a mimosa tree, one of my favorites, and told me to hold still. A body already lay there, a soldier by the look of it, deceased by a gunshot through the chest. If I'd had a heart, it would have skipped a beat as I examined him from my spiritual perch, hoping the man hadn't felt pain. I could tell it was just a body, though. No soul lingered.

Early held a tree limb saw and went to work, dividing the soldier's body in two, blood and guts spilling everywhere, then shuffled it over to connect it to my lower half. Mrs. Ross appeared out of nowhere and started sewing while Early injected my leg with something that zinged up it like electricity and chanted something softly.

Magic tugged at me, a pull that throbbed like a toothache throughout my entire being and I grew sluggish as my soul turned into ribbons that rotated and swirled like water down a drain into my restored body, half of what I had, half of what someone else gave me, but all my spirit.

I settled in like fog dissipating after a prolonged rain. It was a gentle diffusion, as my soul sought the far corners of the new body like an eager five-year-old searching an old house for cool hiding places. I didn't fall in as much as disperse, circulating through my new physical home, exploring, finding it delightfully healthy and fit. I touched down with a sigh, grateful to be whole again, relieved this joining wasn't violent.

Early and Mrs. Ross loomed over me, and I swatted them away with my new arms. "I'm here. I'm here. All's well. Back up. Mrs. Ross, good to see you. I was worried."

Mrs. Ross flickered in a way that made me think of someone holding their breath, and Early clapped my shoulder.

"Oooh. Good musculature there, Waylon. Solid. This guy must have been a weightlifter."

"A soldier stays in shape. I'm sorry he's gone but glad to use what he left behind."

Early chewed his lip. "He was gone, wasn't he?"

I nodded. "Totally gone. We're not using anything he needs."

"Good."

The process had either dimmed my hearing or made me oblivious to it because sound popped in like my ears were recovering after a heavy metal concert, suddenly and at a loud volume.

"What the hell is going on?" I asked, blinking as flashing strobe lights lit up my yard.

"The factions are going at it. The Sheriff's team, with Perkins in there somewhere, Eddie's team, and Quint's are all fighting. Peter's is in the mix as well. No one knows who to trust."

"I have to get in there."

"Be careful! This body's center of gravity might be different than you are used to…"

He trailed off as I tripped over my feet, landing hard on my knees.

He cleared his throat. "As I said."

"And you weren't the most graceful before, either," added Mrs. Ross.

"Not helpful," I growled. Hey, my voice was deeper.

I waded into the mêlée, grabbing men by their collars, pulling them to the ground. "Stop shooting!" I yelled, but only a few heard me. I pointed to those I'd taken down. "I'm not kidding. Stay down and stay put. This has to end."

One of them, Quint's by the black ninja garb, leaped toward me, and I punched him in the mouth, sending teeth flying.

Hunh. I liked this.

I moved on, slipping behind a police officer sharpshooter whose partner whirled on me with a handgun. I put my hands in the air.

"Stop. I'm Waylon Jenkins. This is my house and my yard. Well, it was my house, before it blew to smithereens. I know what to do. Tell your boy here not to shoot me, okay?"

The young cop studied me. "You don't look like your picture."

"It's been a hard evening."

"Still…"

"Look, I was here when Hodges and Cooper came to take Mitzi to the hospital. No one else knows which officers escorted her, right? We kept it a secret, taking her out the back door."

The young man wasn't convinced.

The sharpshooter spoke to someone in his ear. "Roger," and pfft, pfft, two shots took out the strobes. I shook my head to clear it, instantly better now that the seizure-inducing lights were gone.

"Give me your radio," I said to the young guy. He handed it to me.

"Perkins, can you hear me?"

"Waylon?"

"Yeah."

"I thought you were a little under the weather."

"I got better. Did you hear what Quint said?"

"Heard it all. We'd like to move in. We've got him surrounded, but your friend's team is still wrangling with him."

With the lights gone—Quint's work, I imagined—the scene wasn't as chaotic as I had believed. The police were in good position, calmly watching a brawl between Everest, Clipper, Eddie, Peter, Mikey, and a couple of other guys, the black ninjas belonging to Quint and the ones wearing fatigues belonging to Peter.

The only problem was that Quint wasn't anywhere around.

I waded into the fray, ducking and weaving as I went, and yanked at Mikey, who was wailing away at Eddie and Clipper. Mikey backhanded me one right in the jaw, and I flew several feet, stumbling and falling on my ass.

"That's it!" I yelled. "Everybody hold still!"

I got a few suspicious looks, but they kept at it. I motioned to an officer who threw me a megaphone. I held it to my mouth, wondering what would catch the attention of a bunch of hardened soldiers, most of whom had died and come back to fight another day. I settled on a simple, tried and true technique.

"Stop, motherfuckers!"

They froze mid-punch, mid-hair pull, and mid-kick. One stopped mid-bite. But they stopped, so that was just fine.

19

Every single person, or zombie, was under arrest until Perkins gained control and convinced his boss, the Sheriff, to let him handle things. Happily, and to my complete surprise, none of the police officers were seriously hurt, although they were mightily pissed off. They tromped off bitching and moaning about military operations in their territory, endangering civilians, and reckless destruction of property, but they all went home that morning, so I considered it a win.

I'd rubbed dirt on my face and donned a baseball cap, something Early shoved into my hands, to hide my different visage. Everyone was so tired they didn't give me a second glance anyway.

Perkins buried his fury beneath cold competence, sorting out who would write which reports with practiced efficiency, but he kept a cold eye on Peter, Eddie and their men, who dozed on what remained of my lawn with the nonchalance of soldiers who knew how to catch their Zzs wherever they could. The zombies curled up or spread out under foliage, preferring to be out of the morning sun and as cool as possible.

Eddie was the only one awake, in a deep, urgent conversation with Early, stabbing at the ground with the forefinger of his remaining hand.

I roamed the wreckage of my once beautiful yard, noticing flower beds that I'd planted now trampled. I touched my mimosa tree, glad it was still standing, and hurried to my Evergreen Pear, worrying all was lost. It was missing a huge branch that was now on the ground, cracked into three sections, and the main trunk canted at a disturbing angle, but the root system seemed intact, so I thought that if I staked it well, it would recover. I knew I had an arborist's name somewhere in the house.

Oh. The house.

Early's cottage was in perfect shape, untouched, but the main house was a mangled mess of wire, rebar, plaster, brick, wood, and any other natural or man-made material that went into building such a structure. The remains of the roof had obliterated the back porch, and what had been my kitchen was exposed to the rising sun.

My office and all its equipment and products were a complete slag. I rounded the front, shocked to see the main door standing, connected to the vestiges of the entryway like it was waiting for a visitor to ring the bell. Even the welcome mat rested in its customary spot, undisturbed. I had the distinct impression it was waking up, stretching, and wondering what was going on and who had made all that racket.

"You."

Huh? I looked around. Perkins stifled a yawn and beckoned me with his hand.

"You," he said, shrugging on a jacket, "are coming with me."

"Where are we going?"

"After Quint."

"Don't you want police officers? Maybe Peter?"

"I'll have officers ready. Peter is under arrest, as are all the Rambos that invaded your property and made this nice neighborhood a warzone. They're not going anywhere."

I wasn't so sure about that, being confident that if Eddie and his crew didn't like the party, they'd leave whether Perkins wanted them to or not. Same for Quint's guys, but I hoped that the police had a couple of large men guarding Mikey because if he did a runner, no one could stop him.

I was anxious to see Quint behind bars. "Happy to oblige, Captain. That man hurt my pear tree."

"And *murdered* three people, Waylon, not to mention starting a gun battle in the suburbs," he said, gesturing to the yard and street, his voice tight. He opened a squad car's passenger door and pointed to the seat. I slid in, buckled my seatbelt, and watched him get in the driver's side.

Perkins cleared his throat as he started the car and flipped on the red and blue lights. "I am sorry about your trees, though. You don't seem as upset about the house. Why?"

"I'm not happy about it, Captain, but I worry about things with heartbeats more. People first, animals, and plants. Living creatures."

"Trees don't have heartbeats."

"Yes, they do. All life has some rhythm. When you're technically dead, Perkins, you notice these things."

"I never thought of it that way."

I changed the topic. "You're taking my change in appearance pretty well, Captain."

He spared me a glance, then turned his attention to the road, pushing his speed, veering in and out of traffic. "What change? They reattached your body which, when I think about it later, will weird me out, but you look like you always do."

I lowered the visor and checked myself in the lipstick mirror. Sure enough, my hair had grown back like it always did, and my eyes were my own. The features had softened and were settling into my old face.

I'd lost pieces of my face before, mostly my nose, but never had the entire head replaced, so this was new to me. I checked my arms and was happy to see the muscles were still there. I shifted in the seat and was delighted *that* was there, too.

I glanced out the window and didn't recognize the scenery. "Where are we going?"

Perkins' grin was feral. "Quint Addington's home. I have eyes there, and they say his car is in the drive and there's movement inside."

"Wouldn't he run?"

Perkins scoffed. "Who knows why a guy like that does what he does? He's a murderer, but he believes the ends justifies the means. I've got people watching the airport, too, and I've got his name and photo out there—all hands on deck and everyone on watch. The Sheriff is on the warpath. He wants this guy, but not more than I do."

"That's why we are going to his house personally?"

Perkins lifted his hands from the steering wheel for a moment to rub them together. "Yes. I want to arrest that son-of-a-bitch myself."

"You really think he's just there, waiting?"

"He has to know he's caught, that it's only a matter of time. Maybe he wants a clean arrest."

Quint's house lay at the end of a quiet cul-de-sac. Marked and unmarked police cars lined the street.

Perkins jerked his chin at the cops. "We've cordoned off the area and have cars on every block. He's not getting anywhere."

The modest brick house had a medium-sized yard with a simple porch sporting one outdoor rocking chair. Like everything about Quint, it was unremarkable, a part of the dull and unnoticeable exterior he'd cultivated to hide the fiend beneath.

Perkins pulled up in the driveway, not bothering to hide his appearance. Several police officers, all wearing tactical vests and helmets, joined us.

"Sir, let us go in and get him," said one. "You shouldn't even be out here without your gear."

"This guy isn't going to shoot us in the street," Perkins said. "He thinks he's too smart for us."

"Fine, but I go first," and the man shifted his position to be in front, Perkins behind him.

We walked to the front door and knocked, flanked by loyal cops ready for anything. Those same cops pushed me out of the way and wouldn't let me near the door. I followed anyway, earning angry glares until Perkins barked, "He's okay."

A woman with dark hair in a bun answered the door holding a toilet brush. She licked her lips, and when she spoke, her voice quavered. "I've seen you on the street. What's going on?" she said. "Is there trouble? I have my papers. I'm legal." Her eyes were nervous but defiant.

"We're not Immigration, ma'am. We're here for Mr. Addington. Is he home?"

The woman shook her head. "He's been gone for hours. No one here but me."

"His car is in the driveway."

"That's his second car."

"He only has one registered."

She shrugged, more relaxed now that this wasn't about her. "He drives a black Range Rover, too."

Perkins turned to his team. "Search the home. We have the warrant. Please step aside, ma'am." While his team stormed the beach, he got on the radio. I stood there feeling stupid and tired, but also angry. Quint had murdered three people, destroyed my home, hurt my trees, and escaped. Deep in thought, I jumped when Perkins called my name.

"You won't believe this, Waylon, but he's at *work*."

"At The Industries?"

"Wearing a suit and everything like today was a goddamned normal day. I've got people there, and they've placed him in a conference room under guard." He jogged to the man who'd insisted on going to the door first and issued some instructions. Plainclothes detectives were in the house, turning everything over. The housekeeper sat on the front porch chair, smoking a cigarette, unconcerned but also unsurprised. Maybe she'd seen the beast behind the mask.

20

The Industries' parking lot was quiet. The entrance guards waved us through this time without a word, not that Perkins would have given them the time of day if they'd asked for it. He needed them to lift the gate, and that was all. He was done asking for permission.

The security guards snapped to attention as well, perhaps sensing that today was not the day to mess with the captain. He radiated anger in every step, his heels tapping sharply as he came up the walk. He raised an eyebrow, and they opened the door. One of the internal guards brought us to the first-floor conference room without saying a word.

"He's in there?" Perkins said to the cops on guard.

"Yes, sir. We put him there ourselves," said the one on the right. "No weapons. No windows in there. This is the only way in."

"Open the door. One of you stay here, the other, follow us in and stay by the door."

Quint wore a navy suit with a crisp white shirt and a red tie, every inch the executive, and sat with one leg crossed over the other.

"What's going on, Captain Perkins? I heard about the dustup over at your house, Waylon. Was Early involved? Is that why I'm being held?"

"Dustup?" Perkin's voice cracked with incredulity, and the cop at the door coughed as if he was choking. "Oh, come off it, Quint. You were there. You know exactly why we're here."

Quint shook his head, a puzzled look on his face. "I have no idea what you are talking about, Captain."

"Bullshit. Stand up. You're under arrest."

Quint stayed where he was. "On what charge?"

"Murder, three counts, plus a bunch of other charges that I'll add to the list as I go."

"Murder? That's absurd. What proof do you have?"

"I was there, Quint. I heard your confession."

"You were where, Captain?"

I couldn't stay silent. I was seething with rage. "At my home, Quint. When you played ninja and brought a strike team to my house to take out Peter, Eddie, and his team."

"I never did that."

"You destroyed my home! You admitted to killing three people for the sake of your zombie research."

"Oh, is that what this is about? The zombie research? Well, I admit it. We do that kind of research, strictly for the military, mind you."

"For your own gain, Quint, and how old are you anyway? You said you eat zombie flesh every month to stay young."

"That's disgusting. I do not."

Perkins was silent, so I turned to him. "Aren't we arresting him?"

"You can't," Quint sneered. "You have no evidence."

I thought about it. Quint had never revealed his face. He'd been wrapped up like a mummy the entire time, only a tiny strip open for his nose and mouth. He'd never said his name, either.

Quint stood, feeling his victory. "And while you might not like our research, that's not for you to decide. We're making our military stronger, fighting the good fight."

Perkins cocked his head.

I answered, "You stand for truth and justice?"

Quint crossed his arms. "Exactly. We decide who leads and who follows, who is best for strategy, and who is best for blunt trauma."

"Good enough for me," said Perkins, pulling out his handcuffs. "Quint Addington, you're under arrest. We have multiple witnesses, including myself, who heard you say those exact words at Waylon's house. In fact," Perkins pulled out his phone. "I have you recorded."

Perkins moved his thumb over a red button, hit play, and held up the phone, so we could see it. The video was dark, but a black swathed Quint was center stage saying the exact words he'd repeated for us now.

Quint jeered, his voice mocking. "That's your evidence, Captain? A recording of a man in black?"

"Well, that and when Eddie referred to you as Quint, you didn't deny it. It's enough to hold you while we build our case. Turn around."

We drove, Quint in the backseat, in cuffs, but his calm unsettled me.

"You can hold him, Jacob?" I whispered.

Perkins startled at my use of his first name. "Yes, Waylon. We've got him. Don't worry."

I was a zombie who'd been born before the Civil War and somehow survived intact. I'd been nervous every day of my post-life. Not to mention that I had Post-Traumatic Stress Disorder from my turning. Worry was my middle name, but I trusted the Captain. I decided to let go of the anxiety for once. It felt good.

I set up shop in the cottage, and Early moved to a rental a mile away. I told him he could move back once I had my house rebuilt.

Mrs. Ross floated into my small bedroom. "You have a visitor."

"Who is it?"

She sniffed. "One of those men from the skirmish."

"The *skirmish*? Which one? What does he want?"

"How should I know?"

"Didn't you ask? Mrs. Ross, haven't we been through this? It's your job to ask. You're my executive assistant."

"Then, I want to be your partner."

Rolling my eyes, I followed her out the door into the main room and found Peter Shunk waiting there, crushing a ball cap in his hands.

"Hi, Peter."

"Waylon." He bounced on his toes but didn't say anything.

"What can I do for you?"

His words burst forth. "Is it true that a zombie's spirit stays earth-bound where the body is?"

I nodded.

"It never leaves?"

"Not as far as I know, no."

Peter ran his fingers through his hair. "I need your help then, Waylon."

I sat and motioned to a chair, but he didn't sit. "What's going on, Peter?"

"Several months ago, Eddie's team deployed."

"Where?"

"Let's say it wasn't in California. Or in the United States."

"Okay. You deployed a zombie team in a foreign country under dubious circumstances."

Peter paced. "It wasn't dubious, and we had orders, but let's say we weren't invited in by the present government."

"What happened?"

"We left a man behind. Zed, one of Eddie's team. He got dismembered, and we left him there. Well, we left the pieces there."

I rubbed my eyes in disbelief. "We'll get to the dismembering later, but Eddie was okay with that?"

"No, but I ordered him to withdraw, and we thought that he'd lived an honorable second life, we couldn't put him back together, and there's no family to claim remains, so it was an acceptable loss."

I folded my hands in a prayer position and leaned my elbows on my knees. Was there no end to their stupidity and ignorance?

Peter continued, speaking fast now. "We want to go get him, or whatever we can find of him. We need you and Early to come with us. You're the only two people with experience in this."

I thought of Zed lingering near his body parts as they decomposed, wondering what he should do. Realizing there was nothing he could do.

"I'll talk to Early."

Peter let out a sigh of relief. "Thank you, Waylon."

"When do we leave?"

"As soon as possible. First thing in the morning, if you can."

"I'll see you tomorrow."

Peter left, thanking me again, promising to pick me up at six a.m., sharp.

Mrs. Ross sighed, watching him leave. "It's the right thing to do, Waylon, but before you go, you need to speak to someone."

"I know." Before I traveled anywhere, I needed to talk to Sorya. Our date night was ruined and I owed her.

I stopped by her office, which was as cluttered as ever. She was sitting at her desk, and her eyes lit up when she saw me. My guilt rose even more.

"We're going to have to postpone our date, Sorya. I'm sorry." I explained the situation.

Sorya chewed her lip the whole time I spoke and stayed silent.

"I really am sorry, Sorya. I can't leave a man's spirit hanging like that. It's cruel."

She nodded and rose, coming round her desk to stand in front of me.

"I understand, Waylon. I'm a little disappointed, is all. I've never asked a man out before, you know."

I closed the distance between us and lifted her chin with my finger. She was so tiny. I gentled my touch, afraid I'd hurt her.

"I'm looking forward to our first date, Sorya. And our second."

That made her smile.

"I hope so, Waylon."

I dropped my hand and turned to leave. Just as I passed through the door into the hallway, she called my name.

"Waylon."

"Yes?"

She walked to the door and put a hand on the frame. "Maybe we'll make it to a third date." Sorya winked at me. "I'm sure it will be colossal."

She closed the door with a click.

HIDE & CHIC

1

Everest lost his head, and Peter caught it.

I watched the zombies as they trained in an old gymnasium, wrinkling my nose against the stagnant funk of gym socks and jock straps that had built up over decades. The Industries, the organization that funded the undead military squad, had paid for the building, totally unaware of the purchase thanks to Peter's financial shuffling. Externally, it looked like an abandoned lot with a broken-down basketball court and a padlock on the door. Inside, it served an important purpose—letting unkillable, dead people hack each other to pieces.

Right now, antipathy and frustration ran amok and machetes swung with abandon. Eddie, atypically for the seasoned soldier and the leader of the group, lost control and sliced off Everest's head in one wild stroke. It flew in a languid arc, Everest's brown eyes rolling in disbelief, until Peter dove, caught it, cradled it like an experienced wide receiver, and landed on his back, holding it up in the air.

"Don't spike it!" I yelled, jumping from the bleachers and running to grab the head from Peter.

"Jesus fucking Christ!" Everest yelled, his face thunderous, his dark skin blushing a furious, mottled purple. "What's wrong with you, Eddie?"

Eddie flushed with embarrassment. "I'm so sorry, Everest. I'm not used to machetes."

"None of us are, but you don't see anyone else slicing off heads." Everest jerked his eyes in Eddie's direction. "Waylon, turn me around."

I pivoted, holding his head in my arm so he faced his commanding officer.

Eddie grimaced and pleaded his case. "I'm a little off with the whole Zed thing. It's my fault we left him."

"We didn't know he couldn't move on," Everest said from the crook of my elbow. "It's not your fault. We'll go get him and make him whole again."

I wasn't sure this would work, but I'd agreed to go on this cockamamie mission because the zombie military unit left a soldier on the battlefield, not realizing that zombies never die. Even if you pulverize our bodies in a blender with spinach to make a zombie smoothie, our spirits stay tethered to the earth, unable to move on or interact with the outside world. We linger in endless limbo, a hellish scenario I'd experienced personally until my doctor friend, Samuel Early, reconstituted my body, and I'd returned to it. Early was the Civil War doctor who'd turned me into a zombie in the first place, and I'd kept him alive by feeding him some of my flesh each month so he could research how to kill me.

The zombie unit, a black-ops group so unofficial that not even the President knew about it, hid in plain sight under the rubric of an aboveboard company called The Industries, headquartered near me in Calabasas, CA. The unit got sucked into a skirmish on my property, and we'd become allies of sorts. It was a violent skirmish with guns, bad guys in black, and the authorities. I lost my torso and head for a while, but it all worked out in the end. Our local police captain arrested the evildoer, a vile man named Quint Addington, and I thought I'd go back to my day job as a cosmetologist to the Hollywood movers and shakers, smoothing out wrinkles on celebrity foreheads and hiding under-eye circles.

Now, here I was, volunteering for a mission I was not qualified for.

Without my personal assistant, Mrs. Betsy Ross, the nation's most famous seamstress, to sew Everest's head back on, Dr. Early would have to do the surgery. He gathered his supplies from the emergency medical kit he always carried with him and set about fixing Everest's head on straight.

"You can shoot someone before you get close enough to use a machete," said Clipper, the taciturn member of the group, motioning to a 3-D printer he cradled like his precious from *Lord of the Rings*. Wire-rimmed glasses perched on his nose; he was the only one who hadn't tested the machetes. He'd set the thing on a table he'd brought in a few weeks ago.

The printer made plastic parts that snapped together, and with a few metal pins, screws, and rubber bands made passable guns.

"What if they take you by surprise, Clipper?" asked Peter.

"That's never happened."

"Oh, come on. You've been taken by surprise at least once or twice."

Everest turned his massive neck left and right, adjusting the fit. He stared into a hand mirror Doc Early gave him to examine his new scar, and said, "Not since I've served with him."

"Well, there's always a first time," said Early, as he motioned Everest closer to tighten a few stitches.

"Clipper, what did you do before you died?" I asked.

"Classified," he replied, returning to his work on the computer and printer.

"Clipper's an expert in what the Russians call *maskirovka*," Everest said. "Misinformation. Deception. He's our chess master."

"Right now, he's going to stop playing with the printer and turn his considerable brainpower to figuring out how to get to our destination," explained Peter.

"You guys got in before. Why don't we go the same way?" I asked.

"Because we used it before and now it's closed to us," said Clipper, his voice telling me I was an idiot for even asking. "Obviously."

"Why do you wear glasses, Clipper?" I asked, going all-in on the annoyance factor. He couldn't kill me a second time. "Can't you get new eyes with 20/20 vision?"

"No. They always return to this."

I thought about it and realized my eyes did the same thing. Even if I got a new body, and I had, in fact, settled into a completely new torso, neck, arms, and head two days ago, my eyes became my own. My brown, human eyes stayed with me, as did my hair, no matter what other replacement parts I received. Hair and eye permanence made me recognizable to friends, even if I gained muscle through a replacement torso, or new legs added to my height.

Eddie clapped his hands. "Let's chat, gentlemen."

We gathered round, Eddie taking a moment to whisper an apology into Everest's ear. Everest slapped Eddie on the back and, just like that, the whole thing was over. I studied the group, wondering how we all got here.

The soldiers had volunteered for the zombie program, but I was a Civil War soldier for the North, turned at the Battle of Shiloh by Doctor Samuel Early. Desperate to have as normal a life as possible, I'd studied special effects make-up and cosmetology to hide my scars, and built a nice practice in Calabasas, CA, taking care of actors, actresses, and the like.

I was a cosmetologist, dammit, not a soldier.

I considered reminding the team of this fact, but one look at their set jaws and determined eyes made me stop. Whining wouldn't get me anywhere, and there really was a zombie to rescue, so I decided to put on my big-boy pants and zombie up. Game on.

Peter gestured to Eddie to start.

Eddie nodded, took a breath, and looked each of us in the eye. "Our mission is simple. Sneak in, find Zed's remains, reconstitute him, or whatever the right word is, apologize for leaving, and then get the hell out. That's it. Nothing else. No big hero stuff, no drug crime fighting, nothin'."

"What about kung-fu fighting?"

"Shut up, Everest." A little upturn at the corners of Clipper's lips might have been a smile. It happened so fast, I couldn't be sure.

Eddie continued. "Dr. Early will brief us on what it means to 'find' Zed."

Early adopted the air of a professor lecturing to medical students. "We will restore Zed directly where he lies, if at all possible. I understand he was shot?"

Clipper pushed his glasses up his nose. "By a *machine gun.*"

"Yeah," said Eddie, looking at the floor. "Torn to pieces. If he'd been whole, we'd have grabbed him, but they carved up his chest something good."

"It doesn't change much. We still need to find the largest remaining sections of his body. Did you leave him where he lay, or did you bury him?" There was no judgment in Early's tone, but Eddie, Everest, and Clipper fidgeted.

"We were running for our lives," offered Everest. "We dug a quick grave and covered it with rocks. We'll be able to find it."

"Animals may have gotten to it," mused Early, which made Eddie glare a hole in the gym floor. "Regardless, we stick with the plan of finding his body, or as much of it as we can, and restoring him where he lies."

Clipper cleared his throat. "How long will it take to restore him?"

"I won't be able to say until I see the state of his body."

"Let's say, for argument's sake, that we're attacked by hostiles. We didn't make friends down there. What do we do then?"

This made me squinch my eyebrows together. Attacked by hostiles? I knew we shouldn't be there and had to avoid getting caught, but I hadn't considered active fire.

Early sighed. "Then we gather what parts we can, tie 'em up in a bag and bring 'em home."

"Can you restore him here?" asked Peter.

"Yes, but it might take longer."

"Okay. What's involved in the restoration?"

I leaned in for this, too. I'd been on the receiving end of restoration but had never seen Early do it. The original attempts were exquisitely painful, but the last one, only a few days ago, had been gentle.

Early rocked on his heels. "It involves a shot of adrenaline and an incantation. Depending on the state of the body, I may need to provide replacement parts to meld together magically, and with sutures. It's as much an art as a science."

Peter handed Early a pen and paper. "Write the incantation down."

Early shook his head. "It won't make sense until I teach it to you verbally. The pronunciation of the words needs to be right. The magic is particular in that regard."

Peter crossed his arms and gave Early a hard stare. "Fine, but you will teach us. All of us. You can't keep this important knowledge to yourself. Given our unit, this should be a part of basic training."

Clipper's fingers flew over the computer keys. "I'll work with Early to record it. We'll keep it as a shareable audio file."

Peter nodded. "Good idea."

I raised my hand. "What's my role?"

"You are Dr. Early's assistant and Zed's psychiatrist. I'm assuming restoration may be confusing for Zed and that he might be a teeny-tiny bit pissed about being left behind. Your job is to support him. You're the only one with experience, after all."

A fair point, but now I had another question. "Early, how much adrenaline do you need?"

"A lot. Enough for Zed, plus extra. In case."

Peter clapped his hands together again, this time to adjourn the meeting. "Then we'd better go find some. Everyone gather their supplies, and remember, we're traveling light. In and out, people. In and out. Necessities only."

I raised my hand again. "I suppose you don't consider moisturizer a necessity?"

He ignored me.

"Fine," I grumbled. "But I am bringing sunscreen."

Everest smacked me on the back and whipped off his shirt as he headed for the door. "Don't think about the sun, hoss. Think about the bugs."

"Why? Mosquitoes don't bother us."

Everest laughed so his tight abs jiggled, like about a half-inch, but for him, that was a full-on Santa belly laugh. "Not the skeeters. The flies, man. The flies. Flies and dead bodies? Get what I'm saying?"

The mental picture almost made me throw up; or would have if I had any food in my stomach, which I didn't because zombies can't eat. "We have bug spray, right?"

"Don't worry. We've got military-grade stuff. We'll keep the critters off you." He walked away, chuckling.

I turned to Early. "This is all your fault."

"You always say that, Waylon," he sighed.

"I'm bringing floss, too."

He huffed at me, annoyed. "Why? You don't get cavities."

"It's about humanity, Sam. We have to retain our humanity. Behave in civilized ways, and we retain it. As soon as we start thinking about ourselves as nothing but animated corpses, we lose that. I'm not willing to give that up. It's the whole reason we're going to get Zed."

Early pursed his lips. "I hadn't thought of it that way."

Now it was my turn to walk away. "It's all I've got, and I think about it all the time."

2

We took a boat.

That was the first god-awful thing.

The second god-awful thing? It was a cruise ship.

A *cruise* ship.

Everything you've ever read about cruise ships is true. Too many loud, Panama hat-wearing American tourists in a giant petri dish far from land. Picture never-ending mediocre buffets in a floating hotel with rough seas, karaoke, whirlpools, alcohol, and shuffleboard. Everyone on the ship was named Phyllis and George.

At least that's how it seemed to me. Some people love the damn things, but this zombie wasn't one of them.

Maybe I was grumpy. I mean, two of the main things people do on cruise ships are eat and have sex, and I couldn't do either.

The other members of the team were having a great time pretending to be tourists, even Clipper, who took to his Panama hat like a native. Everest walked around without his shirt, and the eighty-year-old women ogled his muscles and rubbed their hands over his scars. When they asked where he got them, he held back a sob and said, "Car accident. I lost my wife, too. I...can't talk about it." That earned him hugs. It would have earned him more, but he politely declined.

Peter wore board shorts and collared Lacoste shirts, and Early carried a clipboard, making sure anyone who asked knew the guys were here for a sales meeting. Eddie handed us each blue pocket-folders filled with charts and graphs and a complicated Excel spreadsheet that said nothing. The Phyllises and Georges of the ship thought the team was a group of gay swingers.

The crew didn't bat an eye. I got the feeling they'd seen and done everything and got through their days by staying slightly inebriated.

I slathered myself in sunscreen and nursed a banana daiquiri in the shade by the poolside bar. The seas were calm, but I swayed with every wave, ebb, and tide. Two couples, both in their mid-sixties, took seats next to me, raving about the mini-golf on the upper deck.

"I can't believe how nice the facilities are," said one of the women, fanning herself. "Our last cruise wasn't this nice, Marvin."

"Only the best for you, hon," said her husband, but he wasn't looking at her. He had his elbows back on the bar, checking out the women entering and exiting the hot tub from behind his mirrored sunglasses.

The second woman wiped her brow and ordered a whiskey sour. Her husband, paunchy and sunburned, ordered a beer.

"You need to put some lotion on your skin, dear," she said. "You're burned to a crisp."

"I'm fine. I don't burn. I tan." He didn't look at her, and his voice said this was a version of an argument they had all the time.

I tried. I really did, but I couldn't resist. "You are actually quite burnt, and letting your skin sit like that without moisturizing is asking for peeling later. A simple mix of vitamin E oil and an essential oil could work wonders."

"What do you know about it?"

"I'm a cosmetologist." Inside, I kicked myself. I didn't know what kind of salespeople we were masquerading as, and here I was volunteering DIY moisturizer recipes.

The man dismissed me with a roll of his eyes, but his wife was intrigued.

"You're a professional! How exciting. Do you have any anti-aging tips?"

I smiled at her, glad for a topic I could get behind. "Argan oil is my favorite for mature skin. The lighter version is fine, don't feel like you need the heavier distillation. And for a touch of decadence," I gave her a sly look, "add a drop of lavender oil. You'll feel like a million bucks."

"Wow. Did you hear that, Steven? A man who understands his oils." She batted her eyelashes at me and touched my arm with her fingertips. "That's a man I'd like to know."

I blinked several times, trying to formulate a response, but Eddie rescued me. "Giving away our secrets, buddy?" he asked, and no one but me noticed the tension in his jaw. "We've got to review those numbers now. I've got a meeting room reserved. Can't chit-chat the whole day."

"Bye," I said, hopping off the stool. "Good luck with that burn."

Steven flapped his hand at me and drained his beer. His wife wiggled her fingertips my way and licked her lips.

"Oh my goodness, I wasn't ready for that," I said as soon as we were far enough away.

Eddie clamped his hand on my elbow. "I'll have to tell everyone we're cosmetics salespeople now, Waylon! What were you thinking? Don't talk shop with the passengers. They could recognize you, of all of us. You're the one who's been on TV."

"No one will recognize me here, Eddie."

"Waylon? Waylon Jenkins? Is that you?" A woman's voice floated over the deck. "Whoo-hoo! Waylon! Whoo-hoo!"

I turned and cringed, preemptively wincing from the daggers Eddie considered plunging into my back. I also caught the pointed looks from Clipper and Peter. Early, luckily, wasn't in sight. Everest, sensing trouble, ambled over, his gait casual but his eyes sharp.

"Mitzi! What are you doing here?" I kissed her on both cheeks. She looked lovely, completely recovered from the beating she'd taken at the hands of Jason Teague. Jason had died shortly afterward; not my fault *per se*, but I now owned his penis.

His colossal penis.

"I'm on a business trip. Shh, though. I can't tell you why. I decided to take the scenic route with my sister." She pointed at a beautiful young woman in a bikini. Out of the corner of my eye, I spied Steven and Marvin watching me talk to Mitzi. They followed the path of her arm, spied her hot sister, and re-evaluated my worth. I had suddenly become interesting.

Mitzi noticed the two older men and shook her head with a wry grin. "Those two idiots don't stand a chance with her or any of the other women here." She turned to me. "What are you doing here, Waylon? And without a hat! Shame on you."

"You are right as ever, darling. I did forget my hat. I'll go inside and get it. This is my, uh, friend?" I gestured vaguely to Eddie, slightly panicked.

He jumped right in, holding out his hand. "Edward. I'm so honored to meet you, Mitzi. You're a wonderful actress." Eddie sounded smooth and sexy, his voice pitched lower than usual. He straightened his shoulders in a way that made him broader and taller. That's all it took to transform him into a different person.

"Oh, thank you," fluttered Mitzi, entranced. "What is it you do?"

Eddie lowered his voice even more and leaned in, confiding a secret. "My business partner and I are considering investing in a new line of cosmetics." He motioned to Everest, who smiled wide and gently took her hand, kissing the back.

Mitzi blushed. "Oh, I didn't know you kept such charming company, Waylon. Who is this debonair fellow?"

Everest bowed slightly at the waist. "Michael, and I'm a fan, a true fan."

"It is a pleasure to meet you, Michael." Mitzi eyed "Michael" like an ice pop she wanted to lick, then clapped her hands like a child. "Waylon! Are you finally going to market that magic cream of yours?" She winked at Michael. "I've always told him that stuff is a miracle. It's rescued my skin numerous times. In fact, I think you should call it Rescue Remedy."

My throat was dry, but I managed to croak a response. "Thanks, but it's exploratory, and secret, by the way." I held her eyes with mine. "Proprietary, classified stuff."

Mitzi nodded, her eyes wide. "I understand. Mum's the word." She zipped her fingers over her lips.

"Thanks, sweetheart. Now, remember to use that SPF."

"I will. But Waylon?" Mitzi looked right and left and lowered her voice.

"What is it, love?"

She looked in my eyes and pouted. "Promise me you won't take on that new actress Joy Lucky or whatever her name is. She says she's my 'biggest fan' and is 'following in my footsteps' but she's not being very nice about it." Mitzi giggled an embarrassed titter. "Watch out for her, won't you, dear?"

This wasn't like Mitzi, who supported new actresses, generally speaking. I'd have to look into this when I got home.

"I'll keep an eye out," I said. "I haven't heard of her yet."

"Thanks, Waylon." She smiled, happy again.

"I will. Toodles." Mitzi sashayed to her sister, and Eddie guided me away with a firm grip on my shoulder.

"'No one will recognize me?'" he said, seething.

"Hey, you guys decided to take a cruise ship. Celebrities like cruising. What can I say?"

Everest jabbed me with a finger. "So, I'm a cosmetics executive? Is that it? I don't know shit about cosmetics. What do I say if someone asks me something?"

I waved his words away. "Simply say, 'You can never go wrong with more mascara.' Works for every situation."

"You can never go wrong with more mascara," Everest repeated.

Eddie rubbed his eyes in frustration. "We need to go over the plan. Everest, find a shirt. Waylon, go change, and I'll gather the others."

"Why change? I'm not dirty."

"You smell like banana daiquiri."

"I only have one change of clothes. You told us to pack light."

"Get a t-shirt in the gift shop, then, and meet us in this room." He pulled a map out of his back pocket and showed me where. "Ten minutes."

"Fine. I'll get a hat, too, but not one of those stupid Panama hats. A cap."

"Get whatever the hell you want."

"Maybe I'll get us all caps. Matching hats for the unit."

Eddie's look would have withered a cactus. "We aren't a Little League team. Soldiers don't want matching caps."

"Speak for yourself, boss." Everest scowled. "I'd love a new cap."

We high-fived. "I'll get one for Zed, too. It might make him feel better."

Everest shrugged. "Not necessary. I brought his old ball cap. I hope to give it back to him."

"The University of Maryland one?" asked Eddie, surprised. "The one with the stupid turtle on it?"

Everest glared at Eddie. "It's a diamondback terrapin, and his name is Testudo."

"Testicle? The University of Maryland mascot is named Testicle?" said Eddie.

"*Testudo*, and don't mess with diamondbacks. They bite toes off the unwary and the rude."

"Isn't it enough that you left the man? Do you have to make fun of his alma mater, too?" I spoke without thinking and immediately regretted it. "I'm sorry. I didn't mean that the way it came out."

Eddie turned his back to me. “Well, it came out bad.”

Everest slapped me upside the head. “Way to go, hoss. What’s wrong with you?”

They both walked away.

“I am sorry!” I called after them, but they ignored me.

God, I was stupid sometimes.

I set off for the gift shop. I’d get Eddie a hat, anyway.

3

Peter, Eddie, Early, Everest, and I disembarked for the third port of call carrying our small backpacks, our new black caps with the red cruise ship logo firmly on our heads. We carried pens and pencils and had our guidebooks at the ready.

And promptly tossed them aside.

We walked farther than the tourists, away from the brightly colored booths, food stands, and kitschy souvenir shops. Away from the parrots and straw hats and knock-off purses, and as soon as we did, literally turning a corner, the landscape changed. The streets were dirtier. Motorcycles belched smoke, and people stared at us with undisguised derision. Music blared from every doorway. Men lounged on plastic lawn chairs next to advertisements for orange soda pop.

"You lost, *Americanos?*" asked a skinny guy chewing a toothpick.

"No, *amigo,*" said Clipper, storing his cap in his bag, his accent perfect.

We followed suit, and the experienced soldiers let their natural demeanor seep through, holding themselves differently, their eyes hard and their arms free, swinging with practiced ease that spoke of an ability to take and give a hit.

Clipper took point, and I slunk after him, trying not to let my nerves show. Everest and Eddie followed behind Early and me; Peter walked behind Clipper. The formation gave Early and me the most protection. It was embarrassing, but I was also grateful.

We walked to a new market square with beautiful buildings painted in bright colors. Many had flower boxes brimming with blooms. We entered an outdoor plaza with benches in a spacious courtyard, and restaurants with small tables on the sidewalk. Someone sold ice cream in bread or on a cone, and a man wearing a pink shirt hawked t-shirts from a rolling cart. Oranges, bananas, mangoes, and papayas lay in piles on food carts, and busty women haggled at the market, carrying bags they brought from home. The smells were overwhelming: spicy rice and beans, fragrant limes, and fish, all mixed with cigarette smoke, body odor, and something that smelled like feet. Two men played checkers while three others watched, a small dog lying at their feet. Deeper in, women cooked stews over fires burning in barrels. Metal pots burbled with red sauces, yellow rice, and thick beans. Trash littered the street. The heat beat down on us in the still air unless we were in the shade. Rapid-fire Spanish came at us from every angle. I understood most of it, but some was too colloquial. We passed a candy store called Confitería Freddy.

Clipper approached a butcher selling pork on a table without any refrigeration, which he sliced with a wicked knife more appropriate for human sacrifice than the delicate task of creating the perfect chop or pork belly sliver. The man glanced at Clipper, blanched, and resumed his task. "What do you want?" he asked, still staring at his hands.

"We need a ride."

"Where to?"

"Same place."

"It's not safe."

"We'll be quick. Pick up twenty-four hours later."

The man's lips twisted in a grimace of distaste. "It'll cost you."

Clipper clucked his tongue. "I don't think so."

"Not for me, but for the driver and the gunman. No one goes there unarmed these days."

Clipper glanced at Peter, who nodded.

"How much?"

The man named a number and Clipper haggled a bit, but he handed over US currency, which the man slipped into his pocket.

"Wait here," he said. He barked something to a woman sitting deeper inside the stall. She went behind a curtain and emerged a second later carrying a tray of ice-cold colas, dripping with condensation. Only Early and Peter could drink them, and they fell on the bottles like dying men.

Early slurped his down and grabbed mine. "You drinking that?" he asked, putting the bottle to his lips.

"Ha, ha. Funny."

Peter laughed and did the same to Everest, who wasn't amused. Clipper grabbed his before either man could get to it and held it against his forehead.

"Disgusting. Clipper cooties. Now I won't touch it," said Peter.

Early wrinkled his nose and held out his hand. "That's a waste, Peter. I'll take it. Gimmee."

Clipper smiled, pulled a tattered paperback from his pack. It was a Russian copy of *War and Peace,* according to the English translation on the cover.

Everest tilted his chair back on two legs and closed his eyes; Eddie did a deep breathing exercise while Peter tapped a pencil on the table. I paced the stall and perused the worn movie posters that lined the walls. Our host loved the classics. *The Godfather, Casablanca,* and *Rebel Without a Cause,* right next to a Spanish language ad for *A Fistful of Dollars, Dirty Harry,* and *Sudden Impact.* This guy had a Clint Eastwood fetish.

"What's he doing?" I asked finally.

Eddie didn't open his eyes. "I imagine he's finding someone to drive the chicken truck."

"I'm sorry?"

"The chicken truck." He opened one eye. "It's our mode of transportation."

"That's a euphemism, right?"

"No."

Clipper looked up from his book. "It's the way to get around these parts, and we need to cross the northern border."

"Shh!" the man returned, shoving past the curtain in the back. "Don't say such things out loud. Come on, I've got two men, but they want to do it right now and be back before dark. They'll take you to the border, and that's it. You'll have to walk the rest of the way."

Clipper shook his head. "That's not what we want."

"Too fuckin' bad. That's what you get. No one's looking to cross the *pandillas,* the gangs. Just to get that far is going to cost you American cash."

"It already did," said Early. "He paid you."

"Extortion fees, *amigo.* Don't be naïve. You aren't in Los Angeles anymore. You're dealing with the *Maras* now."

Eddie placed a hand on Early's shoulder. "Serious gangs. We want to stay out of their way."

"This is getting less and less exciting," I hissed at Eddie. "And increasingly scary."

"Don't worry," he whispered back. "You don't feel pain, and you can't die. That's why our unit deals with such situations."

He had a point.

"Fine, but I want a machete."

The man nodded at me. "Wise choice. I've got two you can buy, but we need to get going."

Clipper handed over a little more cash, and suddenly, I was the proud owner of a twenty-two-inch blade and no sheath. Everest took the other, touched his thumb to the edge, and nodded appreciatively.

The man grunted. "No use having a dull machete."

"None at all," said Everest with an evil smile.

Two men met us out back, one wearing a tobacco-stained wife-beater tank, his belly straining it to the limit. The other, heavily tattooed, wore a black t-shirt and a bandana around his neck and carried a machine gun. Neither spoke, but the tattooed man gestured for us to follow. He led us to an actual chicken truck, one you'd see in rural American carrying hens, and we piled in the back, where he'd removed cages so we could sit. Wife-beater got in the driver's seat, and the other man hung over the top of the truck with his machine gun, keeping an eye out.

The driver started the car, but before we left, a little girl in a pink dress ran out from behind a beaded curtain hanging in a storefront's doorway. She carried a greasy paper lunch bag and reached as high as she could to hand it to the man in the tank. He dropped down, hugged the girl tight, said something quietly, and took the bag. She kissed his cheek, and he let go, gently pushing her back to the door. He watched her for a moment before climbing back in.

"Everyone has a family, and everyone has a story," whispered Everest in my ear. "It's tough here, but everyone has something to fight for."

"It's terrifying," I said.

We drove in the heat, the truck's metal floor getting hotter and hotter, and the pressure on my lungs grew until I felt like I couldn't breathe. A second away from a full-blown panic attack, I remembered I didn't have to breathe, and I wasn't being restrained. I counted to twenty and then twenty again.

The truck stopped.

"Be quiet now," whispered the tattooed man. He climbed down the truck and walked to the side. I scooted around to see what he was doing.

He balanced his gun in his arms and chatted with four lanky young men, each with tattoos on their arms, torsos, and faces.

"Who are they?"

"Gang members," said Everest.

I studied them from between the vertical wooden slats. "They're children."

Everest nodded. "They recruit from the schools and get them young. Middle school age, even."

"That's awful."

Suddenly, the young men raised their voices, and two stomped over to the truck screaming at us. Our driver jumped down, opened the door, and grabbed at our arms and legs, pulling us out. I left my machete in the truck, not knowing if it would help or hurt.

"Hey!" said Eddie, shaking the man off. "What's going on?"

The man didn't answer but pointed to the gang members. One of the youths pulled my bag off my shoulder, opened the zipper, and rummaged through it, pulling out my clothes and my black hat, which he studied and then crammed on his head.

"I like," he said to me.

"Keep it," was all I said back.

Everest, Peter, and Eddie stood to the side as the gang members went through their backpacks, too. They left Clipper alone. One of the skinny kids took Everest's, slung it over his shoulder, and sauntered away. Everest bolted and grabbed the teen by the arm. The next thing I knew, every gang member drew a gun, and our guard pointed his weapon at the youth who'd taken my hat. Two of the gang members snatched Everest by the arms, and a third held a serrated knife to his throat.

"Whoa! Whoa!" I held my hands out in gestures of peace. "What the hell? Everest, let them have the bag. Clipper, give them a little more money, man, and let's get out of here. No one needs to die today."

"I agree," said a throaty voice. A woman wearing green fatigues strolled toward us, gesturing for the teens to put their weapons down. Our guard did the same, and I thought he relaxed a minuscule bit at the sight of the woman.

"Americans?" she asked in English. She was curvy with dark hair pulled into a messy bun. Her sweat-soaked shirt clung to her chest, and she scratched an insect bite on her arm. The vicious scar on her cheek made her look like Jungle Guerilla Warfare Barbie.

"Passing through, ma'am," said Clipper. "Not here to mess with you or your business."

"What do you have for me?"

Clipper showed his hand and indicated reaching into his bag. She nodded, and he moved slowly. He removed a pile of twenties and counted off five. She gave him a baleful look, and he counted off a bunch more.

"What else?"

Clipper held out his now empty hands. "That's all we have."

She rolled her neck. "Unlikely," she said, her voice carrying a warning. "I need something more."

"I have something." I spoke before I could think.

"What?" she asked.

My team looked at me like I was crazy. Early mouthed at me, *What the hell?*

"I need to get it out of my bag." I pointed to the pack on the ground.

She waved at me to go ahead.

I reached in and hunted for a little round tub. My fingers wrapped around it, extracted it, and handed it to her. "It's a special moisturizer," I explained. "You can't buy that in stores. It will help your scar. Make it soften and lay flat."

"Really?" She opened the bottle, ran her finger through the cream, and patted it on her cheek. "It's nice. What's that scent?"

"Peppermint and tea tree. They're natural oils that repel insects as well."

She rubbed a little on her bug bite and smelled her arm, smiling. "This is a good gift. I'll keep it and the cash." She circled her index finger in the air, and her team fell in behind her. "Congratulations, you get to live today. Get back in your truck and keep going. Don't get in our way."

We each looked at each other, hesitating.

"Go," she jerked her chin at us, "before I change my mind. But if you come back this way, have more cash, or I'll let my boys do some cutting."

We didn't have to be told twice. We collected our stuff and scrambled into the truck. Our driver took off like a bat out of hell, and we all breathed a sigh of relief.

Eddie shook his head at me. "Rescue Remedy indeed."

4

We discussed the life-saving benefits of moisturizers while traveling over a bumpy road on the edge of a thick jungle. I watched the foliage for animals, excited to see the beautiful birds I'd heard about, or maybe a jaguar.

"Forget it, Waylon," said Peter. "You'll never see a jaguar unless it's right on top of you, and by then, you'll be torn to shreds."

"What about poison dart frogs?"

"You'll need to be deeper in, and they're disappearing."

"You're always so positive, Peter. Always looking on the bright side. That's what I like about you."

"What can I say? They're critically endangered. Facts are facts."

"Maybe we can make zombie poison dart frogs?"

I shouldn't have said it.

Peter sat up, a new gleam in his eye.

"Kidding! No zombie frogs, Peter."

He nodded, but his thoughts were far away, and he muttered, "I wonder if their poison would still work?"

I poked Early, who was sleeping. "Promise me you won't make any zombie frogs."

"Sure. No zombie amphibians. Got it." Early closed his eyes again.

Clipper studied me. "For your information, those weren't gang members."

I turned to face him. "What? What do you mean? Who were they then?"

"*Former* gang members. That was a resistance group. There are pockets of them organized by the mothers and sisters of the boys coerced into joining."

"How do we recognize who is who?" I asked. "Distinguish friendlies from enemies?"

"Easy," Clipper replied. "If they're active gang members, you'll be in pieces."

I stared at him. "Good to know."

"Why did you guys come down here before? What was your mission?"

"To disrupt the drug supply chain," Eddie answered.

"What exactly does that mean?"

As usual, Peter gave me the blunt truth. "Capturing or killing the leader of one of the major gangs that operate in these parts. The drugs move south to north and wind up on American streets. If we infiltrate the middleman cell, we cripple the transfer chain, creating a bottleneck. Turn the northern contingent on the southern cell, so they fight each other."

"Pretty clever," I said.

Eddie shook his head. "It didn't work. We captured the cell leader, but the gang got to us, carved up Zed, and retook their chief."

Everest shook his head. "I still can't figure out how they knew about the extraction point. I didn't even know it until Eddie and Clipper led us there."

Eddie grimaced. "We had a traitor."

"Who?" asked Everest.

It hit me all at once. "Quint Addington."

"Got it in one."

I rubbed my temples. "What's his connection to the cartels?"

"Uncertain," Eddie said, his lips drawn thin.

"Well, he can't bother us anymore," I said. "He's in jail."

Eddie nodded. "Let's hope he stays there."

"Oh, he's not going anywhere. Captain Perkins has him on three counts of murder."

The truck slowed to a stop, and the driver called, "We're here."

We alighted from the truck, and I asked the only question I could. "Where the fuck are we?"

The road we'd traveled wasn't much of a road. More like a path someone cut through the jungle, and the spot we stopped in was merely a clearing about thirty feet wide at most. There were no buildings of any kind, no people, and no way forward.

Clipper shook our driver's hand and nodded to the guard. The two jumped back into the truck and shot down the so-called road like they couldn't get out of there fast enough.

"Uh, guys?" I said. "I understand we're here, but there is no here, here. And why did our ride leave? How are we going to get back?"

"We walk from here," said Eddie. "Grab your gear. Waylon, keep that machete handy."

I secured my backpack on both shoulders and gripped my machete in my right hand. As quickly as I'd moved, the team still waited for me to get situated. Damn, they moved fast, and I had forgotten to ask for the bug spray.

"Where are we headed?" Early asked.

"This way," said Eddie, pointing at a faint indentation in the foliage I hadn't noticed. "Line up, single file. I'll take point. Everest, bring up the rear. Keep Early and Waylon between us."

"Roger that," said Everest.

"Don't 'roger that,'" said a male voice. "In fact, don't do anything. Don't move. Don't even breathe."

The zombies in our party—Eddie, Everest, Clipper, and I—could stand there all day not breathing and could handle being shot, but Early and Peter couldn't. Everyone held still.

A bull of a man emerged from the depths of the jungle, an automatic rifle pointed at Eddie. His silver hair, pulled back in a short ponytail, contrasted with his tan skin, while his beard and mustache accentuated his deep-set eyes and round cheeks. He wore a yellow beaded bracelet on one muscular arm, and a wedding ring. He looked like someone I didn't want to mess with. A slim figure behind him stayed in the shadows, and I assumed that person was armed as well.

"Americans. Why are you here?" the large man asked in perfect English.

Eddie nodded to Clipper, who answered. "We're here on a fact-finding mission for a nonprofit organization. We've heard of the increased drug trafficking in this area and were sent to reconnoiter and report our findings."

The man released his gun but kept it by his side. "Which nonprofit? We've had a buttload through here."

"Industries Foundation."

"Bullshit. Look at you. You scream army." He looked at me. "Except you. I don't know what you are, but you aren't weapon trained."

"What makes you say that?"

"You're holding your machete wrong. Release that death grip before you get blisters."

Clipper covered a snicker with a cough. I glared at him, but for some reason, glaring didn't harm him the least bit.

"And you, Four Eyes, you're a smooth liar, but a liar, nonetheless. Put away your weapons, and I won't shoot you."

"We don't have any weapons," said Eddie.

In one smooth, quick motion, the man lifted his rifle, aimed, and shot a branch whose leaves skimmed Eddie's head. Eddie's hair blew back in the bullet's wake.

"Every weapon you have on the ground now," the man barked, "or I shoot you and leave you for the animals."

I dropped the machete and observed what everyone else did. Eddie, Everest, and Clipper hadn't brought any guns that I knew of, but I watched as they unloaded weapons of every kind. They each carried those plastic parts that, when put together like a Tinker-Toy, formed a gun. They unloaded bullets and cartridges from God knows where, and a pile of knives followed.

The man studied the weapons on the ground and growled. His eyes hardened and grew wary when he approached Clipper. I struggled to hold still when he placed the end of the gun against Clipper's head and pointed to Clipper's throat. Clipper removed his necklace, a bit of paracord I'd noticed and dismissed but recognized from movies. A garrote.

"Amalia," the man called to the shadow. "If any of them move, shoot them. I don't care where." He propped his weapon against a tree and patted each of us down in a professional, practiced way that reminded me of Captain Perkins. He pulled Early's medical kit out of his knapsack, opened it, grunted, and tossed it on the ground.

Clipper and Everest practically vibrated with the need to move, but Eddie caught their eyes and shook his head. A vein in Peter's head pulsed fast. Early stared at his kit and curled his hands into a fist to keep from jumping out and snatching it. I swallowed hard and thought of Zed lying in this place by himself. I hoped we wouldn't join him.

"On your knees and put your hands on your head." We followed his instructions while he rummaged through our bags.

"Jorge, get out here and gather the knives and guns. Also, take this." The man held Clipper's computer. A slim young man with a rifle slung over his back and a bandage on his hand packed our things into two burlap bags. Clipper pressed his lips together in barely restrained rage as he watched the computer slip into Jorge's bag.

"Take care with that computer, old man, or—" Clipper didn't get to finish because the man shot him in the foot. Clipper fell to his side as his left foot disintegrated into a pulpy mush.

Eddie and Everest sprang into action. Everest snagged Jorge in a chokehold while Eddie dropped, grabbed a knife from the pile, and pulled the larger man into his body, the blade a hair's breadth from his neck. Peter emerged from the forest with a young woman, her gun in his hand. Her eyes promised murder, but she didn't say a word.

"Now," said Eddie, "let's talk about this like civilized people, and no one has to get hurt."

Clipper pushed himself to his one good foot and said, "More hurt, you mean! Look what he did!"

The man didn't dare move, held as he was by Eddie, but his eyes widened as he stared at Clipper. "How come you don't bleed? What are you?"

Jorge whispered, "*Diablos*."

Eddie clucked his tongue at Clipper. "We'll get you a new foot."

"How am I going to walk like this?"

Eddie shrugged. "You lost your temper. If you'd followed my directions, you'd have ten toes instead of five."

"What the hell are you people?" Amalia's voice was delicate and light and completely at odds with her furious expression. "You're obviously American. You here to make things worse?"

I flinched. I'd read up on the history of the region. Good intentions aside, we'd botched things down here but good.

"I'm going to drop my knife and order my men to release you and Jorge. Please keep calm, and we'll explain why we're here. We mean you no harm." Eddie withdrew the knife, and the man stumbled to the young woman's side. The resemblance between the two was undeniable. Father and daughter, I guessed, and Jorge was the son, older than Amalia by a year or so.

Jorge joined them, his eyes darting between Eddie's face and Clipper's foot.

"What's your name?" Eddie asked the man. "You don't sound native."

"My family is from here, but I grew up in Los Angeles."

"You still didn't tell me your name."

"Roderigo. Roderigo Flores."

"You carry yourself like a lawman, Roderigo."

The man didn't say anything, but he didn't deny it.

"I wonder," said Peter, who stayed behind them, "what an American cop is doing down here in the badlands."

"Making a life and a family, you putz. How come that man isn't bleeding out?" He jerked his head toward Clipper.

Everest slipped closer to Roderigo, and the man swallowed before raising his eyes to Eddie, his face defiant.

"It sounds like we may have some things in common, Roderigo. We're here to find a fallen comrade. That's all. Nothing more. We'd like to find his remains and leave. If you can help us, we'll be on our way and out of your hair."

"American military. Always thinking you can stomp all over everything without apology. If one of your guys died down here, he was either a part of the drug cartels or one of the pansy Americans who left when the going got tough. I don't owe either group anything. Besides, anybody left down here is rotted through, eaten by king vultures and ants."

"We understand, but we still want to find what we can."

Early stepped forward and pointed to Jorge's oozing bandage. "What's wrong with your hand? You have an infection." He reached for Jorge's arm, but the slim man recoiled.

"Don't touch me, devil."

"I'm not like them. If you'd blown my foot off, I'd be bleeding out, like Roderigo said. I'm a doctor, and I may be able to help you. If that infection spreads, you'll lose the hand."

Amalia placed her hand on Jorge's shoulder and looked at her dad. "Papa, let's see if they can help. If not, you can shoot them later."

Everest hooted with laughter and slapped his leg. "I like her."

"Fine," snapped Roderigo. "No use staying out here while it gets dark."

"Lead the way," said Eddie.

"What about me?" asked Clipper. "I can't walk."

"No problem, buddy," said Everest with a twinkle in his eye. "I got you." Everest picked up the smaller man and threw him over his shoulder in a fireman's carry. "Hey, Peter, make sure you get a picture of this, okay?"

Peter grinned, yanked a phone from his back pocket, and snapped a photo.

"You will pay for this," grumbled Clipper. "Mark my words."

5

Roderigo led us through dense foliage, following red bandanas tied to trees and brush. The humidity made Early's hair curl, and I was glad I didn't sweat, or I'd have pit stains.

The yellow house had a wooden door, a small porch, an adobe roof, and large patches of cultivated land growing different edible plants. It was a sizeable property with a dirt road in the distance. A small black and white dog, thin but not cadaverous, wagged his tail at our approach, nuzzling Early, who patted him on the head.

"Some guard dog, Amalia," said her father. "He's welcoming them like long lost friends."

"Lobo never knew a stranger, Papa."

Her dad shook his head, but his face betrayed affection. "Gentlemen, make camp outside, but don't squash the plants." He gestured to the side yard, and we dumped our stuff.

Everest placed Clipper on the ground, and the injured soldier grumbled.

Doc Early kneeled to examine the foot. "Well, it's completely off. We don't have a lot to work on, so we should get a new one and attach it."

Roderigo crossed himself and hurried into the house, motioning for Amalia and Jorge to do the same. We dropped to the ground, and Early and Peter dug through their bags for water and granola bars.

"How close are we to Zed's body?" Early asked through a mouthful of granola.

"One klick thataway," said Everest. "But I gotta be honest, I'm wondering if there will be anything left to find. Maybe we're too optimistic."

"Doesn't matter," Early replied, swallowing. "His spirit will be there. That's what we came to get."

"But if we don't have a body to put it in?" Everest asked the question we were all thinking.

"Then we need to be prepared to find him a new one."

"One that is unoccupied, Early. Un. Oc. U. Pied. Got it?" I said, giving him my best steely eye.

"Of course, Waylon. Of course." Early patted my shoulder.

It did nothing to reassure me.

"Dead bodies are like rain around here. They drop in all the time."

We turned toward Amalia, who strode toward us, her long, tanned legs reminding me of a colt learning to race, lithe but gangly.

"Is that so?" Peter asked, his head cocked to the side as he examined the dark-haired girl.

Unhappy with the way his eyes roved her body, I ambled next to him, trying to look casual, and poked him in the side, hard. "Jailbait!" I whispered.

He held his hand to his heart and staggered back a step. "You wound me, Waylon. I would never."

"Yeah, just no."

Amalia stopped about three feet away, keeping her distance, leery of coming too close. Smart cookie. "Papa asks if men who don't bleed need to eat."

"Two of us do," I replied, pointing to Doc Early and Peter. "The rest of us are on a special protein infusion diet."

"Protein infusion?"

"It's a new technology designed to keep people alive even when food is scarce. It also contains a special type of hemoglobin that keeps us from bleeding out."

"Really?"

Wow, she had sarcasm down to a science.

"That's the story."

"Fine," she said. "I'll tell him to make two plates. Come up to the porch, but no farther, and leave your stuff here. Papa's going to make you an offer you can't refuse."

As she walked away, Eddie said, "Good movie."

We followed Amalia to the porch, Clipper hopping, since he refused to be carried again. She motioned for Peter and Early to take chairs and grabbed a round table. Once set up, she added three more seats. If you were eating, you got a chair. The rest of us copped a squat on hard concrete. The moon rose, and the jungle erupted with the sounds of nightlife. High pitched chirps coupled with the splashes of four-footed creatures making their way to a watering hole. The low hum of frogs and haunting owl hoots echoed in the night. I heard the growl of something that could only be a cat, but I didn't think was big enough to be a jaguar.

"Ocelot," Amalia noted offhandedly. "The fat-handed cat." My confusion had her holding her hands in a big circle. "Short tail. Big paws. Beautiful, though."

Interesting. I inhaled and got hit with the loamy, earthy smell of rotting leaves, fresh and decaying fruit, and animal scat. It reminded me of my compost pile at home, but ten times more pungent.

Jorge and Roderigo came out bearing plates of steaming beans and rice, tortillas, and lemonade. Once again, I wished I could eat. The living amongst us dug in while the rest of the team waited, some more patiently than others. Eddie, Everest, and Clipper meditated, letting the night flow over them. I, on the other hand, squirmed, as antsy as a five-year-old at snack time.

"You sure you don't want any?" Amalia asked, holding out a tortilla. It was getting dark, so she flipped on the porch light before sitting down, and bugs fluttered to it, creating a halo of moths and other winged creatures.

"I'm sure, but thanks," I answered. "May I ask how old you are, Amalia? Are you in school?"

"I graduated from high school, and I'd like to go to college, but it is hard. We can't afford to send me, but I've got a plan."

"*Mija...*" Roderigo placed a hand on her arm, but she shook it off.

"What's the plan?" I asked.

Roderigo grimaced, using a tortilla to shovel beans and rice into his face. He did not like this conversation.

"Miss Mango," Amalia said, sipping her lemonade.

"I beg your pardon?"

"Miss Mango. It's a regional beauty pageant. I won my local contest and now get to go to the regional one. It will be televised and everything. If I win, I get a scholarship for the *Universidad*."

Roderigo pressed a fist into the table. His face said he'd wanted to slam it but stopped at the last moment. I admired the control. "Amalia, these pageants are ruthless. You know it is a long shot that you could win."

She snatched her arm away. "Papa, it's the only hope I have."

"When is the pageant?" I pressed.

"Next week, as long as I can find a good dress. I don't like the one I have."

"What's wrong with your dress?"

"I borrowed it and hate wearing an old-fashioned hand-me-down. It won't be anything like what the other contestants are wearing. Beauty contests are an Olympic sport around here. Did you know that six of the last ten Miss Universe winners were Latina? Girls around here go to school to learn how to compete."

"We'll find another way, Amalia," Roderigo pleaded.

"There is no other way. It's this, or I'm done. I have to believe in miracles. I have to believe Mama is looking out for me."

Roderigo pushed his plate away and blinked rapidly, twisting his face toward the front door when he realized I noticed.

"Your mother passed away?" I asked. Some sixth sense told me squeezing this information out of them mattered, even if it pained them to relive the memories. Also, I wanted to know the details so I could help. I'd never turn my back on a beauty pageant contestant who'd lost her mother. I wouldn't be able to look at myself in the mirror, and Mrs. Ross wouldn't like it either. I was already devising a color palette for this beauty.

"Yes," Amalia said, sniffling. Jorge simply inclined his head and wiped his eyes with the back of his injured hand.

A slight shift in the air told me the team listened closely to this exchange.

"I'm so sorry to hear that. Was she sick?"

Amalia didn't answer. She got up and walked into the house, clearing her plate.

"No," Roderigo answered. "She was murdered."

"What? That's terrible! What happened?"

"We lived closer to the city then. She was a social media manager for a large bank."

"That doesn't sound like a dangerous job," I said.

"She watched the company's social media accounts, Twitter, Facebook, that kind of stuff."

"Again, that doesn't sound dangerous."

"You don't understand. She noticed strange posts that hashtagged her company by people she didn't know and companies she didn't recognize, particularly three specific accounts. On the surface, the posts were harmless but confusing. They'd compliment the bank followed by a series of numbers that meant nothing."

Jorge took over, and the slight man's deep baritone surprised me. "She figured out that the posts signaled times, latitudes, and longitudes."

"Drop-offs." Eddie spoke for the first time. "Drug exchanges."

Jorge nodded. "Exactly."

Eddie turned to look at Jorge. "Let me guess. She reported it to her supervisor."

"Yes," Jorge whispered.

Amalia rejoined us, carrying a fresh glass of lemonade. "She was 'mugged' two days later while waiting for a bus."

"That's...that's awful." I didn't know what else to say.

"You have an idea who did it?" asked Eddie.

"I have a good idea," said Roderigo, "but no proof. Besides, there's no one on the police force I trust."

"There's nothing we can do," said Jorge, choking back tears. "We miss her terribly."

"Son, it's not true that we can't do anything," said Roderigo, his tears gone, replaced by determination. "And you boys," he said, pointing to the team, "are going to help us."

Peter shook his head. "We're sorry to hear about your wife, but we can't get involved. We came to find what remains we can of our brother-in-arms and go home. We can't get involved in a drug war in Central America."

I wanted someone to say, "or a land war in Asia," but I restrained myself when I saw Roderigo's face. He smirked, an evil, scary expression, and I reflexively stepped backward, nearly falling off the porch.

Roderigo's voice was low and certain. "Oh, you'll help us, alright. You'll help us, or I call the American Embassy and tell them a military unit is tromping through the rainforest and onto my property. They'll, in turn, have to alert the appropriate authorities in the United States, and boy, are they going to be pissed."

6

"Our mission is classified but sanctioned," said Eddie. "All you'll be doing is creating an incident, a lot of red tape, and pestering busy people who will have to smile and make it all go away. Some money might change hands, a few favors exchanged. No one will thank you for it."

Roderigo leaned back in his chair so that only two legs touched the ground. His untied, worn boots waved in the air while his shirt rode up to show a bit of belly. "I'm sure you aren't here with local government buy-in, and the locals can make a fuss. It will cost more money than anyone has, distract from the drug war, and it will be all your fault for being caught, you dumb shits. What's the saying? This will go on your permanent record."

"We could be gone in thirty seconds. You'd never prove we were here."

"Not with a guy missing a foot, you can't, and when I tell my story to the right authorities, I'm sure they'll be very interested in a soldier that doesn't bleed. Someone, at some time, will crawl up your asses, and it's going to hurt like a motherfucker."

Roderigo had us in his crosshairs.

"Blackmail is beneath you," said Eddie.

Roderigo let the chair fall, his face red. "What do you know about what's beneath me? You don't know me. You don't know my family, my history, my life."

Eddie snorted. "You walk like a cop. Hold a gun like a cop. Talk like a cop. Conduct a body search like a cop, so I can guess. You've lost a lot, and now you're crossing lines you swore you'd never cross. Tell me I'm wrong."

Roderigo shoved the table out of the way and stalked toward Eddie, who took a wider stance and let his arms hang loose. Everest stood behind him, slightly to the left. Clipper shifted closer to the two men and, although he couldn't stand, he was still more dangerous on one leg than most people on two. Peter and Early backed away from the porch light and disappeared in the darkness.

I froze, as did Amalia and Jorge, their faces white with fear. Amalia looked like she wanted to say something but kept silent. Jorge pressed his back to the wall.

"What do you want us to do?" asked Eddie.

"Help me get the guy I believe is responsible."

"Define *get*."

"Capture, not kill. I want to question him."

Early spoke up, and his voice echoed across the distance. "Then what? Let's say he is guilty. What then? What if he's innocent?"

"If he's innocent, he goes free. If he's guilty? Well, let's say you don't have to worry about that."

"We won't be a party to murder," said Eddie.

Roderigo scoffed. "The big, bad Americans won't be a party to murder? That's ironic. Your country is knee-deep in murder."

"It's your country, too," I said, my voice quiet. "You were born there."

"Not anymore. Did you know the major gangs here started in Los Angeles? Don't talk to me of morals, you sanctimonious assholes. You've all got blood on your hands."

I didn't, not really, but I'd benefitted from others' deaths many times over. It was a sobering thought. I'd only taken what was left behind. I never killed for body parts. My conscience was clear on that, and right now, all I wanted was to go home. This had gotten too complicated. Cosmetologists help people feel better about themselves. We don't kidnap them.

That gave me an idea.

The tension between the team and Roderigo balanced on the edge of a knife, and Amalia and Jorge would be better off not witnessing whatever came next. I needed to get them out of the way, for their sakes and mine.

Roderigo didn't stand a chance on his own if he forced a throw-down. I prayed he wouldn't be that stupid.

I clapped my hands, momentarily breaking the tension and drawing every eye to me. "Amalia, while your father and the team here discuss our next steps, why don't you show me your dress and make-up for the pageant?"

"Why?"

"I have a talent in that area."

She gave me a blank stare. "A soldier who cares about clothes and make-up?"

I shrugged. "Everyone needs a hobby."

"He's no soldier," muttered Roderigo.

"Come on. What could it hurt? Jorge, will you join us?"

"I'll do the dishes." Jorge picked up a plate and stacked it with the others, placing the utensils on top, and walked into the house.

Amalia threw her hands in the air. "Fine, but don't make fun of me."

I crossed my heart.

She harrumphed and motioned for me to follow.

Amalia led me to her bedroom, a small affair with a tiny window, a narrow bed, and a desk. Her clothes hung on an open rack, the only personal decoration a framed photo of her with her dad, her brother, and a woman I guessed was her mother. She flicked on the light while I studied the picture.

"Vanessa," Amalia said, pointing to the picture. "Her name was Vanessa."

"I can see where you get your beauty."

Amalia smiled, but a sad one. "My dad took one look at her and decided she was the one. He pursued her for months before she would consent to go out with him for ice cream! He loves her still. We all do."

"Did she want you to compete in beauty pageants?"

"No. It's terribly competitive. I wasn't kidding when I said girls go to school to learn how to be the perfect Miss Something-or-other. It's a religion. No one thinks I can win."

"Who is 'no one'?"

"The girls from my school. My brother." She paused. "My dad."

"But you are going to try, anyway?"

Her expression, a picture of loss and desperation, wrenched my heart. "What else do I have?"

"Well, Miss Amalia, I'm going to tell you a secret, but you have to promise to keep it to yourself."

Her eyes widened in surprise. "What?"

"Promise."

"I promise." This time she crossed her heart.

"Your dad's right. I'm not a soldier. I'm a cosmetologist."

"You're a whaaaaa…?"

"Cosmetologist. But more importantly, I worked with the last Miss America on her make-up."

She flopped on her bed. "You're lying."

I shook my head. "I'm not. Let's take a look at what we have to work with here. My thought is that we keep things simple and let your natural beauty show through. The other girls will be overly made-up in sparkly, slinky dresses. Let's show them up with simplicity and elegance."

She furrowed her brow but got up from the bed. "Yeah, about that…" She sighed. "I'll let you see for yourself."

She returned, displaying a pink confectionary nightmare that wouldn't do at all. If a five-year-old's Princess Barbie birthday cake came to life and married a Pepto-Bismol smoothie, it would be this dress.

I kept my mouth shut for the moment and asked, "What make-up do you have, love?"

She gestured to the desk and pulled out a drawer.

I rummaged through the products, and they weren't awful, but we could do better in the city. There had to be more choices available there, especially with the pageant taking place.

"Twirl for me, Amalia. Let me see your walk." I rotated my hand and motioned for her to do as I said.

She obliged, taking three steps forward, spun, and three steps back.

"Okay, good. Now let's talk about the 'model spread' and the 'return turn.'"

"The what?"

"Let me show you."

I walked the hallway, confident, head tall, shoulders up and back, but relaxed.

"This is the key right here. Do you see? The shoulders and neck. No slouching. The neck is long, and the head is up. Now, you try."

She gave it a go.

"Almost. Loosen up your arms. No, no. Don't swing them. The arms must have a natural sway, and the hips are square. Try again."

She tried again.

"Okay, better, but this time, let's do it in heels. You've got some heels here?"

"How do you know all of this?" she asked, as we continued to practice the appropriate strut, one foot in front of the other, keeping her body tall, arms natural, hands delicate.

"I told you that I'm a cosmetologist, right?"

She nodded as I corrected her elbow by moving it closer to her body.

"Neck. Remember the neck. Most important. I'm not any old cosmetologist, my dear. I'm 'the' cosmetologist. Hair, make-up, styling. You name it. Do you know Mitzi?"

Her eyes opened wide. "MITZI?"

"Not so loud, love; you'll have a microphone. Everyone will be able to hear you when you answer the questions during your interview. Yes, Mitzi. She's my client. But not only that…" I whispered a name, like a secret, and she stopped dead in her tracks.

"Miss America?" she asked, her eyes even wider. "No way."

I put my finger to my lips. "As God as my witness. Now, let's do the pose at the end and the twist-turn."

The first couple of times were rough, but she demonstrated a natural aptitude.

"Keep practicing. Show confidence when you walk. Chin up. Now, onto the clothes and make-up."

"What?"

"Do you ever get into town? Because we have shopping to do."

"We don't have much money." This statement came from Jorge, who'd joined us in the hall.

"This is on me." I winked at Amalia. "Those city girls won't know what happened by the time I'm finished with you, baby girl."

She was still wary, but I saw new hope in her eyes. "Ooookay, but my father has to approve."

"He will. Amalia, sweetheart, consider me your secret weapon."

I didn't expect the hug, but it sure felt nice.

Amalia raced past me to the porch. Jorge stepped in front of me, blocking my path. "I don't know you, and I don't understand why you know the things you seem to know, but if you hurt her, I'll hunt you down."

I held his eyes. "If I hurt her, you won't have to hunt me down. I'll be waiting for you."

He studied me a moment longer, then stepped aside.

"Papa, this man is going to help me with the pageant. He said…" She turned to me as I came through the door. "What's your name?"

Ah…good question.

I looked at Eddie for guidance. He gave me nothing, just a deadpan face that could have meant anything.

"Waylon," I said.

"Waylon is an expert in pageants, and he's going to help me get a new dress and make-up." She threw her arms around her father's neck. "If you approve," she whispered in his ear.

He flashed me an irritated glance but hugged his daughter. "Looks like we'll be working together on multiple fronts, gentlemen. Welcome to Casa de Flores."

7

Roderigo cleared his throat before speaking. Everest had retrieved Clipper's computer so the slight soldier could take notes.

"It started simply, about six months ago. We lived in an apartment closer to the city so my wife could take a bus to work. I consulted on security issues for banks and other businesses. The threats around here are constantly changing, and the bad guys are becoming more sophisticated. My company evaluated risks and recommended solutions for technical and physical security."

Roderigo drank more lemonade before continuing, staring at the table, unable to make eye contact with anyone. The story spilled from his lips in drips and drops, until it flowed, an unstoppable waterfall of pain.

"We owned this bit of property and loved coming here, though people told us it was dangerous to live so close to the jungle. I don't think they worried about the animals, more about the gangs hiding out here, but no one ever bothered us. I'm not sure why. Maybe they knew my profession. Maybe we were lucky." He shrugged. "I didn't question it."

"Vanessa returned from work one day troubled about the tweets and posts to the bank's accounts. She said they weren't alarming in any way she could pinpoint, but they didn't make sense. She thought there might be a virus or some technological issue.

"She watched, studying their pattern, keeping track, writing them down in a notebook. She shared them with us, and we couldn't make head or tails of it either.

"She was too tenacious, too curious. She should have left them alone, but Vanessa never turned down a puzzle. I don't know what tipped her off, but she figured it out and mapped the coordinates."

Clipper stopped typing. "How did she link it to drug deals?"

"One day, the newspaper reported a big drug bust, and she linked the most recent numbers to that city. She guessed the rest."

"I'm not trying to be insensitive," said Peter, and I cringed because it meant he was about to be insensitive. "But, didn't she think reporting this would be dangerous?"

"She'd worked for this bank for years and knew her direct supervisor well. They grew up here together. We went to Santiago's wedding for God's sake. She believed he'd protect her."

"Are you saying he betrayed her?" I asked.

"He must have. He's the only one she told."

"That doesn't mean he arranged or even knew about her murder," I said.

Roderigo growled, a low sound more animal than human. "No, but he knows something."

"Okay," said Eddie, who'd listened from the shadows. "We'll help you question this man, but that's all."

Roderigo didn't look happy, but he jerked his head in a short nod.

"Where can we find him?"

Amalia spoke for the first time. "The bank sponsors the Miss Mango pageant. He's the liaison. He'll be at rehearsals."

Everest's harsh laugh cut through the night, giving me goosebumps. "Well, ain't that convenient?"

"Isn't it just?" said Roderigo. "The only problem is…"

I don't know what Roderigo intended to say because the world blew up.

White light split the air, followed by intense heat and a shock wave. The explosion originated near the dirt road, destroying the cultivated land between the road and the house. The impact felt like being kicked in the chest by a horse. I barely managed to keep my feet, while Peter fell on his ass, holding his hand to his forehead. Eddie helped him up and pushed him off the porch. I looked up to see why and stared in stunned horror as a crack in the house's ceiling widened.

Everest scooped Clipper onto his shoulders and grabbed Jorge by the collar as I pulled Amalia to me. Roderigo screamed something I didn't hear and scrambled on all fours into the house, leaving a trail of blood behind.

I hugged Amalia to my chest and pulled her to safety. She struggled against me, pulling away, her face white, holding her hands to her ears, her eyes wild as she searched for her father. I held fast, pulling her back in. I didn't know if Roderigo would live through this, but Amalia would.

Eddie's reactions were fastest. He ducked and weaved as debris from the roof fell and another explosion rocked the porch. The struts holding it cracked and crumbled. He made it to the door before one corner gave in.

The porch and kitchen lights went out, and the world went dark.

Next to me, Everest held Jorge as the young man thrashed in his arms, shouting for his father. Clipper did an army crawl toward the house but flew back as another explosion shattered the air. This one was closer to our position, and it reverberated through my entire being.

Amalia, Peter, and Jorge crumpled. I enveloped Amalia with my body as she curled into a fetal position. Everest and I hadn't collapsed like the humans had, and while I didn't see Clipper, I assumed the same. What was it? The shock waves damaging live tissue? Their ears?

"Amalia?" No response. Everest checked Jorge's and Peter's breathing and nodded to me. Their chests moved, shallow and hinky but moving.

"Breathe, Amalia. Please breathe," I said, over and over. Could I give mouth-to-mouth? I'd never tried. I moved by feel and instinct, tipping her chin and taking a deep breath. I pinched her nose and breathed into her mouth. Nothing.

Two more.

Jorge rolled to her and held her hand.

I did two more, harder this time.

"Please, Amalia," Jorge begged.

Finally. She heaved and wretched, but her chest moved on its own.

"Thank you," I whispered. "Oh, thank you." I had no idea who I was talking to, but I sent the thanks anyway, maybe out of some belief that it couldn't hurt, perhaps out of some belief that it was simply polite.

I glanced at Everest beside me to see how he was doing. He clutched Peter to him, holding him upright. Peter and Jorge had multiple cuts, and Everest pointed to my face. I ran my hands over my cheeks and yanked out a few slivers of concrete or adobe or whatever building material without pain, but knew I'd need to be sewed up. I jumped when something wet touched my hand and then relaxed when I felt soft fur.

The dog nosed Amalia's cheek and curled around her head, licking her hand.

We waited for another explosion, but it didn't come.

Clipper made his way toward me, his mangled glasses in his hand. He pointed to the front and gave Everest a sign I didn't recognize, but Everest got the message. Everest scuttled to where we'd left our gear, slapped a plastic gun together, loaded it, hugged the edge of the property where the high foliage grew, and moved like a ghost toward the front of the house.

Clipper also weaponed up and army-crawled, following Everest.

Now that the explosions were over, the silence surprised me. No birds or frogs sang, no howler monkeys or owls. Amalia and Jorge's sobbing was a relief because it meant they were alive.

The sun peeked over the horizon, and the scene revealed itself.

Once again, I looked at the remains of a house. The first time, it was my house, but no one had been hurt. This time, I feared for Roderigo.

"Peter!" I shook his arm, and he focused on my mouth. "Where's Early?"

Peter pulled himself to a sitting position, cuts and bruises on his face, neck, and hands, dust on his face and hair as he tried to wipe his eyes.

"Don't," I said. A shard of something had lodged a millimeter from the outer corner of his right eye.

He nodded, slow but enough to show he understood, and sank back to the ground.

Everest returned, dragging two bodies. One was Early; the other I didn't recognize.

"Early?" I asked, my heart in my throat.

Everest lay Early's body on the ground, bent to one knee, and looked me in the eye. "I'm sorry, Waylon."

No. No. No. No.

My mind raced as I tried to understand, unable to grasp the idea of a world without Samuel Early. He was my creator, my only connection to my human life, and the one man who could figure out how to release me.

He was also my friend.

Everest already headed back to the house, and I followed.

Clipper kneeled, frantically shifting rubble, looking for Roderigo and Eddie. Everest joined the search, using his bulk to move larger chunks.

I knew I should help but couldn't think about anything but Early. I held out my hand.

"What?" Clipper snapped, but he sounded far away.

I vaguely wondered why my ears would be so affected. They'd been fine a moment before.

"Do you have your computer?"

"Waylon, this isn't the time!"

"Where is it?"

Clipper didn't even glance at me. "Get your priorities straight, man. We need to find Eddie."

"Computer," I repeated.

"Destroyed."

"What about your phone?"

Clipper patted his pocket and removed the phone, which was scratched but still working.

"Did you record that incantation? The one from Early?"

Clipper nodded, his brows furrowed in confusion.

"Show me."

He pressed a few buttons and handed me the phone, cued to an audio file. He turned back to his task and didn't ask why I wanted it. He was done with me, and distantly, I worried about Roderigo and Eddie too, but my focus was Early.

I ran back to our equipment, found the medical kit, and rushed to Early's body.

I was going to do something I promised I'd never do.

I was going to break every oath I'd ever taken, every pledge I'd ever made, every declaration I'd uttered.

I was going to make a zombie.

8

I closed my eyes and placed my hands over Early's body, trying to feel for life, any life. I let my mind sink, closing out sounds one at a time. Amalia's tears? Close that door. Peter's groans? Push them out. Jorge's gasping breaths? Not anything I could address now. I imagined a volume dial and turned all of those distractions to mute.

I looked for that place I visited when I planted my trees, when I touched their living bark and leaves, when I communed with nature.

And there it was.

A tenuous connection.

Early's soul lingered. Maybe because his death was so unexpected, or because he consumed zombie flesh once a month in a morning "protein" shake, but whatever the reason, I could grab it.

Working as fast as possible, I opened the medical kit and found three pre-filled syringes as well as other essential supplies. I twisted one of the syringes so the needle popped out, and before I could doubt myself, plunged it into Early's thigh and simultaneously hit "play" on the phone.

I had no idea when Everest had returned, but there he was, in my face.

"What are you doing? Did he agree to this?" he hissed.

I ignored him.

The music played through, and I hummed along, getting the tune although I didn't understand the chanted words.

No response.

I hit play again, and this time touched Early while humming louder, rocking back and forth on my knees, desperate for this to work.

"Waylon! Is this what Early wanted?" Everest again, louder.

I heard the question but forced it away. My hindbrain noted Eddie's voice, which I vaguely recognized as good, but I didn't want to pay attention to him now.

"Early! Come back!" I pounded his chest with my fist and hit play again.

The chant filled my ears, and I leaned closer to Early's body, feeling for that strand of soul. Once more, I thought about how I talked to my trees, urging them to find water and to grow, promising I'd take care of them.

"Early, you have to come back. I need you. You're not done here yet," I whispered in his ear as the chant faded away once more.

"Hunnnh." Early's chest rose with a giant inhale, and he sat up straight in one sudden motion so quick I almost didn't pull back in time. He floundered, his arms flopping at his sides, his eyes wide with fear. "Hunnnnnnh!"

"Early! It's me, Waylon. You're okay." I cringed at what I'd done. He wasn't okay, not at all, but it was all I managed.

Early twisted his head in my direction, an unnatural move, stiff and creaky, like the Tin Man in need of oil.

I sat back on my heels.

"I'm not dead?" Early asked, his voice uncertain and scared. He touched his cheeks, his eyes, and covered his face, crying without tears, his chest heaving. "It hurts," he said. "I was there, but then I wasn't. I don't…"

I pressed my lips together, and the rest of the team stayed silent. Even Amalia and Jorge quietly stared at Early in disbelief. Jorge crossed himself and reached for Amalia's hand.

Early gathered his courage and scanned his body, starting with his toes. He pinched his arm, wiggled his feet, and placed his hand over his heart.

"Ahhhh…" Early breathed. "Oh, Waylon, what have you done?"

"I brought you back."

"I always wondered if it would come to this," he said, his voice stronger but still low and slow. "I guess payback is a bitch. You did this to put me in my place, to make me live as you have."

I shook my head. "I did it because I couldn't lose you."

"You've given me an impetus to push ahead on my research, huh? It's in my self-interest now." He wouldn't look at me, his voice bitter.

I didn't say anything because that was partly true. I wondered if zombies could go to Hell and figured if we ever died, we most likely would. I decided not to examine that too closely but figured there would be a reckoning. There always was.

Eddie placed his hand on Early's shoulder. "We'll help you through it, Samuel. It will take some getting used to."

"I can't eat."

"No."

"I can't do so many things."

"But, you can do others, and Peter will keep you on at The Industries so you can continue your research. You're with friends."

"I wanted to ask a new woman out on a date. I can't do that now, can I?"

"Unlikely." Eddie stated the facts, straightforward and calm, without inflection or judgment.

Early nodded, bent his knees, cautious about moving too fast.

I scooted back to give him room and hide my face. My mind flashed back to my turning, being held down, the feeling of being ripped from a path that lay ahead and stuffed back into a shell.

I'd done what had to be done. No turning back from that, but I'd have to live with this choice for the rest of my life, however long that would be.

"Where's the kit?" Early asked.

I handed it to him.

He took it silently with a jerky nod and stood, walking to Eddie to look at Roderigo.

"What happened?" he asked, bending to examine him, Amalia and Jorge already there.

"He ran into the house as it collapsed. He's breathing but unconscious."

I scooted another few feet away from the group, distancing, not sure if I was welcome. Everest still hadn't looked at me, and Clipper gave me his back and only his back. I wasn't prepared to see his face, anyway.

I stared at the sky, reviewing my actions, reviewing the events of the last several minutes, reviewing the situation over and over again, wondering who had attacked, mentally berating myself for putting Early through the zombie process, but relieved by his return at the same time. Would I have made a different decision? No. I'd do it again.

By the time I tuned back in, Early had moved from Roderigo's side and sat with Clipper and the body of the strange man Everest had dragged over.

"Who is that? The body, I mean," I asked, hesitant to bring attention to myself but confused.

Everest replied, still not looking at me. "One of the bad guys. He must have gotten caught in the blast, and his boys left him. He's donating a foot."

"He doesn't need it," Clipper said.

Everest followed up on Clipper's comment. "Of course, no one *asked* if he wanted to donate a body part, but at least that is all we are doing. If he had wanted to, say, come back as a reanimated living corpse, we may have wanted to have a word first."

I stiffened at the rebuke. Early and I had never discussed what to do upon his death or if he wanted to be brought back as a zombie. As crazy as it sounds, it never occurred to me that he would die. We'd been cheating death for so long, but now, I'd made a decision that had no "take-backsies."

"It's alright," Early said, then looked over his shoulder at me. "It's okay, Waylon."

I covered my eyes with my hands and refused to look him in the eyes. It was done, and I'd have to live with it, and so would he.

"How is Roderigo?" Clipper asked, twisting and turning his new foot at the ankle.

"Good," Early replied. "He sustained a concussion and burns on his hands and face. We need to get him to a hospital."

Clipper grunted something to acknowledge and then gestured at his foot.

"This is a good foot but two sizes larger than my other one."

"Glad you like it," said Early. "It's the only one available, so take his boot and manage."

"I'll have one black boot and one tan one," Clipper grumbled but nodded. "I'll handle it."

"No hospital," Roderigo groaned. "They'll kill me."

"Which brings us to the main point," said Peter, finally sitting up and getting color back in his face. "Who did this?"

"The same people who murdered my mom," said Jorge, holding his father's hand. "They're trying to kill us."

Peter let Early attend to his cuts, especially the shard of pointiness near his eye, but kept up the questions with his usual sensitivity. "Why didn't they finish the job? They blew up your crops and your home but left you alive. If it were me, I'd used the chaos to slip back here with a knife and slit your throats."

"Nice, Peter," I said.

"Oh, don't be a hypocrite. I'm being practical."

"I can't say," Roderigo said, his voice hoarse.

"Roderigo, why did you go back in the house?" I asked.

He reached into his pocket with a burned hand and extracted its contents. He showed me a photo of Vanessa. He risked his life for one photo.

Amalia's tears fell down her cheeks, and Jorge wiped his eyes.

"Let's sum up our situation, shall we?" Peter brushed Early off. "People of unknown origin are trying to kill you, we still don't know where Zed is, you have no home to go to, Clipper's got a new big foot, and Early is a zombie. Do I have all that right?"

"Early is a *what*?" Amalia stared at Early and then at me.

"I'm not partial to the word zombie," Early said. "There's too many stereotypes associated with zombies. We're resuscitated. Brought back to life through faith and science."

It wasn't the worst description I'd heard.

Amalia didn't say anything. She'd been through too much to process this new information.

Everest retrieved our gear and packed the medical kit. Clipper got to his feet and tested his new appendage. He'd straightened his glasses as best as possible, but they rested on his nose at an odd angle.

Eddie whistled to get our attention. "First things first, Roderigo needs medical care. Where can we take you, Roderigo?"

"I have a friend up the road, Hernando. If my truck is okay, we can go there." He coughed a dry, hacking cough. "Ow."

"Peter," said Eddie, "find out if that truck works and take Roderigo and Jorge to the friend's house. All three of you need time to heal. See if they can find some aloe to put on the burns. Honey also works."

"Gotcha."

"Clipper, Everest, and Early, the four of us will look for Zed's body." The three nodded. "Waylon, take Amalia to the city and help her get ready for the pageant. Clipper will give you money. See if you can get intel on the bank since they're a sponsor. For the moment, we'll assume someone associated with the bank ordered this mess." He gestured behind him to the house and crops.

"How will we get back to the city?" I asked.

"Take a bus," said Amalia. "But I don't have anything to wear. No dress, no swimsuit, no make-up, so it isn't worth it. Besides, I need to be with Papa."

I adopted my best cosmetologist-talking-to-client face. "Kitten, I'm telling you, trust me on this. I got you."

Jorge put his hand to her chin and turned her face to look at him. "I'll take care of him. You go win this thing."

Roderigo pointed at Jorge and nodded, then passed out.

"Let's get him out of here," said Eddie. "Peter, are you well enough to drive?" He pointed to a truck parked behind the house that had escaped intact. Peter pushed himself to his feet, gave Eddie a nod and asked, "Jorge, where are the keys?"

Jorge's blank look said it all.

"Fine, let's hotwire it," said Eddie, motioning to Everest. "Thank the heavens for old cars. Go find yourself a knife. Remember red wire, then black."

"I got it, boss. This isn't my first rodeo."

Clipper handed me a wad of cash, and I still had no idea where he'd stored it. "Amalia, what time will the bus come?"

"We have to walk to the stop first." She stood, wiping her nose on the back of her hand. "I can't believe I don't have anything. No identification, nothing. How will they know who I am?"

"Oh, honey, they have your pictures, right? Besides, when I'm done with you, you'll be the darling of the pageant circuit."

Before I got my prance on and did my best pageant mom interpretation, I had to do the hard thing. I took a moment to stand quietly by Early.

"We never discussed it, Sam. I'm sorry if I did you wrong."

Early sighed. "What's done is done. We'll hash it out later. Right now, let's figure out which assholes killed me."

9

We caught the already crowded bus and took seats next to one another. A man stepped on my foot without apology, a child got on cradling a cat, and a grandmother carrying enough bags to make me think she was moving to Europe squiggled her ample rear end into the tiny space next to me. I couldn't take it after a few minutes and stood, and she settled into the broader space with a self-satisfied, victorious smirk. Amalia slept the entire bus ride, and for that, I was grateful. She needed rest.

We bounced and slid our way to town, and I exited, Amalia in tow, with a prayer of thanks to whatever deity might watch over zombies. Maybe Anubis?

We checked into the pageant hotel, and I ensured we got a suite. It was the government's money, so why not? I placed a call using the hotel phone while Amalia showered. A second call got me the information I required, and with a quick third call, we were in business.

"Amalia, have you rested enough to go shopping?"

"What are we going to do first?"

"Eddie and Peter will work on your identification. They have connections, so we'll let them do that voodoo they do so well. In the meantime, you and I are going dress shopping."

"But where? We can't walk into a department store and pull something off the rack."

"That's why we aren't going to any old department store." I gestured to my notes and waggled my eyebrows at her. "Follow me."

My first call to Mrs. Ross gave me the phone number for my Miss America client, who called her friend, Miss Venezuela, who called whoever she knew, and *voilà,* I had the name and an appointment with the best seamstress in town.

Nothing and no one moved faster than beauty queens on a mission.

Squirreled away in a side street, Abuela Nina's dress shop was only for people who needed it, had the connections to find it, and the cash to afford it. By the time we walked in, the proprietress waited for us, pincushion on her wrist and tape measure around her neck. Though she introduced herself as *abuela*, grandmother, she wasn't old. Her white hair hung long and lush over her back, gathered in a loose ponytail at the nape of her neck. She wore a white shirt with a blue blouse over it and a chunky turquoise and silver necklace, her only jewelry. Her pink-rimmed glasses highlighted her eyes, which missed nothing.

"Let me see you, girl." Nina ushered us in, speaking accented English. "We don't have much time. Why didn't you come see me sooner?"

Amalia glanced at me, at a loss for where to begin.

"Amalia had a dress, but yesterday, her house caught fire, and the dress went up in smoke," I said.

Nina peered at Amalia. "Is this true?"

"Yes," Amalia whispered. "I lost everything, including the only remaining pictures of my mother." Amalia covered her eyes with her hands to hide her tears.

Nina turned away, and when she turned back around, her face was stoic, but her voice was loud and clear. "Amalia, I will make you the best dress of anyone at that pageant. Take off your shoes and stand on this box." To me, she said, "What are you to her? I won't tolerate a sugar daddy." She walked so close she could, and did, tap my chest.

"I'm a cosmetologist."

Nina blinked.

"I'm a friend of the family. Nothing more. Nothing less. And I'll do her make-up and hair."

"Do a partial updo so we can show off her shoulders."

"Yes, ma'am."

Nina examined Amalia, clucking and tucking and offering advice on posture. She handed her a white tube dress, like women wear as a cover-up at the beach, and clucked more.

"White, I'm thinking, with a long skirt, lace upper body, and a cape."

"A cape?"

"More like an outer skirt. Trust me, I know what I'm doing."

"We trust you." I nodded to Amalia, and she lifted her shoulders in a tiny shrug that said, *What choice do we have?* It hurt my heart to see Amalia so apathetic. She should be excited and involved in every detail. Instead, she was traumatized.

While Nina did her thing, I rustled up a piece of scrap paper from the trash can, snagged a pen, and scribbled notes.

Drug dealers kill Vanessa?

Bank involvement?

Roderigo injured. How badly?

Zed's body, where is it?

Cosmetic purchases? Where to get? Research best Latina brands.

Bathing suit.

It made a decidedly eclectic list, murder with a swimsuit chaser, but each thing gnawed at my mind. I chose to focus on the murder.

Vanessa notes social media posts and keeps a record.

Vanessa reports her findings to her direct bank manager, Santiago (Last name unknown).

Vanessa is murdered in a "mugging."

Roderigo pushes for answers? He didn't tell us who he talked to? Who was he pressuring? He hit a nerve because...

...the front yard of the home is bazookaed,

...but they leave Roderigo and children alive.

Nina tapped my shoulder. "Come back tomorrow, same time. I'll work all night to get this dress done."

Amalia hugged Nina. "You don't have to work that hard. Please don't sacrifice for me. Make the dress simpler if needed."

Nina circled her arm in a grand sweeping gesture. "And what else do I have to do? Do my grandchildren come to visit me? No. My children? No. Too busy to remember their *abuela*. Now, hug me again and come back tomorrow."

She all but pushed us out the door.

I snuck a look at Amalia's face, and she smiled. "What's so funny?"

"Abuela Nina. She's like every grandmother I've ever met, including mine." She crossed herself as she said this. "*'I'll sit in the dark. No one visits. What do I have to live for?'* It's all so...so normal. I forgot for a while."

"Know what will really make you smile?" I asked.

"What?"

"Blush! Foundation! Not that you need much and the lights will be hot, we'll need the right products and a light touch. Ooooh, long-lasting lipstick is a must. I'll show you a trick to keep it from feathering."

"You really are a cosmetologist."

"You betcha, baby. I'm the best there is."

We spent two hours testing foundations and powder.

"What do you think of this one, Waylon?"

"Too dark. Try it on the jawline and bring the mirror out into the sun." The salesperson nodded her permission. She wasn't stupid. She saw the big commission coming.

Amalia returned, and I handed her a new one. "This one is the best, I think."

By the time we finished, we were both toast. I didn't need sleep *per se*, but I did need rest, and the cooler, the better. We agreed to return to the hotel so I could crank the air conditioning.

"Amalia? Amalia?"

We stopped on the sidewalk when a young man, eighteen-ish, called out, running across the street to intercept us.

"Juan? What are you doing here?"

"Speaking English? Too good for Spanish?" Juan asked, but he only had eyes for Amalia.

"I don't want to be rude to my friend." She gestured toward me.

Juan gave me the once over and jutted his chin in my direction. "You got a white boy, Amalia? You deserve better. He doesn't have money."

Amalia didn't reply.

"Come on, don't be like that. How are you, *chica*? Are you okay?" said Juan, his gaze trailing up and down her body. Two more boys watched Juan from a distance.

"I'm fine, thank you," she said, her voice cold.

"I'm surprised to see you. Glad to, though. You seem good. In one piece." Juan stroked a finger down Amalia's arm, from her shoulder to wrist, but it seemed for show. He looked at her body as if examining her, not coming on to her.

"You really okay?"

"None of your business." She jerked her arm away, and as I was about to interfere, Amalia stepped out of reach and shook her head at me. I stood down. Sort of. Not that I had any idea what I could do. Attack him with a mascara wand?

"Baby, you don't have to fear me. I'd never hurt you." Juan stepped close to Amalia, and I placed the bags on the ground so that my hands were free. Juan's friends shoved their hands in their pockets and crossed the street toward us.

"I'm not your 'baby' anymore, Juan. That ended when you got that." Amalia pointed to a skull tattoo on his neck.

"It's join or die out here, Amalia. You know that."

"I *don't* know that. You had a chance to go to college in California, and you stayed here and joined up."

Face red, Juan stepped back, flipping her off. "I stay with my boys, be loyal."

"Whatever."

"Trouble, Juan?" one of the new boys asked as they approached.

"Naw. Nothing."

"She's a pretty little thing. Too good for you, Juan. Hey *chica*, you want a real man, you come to me."

Amalia shook her head in disgust. "No, thanks. Come on, Waylon. Let's go."

Juan kept staring at Amalia as if he wanted to say something else. The second boy bumped him with his elbow. "Come on, Juan. Señor Cinco is coming to town, and we'd better be ready."

Juan licked his lips, his foot tapping, and said, "Be careful, Amalia. Take care of yourself."

I studied the boys, grateful my new body was bigger and more muscular than my last. I retrieved the bags but maintained eye contact with Juan, who eventually turned and jerked his head at his friends. They walked off in the other direction, and I let out a sigh of relief. "Who was that?"

Amalia's voice was thin and tired. "Juan and I used to play together when we were little, before his father died. We stayed in touch in high school, but then I cut it off."

"He's in with the gangs."

"Yeah. It was a real disappointment to me. His uncle, Hernando, is my father's best friend."

"The same Hernando your dad is with now?"

"Yeah, why?"

"You ever heard of Señor Cinco?"

"No. What kind of man goes by the name of Mr. Five? Stupid."

When we got back to the hotel, I asked Amalia for the number to Hernando's house, "just to check in," and tiptoed into the hallway.

"Peter?" I kept my voice low.

"Yeah, Waylon. What's up?"

I told him about our run-in with Juan. "I'm wondering if he may have been involved in the bombing."

"He's only a low level gang member. Why do you think that?"

"No one died, and he kept asking if she was okay."

Peter followed my logic in silence for a moment. "You think Juan kept the explosions contained to the front so Amalia wouldn't get injured?"

"It's a possibility. He seemed pretty relieved to see her in one piece."

"And now we're at Hernando's…" Peter's voice trailed off as it all clicked. "Waylon, I gotta go. Good thinking."

He hung up before I could tell him about Señor Cinco.

I cranked the air in my room and lay down to rest, wondering where we could get a bathing suit last minute and whether Roderigo's friend might be a traitor.

10

Putting food in my stomach made me retch, an unpleasant sound, and an even more unpleasant experience, so I declined dinner and left Amalia to order room service on her own. On my way out, I grabbed a cosmetic case and dumped some products in it.

"Get whatever you want, but don't leave this room, okay? I promised to watch over you."

"I'll get a salad and lemon water. Did you see how skinny those girls were in the lobby?"

"They were emaciated. They didn't look healthy."

"They'll be perfect on television, and I'll appear fat. I don't know why I'm doing this, anyway. We should pack up and go to my father." She slumped onto the bed and threw her arm over her eyes.

Lord save me from teenage beauty queens.

"You're going to see this through, Amalia. You stand a good chance. I believe in you."

She snuffled, and tears leaked down her cheeks. Guilt twisted in my gut.

"Hunmph." She flopped on her side and grabbed the room service menu.

I encountered three of said skinny girls in the elevator and listened to their conversation while thanking my zombie status for not having to inhale. The hairspray was thick enough to choke on.

"I'm excited to see who the judges are," said one, a tall blonde which, given her eyebrows and roots, wasn't her natural color. Catty? Maybe, but I was Team Amalia.

The second had a pixie cut, an unusual hairstyle for a pageant that favored long, flowing locks. It framed her face to show off her cheekbones. One glimpse at her green eyes, and I knew this one had come to compete. Her permanent eyelashes fluttered in the distinctive manner of a master stylist in Las Vegas and, boy, were they fantastic. She caught me looking and gave me a little side-eye.

"Armando?" I asked, pointing to her eye.

"Only the best," she replied.

"Expensive," I said.

"Whatever it takes," she said with a wink of those fabulous lashes.

The third girl watched in silence. Shorter than the other two, and curvier, she'd dressed to highlight her assets. "You're with Amalia, aren't you?"

"Yes, I'm her stylist and cosmetologist."

She pursed her lips. "I had no idea she could afford professional help."

I smiled.

She flipped her hair over her shoulder as we reached the lobby. "Amalia is a country bumpkin who can't win, but I'm glad to see her here. Terrible what happened to her mom."

I kept my smile plastered to my face and bowed them out of the elevator.

Oh, were we going to show them. But first, a phone. I wanted to stop using the hotel phone. I'd already exposed myself getting the dressmaker's information, so I searched outside until I found a shop. I bought a burner with an international sim card, paid in cash, and called Captain Perkins.

"Waylon! Where the hell are you? I've been looking for you everywhere. I've called your house, your cell, even Doc Early, and he's gone too. What's going on?"

"Out of town, Captain, no big deal. I wanted to check in with you on Addington's transfer."

"That's what I was trying to tell you. The bastard made bail and is out on his own recognizance."

"What? You promised me you had him."

"The prosecutor made the case, but the judge ruled Quint an upstanding member of an important employer in town and innocent until proven guilty."

"He killed people and dismembered them!"

Perkins sighed. "You don't think I know that? There's nothing I can do but watch your back. That man is devious. Stay out of town, get a tan. Isn't that Spanish I hear in the background? Get a drink with a tropical umbrella."

"Gotta go, Captain."

My eye twitched at the thought of Quint Addington out of jail and a free man, but I pushed *that* anxiety to the back of my brain to focus on the problem at hand. I excelled at multi-tasking.

The amphitheater where the pageant would take place connected to the hotel by a transparent tunnel that reminded me of a hamster trail. One way in, one way out, and it was hot and made me feel vulnerable. I didn't like situations where I couldn't escape if needed. I still suffered from memories of being turned into a zombie the first time, and the experiments Early and I tried attempting to kill me. Even being held down on The Industries' lawn recently made me freak out. I trotted through as fast as possible.

Once through, I wandered around like I belonged there, walking with purpose. I added a little swish to my step with an imperious head nod. No one bothered me. Every girl had her own team, and various primpers and perfectors sashayed about, so if one deviated from the dressing rooms and vanity mirrors, who was to say?

I nabbed an unattended clipboard, snagged a pen from a nearby table, and snarled at a timid production assistant, all while marching toward a roped-off area guarded by a tall, muscular, broad-shouldered man. He had the bland expression of an experienced security professional used to dealing with long, boring hours punctuated by yahoos like me who wanted access behind the curtain.

Instead of approaching him, I pranced right by, paying him no attention. He let me pass without comment since I wasn't trying to get to the curtained area behind him. Bluffing my way past this guy would be impossible. I needed a distraction. Luckily, I knew where to go.

The dressing rooms were packed, but I sought out my three girlfriends from the elevator. "Ladies?"

The three rotated in perfect synchrony on one toe with a quick pivot. Sheesh. They were trained well. Each raised a perfectly arched eyebrow.

"It would be to all of our benefits if we learn more about the judges, don't you think?"

Fake-blondie raised her other eyebrow.

"There's a roped-off section backstage where I believe the judges are hiding and only one man between them and us. Think about it. One. Man. Child's play for the three of you."

"Where's Amalia?" asked Pixie-Cut.

"Final dress fitting," I lied, but it was a good one. Every girl here would get a last fitting within the next twenty-four hours.

Curvy-Girl regarded me with suspicion, but after exchanging looks with her friends, she held out a finger and said, "Turn around."

I turned and listened to the fast Spanish and the soft slip, click, and rasp of clothes being discarded and donned. A tap on my shoulder told me it was time to turn back around.

Strategic. These girls were chief executive material. Blondie wore torn jeans, a rosy tank top, and ballet flats, the demure one who happened to be sexy, and her wide-rimmed glasses gave her that irresistible secretary look. It helped that the tank top strap fell "just so" down one shoulder.

Curvy-Girl had it going on with a black halter dress accentuating her curves in all the right places, and strappy one-inch heels showing off her red toes. Pixie-Cut wore stretch pants, stilettos, and a bustier. All Mr. Strong and Surly had to do was pick his favorite flavor.

He did a double take when the three beauty queens approached, and while I didn't doubt his professionalism, such delicious eye candy merited a second look. His eyes lingered on Blondie and the coquettish strap, so she took the lead. I lingered to the side.

"We understand we can't go in there," she said, batting her eyelashes, "but can you tell us anything about the judges? A teeny-tiny hint?"

"No, miss, I cannot. Good try, though," he said with a grin.

Pixie-Cut sidled next to him, her heels making her almost as tall as him. She licked her lips. "What's your name, *bebé*?"

"Mister."

Curvy-Girl laughed, drawing his eyes to her chest. While they distracted him, I slipped behind the rope. They hadn't even tried hard.

A black curtain shielded the back area, so I had to walk several feet before I found a break in the drapery and poked my head inside to see…boxes.

Boxes and boxes. Black plastic boxes, wooden boxes, and regular old cardboard boxes, but dozens upon dozens of them, all marked with "costumes," and "instruments," and "shoes." One was partially open, and the contents matched the label: "sashes."

Was this a storage area? Why guard costumes and clothes?

A voice got my attention, and I ducked behind a tower of boxes, listening hard, and once again thankful for not having to breathe if I didn't want to.

"What are we going to do with all this stuff?" A male voice.

"After the pageant, we can toss it." Another male voice, older than the first, but smooth.

"Can we sell it?"

"If you guys want it, you can have it. It isn't my interest."

"I'll tell the boys."

The boys.

It clicked.

The younger voice was Juan.

"Move the product when and how I tell you, and you can have everything else, but you'll have to take it that night because it can't hang around here. Señor Cinco will be watching, and he expects everything to go off without a hitch."

"Yes, we understand," Juan said.

"Also remember, I can't help you. I'll be sitting at the judges' table as the bank's representative. You'll have to do this by yourselves."

"No problem. You can count on us. I promise."

"Stay out of the way of the American judge."

Juan whistled. "She's super hot."

"She's beautiful, so it's easy to think she's stupid. Don't make that mistake."

"Perhaps she'd like to meet a young, energetic man?"

"Keep your head on straight, Juan."

"As I said, no problem, Santiago. No worries."

They walked away, and I sat, my head spinning.

Santiago from the bank.

They'd gone to his wedding, and he was from the same area as Vanessa. Her supervisor. Roderigo was right. The product had to be narcotics stuffed somewhere in all of these boxes.

A woman's voice startled me out of reverie and struck fear in my heart.

"So, I'm a judge, and so's that guy from the bank, but who is the third?" she asked, her lilt and tone so familiar.

"We're still working that out, darling. Don't worry." This woman's voice was deeper, an alto, and when I peered around the box, I recognized

Señora Liliana Leoncio, the organizer of the pageant. I'd seen her photo on a poster in the hotel lobby. Tall, buxom, and sophisticated, this woman looked like she chewed nails for breakfast and washed them down with lighter fluid.

And right next to her stood my friend and client, Mitzi.

11

Mitzi was a judge for the pageant. That must be the secret job she'd mentioned on the cruise ship.

What a freakin' mess.

The priority was to tell the team about Juan and Santiago. I didn't know if they were still at Hernando's or not since my phone call with Peter ended so abruptly. I wondered if I could call there again and mentally kicked myself for not getting Clipper's cell phone number.

A tap on my shoulder made me whip around in fright.

"Waylon!" said Mitzi. "What are you doing here?"

"Oh, hi, Mitzi." So lame.

"Who is this, Mitzi?" asked Señora Liliana Leoncio.

I cowered under her stare.

"My special friend from America. Only the world's best cosmetologist! Waylon Jenkins, have you met Señora Leoncio?"

"I have not. It is a pleasure to meet you, Señora."

"Charmed. Now, what are you doing back here?"

Mitzi whispered to me, hand covering her mouth. "You're involved with a contestant, aren't you? You sneaky boy! Like that Miss America you helped. You never let anything slip." She punched me on the arm.

"You worked with the Miss America pageant, Mr. Jenkins?" asked Señora Leoncio.

"I did. I've worked with many pageant contestants."

Mitzi batted my arm. "He's being modest." She lifted her left hand and her right index to tick off several contest winners I'd helped. Most had won.

"That's impressive. We are humbled to have you here as part of our little event. I have to go now, but see that you return to the main area, will you? You can't be here."

"Yes, ma'am."

Señora Leoncio waved a warning finger to me and went off to do whatever pageant directors did.

"Now, Waylon, why didn't you tell me you were coming here?"

"Cosmetologist-client confidentiality, Mitzi. You know that. You never told me you were a judge."

"You overheard that? Yes, it is so exciting! It's a secret because they're going to do a big reveal the night of the pageant. I'm so honored. Now, tell me, who are you working with? I'll keep it secret. You can trust me."

"Amalia Flores, but that's not what's important." I grabbed her elbow and pulled her to a small corner next to the heavy drapes. "It isn't safe here. It would be better if you left. Come down with a cold or something."

She yanked her elbow out of my hands. "Don't be silly. I'm perfectly safe. It's a pageant, not the running of the bulls. I've been in more danger on movie sets."

"You don't understand—"

"Mitzi, will you introduce me to your friend?"

Santiago.

Ugh.

I'd almost forgotten he was backstage. He'd returned to find Mitzi.

Mitzi turned with a broad smile. "Santiago Aguilar, may I introduce you to Waylon Jenkins, cosmetologist extraordinaire. He's here with a contestant, and we ran into each other. Isn't that funny? It's such a small world."

Santiago was a round-faced man with a mustache and beard manscaped to perfection, which I begrudgingly admired. His full eyebrows framed dark brown eyes that studied me with suspicion. He shaved his hair close on the sides but left it full on top. He hid his small paunch under a well-tailored suit, creating an overall impression of a career-oriented man who cared about his appearance and wanted to rise through the corporate ranks. Nothing wrong with that.

His cologne, however, gave him away as a lying rat bastard. Men who wear too much cologne are hiding something.

"Mr. Jenkins, such a pleasure to meet you," he said, proffering a hand.

I shook it and managed not to wipe my hand on my pants afterward. "What is your involvement with the pageant, Mr. Aguilar?"

"The bank I work for is sponsoring the event. We are proud to be part of giving girls a chance at scholarships that could change their lives." He winked. "It also gives the bank a little international exposure, which can't hurt."

"Absolutely not. It's a win-win."

"Exactly! You understand. Now, which contestant are you working with?"

"Oh, Waylon. What did you say her name was?" said Mitzi, snapping her fingers trying to remember.

Oh, God.

I tried to stop her with my eyes, but she didn't get the hint. I let them go wide and sent psychic messages that didn't work.

It's nothing, Mitzi. It wouldn't be proper to say. I shook my head in a frantic, tiny tremor kind of way, a little microburst that any girlfriend should understand to mean, *No, no, no, please don't do this. Abort! Mayday!*

Girlfriend power failed.

She clapped her hands. "Am-something or other...Amalia Flores? Is that right?"

Santiago froze, and a fake smile crawled onto his face.

I smiled an equally creepy grin right back. "Yes. I think her mother worked for your bank. Did you know her?"

Santiago cleared his throat. "Yes, she did. Such a tragic story." He managed to summon a few tears, even. "Murdered after work one day in a mugging. Senseless."

"Oh, how horrible!" Mitzi exclaimed, her hand to her heart. "My goodness. Such a brave young woman to follow her dream after such a loss. I hope she does well."

"She'll do great. She's beautiful and charming."

"I'm sure she is, or you wouldn't be working with her. Well, you must excuse me. I have some things to attend to."

Santiago and I watched Mitzi walk away in silence until he turned to me and crossed his arms. "Exactly what are you doing backstage, Mr. Jenkins? You aren't supposed to be here."

"I got lost." I suppressed the need to growl.

"I think you need to get lost again." Santiago gestured back toward the way I came. He attempted to guide me by the shoulder, but I shook him off.

"I'm leaving, don't worry. Need to get back to my client." My phone rang, and I answered, pressing it hard to my ear. "Hey, Mom, I meant to call sooner."

"What the hell are you talking about?" Peter asked.

I walked several paces like I hadn't a care in the world, past the baffling for soundproofing, thick curtains, and stacks of chairs. I wasn't too far from Santiago, but all he heard was me jabbering to my mom. "I'm still waiting for that pasta e fagioli recipe. Your version is the absolute *best*. Email it to me already, won't you?"

Peter expelled a lungful of air. "Waylon! You aren't making any sense. Listen. We're on our way. Hernando's acting squirrelly. He's spending a lot of time in bed with a headache. We need to get Roderigo and Jorge out of here."

"How are they feeling?"

"They're recovering well. No problem traveling. Be careful, the more I think about it, the more I think Santiago whatever-his-name-is must be involved. He's the middle man, I'm sure."

"Yeah, I kinda figured that out. You're right, the soup goes best with garlic bread."

"It goes what? Wait, is Aguilar there?"

"Waylon! Where are you?"

I whipped my head at Amalia's voice. "Here, darling! Stay there. I'm coming to you."

"Darling?" Peter questioned. "Is that Amalia?"

"Need to go." I pulled the phone from my ear to disconnect the call, but Amalia ran into me and wrapped me in a bear hug. The phone flew from my hands and landed on the floor.

"How did you get past the bouncer?" I asked but didn't get an answer before she started in on questions of her own.

"Where have you been? I've been hunting everywhere for you. Why are you backstage? I didn't like being up there by myself." She flicked her eyes right and visibly shrank back. "Mr. Aguilar."

The phone wasn't on speaker, but Peter shouted loud enough to be heard. "Get her away—"

Santiago's heel crushed the phone.

"Hello, Amalia. I was telling Waylon he needed to get lost. I think that's a good idea for both of you. Juan!" Santiago called toward the back. "Bring the boys, please. We have guests."

"We aren't your guests." I pushed Amalia toward the curtain. "Hey, big guy! Mr. Security Guard! Why did you let this contestant backstage? Isn't that against the rules?"

The guard popped his head through the curtain, mouth open when he realized Amalia and I were there. Embarrassed, he stiff-armed us so we couldn't pass to the main contestant area. "Sorry, sir!" he said to Santiago. "I was…distracted."

"Yeah, I get that, Luis, but I'd like to keep them back here now, please. They've violated the rules. Ms. Flores and her cosmetologist slipped backstage to get intelligence on the judges, and it turns out that Mr. Jenkins is friends with one. This is grounds for disqualification."

"What?" Amalia's gasp broke my heart.

"That was an accident! I didn't know anything about the judges. I was looking for information about what's really going on here," I said, not bothering to keep the derision out of my voice.

"And what would that be, Mr. Jenkins? Think carefully, now." Santiago took a small step closer to Amalia. Though she sidled away, he grabbed her arm and pulled her to him.

This man killed Vanessa or arranged to have her killed, and most likely ordered the bombing at the Flores home.

"Nothing," I said. "A beauty pageant."

Santiago nodded. "Exactly. Luis, please take Mr. Jenkins and Ms. Flores to the empty office and lock them in so I can consult with the governing board about Ms. Flores's standing." Santiago walked away.

"Come on, miss," Luis said, motioning to her and to me.

"No." Amalia dug her heels in.

"Please don't make me do this," Luis said, his eyes worried. "I don't know why you cheated; you didn't need to. You're the prettiest one here."

"I'm smart, too," she retorted. "And I wasn't cheating. I was looking for Waylon. I walked back here without even seeing you."

"Yeah, Luis." I crossed my arms and tilted my head. "She is the prettiest, but how exactly would you know? Checking out the competition?" I lifted an eyebrow.

A blush crawled up his neck, and he cleared his throat in embarrassment. Nevertheless, Luis led us down a hallway, ushered us into a bare office with a simple desk, and shut the door, muttering an apology. I tried the doorknob, but it wouldn't turn. "Amalia, do you have your phone?"

Of course she'd have her phone. What woman her age didn't have her phone?

"I left it in the room."

My jaw dropped. "Are you kidding me?"

"I forgot it. I have my room key, though." She held up the white key card.

"That's great, but that won't help us get out of here, and I don't want to give Santiago time to think about things. He's looking for an innocuous story to get us out of the way, so he's trumping up these 'cheating' charges, but if that doesn't work, he will remove us personally, like he did to your mom."

"He's the one who had my mom killed?" Amalia's pale, stricken face and trembling lip pierced my heart.

I rubbed her arm, trying to reassure her. "I don't know for certain, but I suspect, and so does Peter. And Amalia, I'm suspicious of Juan."

"Juan? That's crazy. He's with the gangs, yes, but he'd never hurt me."

I didn't say anything else because I had no proof.

Amalia paced the tiny room, rubbing her hands together. "What do we do now?"

12

Knock on the door and call for Luis."

"He locked us in here," Amalia said. "Why would he come back?"

"He thinks you're the prettiest one here, which you are, by the way. Tell him you need to go to the bathroom then try to get away."

"That's the plan? 'Try to get away' is your entire plan?"

"Ow. Pull those claws back, girl."

She huffed an unconvincing, "Sorry."

I tried again. "Getting out of the room is a start."

"You're right." Amalia rapped the door with her knuckles, then smacked it open-palmed with urgency. "Luis! Luis! I need to go to the bathroom. Please, don't make me humiliate myself."

Luis cracked the door an inch. "I'll get a female guard to help you in a moment."

"I need to go *now,* Luis. Seriously, what am I going to do? You are way bigger and waaaay stronger than me." She crossed her legs like she really had to go.

Luis snorted but assented. "You," he said, pointing at me. "Stay there."

I held my hands up in mock surrender. "She's the one who needs the lavatory."

"I also have to get to a dress fitting," Amalia said, batting her eyelashes at him.

He grunted, too professional to fall for anything more. "After you." He turned to the side to let her pass. "The toilet is down this hall."

"Thank you." She slipped by him, brushing him with her breasts and belly.

He caught his breath and turned his face, muttering something about never working around pretty girls again.

She moved like a snake, scrambling for the exit, back the way we came.

"*Dios*!" He raced after her, lithe for such a large man, but unfortunately, he didn't forget to close the door, so I was still locked in though I'd jumped up as soon as she made her move.

"Damn it." I pressed my ear to the door.

"Get back here!"

Then, Amalia's voice. "Let go of me! Ah, Juan. What are you doing here?"

I smacked my hand to my forehead.

"Amalia, is this man hurting you?" asked Juan.

"No, no. We've had a misunderstanding, that's all. I got lost and need to get back to my room."

"I'll take you. You shouldn't be running around back here."

Luis's more mature voice broke in. "Sorry, son. Mr. Aguilar asked me to watch her."

"Whatcha gonna do to stop me?" Juan demanded, that little putz.

Amalia gasped. "Why do you have a gun? Put that thing away before someone gets hurt," she said.

"No need for that, Juan," said Luis, his voice low.

Suddenly, I wanted Amalia to go with Luis.

"Luis, protect her from him!" I screamed. "Don't trust him, Amalia!"

I heard a grunt and a slap, then a shot spliced the air, followed by the dull thud of a body hitting the ground. The shot wasn't as loud as it could have been. I guessed the gun had a suppressor on it, but suppressors only do so much. Despite what the movies and video games imply, there is still a distinct noise. For a moment, I hoped people would hear the gunshot, but then I recalled the soundproofing panels I'd strolled past earlier and got a bad feeling that we were on our own.

Amalia screamed, "Luis! Juan! What did you do?"

"Protecting you! Why didn't you and your dad get the hint? You should both be on a plane to somewhere far away by now."

I pressed my mouth to the door crack. "Juan! I know you were responsible for the bombing at Amalia's! I also know you made sure she and Roderigo weren't hurt. You did good, Juan. You protected her. Now, let her go, and we'll help you."

"I don't know who you are, but you can rot in hell. I got things to do. Amalia, you're coming with me."

"Amalia!" I jerked the doorknob, shaking it in a frantic attempt to escape. I pulled every drawer out of the desk, looking for a paper clip, a pen, anything to unscrew the door plate. Nothing. "Amalia!" I pounded on the door with the side of my fist.

I heard a creak followed by a thready breath, and the doorknob twisted. I pushed it down the rest of the way and swung the door open. "Amalia?" I took a rushed step forward and tripped over Luis.

He'd crawled or dragged his body to the door, leaving a blood trail a mile wide on the floor. He lay on the ground, bleeding from a gunshot wound to his gut, his eyes fluttering as he lost consciousness.

"Oh, my God. No, no, don't die. I'm getting help. Stay with me, brother. You've got this." I shook his shoulder and bent my head to listen to him breathe. "Hang on."

Despite my smaller size, I picked Luis up in a fireman's carry and staggered to the entrance area divided by the black curtains and poked my head out. "Help! Help! We need an ambulance. Someone's been shot."

"Get your hands behind your head and kneel! Now!" A burly police officer brandishing his service pistol rushed at me, weapon aimed at my mid-body.

I dropped, placing Luis on the ground, and put my hands behind my head as he demanded. "His name is Luis, and he's a guard here. A young gang member named Juan shot him and took a contestant, Amalia, with him—"

"Shut up."

Another man, this one taller and thinner and carrying a rifle, kneeled at Luis's side, feeling for a pulse. He bowed his head, his face pale, and crossed himself. "He's gone," he said to the burly man, who also crossed himself.

"You!" the burly one commanded. "Stand up, turn around, and spread your feet wide."

"I didn't do anything, sir. I'm trying to tell you there's a girl in trouble, and the man who has her shot this guard."

He yanked me to my feet, threw me against the boxes, and shoved my head down while the burly man cuffed me.

"Sir, I'm so sorry for Luis. If you will allow me to explain," I begged.

The skinny man barked at me. "You're covered in blood, the only one here, and witnesses saw you sneak past earlier. Don't talk and don't move. You're under arrest for the murder of Luis Ortiz."

"How did you know I sneaked past earlier? I didn't murder him, I promise. Please listen to me—unhh." The cop smacked my head, open palm to my right ear, and I fell back to the floor, unable to catch myself because of the handcuffs. My ear rang like a cathedral bell, and my vision blurred. I lay on my side in a fetal position staring at Luis's body and the blood pooling under him. The blood wasn't pumping, just widening and thickening, another sign Luis was really, truly dead.

The rock in my stomach grew heavier, and my worry for Amalia doubled from distraught to frenzied.

I scooted backward and anchored my legs underneath me, pressing my back to the wall, shimmying up to a stand. I'd made it halfway when the thin cop noticed and kicked my legs out from under me.

"Jesus fucking Christ!" I yelled. "Stop! I didn't kill Luis, but I know who did and there is a young woman in danger. Why won't you listen to me?"

He kicked my jaw, and I hit the floor. I wasn't knocked out, but I floated in a twilight listening to the cops while struggling to get myself together. They knew I'd sneaked past earlier, which meant...ah, crap. They worked for Aguilar.

Tall, thin cop: "This shits the bed. Luis is my second cousin on my mother's side."

Burly cop: "Sorry, man. What are you going to tell her?"

Thin cop: "That a cartel leader dropped him while he protected the girls at the pageant. It's sort of what happened, right?"

Burly cop: "Pretty damn close, *amigo*. Speaking of, you know, the bosses, what are we going to tell *them*?"

"It's being handled. The shipment wasn't disturbed; the girl will be eliminated. There is nothing for them to know."

The words "the girl will be eliminated" snapped my mind back into action. I heaved my prone body to the right and log-rolled toward the thin man, bowling into him with my upper torso, knocking him off-kilter and into the burly guy, who fell like, well, a burly guy. The three of us scrambled on the floor like kids playing Twister, but I was at a disadvantage since I didn't have my hands accessible. Thin guy dragged his nails down my face, and I bit his hand while the burly guy shoved his gun into my temple.

"Give me one reason not to shoot you right here," Burly Cop demanded.

"Because I want to."

The three of us stared up to where Peter stood a few feet away, Eddie, Everest, Early, and Clipper lined up behind him. No one else followed. The cops had probably emptied the area.

"Waylon, what have you done?" Eddie demanded, his weapon trained on the two cops.

The dirty police officers held still and wracked their tiny brains speculating about the identity of the new jerks with guns. I climbed to my feet.

Everest tipped his red and white baseball cap at me, motioned for me to turn around, and did something that released my hands with a click.

I rubbed my wrists. "Thank you, and to answer your question, I'm solving our case. Santiago Aguilar definitely ordered Vanessa's death, and he's tied up with the local gangs and someone higher up named Señor Cinco."

The police shuddered at the man's name.

I continued. "One of the members, Juan, knows Amalia and her family. He bombed their house, but he cares for Amalia, so he made sure no one got killed."

I turned to the police officers. "The problem is that these guys don't care and work with the cartel. This one," I jerked my chin at the thin guy, "is going to lie to his own *mother* about Luis's death." I pointed to the dead guard. "Luis was a good guy and this schmuck's second cousin. You can see he's all broken up about it."

Peter snapped at the cops. They stood and faced the wall, hands behind their backs, familiar with the drill. Peter used their own cuffs on them, pressed on their shoulders to push them to the floor, and crouched in front of them. "Who is Señor Cinco?"

"Maybe you'll get to meet him yourself," said Santiago Aguilar from behind us. "But I doubt it. You'll be dead by then. Drop your weapons. Take their guns, boys."

For God's sake.

The team sighed and did as he asked as men wearing bandanas over their mouths confiscated their pistols. It was all very Wild West.

Santiago released the cops, who hung their heads in shame, but he didn't say anything to them, instead turning to his men who snapped to attention.

"Put them in the cold room."

"What about Luis?" one of the men asked.

"Put his body in with them."

Eddie raised his eyebrows at Peter, who did a slow nod and caught Early's eye. I glanced at Everest's boot and thought I could make out the outline of a knife, but he didn't move for it. Clipper, his bored face intact, wore his garrote, and I was certain the team had other weapons stashed elsewhere.

If they weren't fighting, there had to be a reason. What was it? I studied them and focused on Everest.

The baseball cap had a turtle on it. Testudo. Zed's cap.

13

The cold room was exactly that, a refrigerated box designed to hold perishables before serving in the ballroom. It wasn't a freezer, but the normal operating temperature of a fridge is thirty-five degrees Fahrenheit, which I knew because I preferred to rest in one at night. It slowed zombies' metabolisms, or whatever it was that kept us ambulatory, and allowed us to recover, which meant Peter was cold and Early got his first taste of zombie resiliency.

Santiago's men herded us toward the back of the room and cuffed us to the metal racks lining the perimeter of the room. They tugged, shoved, and tightened more roughly than necessary, but we stayed silent and bore it. They dragged Luis's body and unceremoniously dumped it on the metal floor. I wondered how people became so callous toward life.

The door closed, and Eddie turned to me.

"What happened, Waylon? Every detail, please."

I recapped as best as I could, ending with, "...so the pageant is a front for a big drug deal, an international cartel representative is involved, Amalia is with Juan and in danger, and Mitzi has no idea what she's gotten into. Not to mention we're stuck in a fridge and haven't found Zed. By the way, where's Jorge and Roderigo?"

"Safe," said Eddie.

"We aren't stuck."

I turned to Clipper, who held Everest's hand in his own. Everest wasn't attached to it. He slipped his arm stump out of the cuff, did something to Early's cuff with his remaining hand with Clipper's knife, and motioned for Clipper to hand Early the, well, the hand. Early wrapped it in some butcher paper he found on a shelf.

Using the knife and Everest's skills, the rest of us popped out of our cuffs in no time. I removed my shirt and handed it to Peter, who donned it over his own. Eddie grabbed some cardboard so Peter could stand on it as well. The floor was freezing and slick.

"Nice scar." Eddie pointed to the pinched skin encircling my waist.

"Yeah, we replaced a whole torso."

Everest removed his cap, handed it to Early, then one-armed his shirt off and tossed it to Peter, who wrapped it around his head and ears.

We needed to get out of there.

"What do we do now?" I asked.

"First, we revive Zed," said Early.

"You found him?" I asked.

"We couldn't find his body, but we did find one important item." Early wore worn white painter's pants he must have borrowed from Hernando. He dug into a long side pocket and pulled something out.

A knife. A spectacular full tang tactical fixed blade heavy duty knife. Man, Aguilar's guys didn't search my friends well at all.

"Eleven inches of stainless steel with a fiberglass handle. His dad gave it to him. Look right here." Early flipped it over, and I read a tiny inscription that said, "Good on ya." "Between this and his hat, we hope we have enough."

"You don't have any of your stuff."

"It's in your hotel room."

"How did you get into my hotel room?"

Early pointed to Everest and Clipper and shot me a look that said, *Really?*

"Right, never mind."

Peter nudged Everest. He didn't even sway. The man was named after a mountain for a reason. When Peter tried again, Everest belly-laughed.

"Enough. Everest, Clipper, please unlock that door so we can get out of here," Eddie ordered, taking command. "Peter can't stay here."

Everest and Clipper strode to the front of the room to deal with the door. I turned to Early, Eddie, and Peter, about to ask a question, and then remembered Luis. "We're putting Zed in Luis's body?"

Early nodded. "He's not using it."

"True, but I sorta knew him. He was a good guy, and he's got family here."

"All the more reason to get him to the United States as fast as possible," said Peter, rubbing his arms with his hands.

"I don't feel right about this."

Peter shrugged. His lips chattered, and he blew into his hands. "Thhis is wwwhat we came to dddooo, and this is wwwhhat wwwee are ddoooing."

"Who made you so cold, Peter?"

"Har-de-har-har."

"You're an insensitive jerk who wants to use a body of a good man without permission from his family, who might want something to bury. His cousin crossed himself. They're probably Catholic. What are they going to do without a body to bury?"

"Nnnnot my ppppproblem."

"You agree with this, Eddie?"

"We need a body, and it's the only one we have available. Unless you feel like killing someone."

"Shit." That's all I could say.

"Hey, anyone want to get out of here?" Clipper called to us from the front of the room.

"How did you get the door open?" I asked.

"Interior release mechanism," said Clipper, pointing to a handle illuminated by a small emergency light.

"Let's get Luis," said Peter.

They rolled Luis in clear plastic sheeting they tore from the entranceway, hoisted him on their shoulders, one taking the head, another taking the middle, and the third at the ankles. I closed my eyes and rubbed my temples, frustrated and sick by what we were about to do. This zombie business teetered on a thin, gray line of integrity.

"Get off your high horse, Waylon," called Peter. "You're the one who turned Early without his prior permission. We're all doing things that push our moral boundaries."

It was true, but I didn't have to like it.

I remembered to snag Everest's missing appendage and followed them out, amazed that no one guarded us, but admittedly, we had been handcuffed in a fridge with a steel door. Preparing for a zombie who'd voluntarily chop off a hand wasn't in their playbook.

We walked past a multitude of open-mouthed producers, contestants, and assistants. Six of us accompanied a dead body like a floppy carpet, one a shirtless black man missing a hand, another a semi-fit white dude with a scary scar encircling his whole torso. When an assistant gathered the nerve to say something, I held up a finger and stopped him.

"Prop," I said. "One of the contestants is doing Shakespeare."

"The blood makes it so…realistic," he said, pointing at the dark brown drips on the floor.

The guys clasped the ends tighter and kept on walking.

We marched through the lobby. Shocked no one stopped us, I hit the button for the elevator, and we waited, ignoring the staring people.

The elevator paused on the twelfth floor.

Eleventh.

Tenth.

We gazed at the red numbers as each slowly, painfully slowly, lit up. I took a deep breath.

Nine.

Peter tapped his toes.

Eight.

"Pardon me, do you need assistance?" asked a tiny, older woman wearing a shawl, carrying an enormous pocketbook with an umbrella handle poking out the top.

"No, ma'am. We're fine," I said. "It's a prop for a stage set. Nothing to worry about."

"Carrying dead bodies is tricky, young man. If you held him directly at the hip bones, it would keep him from sagging so much."

I cast her some serious side-eye, but Clipper shifted his position, and lo-and-behold, the woman was right.

"Better," she said and walked away.

No one said anything.

Seven.

Six.

People were getting more interested and animated. A front desk person dialed a phone.

Five.

Four.

"Gentlemen, I'm certain there is a good explanation for this," said a man with a skinny, Snidely Whiplash mustache as he strode toward us, his hotel blazer buttoned crisply at the waist.

Three.

Two.

"Not really," I said.

One.

The door slid open, and a stream of chatty young women exited, not even noticing us. The guys swung around in a wide arc to get Luis through the narrow doors and, in doing so, smacked the mustachioed man in the head with Luis's shoes.

The man stumbled backward holding his ear.

We stepped in, and the guys lowered Luis to his feet and braced him against the wall, buttressing him with their own bodies.

"Better put ice on that," I said, hit "close," and wiggled my fingers goodbye at the mustachioed man.

Every elevator anywhere has Muzak. This one was no different. I hadn't expected American country.

I've always been crazy and the trouble that it's put me through...

"Waylon?" asked Eddie.

"Never knew him, no, Eddie."

We stumbled down the hall with the body until we got to my door. I looked at Clipper and Everest while they looked at me.

"I've lost my key card," I said.

"Jesus fucking Christ," said Clipper. "Here, switch."

I ducked under Clipper's shoulder, trying to anchor myself against Luis's hip, but I missed, and his mid-section sunk like a slinky. He slid off the other men's shoulders and hit the carpet with a thud.

"Jesus fucking Christ," repeated Clipper. He got the door open somehow, and we dragged Luis into the room, hoisted him onto the couch, and collapsed to the floor.

I beckoned to Peter. "Give me my shirt, man, and Doc, give Everest a hand, will ya?" I tossed the butcher-papered bundle to Early.

14

As Early re-attached Everest's hand, I asked the most important question of all. "Do you have any idea where Amalia is?"

"That's what I want to know." Roderigo stormed into the main room from the bedroom in back, Jorge on his tail.

"I don't think they've left the hotel," said Eddie. "Too much going on right now. They'd find a place to stash her and interrogate her later."

"Well, isn't that peachy?" said Roderigo. "I'm glad you don't *think* she's gone. That makes me feel a lot better."

Jorge put a hand on his father's arm. "Juan betrayed us. Don't take out your anger on the wrong people."

"They aren't even people," Roderigo muttered, but he walked away and stared out the window.

"They'd move her out of the way," I said, tapping my lip as I considered where Juan might have hidden Amalia.

Everest rolled his hand at the wrist, testing out the new sutures. "Righteous job, Doc," he said.

Early grunted, already turning to Luis's body. He straightened it so Luis lay on his back, hands at his sides. Everest handed over the cap, and Early placed it on Luis's chest with the knife. The rest of us stepped back and, though I couldn't say why, something about the moment felt sacred, or risky, or...momentous.

Early kneeled and placed a hand on Luis's heart and chanted, the rise and fall of the syllables familiar to me now. I lowered my head, not looking. Everest did the same, but Clipper, Peter, and Eddie watched, stone-faced and stalwart.

The first time didn't work, and I reminded myself that it took more than once for Early to re-enter his body. It had to take extra effort given these circumstances. Early placed the cap on the body's head—I had to think of it as a body now—and slipped the knife into his hand. Finally, he removed a syringe from the battered medical kit and shot it into the body's thigh, chanting anew.

"Oy! It took you long enough!" The body shot to a sitting position. Luis's facial features morphed into someone else's as his hair grew into a mop of tousled, honey-brown curls.

"Zed?" Everest gasped and ran to his friend's side.

"Yeah, you big bastard. I've been hanging around the god-forsaken jungle for how long now? You guys left me after I got tagged." Zed addressed the doctor kneeling next to him. "And who the hell are you?"

"Doctor Samuel Early, at your service."

"Well, aren't you a beauty? Thanks for bringing me back."

I nudged Eddie. "What's with the Australian accent?"

"You saw Aussie slang inscription on the knife, right? His father was Australian, and he spent summers there, or winters, depending on how you look at it. It slipped into his speech."

Zed tested his limbs, wincing as muscles and tendons snapped into place, then Everest helped him to his feet. He tottered but got his balance and gave his brother-in-arms a hug. They were almost the same size. Luis wasn't a small man. Clipper approached, hand out, and they exchanged a solemn handshake and backslap, but when Zed turned to Eddie, his face hardened. "You bailed on me, mate."

"We didn't know what happened to downed zombies until we met Waylon." Eddie gestured to me.

Zed looked me up and down. "What's a Waylon?"

"I'm a cosmetologist."

"A wha?"

"I do make-up, hair, skincare. You know, a cosmetologist."

"This dag for real?"

I arched an eyebrow.

Eddie whispered the translation. "A nerd. A geek."

I shrugged. Guilty as charged. "Real enough. Over a hundred-years-old real. How's that? And, I can discuss every episode of *Star Trek* if that adds to my nerd cred."

"No shit. One hundred years?"

"Yes."

"That's a long time. Ever been killed and brought back?"

"Yes, it can be unpleasant."

"Not as bad as drifting unmoored in a jungle. All. By. Myself," said Zed, again looking at Eddie, who crossed his arms in self-defense.

"We didn't know, Zed. We came back as soon as we could."

"I watched my body get eaten by animals! I saw my bones slide apart and slip deeper into the bush. I saw my hair disappear, but I stayed. My spirit lingered with no body, no friends, no way to talk to anyone, knowing my squad hauled ass in a helicopter and left me there to rot, so don't give me 'we came as soon as we could.' You didn't come soon enough!"

Eddie stared at Zed, arms still crossed, unapologetic. "We did what we could, and we've risked a lot returning, but we would never deliberately leave a team member behind. Right now, if you stop your belly-aching and get your new head in the game, you might appreciate that you have your favorite cap, your knife, the nice body you've been given by a good man, and that we are in the middle of a situation."

Zed rolled his shoulders, whispered a prayer, looked upward, and crossed himself.

"Hey, are you Catholic?" I asked.

Zed startled as he realized what he'd done. "No," he said.

I raised my eyebrows. "Luis was."

"Is this Luis's body?"

"Yes."

"Who was he?"

"A security guard. Decent man. Liked pretty girls and tried to do the right thing. He deserved to live a long life, and now his family doesn't have a body to bury, so value it."

"Who killed him?"

"A young, troubled man named Juan."

Roderigo whirled around. "Juan murdered someone?"

I nodded.

"Oh. *Madre de Dios*. I didn't know he was so lost. Now I worry even more for Amalia."

The door opened, and the entire team shifted to defensive stances, hands on whatever weapons they could find.

Amalia cocked her hip in a whole, "don't mess with me," attitude, and gave an epic eye roll. "Don't worry about me, Papa. I'm fine. Boys are stupid."

"Amalia!" Roderigo embraced his daughter, hugging her tight. "How did you escape?"

"Juan left me alone in his room, tied to a bed with a necktie. How *Penthouse* is that?" she said with a toss of her mane.

Roderigo's eyes grew wide, but Jorge muffled a laugh behind his hand.

"It took a bit, but I wiggled out of it," said Amalia, almost nonchalantly.

I didn't buy the whole easy-breezy retelling, but I refused to call her out in front of everyone. Besides, I noticed the bruise on her neck that she'd hidden with her hair. It wouldn't come in fully for a few days, but my eye caught it. That jerk had held her by the neck and squeezed.

I was so going to kill him when I saw him.

I paused at that thought. Before a few weeks ago, I'd never think about killing someone and mean it.

"Amalia, this is Zed, the member of the team we came looking for," I said.

She cocked her head. "He looks a lot like Luis. That's so weird." Then, she thought for a moment. Her father cleared his throat, and she got it. "Ohhhh…"

I clapped my hands. "You know what, baby girl, we've got to get your dress. You still have a pageant to conquer! Let's go get your gown and pick up whatever damn bikini we can find. You'll rock it no matter what."

Peter hummed in agreement, and I waved a warning finger at him, mouthing, "stay away."

I opened the door for Amalia and cast a look back at the team. They seemed lost as to what to do next. Zed sat on the couch, his head in his hands, Early next to him, whispering something surely meant to be reassuring. The rest of the men, including Peter, faced Eddie, waiting for instructions. Roderigo and Jorge disappeared into the back bedroom.

After the door closed behind us, I spoke. "Okay, doll, spill. What really happened?"

Amalia blanched but regained her game face quickly enough. "He's different now. Harder. Uncaring. More interested in pleasing his masters than being a good person. He's convinced that it's either kill or be killed, and the gang is the only way to stay safe."

"He squeezed your neck."

Her hand fluttered to the bruise. "Yes, he slapped me around a bit. Luckily, Santiago summoned him, and he left before..."

"He could do worse?"

"Yeah." She licked her lips, a sign of tension I'd seen many, many times in my career. After the pageant, she might benefit from therapy to deal with being assaulted by a boy she used to trust. I told her so.

"Maybe," was all she said.

We kept our heads down as we crossed the lobby and made our way to Abuela Nina's, who clucked over her charge when she saw the bruise.

"Don't worry, my dear. I'm sure your cosmetologist friend can cover that, can't you?" She gave me the stink-eye, daring me to say "no."

"Of course. Child's play," I said.

"Good. Now, the dress."

Abuela Nina pulled out a garment bag and unzipped the front with great care and as slowly as possible to draw out the moment.

It was worth it.

We both gasped.

I had no idea how she'd pulled this off so fast.

The white dress had a lace top and a deep V neckline. The gorgeous straight satin hem would hit the tops of Amalia's feet in heels. But the cape made it. I'd never seen one like it. Instead of coming from the shoulders, it came from the waistline, and when she walked, it floated around her like ethereal wings.

"Oh, Abuela, thank you," Amalia said.

I thought she might cry. I dabbed at the corners of my eyes with my pinky fingers as if I was crying because, darn, I wanted to.

"Go and do your best, princess, for your mother," the miracle-worker seamstress said. "Make sure you tell me what happens."

"Oh, I will! Thank you, thank you."

I slipped more money into the envelope containing Abuela Nina's fee and left it on the counter. Uncle Sam could foot this bill.

Neither of us wanted to stay out long with the gown in tow, so we literally stopped at a stall that sold t-shirts, flip-flops, and swimsuits, and picked a tiny aquamarine bikini. We liked the color, and that was that. We had two hours to get ready.

15

Whatever Santiago expected would disqualify Amalia didn't happen. We found her chair and mirror right where we expected and grabbed a rolling dress rack for her gown, carefully concealed in the garment bag. A gift bag waited with her name on it containing body lotion, shampoo and conditioner, a razor, sample-size mascaras, lip glosses, butt cream, and eyeliner. It also included a mango-shaped and scented candle. We brushed this all aside, except the butt-cream.

Amalia tried on the bikini, the color as ah-maze-ing as I knew it would be. It fit her perfectly once I did a little nip and tuck on the top with some needle and thread and made sure that she had the butt-cream, uh—roll-on body adhesive—applied so the fabric wouldn't ride up and cause a wedgie.

I did her hair and make-up, carefully hiding the blooming bruise with a fabulous tattoo concealer I'd picked up on our way back to the hotel. Petroleum jelly to make sure her lipstick didn't stick to her teeth, bronzer to accentuate her cheekbones, and a pencil for her strong brows to pick them up and shape them precisely. I secretly added a few of my skin cells to her mascara to help it set, remembering a recent pageant winner's photo where her mascara ran down her face and it was all anyone talked about. The zombie cells kept it in stasis. It was gross, but pageants are extreme sports. You gotta do what you gotta do.

The usual pageant hubbub swirled around us. Girls stared at Amalia, wondering why they hadn't seen her earlier. Then, they were called for a quick run-through, told to get into their gowns, and the pageant would start on time. "On time, *dammit*," I believe the frazzled pageant director actually said.

Amalia had light pink heels to go with the thankfully burned-to-ash pink confectionary dress, and under the long white gown, they looked fine. In fact, they gave a subtle pop of color when she walked. She wore her mother's gold necklace and earrings, and I used one of her mom's combs to pull her hair into a half-up-do. One last spritz of hairspray, and she was done.

I stepped back to marvel at this beautiful, smart, resilient girl, thinking of all she'd been through. "Knock 'em dead, baby girl. Don't even glance at the mean girls. They're jealous."

She smiled gently and tried to kiss me on the cheek, but I ducked. "No kissing! You'll mess up your make-up!"

Once the contestants were ready, all handlers, make-up artists, and parents had to leave the backstage area.

I wandered out to the grand ballroom to find a seat, not seeing either Roderigo or Jorge, which concerned me. I thought they'd be watching from the front near the television cameras, but they weren't there.

"Sir, you need to take your seat," said an usher with an imperious tone.

"One moment," I said.

"No, sir, you must—"

I walked away, then spied Everest and Clipper, both dressed rather nicely, better than me. Everest even wore a tie.

"What's up with the clothes?"

"I wanted to clean up and look presentable," Everest said, straightening his tie. "You should try it sometime."

"Where's the rest of the team?"

"They'll be back," said Clipper. That was all I was going to get.

"Waylon! Waylon! Oh, thank heavens I found you."

Mitzi careened toward us in her high heels. She looked lovely but distressed.

"Mitzi, what's going on? Shouldn't you be in your judge's chair?"

"We are in a panic. Mr. Aguilar is nowhere to be found. The third judge is a local disc jockey, and he's here, but we only have two judges."

"I wonder where he went," I said.

Clipper shifted his stance to get a better view of the crowd.

"In the absence of a judge, it occurred to me that you, Waylon, might substitute."

"Oh, no..."

"Of course not, silly, I dismissed that thought immediately. You're with one of the contestants. But then, I realized..." She turned to Everest. "That Michael here is a cosmetics industry titan and would make a stupendous judge." She batted her eyelashes at Everest, his face frozen in terror.

Clipper coughed into his hand and clapped his friend on the back with the other.

"Please, Michael?" Mitzi tugged on his arm. "We need you. The show must go on."

"Go, Michael," I said with a wide grin. "What an opportunity."

"Yes, you can promote your company! Win-win!" Mitzi trilled. "I'm so glad you're here, and this tie is so handsome. It complements your skin tone." Mitzi pulled Michael away, and he threw us a look over his shoulder, mouthing, "Help me!"

Clipper and I waved goodbye, each pressing our lips together to keep from laughing.

"Let's get some seats, Clipper."

He pointed. "In the back, near the exit."

"Okay."

Music played, an excited introductory trill, then the emcee with a righteous punk hairdo began the show. "And here are our most distinguished judges!" he said. He gestured wide with one arm. "Our first judge is local personality, DJ Rock!"

DJ Rock wore distressed skinny jeans that belonged in the '70s. He threw a peace sign and took his place.

"And needing only one name, star actress, Miiiiitttziiiii!"

Mitzi sashayed onto the stage with a glamorous pout, did a coquettish three-step turn, and took her seat, the crowd clapping wildly.

"And as a surprise judge, Michael West, from America. He is part owner of a new cosmetics company called Reborn Cosmetics. I can't wait to see what secrets they have to share. Welcome, Michael!"

Michael walked out like a man facing a firing squad.

Clipper swore, grabbed his phone and typed, his fingers flying on the keyboard, a pinched look to his face.

"What are you doing?"

"We need a website for Reborn Cosmetics. Guess we have a company now."

I didn't know what to say. "They can set something up that fast?"

Clipper scoffed. "Of course, but we'll need your help to make it look good when we get back. Eddie will have a cow."

"Add the word 'Luxury.' Reborn Luxury Cosmetics."

"Nice touch."

Michael took his seat, his back ramrod straight. Luckily, he didn't have to breathe, or he might have fainted.

"First, ladies and gentlemen, let's meet our contestants in the Parade of Gowns!"

The deep red curtains drew apart, and a bevy of stunning young women marched forward, modeling their dresses, smiling ear-to-ear. Some were noticeably nervous, others more at-ease. The well-styled ladies wore the on-trend colors—ruby red, emerald green, black, and sapphire blue. They sparkled like the jewels they mimicked, but each one looked like the other.

Then, Amalia entered.

The only contestant wearing white and the only one wearing the dropped cape skirt made by Abuela Nina, she shone like a pearl in a bouquet of bright colors. The audience clapped as she walked forward, her steps directly in front of one another like we'd practiced.

Until she fell.

She placed her right heel too close to her left and tripped, catching herself with one hand. She straightened, kept her smile, and took her place. The audience's audible gasp made me hang my head. She'd ruined her first impression.

Her pageant was over.

Even having Michael and Mitzi in her corner couldn't wipe out that kind of error. In this business, the points mattered, and the initial walk mattered the most.

The mean girls gave her the expected side-eye, but some looked genuinely distraught for her. One reached out and took her hand briefly.

Amalia lifted her head high, touched her mother's necklace, and stood her ground.

Clipper nudged me. "That wasn't good, was it?"

"It was disastrous," I replied.

The rest of the ladies made their entrance and stood in a semi-circle on the stage. "Look at these stunning young women!" said the emcee.

"Tonight, you will grow to love them, not only for their natural beauty but for their talents and character. Get ready for an exciting evening! Before we break for commercial, let me thank our sponsors. Let's get a round of applause for Banco Silvestre and our biggest supporter, Santiago Aguilar! Plus, we'd like to thank Grupo Financiero Todo Americano for their help in televising this pageant worldwide!"

"Ever heard of that company, Clipper?"

"No," he said, once again zipping off a message to a contact. "I haven't."

"Seems like a great name for an international cartel, don't you think?"

"Oh, yes."

The pageant broke for commercials, and the contestants disappeared behind the curtain to prepare for the talent portion. I realized I had no idea what Amalia's talent presentation included. I smacked my head with my palm, wondering how I could have been so stupid.

The first contestant sang, as did the second contestant, and the third. The fourth did gymnastics, and the fifth painted an insane impressionist painting of the audience in real-time. The sixth sang opera, hitting the high notes. These women were talented, practiced, not one made a misstep.

Amalia stepped forward, still wearing her gown, while the other women had changed into new ones or costumes to fit their region. She stood in the middle of the stage with only a spotlight and spoke.

"Amarás la belleza, que es la sombra de Dios sobre el Universio."

"What is she saying, Clipper?"

Clipper stared in silence at the young woman on the stage, matching the reaction of the entire audience.

"Clipper?"

"Shh."

Amalia spoke from the heart, her pauses perfect, her tempo slow and deliberate. She ended by lifting one arm and pointing to the sky.

The crowd broke into thunderous applause.

"She's reciting the *Decálogo del artista,* a poem by the Chilean poet Gabriela Mistral."

"Who is she?"

"She *was* the first Latin-American poet to win the Nobel Prize for literature."

I made a mental note to do more research into her, but I was thrilled for Amalia. Her talent was different and beautiful.

The emcee took the stage. "Before we break for commercial, let's ask our judges for advice as we head into the swimsuit and question-and-answer sections."

Clipper and I exchanged terrified glances.

"DJ Rock, what is your best advice for our contestants?"

DJ Rock pursed his lips and leaned into the desk. "Be yourself. Don't try to be something you're not. We can see straight through that."

The emcee moved on. "Mitzi. You're an expert. What's your advice?"

Mitzi smiled like the pro she was. "Take a deep breath and relax. If you are out of breath, we won't be able to hear you well, and you'll appear insecure."

The emcee turned to Michael, who clutched his microphone so hard I thought he'd crush it.

I pressed my lips together and clasped my hands, squeezing my palms.

"Mr. West, what do you have to add?"

Michael stared wide-eyed at the emcee for a brief second but gathered himself and winked. "Well, you can never go wrong with more mascara."

The audience cracked up.

I let out a whoop, proud of my mountain-sized padawan.

Clipper gave me an uncharacteristic high-five and immediately wiped his hand on his shirt.

16

After his moment of unbridled emotion, Clipper reverted to his usual taciturn self. "I'm going to find the team," he said. "You stay here."

"Sure. I want to watch Amalia."

He slipped off to my left.

The break lasted longer than the previous ones, and people milled about, going to the bathroom, getting drinks, or talking amongst themselves. I wondered what the TV audience experienced. Probably a local news update.

It gave me a chance to think, which gave me a chance to worry. Anxious energy flooded me, and I decided to move to burn it off.

I wandered to the exit on my left with the "No Admittance" sign. No one stopped me when I leaned against the door and it opened. No one said "boo" when I walked down a hallway I hadn't seen before, another behind-the-scenes area used by production and wait staff. I mean, I was looking for a men's room, right? Sign? What sign?

Regular fluorescent lights lit the hallway's beige walls and ugly speckled flooring designed to hide dirt, which it did ineffectively. Doors branched off left and right, but they were locked. Except the door at the end. It opened on another backstage area, dressed with black curtains separating this area from the immediate rear of the stage behind the house curtains. A built-in ladder to my right led up to the rafters.

Curiosity might kill the cat, but it couldn't do much to a zombie. I mean, I wanted to look, that's all.

I climbed the ladder and walked the catwalk suspended over the stage, taking care to avoid the wires and clamps holding lights in place. Heading farther upstage, I got down on my hands and knees, crawled the rest of the way, and stuck my head between the horizontal bars to get a better view.

I blanched when I saw the tops of several familiar heads. Roderigo was on top of the pallets, rummaging through contents, the original plastic wrapping, and industrial packing tape discarded on the floor. Eddie, Peter, Zed, and Jorge milled around, keeping an eye out for unwanted company.

"What's in there, Roderigo?" asked Eddie.

"Sashes." Roderigo's face scrunched in confusion.

"That's what it says on the side of the box, but it's probably camouflage. Dig deeper," said Jorge.

Eddie held up a finger. "No, I told you we'd look, but we're running a huge risk being here."

"Yeah," Peter said. "We got what we came for. This is none of our business."

Zed placed a foot on the pallet and hauled himself up. "I don't know if it is me or Luis speaking, but I'm pretty pissed about using the pageant as a front for an international drug deal." He pushed the sash box aside and the one underneath as well and tore the tape from the next carton, labeled "mangos," fishing around inside with his hand. He patted something and withdrew his hand in shock. "What the hell is this?"

He pulled the boxes to the floor.

Peter bounced from foot-to-foot, getting more anxious by the minute.

Eddie scratched his head and gave Zed a hand opening the box the rest of the way.

"Plastic-wrapped mangoes," Eddie said. "What the hell?"

I recognized them, but Jorge explained, "It's the Miss Mango pageant. I saw this on the tables in the audience and on the judges' table. They're keepsake candles. See the wick at the top?"

Roderigo let out an exasperated sigh. "Mango candles. What a stupid idea."

"No, it's not," said Peter, suddenly interested. "Let me see that."

Jorge handed him one.

Peter picked up a utility knife from a neighboring pallet and sliced into the mango. The thin plastic wrapping gave easily. Peter slipped the knife in farther, tearing the bag. Several mangoes fell to the floor and a few split open, spilling white crystals. Zed scooted back several feet to avoid stepping on them.

"Crikey, is that what I think it is?"

"Crystal meth. The paraffin covers the chemical odors and makes it undetectable," Peter said.

"Every guest bag has one," Jorge said. "Every contestant got one."

"I'm sure those don't have anything in them. They're the decoys."

Before I drew the team's attention, Juan walked in carrying a gun like he knew how to use it, which I guessed he did, given that he'd already shot one person.

"I thought I killed you, Luis," said Juan. "What? Your mom pray so hard that He sent you back, too? I thought he only did that once."

Zed shook his head in disgust. "You really are an arsehole."

"He sent you back as an Aussie? Wow. That's weird."

Zed gave him the finger, gun be damned.

"Hey, wait, you're not Luis. Jesus, you look like him."

"Not Jesus, I thought we already covered that," said Zed.

"Language!" said Roderigo, before he could stop himself. He shook his head. "What does your father think of you, Juan?"

"He thinks I'm taking care of business." The young man puffed his chest.

"He's dying a little inside every day. You're killing him bit by bit."

"He's proud of me."

"Your mama? Your sisters?"

"A man's gotta take care of business." His words were tough, but Juan wouldn't meet Roderigo's eye.

"You're not a man, son."

"Fuck you! What kind of father and husband were you? Letting your wife get killed? Who are you to lecture me?"

He hit home with that one. Roderigo flinched, and Juan sneered at the older man's discomfiture. I wanted to punch the kid in the mouth.

"Put that gun down, young man." A new voice joined the group, and I almost cheered when Señora Liliana Leoncio emerged from the shadows carrying an enormous pistol I recognized from Dirty Harry movies. It must have been heavy because she held it in two hands, and I briefly admired the wood grip.

Juan hesitated, but the Señora braced her feet, aimed, and shot a mango. The mango got it square in the eyes, exploded, sent crystal meth out thirty paces, and effectively demonstrated her aim.

Juan placed the gun on the floor and held his hands in the air.

"Gentlemen, would you like to tell me what you are doing back here?" asked Señora Leoncio.

Roderigo explained in rapid-fire Spanish, but the Señora wasn't amused.

"They're the good guys, Señora!" I yelled from the catwalk.

All heads turned up to me lying flat on the metal walkway, my head through the guardrails. I waved like I was hailing a bus.

"Waylon! What the hell are you doing up there?" asked Eddie.

"Uh, well…" I tried to pull my head through the horizontal bars.

And couldn't get it through.

"I mean, I was looking for…" I pulled again but bumped the back of my head with an audible clang.

"He was snooping," said Clipper, coming up behind me, stomping on the catwalk, making it shake. He placed a hand on my back and another on my chin, tilting my head at an angle, trying to help me squeeze back through.

"Clipper! What is it about 'watch the pageant' that the two of you can't understand?" yelled Eddie.

"Watch Juan!" I yelled, pointing to the young man sneaking away.

Zed rolled his eyes, took a single step to his left, and stuck out a giant Luis-sized foot. Juan tripped, hitting his chin on the concrete. His ankle hit the gun on the floor, and it skittered to the edge of a pallet.

Señora Leoncio holstered her gun in a bag I hadn't noticed, and I wondered what kind of hard-ass pageant director carried a Smith & Wesson.

"Please stop fooling around with my employees, Señora. I don't need them, but I prefer them in one piece." Santiago Aguilar entered the room with a small squad of armed punks. He motioned for one to disarm Señora Leoncio, but Peter body-slammed the kid to the ground. Clipper, who I hadn't felt move from my side, suddenly clapped a hand around Santiago's mouth, wrapping an arm around his neck and brought him down in one smooth, efficient motion.

Two of Aguilar's squad carried machetes, which made Eddie smile. He spun to his right like Fred Astaire, snatched the machete out of Punk Number One's hand, and flowed like water to the second one, using the first machete to delicately split the kid's pants ass to ankle. As the second young man took a step, Eddie shoved him from behind, and he fell flat on his face, stopping the fall with his nose. Eddie plucked his machete up in one smooth move.

Punk Number One growled and charged Eddie like a rampaging bull only to get stopped by Zed, who grabbed him by one arm, pulled him close, twisted the young man's hand so it was palm out, and pulled it behind the kid's back and up toward the kid's own shoulder blade. Punk Number One, now less cocky and more injured, rose on his toes to decrease the pain. Zed said something I couldn't hear. The kid spoke to his friend on the ground who was on his hands and knees holding his bleeding nose while flashing his ass. Zed let his neutralized, worn-out attacker go so he could help his buddy to his feet.

I struggled to extract my head and flapped my arms while Eddie, Zed, Peter, and Clipper took down the rest of the ruffians with no more trouble than they would have defeating an unruly kickball team.

The defeated gang appeared ready to beat a retreat, but Señora Leoncio retrieved her pistol and shot at one of the gang members anyway, maybe just to prove a point. She missed, despite her proficiency earlier, and her bullet zinged around the pallets until it embedded itself in a box of mangoes. Maybe her only skill was shooting fruit.

The impact threw a dangerous mélange of meth shards, paraffin, and mango-scented candle wax into the air, causing the humans to rush for an exit before they breathed it in or suffered injuries. The gang members crawled or ran away, some bleeding, all bruised, while Santiago lay unconscious on the floor. My team mopped itself off, flinging the witches' brew of waxy opiates to the ground.

The Señora held a scarf in front of her mouth. "I'll get the police," she said.

Eddie warned her, "Be careful who you call. They're on the take."

"I know the honest ones. Stay here," she ordered.

Still trying to free myself, I smashed my head on the metal bar again, and when everyone looked up at me, Santiago moved.

"Ugh! He's! ARRRGH!" I pointed toward Santiago's crawling figure.

Eddie leaped toward him but didn't get there in time.

Santiago rolled to a neighboring pallet and grabbed the gun Juan had left behind, flipped over, and fired at the approaching zombie soldier.

And shot Juan instead, who'd come back for his boss.

Juan's mouth opened in a shocked "O," and he crumpled to the floor. Santiago didn't even look back. He scrambled to his feet and rushed away, slipping and sliding through the mess on the floor in his designer shoes, but still escaping, the rat.

Eddie ignored Santiago's departure and hurried to Juan's side, but it was too late. The bullet hit the young man square in the chest. Blood, bone, and soft tissue bubbled through the wound, and the boy died before he could say a word.

"Jesus fucking Christ," whispered Clipper.

Zed turned to Eddie, his eyes hard. "We can get Santiago if we go after him now."

"No. We got you, Zed, and that was our mission. We're leaving." Eddie's voice was firm. This was an order. He closed the boy's eyes and motioned to his team. They exited in a practiced, fluid manner, gone before I blinked.

I stared at the carnage, my head still stuck in the guardrails, wishing I could cry.

17

"Come on, Waylon. Let's get you out of here." Doc Early wiped something slick and creamy on my hair and face and helped me get out of my predicament and on my feet. "There you go. Rescue Remedy comes through again."

"It has zombie cells in it," I said, rubbing the cream into my skin. "Not sure the FDA would approve."

"Mitzi swears by it."

"She's a smart one." I swallowed to get rid of the lump in my throat. "Thanks for getting me out, Doc." I could barely speak. "You didn't see what happened. It was awful."

He swung an arm over my shoulder and hugged me. I clung to that hug so hard. It meant everything. "I heard. The others told me and asked me to get you. We need to leave."

"Wait. Where were you?"

"In the freezer. I needed time to rest."

"You took a nap?" I wrinkled my brow at him, incredulous.

He drew himself up and released the hug. "Yes. I took a nap. Sue me. I didn't think we'd have a shooting at the OK Corral or that you'd be Waylon enough to get your head stuck like a three-year-old."

"Unnecessary," I muttered.

"Wait until I tell Sorya."

"You wouldn't dare!" The thought of our medical examiner and my sorta girlfriend made my heart clench. I couldn't wait to see her.

"Oh. I would." I heard the teasing tone, and a knot in my belly released.

"Bully."

"Yeah, but now I'm a zombie bully, so I can keep this up all day."

I stopped short. "About that—"

"We have to go."

I let him change the subject, but I thought things might be okay between us. "What about Amalia? Did the gunshots disrupt the pageant? Did they hear them?"

"We didn't hear a thing. Between the soundproofing, the people and the music, no one noticed."

"How did she do?"

"She won."

"What?"

"The judges asked her a question about drug trafficking, and she shared the story about her mother, and everyone cried. She's Miss Mango."

"I missed it!"

"You did, but it's okay. Roderigo and Jorge got there in time to see it. Hurry. We can catch the end."

Amalia stood in the center of the stage, surrounded by the other contestants, cameras, Roderigo, Jorge, and two of the judges, giving a thank you speech, tears streaming down her cheeks, her hand on her mom's necklace.

Eddie jerked his chin at me, and I joined the group, following them up to the roof, where Clipper and Everest stood next to two helicopters. They motioned us into them, splitting us up, Zed with Eddie and me, and Early with Peter, Clipper, and Everest. Our pilot didn't say a word, lifting into the darkness.

"Wait!" No one could hear me, so I pointed toward the adjacent building where another helicopter waited for two men. I tapped the pilot on the shoulder and pointed again. Eddie peered that way and said something to the pilot on his headset, motioning for us to don ours.

The pilot rotated and illuminated the roof.

Two men held their hands in front of their eyes, looking into the light, and there was no doubt who they were.

The first was Santiago Aguilar, and beside him stood Quint Addington.

"What the hell is he doing here?" Eddie fumed in our ears.

It all made sense. "Quint. A sequence of *five* cards." I leaned back in my seat as the pilot resumed our original course. "Quint is Señor Cinco."

18

What will happen to Amalia now that she's won the scholarship?" Sorya asked.

I'd prepared—ahem, bought—a picnic, and placed a soft blanket on the grass in my backyard. I'd liked to have made the food myself, but it had been decades since I'd cooked. We'd found a pleasant shade tree and lounged against the trunk, enjoying each other's company. While I couldn't eat, I urged her to try the cherry cobbler and other delicacies. It gave me pleasure to watch her enjoy them, and after the past several days, being with her was what the doctor ordered.

"She can go anywhere. I've invited her here to Los Angeles if she wants to come." I leaned over and dabbed Sorya's mouth with a napkin, smiling when she blushed.

She held her hand over her mouth.

I touched my hand to her fingertips and shook my head. "I like your smile. Let me see it."

She shrugged, avoided my eyes.

"What's wrong?"

"I worried you'd be killed, but then I realized you can't die, but I could lose you." She pinched the bridge of her nose. I understood. The whole thing was confusing enough to give anyone a headache. "Zed is having a hard time."

Zed struggled now that we were home. He had zombie post-traumatic stress disorder, Z-PTSD, something I understood all too well. I still had flashbacks about being changed, being held down and not allowed to leave. Zed's nightmares centered on watching his mates depart and his inability to communicate, screaming into the void, unheard. I'd become his therapist of sorts, and Early and Sorya were trying too, although no antidepressants or anti-anxiety meds helped zombies.

"We can only do what we can do."

"I know." She changed the topic. "Want to see a movie on our next date? I hear that old Brad Pitt movie is playing at the drive-in."

"*World War Z*? Seriously? Very funny." I grinned.

"Now that you are home, what's next for you?"

"Trying to get back to my clients, some of whom are not pleased I left without notice, but when I tell them I helped Amalia win Miss Mango, they'll soften up. Her story went viral. It's all over social media and made the news in the US and Europe. She inspired people with her response to the question about drug trafficking."

"Mitzi got some quality camera time."

"She's loving it! It's all good publicity for her. I'm going to ask her to be the face of Reborn Luxury Cosmetics."

"You're setting that up as a proper company?"

"That's the idea, and I get to be Chief Creative Officer." I sounded like a kid who'd gotten a gold star on his homework.

"Oooohhhh, aren't we fancy?" she teased. "Don't let the title go to your head." She popped another bite of cobbler in her mouth.

Her phrasing made me think of how my recent adventure started and how much my life had changed since Captain Perkins marched into my life, accusing me of murder. How much better my life became since I'd met this charming medical examiner.

Before I'd met her, I'd filled my time with fun but inconsequential things, waiting for Early to kill me. Now, I filled my time with fun and meaningful things, appreciating life, not rushing toward death.

I'd lost my mind, but Sorya had caught it.

CUT & DYED

1

The cadaver dog nosed my crotch and whined in confusion *again.*

"I don't mean to insult you, sir," whispered his handler. "But, could you be...?" He looked around, a blush crawling up his neck to his ears. "Impotent? Sick? Maybe cancer? We specifically trained the dog to identify dead people."

The officer who'd met me at the parking lot stared upward, whistling like he'd never seen clouds before.

"Anyway," the handler said, clearing his throat. "I'd consult a doctor if I were you. Wouldn't want any special parts to, you know, rot or anything."

My special part was particularly special. In fact, serious connoisseurs of adult films had deemed it "colossal." Not that I was ever in a movie like that, but this recent acquisition came from a now-dead porn star, a replacement after my original fell off.

With no good way to explain my unusual circumstances, I brushed my stupid bangs out of my eyes, sniffed, and soldiered on, turning to the cop. "Officer, can we please proceed?"

The police officer motioned for me to follow him to a location along the Arroyo Calabasas, a seven-mile-long tributary of the Los Angeles River entirely encased in a concrete flood control channel. The Arroyo Calabasas represented a merging of Dry Canyon Creek from the Santa Monica Mountains watershed and the McCoy Canyon Creek in the Simi Hills watershed.

The officer led me toward his boss and the man who'd called me out to the Arroyo Calabasas in the first place, Captain Jacob Perkins.

"Waylon, get your ass over here. Stop lollygagging." Captain Perkins waved me over, glaring at a body on the ground. I didn't want to get closer to the dead body, so I stopped at the crest of the hill and observed Perkins for a moment.

The captain was a persnickety man, southern originally, but with a flattened accent that spoke of several years in the West. He'd tucked his thumbs in his belt loops and stared hard at the body at his feet.

"Staring at it won't make it talk, Captain," I called to him, my tone joking.

"Second one this week."

"I'm sorry to hear that, but what does this have to do with me? I'm out of the murder business. I'm done."

He huffed out a mirthless chuckle. "Yeah, I heard you're heading up a new cosmetics line. What's it called?"

"Reborn Luxury Cosmetics. I'm the Creative Director."

"Lovely. Just great. Fantastic." His voice was so dry it scraped the *air*. He scowled at me and said, "Scoot your behind over here and look at this."

I screwed up my courage and picked my way down the hill to the body. The jeans stuck to the body's legs. The t-shirt appeared blue, but the mud and debris made it hard to tell, and I didn't want to get closer. It was missing both hands, but I couldn't tell if that happened before or after death. Despite being dead, I wasn't proficient with cadavers. My sorta girlfriend, Sorya Sang, the local medical examiner, was the expert.

Captain Perkins introduced me to a cop standing nearby. "Officer Blake, this is Waylon Jenkins. Can you turn the body over for him, please, and then go help the forensic guys with the water samples?"

Officer Blake carefully turned the body over and then departed. The grassy bank's moisture made me slip a little as I inched closer.

"What do you see, Waylon?" Captain Perkins asked.

"A disgusting mess." Swollen lips, a protruding tongue, and a bloated abdomen. "I've never seen anything like it. What's with the red, mottled skin?"

"Decomposition," he said, nodding. "What else?"

"It's missing hands."

"Good. Yes, what else? Get closer."

"Do I have to?" The t-shirt had ridden up a couple of inches to show the tummy. "What's with the white patches?"

"The white part is normal sloughing of skin called 'washerwoman changes.' You'd see more of it if the victim had hands."

"Yick."

He shot me a look that could have shattered glass.

Sighing, I scooted closer. The neck showed signs of sloughing, too. I also noticed the overall bloat and the tear in the t-shirt from the bottom hem to the armpit. I had no idea what else the captain expected me to see.

I stared at its face some more and got it. "It's missing its eyes."

"Bingo. The first one didn't have hands or eyes, either."

"Don't bugs and stuff like to eat eyes? Couldn't there be a perfectly natural reason a body found in the water doesn't have eyes?"

"Yes, but we found the first one the same afternoon he died, and he wasn't completely submerged."

I put my hands on my hips, narrowed my eyes, and tried to think like the forensic experts on the TV shows.

Perkins frowned. "What are you doing?"

"Contemplating."

"You look constipated, which I know you aren't because you don't eat."

I dropped the pose. "I'm wondering about the hands. You know, on TV they'd say it was to hide the victim's fingerprints."

Perkins rolled his eyes. "You still watching those shows?"

"Possibly."

He pursed his lips. "As much as I hate to admit it, the TV show theory may be right."

"Ha!" I was on a roll. I tapped my lip. "Both male, and this one was in the water before the one you found earlier this week? They killed this guy first?"

"That's what we think."

"Do we know what killed either of them? I mean, they could be unrelated and natural causes of death."

"A very far out hypothesis, but it could be true. Dr. Sang will compare the body she has in her possession to this one."

"Captain?" I asked.

"What?"

I moved close so only he could hear me. "You still haven't told me why you wanted me here. Nothing points to anything supernatural. This is probably an evil person doing what evil people do."

"You say that, Waylon, but the hairs on the back of my neck are standing up. Besides, what better things do you have to do? Mix up a new shade of Siren Red lipstick?" He dismissed my work, my passion, without a second thought.

"Siren Red is a glorious name for a lipstick, Captain. I'll have to use it. Thanks for the suggestion." I clenched my jaw to keep from saying more, turned my back on him, and stalked through the scrub toward the parking lot.

"Waylon!" The captain hollered after me, but I kept going. I'd come when he summoned me because of our friendship and what we'd been through together. The least he could do was show me some respect.

"Waylon!" He rushed after me and caught my elbow, but I jerked away. I didn't like being touched without permission, and besides, with enough rough handling, I could lose an arm like Mr. Potato Head.

"I'm the Creative Director of a company, Jacob, and I'm damn good at it, plus I have clients. I rescheduled two actresses for their weekly treatments to run out here and meet you. You may not care about such things, but there's no reason to treat my career like it means nothing."

"Sorry, Waylon. Didn't mean it like that." His eyes crinkled in the corners.

I turned my back. "Don't call me to look at a dead body without something more than a hunch. I don't enjoy it, and I have work to do."

I got in my car and drove away, swearing I'd never see another putrefying body again. Despite being an animated dead human myself, there was a big difference between me and that decomposing corpse, including the most vital one—I had a soul, or whatever spark that kept me living and made me, well, *me*. Whoever that poor schlep had been, his soul was gone, moved on to whatever came next. I couldn't do that, no matter what happened to my physical form. I may need replacement body parts sometimes, but I couldn't truly die.

Doc Early turned me into a zombie during the battle of Shiloh in the Civil War. Ever since, we'd been searching for a way to kill me. We'd tried everything. Drowning, yes. Slit my throat—that tickled. Cut me to pieces. It didn't matter. My essence stayed right here, unable to leave, ascend, proceed into the light, or whatever was supposed to happen. If my body incinerated or disintegrated, my spirit would linger on wherever I'd fallen, unable to communicate or interact with the outside world. Forever. This happened to another zombie named Zed, and a bunch of us had gone down to Central America to give him a new body to settle into and bring him home.

The point being, decomposing bodies weren't gross. They were a reminder of what I couldn't be, and my greatest fear.

Early connected me to my past, and we fought like brothers. Early had originally extended his lifespan by eating tiny bits of my flesh, promising me he'd figure out the answer to zombie true death. Then, while getting Zed, Early had died, and before he could pass on, I turned him into a zombie—without his consent. I'd panicked, unable to imagine life without him. While we'd made peace, I still didn't know how he truly felt about it.

Once at home, I took refuge on my new plum Victorian-style couch, positioned across from a wingback chair upholstered in Bungalow Rose velour, an admittedly confusing name because the primary color was teal. I'd recently redecorated. Well, I was forced to redecorate because my home collapsed in on itself during a recent zombie/bad guy/police skirmish. I'd gone old-fashioned. The floors were a dark wood, but the plush ivory area rug softened the overall look. Lamps with burnished gold bases and ivory shades sat on delicately gilded side tables. The new curtains picked up the teal in the wingback's print and hung heavy and luxurious on the back sliding glass door. The ambiance tickled my inner aristocrat. Maybe I'd hit a costume shop for some powdered wigs.

"Still channeling Marie Antoinette, Waylon?" Early walked in as I petted the crushed velvet couch. Mrs. Betsy Ross floated in after him and hovered near a painting of George Washington getting his pants shortened.

Before I could answer, my front door crashed open. A beautiful, young, Latina woman posed for a moment in the doorframe, appearing as a dark silhouette against the sunlight.

"Amalia? Are you here for the weekend?"

"In and out, Waylon. Just sooooo much to do. You know how it is." The reigning Miss Mango skipped into my living room and gave me L.A. air kisses, then flitted to do the same with Doc Early, who kissed her back.

A quick look revealed that Mrs. Ross was nowhere to be seen. My personal assistant hadn't shared her status as a transparent, multi-centenarian person with Amalia or the zombies. In fact, while they all knew I had a personal assistant of some sort, they had never met her, and this rankled Amalia. I'd simply explained that my assistant possessed unique qualifications, and when she was ready to meet Amalia, she would. I couldn't, and wouldn't, betray my relationship with Mrs. Ross.

"How's college?" I scooted over on the couch to make room. She didn't notice and flopped into the Bungalow (Teal) Rose wingback.

"School is great," Amalia said. "I'm enjoying my classes, and I've met *so many* people."

"Boy people?" I asked with a frown. I didn't want to be the one to tell her dad.

"Of course, boy people! But no one to tell Papa about." She'd read my mind.

Seeing her so happy made me happy, and had the side benefit of keeping my epidermis attached to my skeleton since her father would skin me alive if she so much as shed a single tear.

"I'm enjoying my American History class, but you know, isn't it stupid to study history? I mean, what can you do with it, anyway? Just a bunch of dead people who fought in wars started by past presidents."

She didn't notice my raised eyebrow. I was a dead person who fought in a war started by a past president named Lincoln.

She stopped, studying me. "What is it?"

"Nothing," I replied.

"Don't lie to me. Your eyes are narrowed."

"That makes no sense," I said.

"You narrow your eyes when you're thinking about something you don't want to tell me," she said.

A tell. I had a tell. Fan-freakin'-tastic.

"It's nothing to do with you. Keep telling me about your day," I said, gesturing for her to continue.

"No. It's your turn," she insisted. "What's going on?"

"Captain Perkins called me to look at a body they pulled out of the water this morning. It was a weird death, and he thought I might know something about it. I can't get it out of my head."

"What made it weird?"

"Eh. Its eyes were missing."

"Yuck. Someone dumped it in the water, or he fell in?" she asked.

That she asked such a pertinent question reminded me she was no ordinary girl. She'd seen her mother killed, her home bombed, and drug cartel violence up close. No pussyfooting around with this one. Just the facts and straight for the jugular.

"The captain thinks it's a murder, and the killers dumped the body in the water."

"That's terrible. Could you shed any light on it?"

"Of course not. All sorts of things happen to bodies in the water," I said.

"Right." She screwed up her face, her beautiful eyes serious. "Bodies?"

"This was the second one, although this one died first. It's complicated. Never mind. Let's talk about something else."

"Okay." She chewed her lip for a moment, the bad thoughts fluttering away like a butterfly on the breeze. She sat up straight, a gleam in her eye. "I want to show you something, Uncle Waylon."

She'd taken to "Uncle Waylon-ing" me while she hatched some plot or project. Or when she wanted something. Last semester, she'd decided she wanted to intern with me. Now, she had classes four days a week and hung around with me for one or two days while I saw clients. I made her study the accounting as well. If she wanted to be a small business owner, she needed to see all the ins and outs. It wasn't all facials and lip gloss.

"What is it?"

"I'm working with Pee-Wees and Playgrounds, a nonprofit that brings kids into nature and outdoor play. It is part of my Community Development class."

"That's great. I love it."

"What are you doing with this organization, Amalia?" asked Early, staring forlornly at a donut. Since he'd become a zombie, he couldn't eat food, and he insisted on torturing himself. Guilt gnawed at my gut, but I shoved it down. Again, I'd had Reasons.

"We're building a park with swings and a swirly roundabout thingamajig, and the best part—a treehouse!"

I leaned forward, my interest sparked. "I've always wanted to build a treehouse."

"I know!" Amalia popped out of her chair. "That's why I volunteered you as a community mentor."

"You did what? You *volunteered* me?"

She clapped her hands like a five-year-old. "It'll be great! We'll get to work together, and it's for charity. You're always telling me to think beyond myself, and the kids are so cute. They're all about five, maybe six? What's kindergarten age here? It'll be fun!"

"I have to work. You can't volunteer me for something without asking first. That's simple courtesy. Would you like me to volunteer you for something without asking?"

She slumped into the chair. "But Uncle Waylon, it's for the *children*."

"Seriously? You're going to go there? That's the best you can do?" I swung my legs up on the couch and lay my head on a fluffy decorative pillow. I didn't need to breathe, but I still did it out of habit and to appear normal. So, I took a deep breath and let it out to the count of three.

"Well," she said, the gleam in her eye telling me she'd thought of something. "By designing the treehouse, you can ensure it doesn't hurt the tree. I know how you'd feel if they just nailed in boards without thinking of the tree's health. They could damage the stomach wood." She batted her hand in the air, grasping for the right word. "The middle wood. The lung wood."

"The *heart* wood."

She snapped her fingers. "That's the word."

That tricky girl had gotten me. I gazed out my window to my beloved Evergreen Pear and shuddered at the thought of someone hurting them. The thought of someone nailing boards into a tree or using ropes to tie the treehouse on made me ill. Ropes damaged the bark, and the tree wouldn't handle the stress and weight.

"Maybe they have someone who loves trees as much as you do, but you know, it's California." Amalia's easy-breezy tone rankled me, which meant she probably did it on purpose. "It's possible someone as devoted to trees as you are will come forward."

"Fine." I gritted my teeth. "I'll consult. *Consult*."

She clapped her hands. "That's great!"

I held up a finger. "But, that's it. I'm assuming they have experts managing the project. Who's funding it?"

"I dunno. I'll give the organizers your contact information. Thanks, Uncle Waylon." Amalia hopped out of the chair, gave me another air kiss, waved to Doc Early, and skipped out the door, snagging an apple from the dining room table's fruit basket on the way. She stopped and turned at the door. "Why do you have fruit when you can't eat?"

"It's pretty," I grumbled.

"What do you do with it once it goes bad?"

"Compost."

"I should have guessed. You're the perfect person to help with this project. Thanks again! Be back later. Hitting the mall." She left in a flash, leaving only the faint trace of a floral eau de toilette I didn't recognize.

"She's got your number," said Mrs. Ross, emerging from wherever she went when she disappeared.

"Hmmm." I studied the pear tree some more, thinking about the treehouse. Would I get to pick which tree we used?

"She knows how to play you, get you to do what she wants. You're wrapped around her little finger. All the clichés."

"Right." The tree couldn't be too high from the ground, and any design required strong cradling branches to support the weight of the structure and the kids climbing on it.

Mrs. Ross tried again. "Waylon, I need to speak with you about something."

The size of the tree mattered. I'd need to take measurements.

She cleared her throat.

"Mrs. Ross, can it wait? Hang on for a little bit, okay? I don't want to lose my train of thought." I went to my office, booted up my computer, opened a web browser, and searched "treehouses." I fell down a long, dark rabbit hole of information and had designed a multi-level arboreal condominium in my mind before I remembered I was only a consultant, and this was for small children.

Sighing, I dragged my mind back to work, back to Reborn Luxury Cosmetics. Conceived during an inadvertent Miss Mango miscalculation, the zombie team sat on the idea, incubated it, and finally hatched the company into reality. The point was to provide an up-and-up revenue stream to finance the research on how to kill us. Reborn's signature product, my facial cream, worked like magic because the little bits o'zombie in it made it literal magic.

The Federal Drug Administration's labeling requirements certainly didn't address this particular scenario, but the regulations deemed a cosmetic "adulterated," their term, if it consisted of a "decomposed substance." Since we harvested zombie cells from individuals who were technically dead, the cells would read as dead human tissue on analysis. It was a stumper.

In the meantime, Doc Early and the team planned experiments to see how long the rejuvenation effect persisted and how long the zombie cells lasted, separate from their original owner. They'd do this as they had before, as part of The Industries' military wound care research contracts.

The Industries, a private company with extensive armed forces connections, employed Doc Early as a scientist/doctor who experimented with renewing skin for wound care. As part of this, he'd done his more personal research, hiding it within his legitimate company work.

The former head of The Industries, Quint Addington, had oddly abetted us. Since he was a criminal who focused on his own pet projects, including creating his own pet zombies and running a giant narcotics conglomerate, Early had siphoned off research funds without notice. With Quint now wanted for murder, disappointingly competent people monitored The Industries' accounts and required our department's numbers to add up.

Much to my dismay, Quint, that vile, corrupt mass of malodorous putrescence, had slipped away like the naked mole-rat he was. Bastard.

Given our FDA and Industries concerns, I wanted the launch to be an intimate, luxury brand, appropriately priced for the rich and famous. I wanted to maintain the caché and make the brand a secret women and men whispered to their best friends. We didn't need to attract unwanted attention, and since the whole point of doing this was to fund research into zombie true death, it didn't need to become a big commercial success like Clinique or even L'Oréal.

Early vowed to find a solution, spurred on by his loyalty to me, but now with the extra motivation of being a zombie himself.

2

I violated my oath about not seeing decomposing bodies the very next day. But, this time, I did it in the name of love.

Sorya called me in to the Medical Examiner's office. I was happy to hear from her but had hoped for an invitation to go on a date. Maybe a picnic or even dinner at a restaurant. Though I'd long since lost the desire for food, it pleased me to feed her.

"Hi, Waylon." She stutter-stepped toward me, and I leaned in so we bumped into each other, not quite a hug, definitely not a kiss, but wholly awkward. It had been a while since we'd seen each other, and we'd lost our rhythm.

She cleared her throat as I cast my eyes to the floor, the ceiling, and anywhere but her face. "Well, ah, thanks for coming," she said, taking a seat in her rolling chair. "It's good to see you. It's always good to see you, but you know that, of course. I don't have to say that, right? I mean, you've come here before to look at bodies." Sorya always moved and spoke like a hummingbird on meth.

"I will always come if you ask."

She blinked but grinned as well. "Captain Perkins wanted you to examine some bodies. They're ready."

"I already looked at them. What's he want me to see this time?"

She looked away, embarrassed that she'd had to call me at his insistence. "He said he wants you to look again with an open mind."

"Oh, Sorya, why? Someone or multiple someones killed two men and threw them in the water where they decomposed, as expected, and the eyes are missing. Eyes regularly fall out. What's the big deal?"

She scrunched her face and gave me a tiny shake of the head. Yeeeah, that hadn't come out right.

"I mean, not for everybody. Eyes don't go missing for regular people. I just meant…" With no way to rescue this, I rushed forward. "What I'm trying to say is animals like the soft bits of dead bodies."

Worse and worse.

I blew out a breath and said, "Scavengers eat them first, right?"

I expected Sorya to respond with a scientific point about scavengers, but instead, she froze in her seat. Sorya, sitting still? Unheard of. Ridiculous.

"Sorya, what's going on?"

"Just come see." She stood and opened her door, moving with quick, precise steps, her shoulders and back straight.

I followed her to the morgue, more uncomfortable every second. I didn't want to get involved in anything nefarious, but it seemed inevitable. I bit the inside of my cheek, hating the situation but seeing no way out. I'd never leave Sorya in the lurch.

Stacked stainless steel drawers lined the back wall of the blue room. One drawer's door rested open, and a body lay on the shelf, pulled out for my view. A sheet covered it from the toes to the neck, so I couldn't see its absent hands. He was tall, over six feet, I estimated. She'd pinned back the lids, and the empty eye sockets made my skin crawl.

Sorya took a breath and pointed at the face. "This is body number one, as in found first, but killed second."

"And, the one we found yesterday?"

"First killed, but found later, so it had been in the water for longer."

"Got it." I swallowed in distaste but did as she asked and studied the body. "Give me a hint. What am I supposed to see?"

"The eyes."

I crossed my arms. "I'm only doing this because *you* asked me."

She nodded, biting her lip.

The lip-biting got me. Sorya flitted, moved, darted, and swooped. What she didn't do was get grossed out by anything. What the hell could it be?

I leaned close to the face, holding my floppy bangs out of the way, and studied it. Dark hair, short on the sides, longer on top. Eyebrows, normal.

Nose, Roman, long and angular, with an Enrique Iglesias mole on the right side. The lips would have been full if they hadn't been blue and desiccated. The skin was yellow and bruised, with deep splotches of red under the eyes and settled along the jaw and cheeks.

There was nothing left of the eyes. No connective tissue at all. The murderer had removed the eyes, iris to optic nerve. Nothing left, just smooth-skinned pits of emptiness.

Smooth?

I looked again. No bite marks. No cuts, scratches, or incisions. It looked as if this person never had eyes.

"I'd say this person was born without eyes, but the second body is the same, right?" I asked.

"No nicks or punctures. No gnaw marks at all."

I stood straight, exhaling a long, frustrated breath. I hated admitting, even to myself, that Perkins might be right, but this had the feel of old, ugly magic I hadn't encountered in a long time. It jangled my nerves and reminded me of an old song lyric. "Friends might say I've always been crazy, but it's kept me from going insane."

And when magic stares you in the face, you must stare right back.

"Waylon?"

"Let me think about this." I kissed her cheek, so distracted that I didn't have time to be nervous, and executed the kiss flawlessly. I walked past the surgical suites and waved at some of the staff, but didn't stop to chat. I nodded at the receptionist, dropped my guest badge, and walked out the door, the little bell tinging behind me.

Sliding behind the wheel of my car, I cranked the air and took off toward home, mulling over the situation, humming to the oldies. I parked in my drive, kept it running, the music still playing, and sat there, stuck in my thoughts.

Early tapped on the window, and I jumped.

"You okay, Waylon?"

I rolled down the window. "You scared me!"

He shrugged. "Sorry. Saw you from the house and came out to check on you."

I turned off the car. "I'm trying to wrap my head around how bodies lose their eyes."

Early examined my face. "Did you lose your eyes today?"

"Not me!"

"Well, what exactly do you mean by 'losing their eyes'?"

Exiting the car, I walked toward the house, and he trailed me. "They're gone. The eyes, I mean. As if they never had them, but Sorya and I don't believe that's true."

Early opened the house's front door and indicated I should go in first. He considered what I'd said, his face screwed up in concentration. "There are plenty of ways to remove eyes. I don't know what modern tools exist, but it happens. People have cancer, for example, or whatnot."

I grinned, despite the serious topic. "Whatnot?"

He lifted his hands, palms up. "I learned a new word. Sue me."

Reverting back to the original subject, I said, "But why do it to these victims? And how did they do it without leaving a single tear or cut? They're gone, poof! Like magic. Like old magic, Early. Louisiana magic."

Early shifted his feet, leaned against the wall separating the kitchen from the living room, and stared at the ground. "You don't know for sure they were victims, and it is entirely possible someone invented a stunning new technology that leaves no sign whatsoever. Science looks like magic to people who don't understand it."

I flopped on the couch, eyeing him carefully. Beyond him, Mrs. Ross silently floated into view.

"Occam's Razor," Early said, with a crisp flick of one foot as he crossed his arms. "The simple answer is usually the right one. Don't reach for the supernatural when a new technology will do. I'll check with the brass at The Industries and see if anyone knows anything about a new ocular treatment or some such whatnot. You forget about it and focus on your work."

Mrs. Ross solidified and walked by the painting of George Washington, brushing it with her fingers. The painting wiggled a little as she touched it, and she absentmindedly straightened it.

"Mrs. Ross, what do you think?" I asked.

"Huh?" The ghost swirled around to look at me.

"Anything you'd like to share? Did you hear what Early said?"

Mrs. Ross sniffed. "When I have something to share, I will inform you."

"Geez," I said, raising my eyebrows. "Attitude much?"

Mrs. Ross clasped her hands in front of her and stared me down until I looked away, unwilling to deal with her rudeness. She'd always been smart-mouthed but in a funny, endearing way. I didn't recognize this behavior.

I gazed out the window at my favorite Evergreen Pear tree instead, thinking about its overall health. Nothing to see here, just a zombie admiring his foliage. The poor thing was still recovering from the battle with Quint Addington's mindless creations, but it looked to be doing well.

"The eye thing's got nothing to do with us, Waylon," Early assured me, interrupting my thoughts. "Tell Perkins and Sorya to keep you out of it. Let them concentrate on these bodies, and you concentrate on Reborn."

"You sure, Doc?"

"Don't lose focus." Early ran his hands through his hair, and his voice rose in pitch. "They have no right to do this. You've got important work to do."

"Why are you getting so upset?"

"I'm not. I'm aggravated they want to pull you away from Reborn. Getting funding to continue our research is the way we gain control over our destinies."

"I don't think Sorya is trying to distract me from that. Perkins? Maybe. He's being a bit of an asshole right now, but Sorya's confused and worried that she can't explain it."

"Sorya is lovely, but since meeting you, she's looking for mystical explanations when anything is even the tiniest bit unusual instead of focusing on good old-fashioned science." He blew out an exasperated breath. "Speaking of science, I'm going back to the lab. I've got work to do." He marched out of the room, closing the door with a solid thump.

"What was *that* all about?" I asked Mrs. Ross, but she was nowhere to be seen. Where'd she go?

It didn't matter because my next client rang my doorbell. I let her in, saying, "Hey, pretty lady."

"Hallo, Waylon," Mitzi said through a stuffy nose.

Alarmed, I took her by the elbow, scrutinizing her face. "What's going on with your eyes, my love? You've been crying." I walked Mitzi to my treatment room and set her in my chair, then grabbed a bottle of water from my mini-fridge. "Drink up. You must hydrate. You've gotten too much sun. Look, you're peeling." I tut-tutted over her for a minute, placed an ice pack over her sinuses, and after a few minutes, the swelling subsided.

"Oh, thank you, Waylon. That feels so nice." She patted her own cheek. "I know I need to take better care of my skin, but I love a tan! I'm upset because my homeless man isn't at his corner, and Joy Lucky, remember her? That obnoxious B-lister who wants to steal all my roles? She follows me everywhere. She spied on me at a lunch meeting yesterday."

I focused on the first problem. "I don't understand. You *have* a homeless man?"

"There's a homeless man who lives on the corner of this little strip mall near my house. I used to shop at the dollar store there when I started out, you know? I got to know him, and I've stopped by every week to give him some money and see how he's doing, and suddenly, he's not there!"

It didn't surprise me that Mitzi continued to check on a homeless man every week. She was sweetness personified and grateful for her success. Her recent stint as the Miss Mango pageant judge had catapulted her into a judge's chair on the uber-successful TV show, *Our Nation's Talent*. She'd combined a little natural aptitude with a lot of hard work and now made millions. Of course, she'd want to share it. She hailed from a rural farm town and remembered what it was like to be poor.

"I'm sorry he's not there, but maybe he found a place to live? I mean, no one wants to stay homeless, right?"

She drummed her nails on the chair arm while I cleansed her face. When I finished, she said, "I've offered to find him an apartment, but he always refused. He preferred to live on the street. It is so unlike him not to be there. He's been there for years."

"I hate to say this, Mitzi," I said as I laid new cold compresses on her eyes and exfoliated her lips with a brown sugar scrub, "but you didn't really know him. Anything could have happened."

She pulled the compresses off her eyes and pushed my hand away. "That's just it. Anything could have happened, and when I tried to talk to the police about it, they said they couldn't do anything."

I replaced the compresses and prepped a facial mask. "Do you know his name?"

"Travis."

"Last name?"

"I don't know."

I stirred the mask, trying to think of what to say. Working around the compresses, I slathered the concoction on her face. "Oatmeal to bring down the redness and honey for its antimicrobial properties. Plus, avocado for moisture. You'll be feeling better in no time, darling."

"Thanks, Waylon. What do you think I should do about Travis?"

I continued to paint her face with the mask, moving down to her neck and décolletage. "Nothing. It's probably good news he's not there." I set the mask bowl aside. "I mean, you can't expect the police to hunt for a homeless man with only a first name." I lifted her left wrist for her forearm massage. "Not to be insensitive, but it's not like you found his body."

She looked at me askance.

"Thank goodness," I added.

She gave me a rueful look but relaxed into the bodywork. "You're right. I always thought he could have been a model. He has the prettiest blue eyes and is quite tall. With those full lips and that long, Roman nose, he's quite striking. He gets his hair cut somehow and keeps it short on the sides, long on top. Like a rock star. He even has a beauty mark under his eye like that Mexican singer before he got it removed?"

I stilled. Probably coincidence. I mean, what were the odds, but the description reminded me of the body lying on Sorya's table. "Enrique Iglesias?"

"That's the one."

"He's Spanish by birth, actually."

"Ah, right. I remember now."

I cleared my throat. "Anyway, anything else you can tell me about him? I'll mention it to Captain Perkins if I see him." I kept my voice casual.

"Oh, that would be great, Waylon. He always wears jeans and a superhero t-shirt. I don't know where he gets them, but I've never seen him wearing anything else."

"Okay, I'll mention it to the captain. In the meantime, sit back so I can remove this mask. Are you going out tonight?"

"I'm attending a fundraiser for Pee-Wees and Playgrounds. I'm helping them raise money for a new play space."

"Oh, Amalia roped me into that, too. Something about consulting on a treehouse."

"Awesome! I can't think of anyone better for it. It's nice that you do things for the community."

"It was Amalia's idea."

"She's such a good girl. How is she doing?"

"Great. Likes college."

"When she gets her degree, make sure she calls me. I've got contacts." She held up her phone and waggled it in front of me.

"That's nice of you. I don't know what she wants to do, but I will tell her. So, what kind of look are we going for?" I sat her up in the chair and rotated it so she could see herself in my mirror.

She leaned forward, rotating her head back and forth. I fluffed her hair while she pondered, but my mind stayed on the Roman nose, beauty mark, and black hair of the eyeless man on the slab in the morgue.

She sat back with a cluck of her tongue. "Glam but natural, I think."

I mentally considered what glam but natural meant.

"Big eyes?"

"Always."

"Got it. I'll get the false eyelashes."

I walked to the makeup drawers, my back to Mitzi, and pulled out my phone. I texted Sorya. *What was Dead Body number 1 wearing?*

The message came right back. *Jeans and a Captain America t-shirt. Why?*

Well, son of a gun.

3

"Oh, you're talking to me now?" Captain Perkins looked up from his desk when I knocked and walked in.

"Against my better judgment. I have some information." I told him what Mitzi had said.

Captain Perkins wrinkled his nose. "It's a long shot." He picked up a pencil and snagged a piece of paper from his top drawer. He blinked at the paper and, with a sigh, perched a pair of reading glasses on his nose. "What did you say the name was again?"

"Travis."

"Last name?"

I shrugged. "She didn't have one."

He looked over his glasses at me. "She's known this man for years and never asked his last name?"

"Well, *she* doesn't use one."

"Yes, but she's Mitzi. *The* Mitzi."

"And he's Travis. *The* Travis."

"Okay, smart-aleck, I'll send a patrol to the corner and see if any of the store managers can pull a shot from their security cameras. At least it is a place to start. Unfortunately, Captain America t-shirts are a dime a dozen in this town. Everybody wants to be Cap."

I raised an eyebrow. "Including you?"

He pulled his shoulders back, affronted. "Of course. Team Cap all the way." He rolled his chair back and stood, hands on his hips. He hesitated, removed his glasses, carefully folded them and placed them on his desk, then looked at me again.

"Waylon, I'm sorry for before. I didn't mean to insult you. I understand what you do is important."

I stood, too, and extended my hand. "Thanks for the apology."

He shook, and our kumbaya moment ended, his face reassuming its normal impatience. "I'm telling you something is weird about this case. It involves woo-woo stuff. Your kind of stuff." His voice gruff, he said, "Don't dismiss my Spidey-sense."

I wasn't, but I had nothing to go on and a fundraiser to attend. "At least you're keeping it all Marvel, Captain." I closed the door after me.

Mitzi had invited me to the Pee-Wees fundraiser that evening, even giving me a free ticket. Since I'd "volunteered," going seemed like a good idea. I wanted to learn more about the organization and a night out was just the right thing to get my mind off the dead bodies.

While I drove to my house, I mentally calculated how much time I'd need to prepare. Getting ready took some time, not because of the clothes, but because of my scars. Replacing limbs and reattaching various parts required stitches, and while I could hide most with sleeves and pants, my hands and neck always required extra care.

"Mrs. Ross?" I dropped my keys in the bowl that sat on a small table in my entranceway.

Silence.

"Mrs. Ross? Where are you?" She'd disappeared on me before and now wasn't answering when I called. Where was my usual snarky, impatient toe-tapping personal assistant?

I tried again. "Mrs. Ross? Anyone call to make an appointment?"

Mrs. Ross emerged from the hallway, her milky white body filmy and tattered. She could be solid enough to answer the door for guests, but now she looked like an extra from *A Christmas Carol*.

"Hey, what's wrong?" I would have hugged her, but I'd never tried and wasn't sure how she would react.

She sighed a long, drawn-out sigh best punctuated by the rattle of chains.

"For goodness' sake, what is the deal?"

"I'm useless!" She threw her hands into the air. "Useless!"

"You aren't useless. I need you. You're my personal assistant. Who else would keep my appointments straight? Warn me when Mitzi was coming?" I winked at her. "Sew important bits back on?"

She crossed her arms, tapping her fingers on the opposite bicep. "Early can sew on parts."

"No one stitches and fixes limbs like you, Mrs. Ross. I lost a whole torso not so long ago, and you got me fixed right up."

"Early brought you back." She opened her arms wide. "All I did was sew."

"I'm serious. You're necessary. I wouldn't trust just anyone to sew on a new penis. Only you." It was true. Mrs. Ross's flag expertise meant she knew the difference between flying half-mast and full mast. If you weren't using your penis, and zombies couldn't, you wanted that baby *down*. Otherwise, certain social situations could be badly misinterpreted.

"Penises are my specialty, yes, but you don't lose them often, and the last time someone lost a head, Early took care of it."

She paced into the living room, and I followed. Spinning back to face me, she pointed at my chest. "I've lost my purpose."

"What exactly was your 'purpose'?"

Her glare froze me in my tracks. "That's the problem. Or have you not been listening?"

I twisted around to avoid her eyes and think about what she meant. Gee, that Evergreen Pear needed more water. Or maybe less. Okay, I was disseminating. I didn't know what to say to her, so I settled on the simplest.

"Tell me how to help."

"I need to get out more."

"You don't go out. Ever. You can't. It doesn't move." I jerked my chin toward the painting.

"That's my point," she said.

"I'm confused. You told me you bonded to it."

"Yes, I am, but maybe you could carry a piece with you?"

"You want me to cut off a square and stuff it in my pocket like a hankie?" My jaw fell open.

She literally wrung her hands. I didn't know people, even ghosts, actually did that. "It's the only thing I can think of!"

"What if cutting it fails and you...leave or fade or whatever happens to you?"

"It won't fail."

"It could!"

"It won't!"

"Arrgh!" I grabbed a handful of my hair and pulled. "You can't be sure! This could go horribly, horribly wrong. We could ruin it, and you could disappear forever."

"I've been with you so long, helping you go to school, build a business, start over when needed, and I'll help you reinvent yourself again, but in the meantime, I've got nothing to do. Amalia even helps with the books."

"I'll think about it. I'm worried that cutting the, well, you know, will fail. I couldn't be happy without you."

"It's not about you, Waylon!" Her body flashed red, and I jumped back several feet before her figure settled into a pulsating yellow.

Mrs. Ross defaulted to snarky and snarkier, but she's also helpful and supportive. She was sometimes irascible, and occasionally sad, but never furious, and I'd never, ever seen her turn colors.

A knock at the door tore my attention from Mrs. Ross for a moment. When I looked back, her whole body throbbed an angry red again.

"Okay, okay." I backed up farther and swallowed hard. "I'll do it, just give me a minute to think of the best way."

The thump-thump from the door became a sharp rat-a-tat-tat. I took a deep breath and rubbed my temples while the knocking grew even more insistent.

"Waylon, open up."

"Stop pounding. I'm coming."

"Mrs. Ross…" I whispered, then looked around. She'd disappeared.

I opened the door to a mountain of a zombie in jeans and a simple blue Henley. Scars marked his dark skin, including one circling his entire neck. He'd lost his head after a recent run-in with a machete, but Early sewed it back on, one of the things Mrs. Ross resented.

"No need to go all Hulk-smash with the door, Everest." Beside him stood his direct opposite, a thin, shrewd human who almost always wore a dark suit.

"Oh. Hi. Peter."

"Hello, Waylon. Thanks for inviting us in." Peter pushed past me, and Everest followed like a Newfoundland tailing a Yorkie. They stepped into the living room, and Everest noticed the couch right away. He ran his hand over the crushed velvet. "Sweet."

I smiled. It was nice to have someone around who appreciated the finer things. "Thanks. I got a good deal on it, but I had to bargain hard…"

Before I could tell the story of my beloved couch, Peter interrupted. "Got a call from the FDA today."

I stared in alarm. "Why? We haven't released it yet. How would they know about Reborn?"

Peter tramped on my beautiful rug, and I worried for the integrity of its knot count. "Isn't that a brilliant question? Someone put them on our scent," he said.

"But who? I mean, few people know about the company yet."

Peter speared me with a look. "Except all the people you've told, Waylon."

"What do you mean?"

"Perkins. Sorya. Mitzi. Amalia. Everyone who watched the Miss Mango pageant."

I shrugged. "Ach, nobody at the pageant took it seriously."

Everest took a seat on the sofa, closed his eyes, and stretched his tree-trunk legs. "Someone got to them, though, and they want to know whether we'll be marketing our products as cosmetics or drugs."

"Didn't you tell me the FDA is badly understaffed? Why waste resources on a company that hasn't launched a product yet?"

The slim man tapped his nose. "A damn fine question."

"Besides, they aren't drugs," I said.

"Dandruff shampoo is a drug, Waylon," said Peter. "So is antiperspirant, toothpaste with fluoride, and sunscreen. Anti-aging products are considered drugs."

I sat in my chair, mentally reviewing the ingredients, considering the larger goal. "That means it's more than the zombie cells as ingredients. It's the whole concept."

"Exactly."

"Well, shoot."

I jumped as another fist pounded my front door. "Oh, for Heaven's sake, what is going on here?"

I yanked the door open without asking who it was, and Captain Perkins barreled in, already talking. "The FBI is sniffing around my murder investigation, Waylon. The damn Federal Bureau of Investigation is interested in my case! What makes the FBI jump into a local murder investigation? We don't even have an ID on one of the bodies yet." He held up a finger as he remembered something and looked at me. "Oh, I should say thanks. Your lead was a good one. We got a match. The homeless man, Travis? His name is Travis DeMarco, and he's one of the John Does. Tell

Mitzi I'm sorry." He finally noticed the other people in the room. "Peter. Everest. What are you doing here? Do I have to pre-emptively arrest you to stop a riot before it happens?"

Everest gave the captain a lazy grin, but Peter couldn't help poking the cop where it hurt. "No. Find Quint Addington yet?"

I smacked my palm to my forehead. "Peter! So unnecessary."

"What?" Peter said, checking his nails. "Quint escaped on the captain's watch. Might as well be honest about it."

Everest growled. "Don't be rude."

"You have no room to talk." Perkins squared off with Peter, his face red, and hands balled into fists. "He was your boss, yet he made zombies right under your nose while grifting money for a drug operation."

Peter stepped into Perkins's physical space and stood toe-to-toe with him until I grabbed Perkins and Everest, seized Peter, and we forced them to opposite sides of the room.

I glared at them both as the two men huffed and puffed like bulls. "Gentlemen, this is not happening in my house. Quint is a slippery, nefarious devil of a man, and he tricked everyone. He got away from us at the pageant, too. You're both upset about other things, and taking it out on one another is stupid."

Peter's snide smile only disappeared when Everest stepped on his foot, but Perkins got himself under control.

"Waylon's right. This is a waste of energy," said Everest. "Seems to me like someone is poking the federal agencies and pointing them our way." He didn't continue because Peter's phone rang.

Peter answered, said a few choice words, and disconnected with a grimace. "The IRS is auditing our books."

"Fuck me," said Everest, dropping back on the couch.

Perkins exhaled and dropped into a rocking chair I'd positioned in a corner beside a small table with a lamp. "This is not coincidental."

I shoved Everest's feet out of the way and sat beside him while Peter stood at the sliding glass doors. "Let's break this down," I said. "We've got two men dead, without eyeballs or hands."

Peter whirled around, and Everest shuddered. "No eyeballs?" asked Peter, shocked. "What the hell? Why didn't you tell us?"

"I thought Early mentioned it. The eyeballs are missing, completely, as if they never had eyes. Hands too."

"No, he didn't mention it."

"That's grody," said Everest.

I sighed. "Continuing on. We have two eyeless, handless victims, and someone is poking the Federal bear to investigate the murders and scrutinize Reborn."

Perkins narrowed his eyes at Peter. "Are you experimenting again? Why would the Feds investigate both of us at the same time?"

Peter held his hands up in mock surrender. "I assure you, we had nothing to do with those deaths."

"Not sure I believe you."

"Fine. Don't," Peter snapped. "But don't waste your time looking at us."

"What do you think about the eyes thing, Peter?" I asked.

Peter turned to me but kept flicking his eyes to Perkins. "You say completely removed?"

"Yes. No signs of surgical removal or bite marks."

"Removing the hands could be to slow down identification, but the eyes are weird." Peter rubbed his chin. "Honestly, it sounds like a witch to me."

"How would you know?" asked Perkins, standing, looking ready to whip out his handcuffs.

Peter ignored Perkins, addressing Everest and me. "Witches can do that sort of magic, but dark witchery always has a cost. Blood. Bone. Flesh. Sacrifice. It's hard magic, and messy. So, the better question is, what does a witch get out of killing men and removing their eyes? What's their motivation?"

"Can they re-use them?" I asked.

Peter shrugged. "Seems unlikely, but what do I know?"

"Can they be transplanted?" asked Everest.

Now Perkins shrugged. "I can't imagine how. Corneas, yes, but whole eyes?"

"I asked Early, but he's focused on Reborn," I said. "He thinks this is all a distraction and has nothing to do with magic."

"Still, you would think Early would have mentioned it," said Everest. "We always like to hear about weird stuff. It makes us feel less weird by comparison."

"This doesn't help Reborn," I said. "Perkins, let us know what we can do on the murder investigation, since, it seems like 'woo-woo' stuff, as you suggested."

Perkins gave me a brief nod.

"Peter and Everest," I continued, "go back to The Industries and figure out what to do about the feds on our end. I'm sorry, I'd like to help…" I rubbed my face. "But I have to get ready for a charity event."

"What charity?" asked Everest.

"Pee-Wees and Playgrounds. I'm consulting on the construction of a treehouse. Amalia dragged me into it."

"That's cool."

I smiled at Everest. I liked the guy. "Make sure to talk to Early."

"I hate talking to federal agencies," Peter grumbled.

"Like it or not, we have to face them," I said. "We need the revenue, and we can't move forward without at least FDA approval."

Everest stood and stretched. "Yup. Can't *see* a way out of it. We're *blind* to what they want. Might have to *feel* our way through."

We all scowled at him.

"Too soon?" he asked with a grin.

4

A huge number of big celebrities showed up to the Pee-Wee event. TV actors, movie stars, producers, and directors wandered the gorgeous, palatial estate of one of Hollywood's most notable leading ladies, Ebony Ahn, and her wife, a tall, willowy model that once graced the cover of *Vogue* four months in a single year.

Ebony's star had faded a bit with age, as most actresses discovered, but she'd reinvented herself as a society lady and supported several charities, living off her residuals and royalties from two best-selling autobiographies. Plus, she made some small prestige appearances whenever a production company wanted to add a little gravitas to their film.

Ebony spotted me as soon as I entered.

She looked great. She used a light coco butter-based moisturizer for her cheeks and neck, plus a hyaluronic acid gel for her T-zone, forehead, nose, and chin. Her eyebrows, once too thin, were now full thanks to a new vegan serum, and her blush complemented her darker skin tone perfectly. I color matched and mixed it specifically for her.

Once a month, I saw her for a deep skin treatment, and we always discussed her charity work, but she hadn't mentioned the playground before. I felt much better about being wrangled into this endeavor with her involved.

I held out my arms for a hug as she approached.

"Oh, Daaaaahhhhling! Mitzi told me you are helping with the treehouse! Faaannntastic. We are so lucky to have you on-board." She embraced me, took my arm, and walked me through the crowd, giving little finger waves to all of the A-listers. A few B-listers studied me like a bug, trying to figure out why I merited her attention. We sailed through the crowd with gracious smiles, stopping here and there for chit-chat.

She tapped my wrist. "I know we can count on you for a little donation, too, of course."

"Naturally. I brought my checkbook with me," I said.

She kissed my cheek. "You are the type of donor I like! Prepared." She giggled, which was cute on her. "Oh, look. Harrison just arrived in his helicopter. I must say hi."

"You have a landing pad?"

"We got sick of the traffic. A helicopter is an absolute must these days."

I kissed the back of her hand. "Go be a hostess. You look wonderful. Radiant."

Ebony winked at me. "Thanks to you."

"I was hoping you'd ask her to invest in Reborn." The voice came from behind me.

I turned to see a tall, handsome man, about sixty, with the most luxurious facial hair I'd seen in a while; sideburns melded into a full Bandholz beard. His mustache and eyebrows were darker than his silver beard and sideburns, creating a sophisticated, natural two-toned look. His mouth disappeared into the facial hair. I wondered how he ate without leaving half his food on his face. I'd recommend trimming it if he were my client. He wore his hair combed away from his face so we could see his forehead. His dark eyes peered at me, friendly, but a little on edge, like he didn't know how I would react to him.

"I'm sorry?"

He transferred his two-olive martini to his left hand and held out his right, which I shook out of habit. His handshake was firm but not too tight, and he let go as soon as he introduced himself. "Oliver Bramwell. I'm the new CEO at The Industries. We haven't met yet. I didn't realize you were so young."

Didn't the new director know about the zombie team and how we didn't age?

"Nice to meet you, Mr. Bramwell. I suppose Dr. Early told you about me?"

"Call me Oliver. Not Dr. Early, no. Peter spoke highly of you. Said you were invaluable." He clapped me on the shoulder.

"I sorta doubt that."

Oliver quirked his head. "Why do you say that?"

"I'm kidding. Where were you before The Industries?"

"Banking. Venture capital. Finance."

That told me nothing. "I mean, specifically, where did you work and what attracted you to The Industries?"

"I like the challenge of taking a company that has been through so much trauma and righting the ship. I'm intrigued by Reborn as a subsidiary. I understand you came up with the name."

"Yes. I liked the idea of helping women feel reborn as they age. It really plays to the growing forty-five and older market."

"I've studied the finances behind it, and we need private investors to make this work. It's fiscally irresponsible to expect The Industries to subsidize it all." He clapped a hand on my shoulder, again. "But that's not a subject for today. Tonight, we party."

I squinted at him. "If you say so. You're the boss…?"

He belly-laughed. "Yes, I am. Let's go get another drink."

He offered me a *drink*?

He didn't know I was a zombie.

How was this possible? He had an entire zombie team working at The Industries. Did this mean that the higher higher-ups didn't know or didn't tell Bramwell? Did the knowledge of the zombie unit stop with the missing Quint Addington? Certainly, it meant Peter and company hadn't mentioned it.

Two steps toward the bar, Oliver turned to look at me. "Coming, Waylon?"

I smiled and gave him a little Queen's wave, all five fingers together. Veeerry cosmetologist. "No, thanks. I'm going to mingle. I'll see you soon, I'm sure."

"Absolutely. I'm going to hand a generous check to the nice folks collecting donations on behalf of The Industries, of course. We need to be good members of the community." He gave me a manly cuff on my upper arm and departed.

I studied Oliver as he swam through the waves of people flowing through the now crowded house. He worked the room, stopping to pump hands every so often, winking flirtatiously at the pretty actresses. My mouth must have dropped open because Mitzi gave me a shake.

"Waylon? You look like you got hit by a two-by-four."

"I just met the new CEO of The Industries."

"Oh? Is he nice? I haven't met him." She bit her lower lip as she caught sight of him chatting up two people I didn't know. "He's very good-looking. Suave. Debonair."

"I guess so."

"Introduce me later. For now, follow me so you can meet the rest of the Board of Directors." She swept me along, and I followed in her wake, lost in thought, not noticing anyone around me.

Oliver didn't tell me where he'd worked before when I'd asked specifically.

And he didn't know I was a zombie. Curiouser and curiouser.

I snapped out of my reverie and forced a smile when Mitzi introduced me to the additional members of the Pee-Wees and Playgrounds Board of Directors, a veritable who's who of Hollywood. I'd worked on three of the six faces, but we all pretended we didn't know each other.

"Waylon, you say? A cosmetologist? Must be a pretty good living here in California, with all the women around. Everyone struggling to recapture their youth," said a man who knew darn well what I did for a living.

"Well, yes, Hal, is it? But men too, you know. Waxing your own back can be a real bear."

A woman I didn't know, but recognized as an anchor for a nightly entertainment news show, wiggled her fingers in front of my face to get my attention. "Pardon me, but didn't you know Jason Teague before he died? Weren't you on set when it happened?" This poor woman needed a good meal. Those collarbones would have looked appropriate on a starving child. What was her name? Holly.

"Oh, everyone knew Jason Teague, and I do mean, *everyone*." I winked at her, reminding her of Jason's womanizing past and, for those in the know, his super-now-not-so-secret past as the porn star, Mr. Colossal.

"How is a cosmetologist going to help with the playground? Other than make sure we all look good at the ribbon-cutting ceremony?" asked a third woman, slightly older, a little pudgy, but she'd inherited a fortune from her father and fancied herself a talent agent. I knew the doctor who did her nose. Her name was Vivian Something-or-other.

"My other passion is plants and trees. I'm something of an arborist, and I'll be helping with the treehouse."

"You almost look young enough to play on the swings yourself." Vivian batted her eyelashes at me, and I was glad I hadn't puked in a century. That kind of practice helped keep my gorge down now.

A blond, busty woman I didn't recognize joined us, elbowing past Vivian, who had the good graces to step aside although she sniffed like she smelled something rank. The blonde dragged a fit, older man behind her who watched her rear-end with reverence.

Mitzi tensed beside me.

"I wanted to say how happy I am to be here," the new blonde said, waving with her right hand, her cosmopolitan sloshing over the sides of the glass. She wore a navy blue dress which highlighted her spectacular blue eyes. Too bad she'd used blue eyeliner. I wanted to grab her and whisper, "Brown is your friend."

She continued, leaning over so I got a good glimpse of her impressive cleavage. "Such a good cause. Sooo happy to help, and I'm ecstatic to be the face of the campaign. Right, Roger?" She grinned at the gray-haired, besotted man behind her and clutched his arm.

"Absolutely, honey. Nobody better for it. Especially with *Joy Lucky Does Ducky*, premiering next month."

Were they kidding? Her name was Joy Lucky? *This* was Mitzi's rival?

"Are you Waylon Jenkins?" Joy asked, releasing Roger to grab my hand. Hers was wet and sticky. "I've heard you are the man to see about my face."

I peeled her fingers off of mine. "Your face is lovely as it is." Along with the stunning blue eyes, she had the natural supple skin that comes with youth.

Mitzi elbowed me in the ribs again. Mustn't compliment the competition. Got it.

"Well, of course, but we must keep it this way, right?" She batted those baby blues, and I knew how seals felt in the presence of a shark. Drunk or no, she was sizing me up, deciding how much use I could be to her. Joy beamed another megawatt smile. "I'll be in touch, Waylon. With my new show starting, it's important I look my best." She wiggled up to her beau. "Roger, where to next?"

"Let me introduce you to that producer over there. He's considering a movie you'd be perfect for."

And off they went.

Victoria rolled her eyes as soon as they were out of earshot. "Joy Lucky. Can you imagine? What a name."

"Better than her real one," said Back Hair Hal.

"What's her real one?" I asked.

Mitzi let out an uncharacteristic snigger. "Joy Lunkenderwenschitz."

My jaw dropped. "What?"

Nightly News Holly lifted her eyebrows and raised her glass. "It's true. Joy Lunkenderwenschitz came to Hollywood and changed her name to Joy Lucky, because that's so much better. She's got a reality show called, yes, you heard it, *Joy Lucky Does Ducky,* where she travels to all her favorite spots around Los Angeles, explaining how she came here with nothing and made her own luck. It's meant to inspire new actors." Holly stuck her finger down her throat and made a gagging noise.

Mitzi turned to leave, eyes pinched, and muttered under her breath so only I could hear. "The marketing firm publicizing this shindig originally picked me to be the face of the Pee-Wees and Playgrounds campaign, but Joy's boyfriend bought her into it." She sniffed and straightened her shoulders, turning so only I could see her face.

Just then, I remembered I had something awful to tell her.

I touched her elbow. "Mitzi, can I talk to you privately?"

She cocked her head at me in a way that reminded me of a springer spaniel. "Certainly, Waylon."

"Excuse us," I said to the board members, who turned to the next victim, I mean, person to approach.

I escorted Mitzi to a secluded spot on the veranda. "I'm sorry to tell you this." I took both of her hands in mine. "Captain Perkins had two dead bodies and identified one of them as your Travis."

Mitzi yanked her hands from mine and brought them to her mouth, choking back a sob. Her eyes filled with tears, and I wrapped my arms around her. Her grief poured onto my shoulder, wetting my suit jacket.

"I'm sorry," I whispered into her hair. "I'm sure Perkins will find out what happened."

She stiffened, took a deep, shuddering breath, and then shoved me away, her face red. "When did you find out? You're just telling me now? A man died, and you partied and chatted with Joy Lucky, of all people, before telling me?" She thumped my chest with both fists.

"Mitzi, I'm sorry. I forgot to tell you right away, but that doesn't mean I don't care." I tried to grasp her shoulders, but she twisted out of my grasp.

"You callous monster!" She wrung her hands and then wiped at her eyes. "Just because he was homeless doesn't mean he wasn't worth something."

"Of course, of course…he was…he was worth something. That's not what I meant. I'm sorry it came out that way." I tried to catch her hand.

She shoved me again, tears streaming down her face, but her mascara hadn't run. My formulation was truly fantastic. "I'm leaving. Don't follow me."

"Mitzi, wait!"

With a wail, she flicked off her shoes, grabbed them by the straps, and headed down the stairs, her tight, sexy, white sequined dress forcing her to take them one painful, mincing step at a time. Multiple well-dressed, handsome men approached her with handkerchiefs at the ready, but she extended her arm and refused them all.

I started after her, but a burly member of the private security staff held one meaty arm against my chest and shook his head. He glared at me with steely, accusing eyes. "You're the one that made her cry."

Helpless, I watched her go.

Without her shoes, her dress trailed behind her, and a member of the waitstaff dropped a tray of appetizers and hurried over to lift it so the hem wouldn't get ruined. An elderly stateman of the crowd, an actor's actor if there ever was one, offered her his elbow and escorted her down the hill, patting her arm while she wept.

I slumped, aware I'd messed up. I should have called her as soon as Perkins told me, or at least told her immediately upon seeing her. As I turned to go back inside, I found a cadre of Hollywood heavy hitters gaping at me in shock and malice. Ebony, our hostess, stared at me with her hands on her hips.

Back Hair Hal tilted forward and pointed at me. "What did you do to her?" he demanded.

"Did you hurt her?" demanded Holly. I expected her to thrust a microphone in my face.

"No! I would never." I held my hands to my heart, begging them to believe me. "I delivered bad news, but I did not hurt her."

They turned as one, and their exit made it clear I was not welcome back inside.

Ebony shook her head at me and gestured for me to go, but she also mouthed, "I'll call you."

A tall man slipped next to me. He must have come from the lawn behind me. "Way to go, Waylon. You aren't just a local businessman.

You're a representative of a new company now. Don't forget it. Your behavior reflects on The Industries and Reborn."

For all his "join me for a drink," talk, Oliver's glass didn't have any condensation on it. It was dry as a bone, and whatever ice it once had was long melted. I suspected he'd been nursing the same drink all night and used it as a prop for whatever game he played.

I frowned, affronted. "I'm well aware of who I am."

"Good." He leaned toward me, lowering his voice. "See that you don't forget it." He pivoted, and I watched his back as he walked to the house.

I knew who I was, but who was he?

One of the eager valets jogged over. I gave him my ticket and waited for my car, considering my situation from every angle. I needed to make things right with Mitzi, find a murderer, help Reborn dodge the FDA and the IRS, and now figure out the mystery of Oliver Bramwell. Beyond that, I still had a business to run, and if I hadn't made a total mess of things, design a treehouse. It was an eclectic to-do list, and I didn't know where to start.

I drove home on autopilot, thinking. Usually, when I wrangled with a problem, I used Mrs. Ross as a sounding board, but I wasn't sure of her mental state given our discussion regarding her purpose in the afterlife. Wasn't a ghost suffering from ennui almost a cliché? I mean, think of all the ghosts from movies, books, and TV? Other than Casper, did we know of a happy one?

That brought me up short. Mrs. Ross had been happy, or at least, spirited. I cringed at my pun. Now she wasn't.

I parked in the garage and entered through the back.

I tip-toed into the living room, with the grace of Elmer Fudd hunting wabbits, hoping to find my personal ghost in an agreeable mood, and whispered, "Mrs. Ross, may I speak with you?"

One of our most famous founding mothers emerged from the bedroom hallway trailing water that soaked the carpet before evaporating in a diaphanous smoke.

"Mad special effects budget, Mrs. Ross." I tried for teasing, but she slumped at my words.

"Shut up, Waylon."

"Oh, come on. I want to help. Let's try this possibly disastrous thing before you flood my house." I gestured to the painting. "Shall we?"

She flashed red, then yellow, a dizzying stoplight effect.

I held up a hand to block the light show. "Hold for a moment. Let me go to the kitchen to get the scissors."

"They're in the junk drawer," she called to me as I rummaged around.

"Got'em." I came back with the scissors.

Back in the living room, I lifted the painting of George Washington down from the wall. I had to spread my arms wide to do it. The heavy painting threatened to plunge to the floor, but I managed to lower it without cracking the frame or injuring the oil paint. Mrs. Ross clapped her hands in anticipation as the safe came into view.

"Don't get excited yet. This might not work, and we don't know what will happen. We're taking a risk."

"It's my risk, Waylon. Do it."

It wasn't just her risk; it was also mine, and Early's, but it was her life, or death, or undeath, whatever the word, and I wanted to help. Early would too. If there was anyone who could understand being stuck halfway between life and death, it was us.

My fingers entered the code on the safe and waited while it sent a message to my phone. Gotta love two-factor authentication.

I confirmed the code, and a second later, the safe clicked and popped open a fraction. I took a deep breath and grasped the edge of our prize.

We'd folded it into a ceremonial triangle, the blue field of stars on the outside, though far fewer compared to modern day. The worn, delicate fabric smelled slightly of earth. Several holes dotted the expanse where the fabric had torn. Mrs. Ross touched it, her hand solid, and breathed a sigh.

"What do you feel?" I asked.

"A little like I remember sex, a pleasurable, satisfying sensation."

I blinked, reminding myself that she was once alive and had children. Swallowing, I said, "This is why I don't want to cut it, Betsy. If it feels good to touch it, won't cutting it hurt you?"

"Only one way to find out." She pointed to the dining room table, visible from where we stood thanks to the open floor plan.

I nodded, though my hands shook as we carried this priceless piece of history to the dining room table and spread it flat.

The scissors shook in my hand, and I opened them with a *schwick* of the blades and placed them to the fabric.

"Not the wreath," Mrs. Ross said, staying my hand. "The stripes."

My trembling fingers positioned the blades at the side hem, and I looked at Mrs. Ross one more time. "Are you sure?"

She fixed her eyes on the scissors and whispered, "Yes, I'm certain."

I used my left hand to hold down what was probably the most treasured and expensive fabric in the world, and...

...cut.

At the scissor's first score, Mrs. Ross snapped upright, taut as a violin string.

"Mrs. Ross?"

"Keep going," but her voice was tight.

I closed my eyes and sheared the fabric a second time. Mrs. Ross cried out, and when I looked at her, she held her hand to her mouth.

My jelly legs wouldn't hold me, and I had to sit down. "That's it. I'm not doing any more!"

"We've already done the hardest part." She forced words through gritted teeth and her aura pulsed purple. "One more cut, to make a small rectangle."

"No."

"It's too late. Let's see this through."

Hot, thick blood swelled at the flag's torn seam and dripped onto the floor. I touched it as it fell, crying out as if the injury were my own.

"One last snip, Waylon. Do it!" She clutched the dining room chair with both hands, panting with pain.

I pressed my lips together and cut the flag again.

A small rectangle of red and white cloth separated from the flag. I carefully placed it on the table.

Mrs. Ross released the chair, losing her solidity, becoming translucent again. She heaved, breathless, as she recovered from whatever just happened. The flag slowly stopped bleeding and clotted at the raw edge. I smoothed it and re-folded it, whispering words of apology as I replaced it in the safe and re-hung the painting.

"Mrs. Ross?" I looked over my shoulder toward the dining room, where I'd left her.

"I'm fine," she said, righting herself. "Let's take it for a test drive."

"Literally?"

"Yes."

I folded the flag square and, not knowing what else to do, put it in a baggie and tucked it in my pocket. I kept my head down as I walked to my car, plagued by thoughts of Orpheus and Eurydice from the Greek myths. Was it my imagination, or did I hear footsteps behind me? I didn't provoke the Fates and check.

I pulled out of the driveway and drove down the road, a light breeze picking up, the moon a crescent in the distance. After a quarter of a mile, I dared to look at the passenger seat.

There sat Mrs. Ross, smiling from ear to ear, her eyes shining, semi-translucent but clearly visible in the streetlights. "We did it, Waylon! We did it."

5

My cell rang in the cradle on the dash, and I motioned for Mrs. Ross to answer and put it on speaker, like she answered calls in my office. She swiped at the phone, and her hand passed through it. Eyebrows scrunched, she tried again, but her hand swished like a basketball through a net. She stared at her palm and wiggled her fingers.

I hit the speaker button and said, "Waylon."

"It's Perkins. We have another body." The wind whooshing by made it hard to hear him.

"Where?"

"Same place. The creek." He issued an order to someone who responded with a "Yes, sir."

"Somebody likes dumping there."

"Yeah, we've been patrolling, but we missed them. Ouch. Damn. Sorry, a tree branch just whipped me in the head."

"It's the winds. Was it another male?" I raised my voice so he could hear me.

"Yes. Shorts, Nikes, reflective vest. Lean. In good shape."

Headlights blinded me, and I blinked to clear the after effect. "A runner."

"Seems so."

"The eyes? The hands?"

Perkins' voice tightened. "The same."

"I need rest, Perkins, and I'm sure you do, too. I'll come by Sorya's in the morning, if you want?"

"Nothing new for you to see. Think about the witch angle." He barked out a laugh. "Christ. I can't believe I just said that and meant it."

"The world is a mighty strange place, Captain."

"And getting stranger every day."

We hung up, and I turned the car for home. I had a question to ask her, but I hesitated a moment, considering how to broach the topic.

"Mrs. Ross, why weren't you able to touch the phone when you can touch things in the house?"

She didn't answer, and when I glanced her way, I realized why. My formerly housebound ghost was staring out the window, her face practically pressed to the glass.

"There are so many lights," she said, her voice soft. "You can't see the stars. And the cars move so fast. The rain's the same, though."

My personal assistant hadn't seen the big, bad outside world in, I didn't know, decades upon decades. Selfish me had never considered it. I slowed down and turned left into a strip mall, circling the parking lot. "Maybe not the best of human inventions, but this is a shopping center."

"I've seen them on TV. This one seems big. Is it?" She turned to me, eyes wide.

I shrugged. "Medium sized? Over there is a movie theater with twenty screens. Now that you can leave the house, maybe we can go there some time."

She pressed her hands together in front of her chest. "Oh, I'd like that."

Speaking in a measured tone, I asked my question again. "Why couldn't you touch the phone?"

Still staring out the window, she said, "I don't know. Probably something about not being near the principal part of the flag. I'll test it when we get home. I'm not worried."

I didn't push her because I didn't want to ruin the moment.

Besides, fatigue clouded my thought processes. I looked forward to falling into a meditative state in my walk-in freezer. It wasn't sleep, but it acted similarly for me. Maybe the details of the day would shake out into something while I relaxed.

I emerged in the morning scratching my ear, dismayed to discover it had become loose and floppy. I was going to have to get another one.

"Mrs. Ross?"

She usually responded, chastising my choice of footwear or reminding me of my appointments that day. I worried the outing last night had zapped her energy. Maybe she needed rest and time to recuperate. I decided to leave her alone until later. If she wanted some more autonomy, I'd give it to her.

I forced my concerns aside and dressed, did my makeup to cover my scars and make me look as human as possible, then drove to The Industries, using my pass to get by the surly guards stationed in the parking lot and at the front doors. I'm certain they had fun once in a while, but you'd never believe it if you saw them on the job. They had permanent blank stares punctuated by looks of active concern, and that was it.

I sometimes tried with the elevator guards while waiting for the car to arrive.

"Knock knock."

They blinked.

I filled in their part. "Who's there?"

"Voodoo." I answered myself.

Nothing. No reaction, so again, I answered for them. "Voodoo who?"

I delivered the punch line with a flourish. "Voodoo, you think you are, asking so many questions?"

Maybe. Maybe, I couldn't quite tell. One of them smirked.

I didn't have an office at The Industries, but I did have a desk in the Dead Zone. It wasn't the section's official name, but we zombies gave it the nickname. Formally, it housed the headquarters of Reborn Luxury Cosmetics, but despite the mock-ups of logos, packaging colors, and a myriad of chemical equations, it resembled a military war room. Eddie and the other military men knew no other way of doing things.

The room had a large, oval, cherry table in the middle surrounded by swiveling, rolling chairs. Individual cubicle desks, like mine, lined the outside edges of the room and still left more than enough space to walk around the table. The industrial weave carpeting provided little foot cushion. The lighting was on a dimmer to enable slide show or video viewing in a snap. Never having been in the Pentagon, it still reminded me of it.

My wobbly rolling chair almost got away from me, but I managed to snag it and sit at my desk, stuffing my legs underneath. I grabbed a pen and a legal pad from a side drawer and scribbled notes about everything on my mind. The murders. Hands. Eyes. Magic with a big question mark. The IRS. The FDA. Mitzi. Joy Lucky. Mrs. Ross and the flag. I dumped my brain on the paper, drawing circles and lines where things connected.

It looked like a cat's hairball left in your slipper.

"We've got a problem."

"Argh!" Surprised by his voice, I jerked backward and banged my knees, trying to swivel around. Finally, I extracted myself from the desk and turned to face Eddie.

"Another one?" I asked.

Eddie stood at parade rest. "The Industries' new management wants to fingerprint us," he said.

I blinked at him. "What for?"

"New ID cards for entering the building."

"This Oliver Whats-his-name's idea?"

"Bramwell."

"How does he not know about zombies? Who hired him?" I asked.

"The bigger up and ups? I don't know what they know. I don't even know who they are. Maybe the zombie knowledge stopped with Quint?"

"Too many 'knows' in that sentence. I can't keep them straight. They can't fingerprint us. How will we explain new fingerprints when we replace a hand?"

Peter came in, followed by his much bigger, hulking shadow, except the shadow, Everest, smiled when he saw me; Peter grimaced.

Everest shoved a monster fist in my face, and we did a bump thing that I think I got right. "Heard about the fingerprints, dude?" he asked.

"Eddie told me." I added this new problem to my legal pad and stopped, staring at the intertwining lines. Hands and eyes. Eyes and hands. I gazed at the paper while my brain made connections.

Eddie noticed me thinking. "What is it?"

"Our eyes look the same. If we lose our heads, or an eye, and replace it, our eyes return to their original shape and color."

"Yeah?"

"Do they scan the same? I mean, are they the same structure inside? Could we suggest retinal scans instead of fingerprints?"

Peter and Early exchanged glances while Everest and I waited.

"Let's get Early." Eddie pulled out this phone. A quick text later and Early arrived in the Dead Zone. We posed our question.

"I have no idea," Early said. "But we could test it. Remember when I worked at that other super-secret medical facility, Waylon?"

"The one associated with that federal agency beginning with an N?"

"They all begin with an N," complained Peter.

"Yeah, well, whatever." Early waved him off. "The point is, I had a retinal scan to access the microscope room. I bet I can get those scans and compare them to my eyes now."

"They think you're dead," I said.

"Immaterial. I'll work with Clipper."

I'd never seen a system our resident zombie hacker couldn't get into, but this one might be hard even for him, and I said as much.

"Too much for me? What system?" Clipper entered the room, silent as a wraith and sat at the table. I really needed to put a bell on him.

Early whispered in his ear and Clipper smiled. "I've cracked that twice already. Left myself a back door the last time. No problem."

I shook my head. And here I'd been impressed with my safe's two-factor authentication.

"Okay, you guys get on that," said Peter, going into administrative mode. "Good idea, Waylon." He patted my shoulder.

"No need to sound so surprised," I said, a tad affronted.

"You aren't known for them, is all," he said.

"Hey!"

He ignored me.

I huffed, my goofy bangs rising with my breath. "Let me show you what made me think of it." I held up my legal pad.

The team stared at my squiggles as if deciphering a Rorschach test.

"It represents man's search for meaning?" said Peter.

"It's a turtle?" said Everest. "A beam? A bear?"

"Oh, I know!" said Early. "It's a spell. Eyes, an ear, toe of newt."

"No," I said, then stuck my tongue out because I was that mature. "I wondered why someone would cut off the hands and steal the eyes out of dead bodies."

"They also threw them in the water," said Everest.

"Ugh." Early threw his hands in the air. "This again. It has nothing to do with us."

Peter ignored him. "It's to slow down identification, Waylon. No hands, no fingerprints. Eyes are important for facial recognition."

"But you said it could be witches."

"Even witches want to make it hard to ID their victims."

Early slapped the table. "It's not a witch. We're wasting time on this."

Clipper rapped his knuckles on a nearby desk. "Murder? Victims? Eyes? Report, please."

"It isn't important," Early insisted.

Frustrated with Early, I closed my eyes and counted to three before speaking. "Yes, it is, Early. What's with you? We can focus on Reborn and the murders at the same time. We're all capable of multitasking." I shifted my attention to our computer hacker. "Forgot you didn't know, Clipper." I brought him up to speed.

"Why does no one tell me these things?" Clipper muttered, whipping out his computer from a bag he'd placed at his feet. He typed in something and reached for a coffee cup that wasn't there, and that he couldn't drink even if it was.

"Old habit," he growled.

Surprising how long those routines stayed with us.

"Anyway," I said, "my brainstorming made me think of fingerprints and eyes, and that led to the idea of retinal scans. Right? Because cutting off the hands and removing the eyes prevents the identification of the victims. We only caught a break on one because of Mitzi."

Clipper shot me an exasperated look. "What does Mitzi have to do with it?"

I told him.

"Anything else?" he asked, immediately followed by, "Never mind, I'll hack into the police reports and the medical examiner's office. You guys are useless."

I studied the group and noticed the lack of our Aussie zombie, who was currently walking the Earth as a dead Latino former security guard. "Hey. Where's Zed?"

"On walkabout," said Eddie, taking a seat at the center table with a manila folder and a pen. He flipped the folder open and sorted through some papers. His calm exterior belied his concern. "He's not ready to join us yet."

Zed's recent destruction and reconstitution traumatized the Australian, leaving him with zombie post-traumatic stress disorder. My ZPTSD flashed back to when Dr. Samuel Early had shoved my soul back into my dead body without my permission on the battlefield at Shiloh.

Unlike my original zombification, Zed had wanted to come back, but his soul had lingered in the jungle for months, abandoned and alone while his body disintegrated in the underbrush. When we'd brought him back, we'd put him into a stranger's physique. It was enough to give anybody the heebie-jeebies.

Eddie worried about Zed's mental health, as did I. But if Zed wasn't here, I couldn't do anything to help him. I tugged my ear thinking about it and winced as it dangled unnaturally.

"That doesn't look good, Waylon," said Everest, ever helpful.

"Thanks, buddy. I have to stop by Sorya's and see if someone can lend me an ear."

"You couldn't hold back, could you?" said Early.

"Nope," I said. "It was too easy."

"What was too easy?"

Eddie and Everest jumped to their feet while Early, Peter, and I stood a tad more leisurely. Clipper didn't stand at all. He didn't even look up from his screen.

Eddie took the lead. "The FDA finding us, sir. We haven't announced our product line yet. We were wondering how they found out."

Oliver motioned for everyone to take a seat. He chose an armless chair from one of the side desks for himself. He spun it around and straddled it, chest against its back. The move looked unnatural for him, and I considered why he did it. If he'd worn a baseball cap, I'd bet he'd turn it around too. Just a good ol' boy. Never meanin' no harm. No, not him.

If he leaned forward too hard, he'd tilt over. I watched in morbid fascination, sort of hoping it would happen.

"Listen, team," Oliver said, voice low and conspiratorial. "The evidence is clear. We have a leak in The Industries, and when I find out who it is, we will prosecute them for industrial espionage. To the fullest extent of the law."

Eddie crossed his arms and cleared this throat. The rest of us sat in silence. Clipper put on his headphones.

Oliver searched our faces and steepled his fingers. "Didn't you hear me? I'm taking this seriously."

"We are too, sir," said Eddie. "It's not that we aren't grateful for your support, but the bigger issue isn't how the leak happened. It's what do we do now that it has. Reborn's product line may never get off the ground."

Oliver held up both hands to stop Eddie from continuing. "I need to be honest with you guys. We'll do what we can to support Reborn, but it isn't my priority. Don't forget Reborn is a happy accident, an offshoot of our wound care research."

"It has the potential to bring in strong revenues," Peter replied. "You saw the financial analysis."

Oliver held up a finger. "If we find venture capital. I'm concerned about the leak, but not as fussed about the cosmetic company. If it continues to cause us trouble with the FDA and we can't find investors, we may not pursue it."

A frisson of anxiety chilled me. We needed Reborn to fund the zombie true death research. When Quint, uh…left, oversight tightened. Early couldn't funnel contract funds into his own research anymore.

"At least it's only the FDA," Peter said. "They're primarily a bureaucratic agency. I'm sure we can find a solution. It's all about wording, packaging, and money."

Oliver patted his pocket and pulled out his phone. "Hello?" he said.

We couldn't hear the words from the person on the other side, just a mwa mwa mwa, like Charlie Brown's teacher, but Oliver's face paled. He punched a button, putting the phone on speaker. "Can you say that again, Marjorie?"

A voice that could shatter glass crackled through the phone. It said, "The DEA is on the phone for you, Mr. Bramwell. You know, the Drug Enforcement Agency."

6

My stomach sunk to my toes, and Oliver's face turned an interesting shade of puce. Peter slammed his hands on the table while Eddie and Early paced. Everest leaned back in his chair and whistled. Clipper might have typed a little faster, but I couldn't swear to it.

If Oliver considered dumping Reborn before, this might be its death knell. The addition of the DEA to the federal agency alphabet soup harassing us raised the stakes to a frightening new level. We were standing in shit and sinking.

My phone buzzed with a message from Amalia asking if I could stop by the Pee-Wees and Playgrounds site to see the maple for the treehouse. It was the distraction I needed.

I signaled my departure to Eddie. He stopped me at the door and pulled me into the hallway, his voice low. "Waylon, we may need to abandon Reborn if it means risking the zombie project. We can't have the DEA discover zombies exist."

"I know. It isn't worth the risk. You'll continue working for the military, but I'm not a soldier. I don't want anyone knowing about me."

"It's far worse than that." He dragged me into an alcove. "We'll all be prisoners. The zombie military program is in disarray. I've tried to get in touch with command multiple times."

"What do you mean?"

"The entire command structure evaporated. Quint was our guy, and we followed his orders. Now he's gone, and no one answers my calls."

I stared at Eddie in horror, considering the implications. Eddie and his team were now soldiers without command, either forgotten or abandoned. If a new federal agency discovered them, or me, I didn't know what would happen, but I'd bet my useless left testicle it wouldn't be good.

We heard footsteps, and I waited for the people to pass us before speaking again. "You need to get away from Oliver. All he knows is Early brought you in to help with the 'wound research,' but he doesn't know why. Once he figures out you aren't actual scientists or trained technicians, he's going to ask questions."

"Early is a real scientist. Now that we know the truth about our inability to die, we have to keep searching for answers. I'm not willing to bug out yet," Eddie said, the set of his chin telling me it wasn't worth arguing, but I had to try.

"I agree, but you can't risk—"

He stopped me with a hand in my face. "I will prep to decamp if needed. The team can slip away in three minutes."

"Where will you go?"

His face hardened. "We'll contact you when we get there."

I bit my lower lip with worry. "Promise you won't disappear on me."

"We'll contact you when it's safe."

That was the best I was going to get. I had to trust Eddie.

He gave me a handshake that was more elbow and shoulder than palm and fingers, and I left rubbing my temples, anxious about everything. The FDA, IRS, and the DEA were going after Reborn. The local police had the FBI on their door. I was entangled in both investigations. Mrs. Ross could travel but not touch, a shocking departure from her normal existence, and my friendship with Mitzi was on the fritzi.

Oh, and not to mention a murderer with a disturbing fascination for peepers and phalanges.

I headed to my car with a lump in my stomach.

Rolling down my car windows, I blasted my radio as I drove to the playground, trying to clear my head. I parked near the top of the hill where the treehouse would be situated and studied the landscape as I approached. Grassy, flat at the top, but a long hill ran down from the treehouse area to the bottom half of the playground. I imagined kids rolling down the slope and smiled at the thought.

Halfway there, I noticed a vinyl banner tacked to the side of the restroom facilities. It said, "Welcome to the Pee-Wees and Playground new construction site!" Joy Lucky's giant face beamed at me, her hands forming a heart over her chest. I glanced to my right and left. No one had seen me yet. I grabbed the corner of the banner and tore it down. I rolled it up like wallpaper and dumped it in the nearest trash can, making sure a half-empty green smoothie dripped all over it.

Stifling an evil chuckle, I stuck my hands in my pockets and hummed a song under my breath as I got closer to the treehouse site.

I couldn't have picked a more perfect location for the treehouse. I knew which tree it was the second I saw it, and only a small part of me regretted drilling into its heartwood. It would adapt, and I could protect the beautiful maple while creating the world's best elevated play space, if we built it right. I loved the squat, thick trunk we had to work with. Maples were usually thinner and more graceful, but this runt had a beauty of its own if you knew how to look. I excelled at finding and highlighting beauty where others couldn't, and it thrilled me that someone else had noticed this tree before me.

"What do you think, Uncle Waylon?" Dirt streaked Amalia's face and stuck like ants on her eyelashes. Her eyes shone as little kids ran after her with plastic shovels.

"It's amazing, the perfect tree. We won't need a ladder. Look here." I pointed at a low branch. "The kids can step on this to get the first platform."

"The *first* platform?"

"Oh, yes." I rubbed my hands together. "I've got plans. Lower levels for the smaller kids, but this tree can support higher levels for the older kids. See the higher branches there and there?" I pointed at several lovely sturdy branches that formed a perfect notch. "Those will make a great upper story."

"Isn't it a little high?"

"It's a treehouse! Height is the point."

"We'll see about that, Mr. Jenkins. The Board has the final say." I turned to see Vivian Something-or-other striding toward me. I froze in place at her cold gaze. With her re-done nose turned up so far, I could see inside her nostrils.

I stammered out a greeting. "Hell-hello, Vivian. It is good to see you."

"I wish I could say the same," she said, wrinkling that perfectly sculpted nose. "I saw what you did to Mitzi the other night."

"That was a misunderstanding."

"Reallllly?" Her voice rose an octave. "Then if I call her, she'll tell me you've cleared the air and apologized?"

"Not yet, no, but I will." I wanted to smack my hand to my forehead. Despite my years, women still confused me. First Mrs. Ross, then Mitzi. "It's complicated."

Amalia's eyes ping-ponged back and forth between us.

"You'd better, or I'll kick you off this program. I don't want abusers here."

"Abusers? We had a verbal misunderstanding. No abuse. I'm offended you would say something like that!" Affronted, I leaned in, and my ire must have shown on my face because she glanced at Amalia and then back at me and took a step back.

"Still, she shoved you away." She lowered her nose at me. Who knew a nose could be so expressive. Did the doctor add extra muscles to it?

"I gave her some bad news that she found distressing. I tried to comfort her."

She sniffed. "You did a terrible job of it."

"Well, obviously, but Mitzi and I go way back." I sighed and rubbed my temples. "I'll fix it."

I hoped.

"See that you do." Vivian sauntered away. No children followed *her*.

Amalia's mouth opened in shock. "Waylon!" No *Uncle Waylon* now. "What did you do?"

I sighed. "We had a misunderstanding."

"Well, get it locked down. I need you on this project." Mouth pinched in worry, she pecked me on the cheek and led her little minions down the hill, and left me with the tree.

I rubbed the bark. "You're the only one who understands me."

A branch brushed my shoulders, and I chose to believe it did so on purpose.

I climbed its branches to the notch where I planned to build the older kids' level and sat there in the relative quiet, letting the children's laughter waft up and over me. It was higher than I originally estimated, but they could handle it.

I modified my "to-do" list.

First things first. I called Mitzi.

Two rings, then, "Hello, it's me."

"Mitzi, it's Waylon."

"Leave a message at the beep."

Oh. It was her voicemail. Tricked again.

"Mitzi, hi. It's Waylon. I'm calling to apologize for not notifying you immediately about Travis. I do care, and I didn't want to tell you over the phone, but I should have done it as soon as I saw you, not waited. Forgive me." I waited a beat, trying to think of what else to say. "Call me back, please. When you can. Oh, I saw a Joy Lucky sign when I walked into the playground space. I tore it down and dumped it in the garbage."

I hung up. What else could I do?

Moving to the next item on my modified to-do list, I texted Amalia a list of materials I needed for the treehouse, plus a link to the plan I'd mapped out in a shared drive. I'd build this thing one way or the other. Vivian be damned.

Not a second after I hit send, the phone rang. I checked the display, hoping it was Mitzi, but no dice. Perkins.

"What's wrong, Captain?"

"It's what's going right, finally. Come to Sorya's office. I've got something to show you."

I almost objected but smiled at the thought of seeing Sorya. Besides, I had a little ear problem to resolve.

My drive took longer than it should have, thanks to traffic, and by the time I walked into the waiting room, Perkins had worn a path in the carpet. Sorya bounced on her toes and picked at her cuticles. The zombie team waited in perfect, calm silence in one corner, except Early, who scowled at his feet.

I nodded to Eddie. "Hey, guys, whatcha doing here?"

"I asked them to come," Perkins said. "Since we've agreed this involves 'woo-woo' stuff, I'd like them to see this, too."

I narrowed my eyes at him, confused. "Ooookay, well, show us."

We followed him to a moderate-sized meeting room with a projector and a computer connected to it. As the team took seats, Perkins turned off the lights, clicked a remote to start the video, and leaned against the wall. I stood next to him. He was playing a game here, but damned if I knew what or why.

"What are we seeing?" I asked.

Perkins shushed me. "Just watch. People, this is video only. No audio."

The surprisingly sharp footage came from a corner camera overlooking an outdoor strip mall walkway. An entranceway to a grocery store stood in front, followed by a nail salon, a liquor store, a hardware store, and a sandwich shop on the end farthest from our view. The mall continued around the corner, but we couldn't see what lay past. The dim lighting didn't illuminate the area well, but it appeared to be that odd orange-pink stucco we had all over California. I spied the far-away stone garden display boasting several cacti and plastic pink flamingos. Tacky, but common around these parts.

The natural light faded, and the streetlamps in the parking lot must have flickered on because shadows cast the area into sharp relief. That's when I noticed the familiar sign in the liquor store, *Salute! Spirits*.

I knew this shopping mall.

"I'm going to be upset by this, aren't I?" I asked.

"Uh-huh," he said, without an ounce of remorse. "But, you guys have seen worse."

Early snorted, and Sorya stalked out, her face clouded with fury and... something else? Grief? No, more than that. Anguish.

I elbowed Perkins, my voice accusing. "Sorya is distressed."

He had the decency to look mildly ashamed. "I'll apologize to her later. Now, watch."

A man carried a laundry bag to the corner of the sandwich shop at the far end of our vision, so we could only see half his face and body. He dumped the bag on the ground, rummaged through, removed a blanket and pillow, and laid down, pulling the bag close. He moved stiffly like his joints didn't work right. After a few seconds, he sat up, extracted a water bottle and a baggie, brushed his teeth and wiped his face, then lay down. He kept his shoes on. He looked to be in his late twenties, but it was hard to judge. He was thin but not emaciated; still, I'd want to give him a good meal or two.

"When was this?" I asked.

"Night before last," Perkins answered, eyes focused on the video.

The man curled into a fetal position, a small boy hiding from the monsters in the night, the laundry bag clutched to his stomach. He threw his right arm over his eyes to block the light. My stomach clenched as he twitched in his sleep and brought his left fist to his mouth in a remnant of the childhood thumb-sucking he hadn't truly kicked.

A shadow approached, human but blurry, as if Vaseline coated the camera lens. The barefoot figure approached the sleeping figure on tiptoe, pausing every so often to make sure he hadn't woken. It carried some kind of stick in its right hand. The homeless man had fallen into a deep sleep, his breathing easy and steady.

We all leaned forward. Early's face froze with his lips pressed together tight; his eyes squinted like he couldn't bear to look. He held his hands together in prayer. Even Clipper gripped the table. I'd never wanted to close my eyes so much in my life.

As the figure stepped into the light, the image sharpened into a man with dark skin wearing a dark, sleeveless shirt over dark pants. He was bald and, if the muscles in his arms meant anything, quite strong. As he got closer, the object in his right hand became clearer—a spear, of all things.

Early rocked in his chair, and his hands seized the armrests. Everest grunted a "Huh?" and Peter whispered, "What the ever-lovin' fuck?"

"A spear is an odd weapon," Eddie remarked.

Clipper replied, "If I could get a look at the tip, I could tell you where it's from."

Ice ran through their veins. I was more the *A spear! A spear! Run for the hills!* type. My feet itched to flee, and I clasped my hands together to keep from throwing the door open and running out of the room.

We fixated on the video, but like a horror movie or a train wreck, we couldn't look away. We all knew something terrible was about to happen, and we couldn't stop it.

I blinked for surcease. I rubbed my eyes. It didn't help.

The images kept moving, and I couldn't look away.

The shadow man bent next to the sleeping man, pricked his hand, and then held the spear to the man's neck. The sleeping man's eyes and mouth gaped wide, and he grabbed at his neck. His body arched in a painful bow, his stomach to the sky, his feet and skull pressing into the earth, straining side-to-side, until he collapsed to the ground, still conscious. His mouth opened and closed like a dying fish, and wisps of white smoke wafted from his body into the air. The attacker poked him with the spear three times, once on each side and once on the belly, not hard, but enough to draw blood, and the man writhed helplessly.

I held my hands to my mouth, wanting to tear my eyes away from the screen. But the video transfixed me as much as anyone else in the room.

The attacker drew the bleeding, spent, shocked man to his feet, speaking to him in his ear, and guided him off-camera by the elbow, abandoning the man's meager belongings. As they passed under the camera, the attacker glanced up and smiled, unconcerned that we could see his entire face, indeed, happy that we could. His black eyes glittered, and he grinned, like he was issuing a challenge to us, or, I thought, to someone.

7

Perkins flicked off the projector and snapped on the lights, his moves swift, economical, and angry. The rest of us remained silent, absorbing what we saw, each in our own way. I stared at the floor, shifted from one foot to the other, and replayed the scene in my mind, trying to make sense of the images careening through my brain.

"Have insights to share?" asked Perkins. I looked up just in time to see him walking to stand behind Early, his hands behind his back.

Each of the men around the table was doing something similar, except Early. Early sat frozen. He grasped a pen so hard that his index finger and thumb turned white, and he clenched his jaw tight enough to shatter teeth.

All eyes shifted to the zombie doctor.

I considered Early's comments from the last couple of days. He'd insisted we not get involved in this investigation, pointing to Reborn as the reason, but maybe that wasn't it? Sam Early and I had a complicated relationship, but I considered him my closest friend and confidante. Now, I wondered, what didn't I know?

"He's a *boker*. A Voodoo sorcerer," Early said, eyes on the table.

"How do you know?" asked Perkins.

It hurt to hear Early's scratchy, raw voice. "Because he's my brother."

I took a seat because my legs wouldn't hold me, then I said the stupidest thing. "He's Black."

"He's not my biological brother. I grew up with him over a hundred years ago. My father hated me, blaming me for my mother's death. If he hadn't married a fourteen-year-old and forced her to have a child, she might have survived. The slaves took pity on me, the Master's son, rejected, alone, helpless."

"When was this?" asked Eddie, his voice a monotone, controlled hum.

"I was born in 1834 in New Orleans and, as I said, my mother died in childbirth. The woman I called Aunt Adah was only eighteen but already had a baby, Thomas." He gestured to the screen. "Adah became my wet nurse. She and Thomas slept in the main house with me, but as I got older, my father demanded that I stay in the main house by myself. I cried whenever she left. Eventually, Papa got sick of my crying and let me be with her. During the day and as late into the night as Papa allowed, I stayed with her, Thomas, and Victor, Adah's husband and Thomas' father. I ran to Adah after school when I was older. Thomas and I became inseparable. I learned voodoo at my Uncle Victor's feet as he taught Thomas."

"Victor instructed you?" Eddie asked.

Early stared at an empty space on the table, eyes unfocused. "Not directly. I was White, after all, and the son of the Master. His wife cared for me, and I think it tweaked his sense of retribution that the Master's son liked him more than I liked my own father. He let me watch as he taught Thomas, and I absorbed it like a sponge. I was so starved for affection that even secondhand attention was better than none."

Sam wiped his tearless eyes, a reflex from human days, and continued. "When I turned fifteen, I begged Victor to teach me formally, but he refused."

Early huffed as if it didn't mean anything, but his mouth twisted in pain with the memory. "Of course, I didn't know he wasn't a *houngan,* a voodoo priest, a man who called on the *loa,* the spirits, to help people. No, he was a *boker,* a sorcerer, a man of the black arts. They were the only family I had." His voice broke, and he covered his face with his hands. Then he looked at me. "I wanted to prove my worth."

My friend's voice shook as he continued. "Victor wouldn't teach me, but I'd learned a lot by watching, and I found others who would teach a white boy for a little coin. They laughed at me behind my back at first, but they underestimated my anger. I poured all my emotions into my magic. My fury at my father, the loss of my mother, Victor's rejection. The only people I loved were Aunt Adah and Thomas."

"What did you do?" I asked.

"I delved into the blackest of the arts," Early said, his voice a whisper now. "The Civil War came, and I thought I could prove myself to Victor and my father. I raised my first zombie at the first Battle of Bull Run and brought it home. Showed my father how I could help the South win the war without sacrificing her sons. He cast me out. I left, but not before I ordered the zombie to kill him."

I stifled my shock.

"I thought Victor would understand, but when I went to him, he snarled at me. Not because I'd raised a zombie, but because the zombie wasn't perfect. He critiqued my *technique*; can you believe that?" Early slammed his fist on the table.

No one batted an eye or lifted a finger.

"I ordered the zombie to kill him too, but he escaped."

"How did Victor escape?" Eddie asked.

"Victor didn't escape. The *zombie* did. I lost control, and the zombie escaped the house."

"Wait," I interjected. "What happened to it?"

"I don't know. I never saw him again. He's your first sibling, Waylon."

"My *first*?" My voice rose an octave.

Only then I noticed Perkins holding a phone behind his back. He'd been recording this whole time.

Early caught sight of my eye movement and turned around, twitching when he saw Perkins. The captain showed him the phone.

Early pushed back his chair. "I'm not saying any more. I've been paying for my crimes for more than one hundred years. I tried to keep our team out of the investigation to avoid any evil magic. I did not know that Thomas was alive. That's the truth."

"You suspected a *boker,* though," said Clipper, an uncharacteristic comment from the taciturn zombie.

"I suspected, but I wasn't sure," Early snapped. "Sue me for wanting to keep my people safe."

"You withheld important information, Early, and people died. That man suffered and is probably dead now. You saw it yourself," said Perkins, the slump of his shoulders more sad than angry. "You can go, but once I update Sorya, I'm going to ask more questions, and you'll answer them or I'll throw you in jail."

"For what? What charge? Magic avoidance?"

"I'll think of something."

Eddie circled his finger in the air, the signal for the team to get moving. He stood, and paused a moment before exiting. "Early, you've kept a lot of information from us, and from the look on Waylon's face, a lot of information from him. Now, we're obligated to find this *boker,* but we don't know the full extent of the problem. How many zombies are out there? How many did you make? How many has Thomas made over the years? Where are they?" Instead of waiting for an answer, the team slipped out the door without a sound.

Only Peter stopped to address Early. "A *boker* is close to a witch, a suggestion I offered twice, and you dismissed. You knew, you bastard. You *knew.*" Peter was close enough to spit on Early's cheek. "Don't come into work tomorrow."

Perkins followed Peter, already talking on his phone.

Early's face dropped like someone had kicked him in the gut. He turned to me. "Waylon, I—"

"Don't." I held up a hand. "Just answer my questions. How many did you raise?"

"Five, including you." Early slumped into a chair, one hand covering his eyes. "You have four siblings."

"When did you make them?"

"I made the other three at the Battle of Shiloh, when I made you. Two other men and one woman. You have three brothers and one sister."

My head spun like Dorothy's tornado. "I don't know how to react to this. You don't know where they are?"

"The first escaped. The other three were cut down at the Battle of Shiloh. I tethered their spirits to those spots. Don't judge me so harshly, Waylon. It's why I've worked so hard on true death. I intend to release them, too."

I ran my hands through my hair. "This is the most absurd day in months of absurd days. I cannot believe how many secrets you've kept from me. When was the last time you saw your brother? You said you believed he was dead? Did you think he died a natural death a hundred and something years ago?"

Perkins blew the door in. "We found the body."

8

We waited for the ambulance, gloved and ready to go. Sorya stood as far from Early as possible, her back ramrod straight, reminding me of Eddie. She refused to look him in the eye, and I couldn't blame her. He wouldn't get any quarter from me either. I gave her a one-armed hug, and she briefly relaxed against me.

The medics rolled the corpse into the room and left. Sorya noted height, weight, and other preliminaries for what would be her report. She also took pictures.

I couldn't take my eyes off the wounds. Thomas had punctured the man's abdomen, and those injuries gaped in the stark light of the examination suite. Blood stained the surrounding skin a dark, cherry red.

"Thoughts, Sorya?" I asked.

"What's there to say?" Sorya asked in a brittle voice. "The eyes are the same. The hands are the same. The abdomen stab wounds are new. Do you have any guesses what those are, Dr. Early?" She still didn't look at him.

Early crossed his arms and stared at his feet. "Vents for the soul to leave so he could put another one inside. Instead of trying to trap this man's soul, he wanted to put a new soul in the vessel."

"The vessel!" Sorya's voice echoed. "The vessel? A person!" She whirled on the doctor. "A living, breathing human being! You call the man who did this your brother? Is he a zombie too? How has he lived this long?"

"He must have eaten zombie flesh like I did," Early said softly. "He stopped being my brother long ago."

I shook my head in frustration, and my loose ear flew across the room, landing with a wet *plop* on the linoleum floor. Of course.

I sighed. "Sorya, could you lend me an ear?"

"You've used that joke before, haven't you?" she said, her mouth twisting in a pained smile.

"I can't help it. When else can you use that line and mean it literally?" I held my arms out wide. "Can you blame me?"

"Never," she agreed. "Unfortunately, the only fresh ear I have belongs to our murder victim." She gestured at the man before us.

Perkins covered his eyes. "I'll leave. Do it. Since you're going to catch the man who killed him, I doubt he'd mind donating." He left, closing the door behind him with a soft click.

I sat on a rolling stool. Early chose a scalpel, removed the ear in one neat stroke, and sewed the new one to my head. I mentally reminded myself not to tell Mrs. Ross that he'd done her job. As he tied off his last stitch, I heard whispers. I jumped to my feet, looking around. "What is that?"

"What is what?" Sorya asked, touching my arm in concern.

I closed my eyes and listened, truly focused on the words. "I think these may be the last words our victim heard."

"How is that possible?" Sorya asked.

"I don't know. Why does Zed now cross himself though he's not Catholic? Now, hush…let me listen." I waited as the voice repeated a single sentence in a whisper, on the edge of my hearing. It scratched like nails on glass, and my shoulders drew up to my ears in response. Finally, I caught it.

"Sam," I said.

"What? What do you hear?" He stepped closer, his hands clenched at his sides.

I wrinkled my nose and closed my eyes. "Revenge, revenge, revenge."

Early stiffened and hung his head.

I clapped my hands together. "Well, this is great. Just great. Your voodoo witch doctor brother comes back from the past, kills people in freaky ways, makes more zombies, generally makes himself enemy number one, and you kept all this history a secret from us, from me, for decades, and now I can hear his last words to this man."

Early covered his face with his hands again and rocked in place.

Sickened, I shook my head and turned my attention to someone who made me feel good, and could help me with my updated to-do list. "I'm out of here. Sorya, come with me. We're going to do something nice and normal." I claimed Sorya's wrist. "You want to play with some kids and build a treehouse?"

She held up a finger. "Let me put the deceased away properly, and then, yes, I'd like that very much."

I waited in silence, and when she finished, we left Dr. Samuel Early alone in the cold room.

We drove to the playground listening to music, both eager to calm our nerves. Luck was with us. We made it to the park quickly, and it pleased me to discover that the materials I'd texted to Amalia had arrived along with a few strong, capable-looking men. They'd staked out a nice border with yellow tape so the children wouldn't come near us, but a few played in the grass nearby.

"Hey, you Waylon?" asked one of the guys.

"Yeah. Did Amalia tell you what I have planned?"

"She did. I like it. Appreciate the effort to give the tree a chance to grow around the bolts. I'm George. This is Mark."

Mark grunted.

I grunted back, and that seemed good enough. "This is Sorya. She's a doctor, so if we accidentally hit our thumbs with a hammer, she can help us."

"Only if you're dead," Sorya said, straight-faced.

George and Mark gave each other an alarmed side-eye.

"Medical examiner," I explained.

"Oh! A joke. Pretty funny," said George. "Maybe we should get to work? As you can see, we started with the upper portion."

I craned my neck to see, and Sorya whispered, "Isn't that rather high?"

"Wow, guys, that's higher than I thought."

George rubbed his hands together with glee. "We thought you might have meant these slightly lower branches, but Mark and I here always wanted a big treehouse." He punched his buddy in the shoulder, and Mark *oomphed* at the hit. "So, we went a little higher. The kids are going to love it."

"You boxed in the higher section almost completely," I said.

"Yeah, you know, for safety."

"Did you consider tree sway? We need flexibility for wind. The higher the floors, the more the beams have to flex to give with the natural movement of the branches. The bolts may not hold. We need specialized tree house engineered bolts."

"Eh! What do you know? Look at you. You're what? Twenty? I've built plenty of tree houses."

Mark kept laying boards and nailing them in place as George and I talked.

"How many of those tree houses are still standing?" Sorya asked.

"Almost all of them. At least half," George bragged. "Here, hold this board, right here, see?" Sorya held the board in place where he told her. "That's right."

Vivian marched up the hill. Did she ever do anything but march? "Waylon, I see you've met George and Mark. They're experienced builders, and since I don't feel I can trust you to do this properly, I've asked for their assistance. They're using your plans, so I'm sure you won't mind." Her nose twitched. "You're lucky we're including you at all, but Mitzi said you apologized."

"Vivian, can I talk to you?" I touched her elbow, and she shot me a pointed look. I withdrew it immediately but led her away from the tree for privacy.

I lowered my voice. "George and Mark altered my plans and made them unsafe. The higher level is significantly higher and did it without making accommodations for tree sway, which concerns me. It might be unstable."

She pointed a finger at me, one long nail touching my chest. "This is your plan. Make sure it *is* safe. You're responsible." She strode off, better than marching but not by much.

I stared at the treehouse, now rising high in the tree. Vivian's bitchiness billowed behind her, leaving a stench in the air that I struggled to shake off.

But then, Sorya smiled at me from her position at the base of the tree, waving while she helped George and Mark measure and saw, and it was as if the clouds parted. It was the first time I'd seen her relaxed all day. I could make some suggestions to fix the top section. We could also add a soft surface underneath. This was salvageable.

The rest of the late afternoon passed quickly in a kind of peaceful meditation as I thought about the tree, changes to the design and construction. I considered asking Sorya to a movie or maybe roller skating.

Sorya shook my shoulder when it was time to leave, and I packed up my stuff while she grabbed her bag. I swatted at the gnats humming next to my new ear. Those tiny no-see-ums loved the dusk, and they buzzed and snapped at my skin.

As I shooed the bugs away, I glanced up at the treehouse, silently reassuring myself that it could be modified properly.

A bug buzzed toward my new ear again, and I swatted it.

The buzzing faded, but then a low tremor thrummed at the limit of my hearing, only in my new ear.

Or, not bugs?

I whirled around, searching for the source. The gurgle of sound throbbed low and mean, glug-glugging like something thick and fetid from a sewer. I could almost smell it. It rose to a loud thump, thump, and then settled into a crooning, malevolent dirge.

"What is this?" I whispered. "Who is this?"

The cruel music subsided, and a vicious laugh increased in volume until it rose to a fever pitch. I held my hand to my ear and cried out.

Sorya rushed to my side, "Waylon! What is it?"

"Soon," the voice said and faded away.

I hugged her tight and said nothing.

9

The next day, Sorya and I returned to the treehouse. Early joined us, not saying much, but he sawed boards like his life depended on it. He soon found the nail gun and made good headway getting the floorboards down on the lower level. He raised an eyebrow at the height of the second level but, wisely, said nothing. I caught him looking at me from time to time, but I couldn't bring myself to talk to him yet. We'd let him help, and that was enough for now.

George and I added a small table with benches at the bottom of the tree, straddling the notch where the main branches formed a V from the trunk. The whole thing looked amazing. I measured cut-outs for the windows on the upper level and ordered the soft filling for the ground beneath. I "accidentally" broke another Joy Lucky Pee-Wees and Playgrounds sign as we labored. *Oops.*

I'd told the team about my experience with the ominous laughter, and I'd still been creeped out when I'd emerged from my freezer that morning. But by mid-morning, with the beautiful sunshine, the crowds of cheerful people milling about the park, and the kids playing down the hill, I pushed the abstract fear away. I even took off my shoes to enjoy the feel of the grass between my toes.

Then Eddie called.

I walked away so Sorya couldn't hear.

"We've tracked the *boker*, and he's hanging out around that area. He could be watching you guys this very minute."

"How did you track him?"

"A satellite or two may have moved without permission."

"Jesus."

"No," Eddie said. "Clipper."

"I'm glad he's on our side."

"Yeah, some asses are getting spanked in Washington today."

"What do I do about it?"

"The asses? Nothing. You can't help them."

"Har de har har. No, I mean our bad witch. Why do you think he's hanging around? Do you think he's going to make a move during the day? Is there someone here he wants?"

"Doubt it. We'll join you at dusk."

"What are you doing until then?" I asked.

"Things."

"What things?"

Eddie sighed. "Things, Waylon. We've got other problems here, remember? Federal agencies trying to hump our asses. We're looking into it."

"How?"

"Oh, for God's sake, if I wanted to tell you, I would have. Keep an ear out and let us know if you hear from the witch doctor again. We'll be there later." He disconnected.

A small hand tugged at my shirt. "Mr. Waylon?"

"Yes, buddy?"

A child, maybe five years old, pointed. "It's a doll. Mommy said to tell you." He talked around his thumb, making it hard to understand him, but I couldn't miss what he showed me.

I ruffled the boy's hair. "Thanks so much. That is very sweet of you." I bent to look at the doll and picked it up with my thumb and forefinger.

A poppet.

With a white felt body, red felt heart, and two buttons for eyes, the doll reeked of dangerous magic. It pulsed with black energy, and I hurried to move it away from the child. Evil emanated from every fiber, and I didn't want him touching it.

I dropped it to the ground but kept it between my feet, protected so no one else would pick it up.

I dialed Eddie, but it went to voicemail. Without leaving a message, I called Perkins next.

"Keep it safe, and don't let anyone else touch it. Get rid of the families loitering on the top of the hill," he said.

I dialed Amalia, who was down the hill, and soon the kids ran down the slope for a balloon show and ice cream.

Sorya dusted off her hands and walked over to me, Early following. I didn't say anything, just pointed at the felt figure.

"Ah, shit," said Early.

"Is that what I think it is?" asked Sorya. "I've only seen them on TV shows."

"It's the real thing," said Early. He knelt, studying it. Doing what I had done, he nipped the edge with one finger and his thumb and brought it closer to his face to see the detail.

"Oh, dammit, this isn't goo…" Before he could finish his sentence, he inhaled a ragged choking breath and fell to all fours, retching.

"Hey! Zombies don't throw up," I said. "We have a no vomiting clause. It's one of the perks."

"That doll is potent," he mumbled and sat on the grass, staring at it. "It's truly awful."

"Yeah," said Sorya. "You look green around the gills, Early. You want to sit on a bench?"

He didn't respond. He lay there, stretched out on the grass, barely moving, muttering to himself, eyes wild.

Sorya sat next to him. "What's going on?"

"You want to know why Thomas is so hell-bent on getting even with me?" His voice rattled in his chest.

"Yes, I do," I said, hands on my hips, more than a little freaked out. "That would be excellent information to know."

"Remember the zombie I lost control of?"

"Yes."

Early rolled to his side and retched again.

"What the hell?" Sorya scrambled away from him.

He gasped and blew out a strangled breath. "Well, after I left, it came back, still under my compulsion to kill Victor. It fell on him, gnawed his neck right through the carotid, finished the job I assigned it. Thomas couldn't get it off him. It was super strong and single-minded. Once Victor died, it collapsed."

Early convulsed, a frightening shiver of pain. "Thomas burned the zombie, but basically—oh, God, God forgive me—he watched it eat his father."

Sam brought both hands to his throat and let out a brittle cough, followed by a shaky inhale, and I pulled Sorya to my side. She buried her face in my shoulder as we both contemplated Early's horrific words, unable to move.

The doctor pulled his knees into his chest and rocked, chanting Creole words I couldn't understand.

Sorya and I backed up several feet. I wrapped one arm around her and called Perkins with my other hand, stabbing at my speed dial with my thumb. "How far out are you?"

"Ten minutes."

"Make it two."

Early jerked and strained. His neck pulled as far from his shoulders as it could without popping off. He shouted words to the sky as he threw his arms to the side, his hands splayed wide, then shrunk into a ball again, whimpering like a baby. His eyes grew enormous, and his irises rolled up into his head so we could only see the whites. He bit his lower lip so hard his teeth sank through.

Perkins jogged to us, his duty belt jangling with every step. "Is he having a seizure?"

"I think Thomas made a poppet targeting Early. Thomas probably has Early's blood, hair, or skin and is now using that doll to control him." I pointed to where the poppet lay on the grass.

"You didn't pick it up?"

"Aw, hell no," said Sorya.

Fading sounds of car doors slamming told me the kids and parents were leaving, thank the heavens, but that left Sorya, Perkins, and me alone with a compromised Early and possibly the *boker*. I didn't like the odds, and I had a horrible thought as I recalled the vicious laughter from the night before.

"Perkins." I caught the captain's attention as he raised the radio to his mouth to call for backup. It crackled, but I stopped him from saying anything. "We can only have humans. I'm telling Eddie and the team not to come here no matter what, and I've got to leave." I released Sorya so I could text with both thumbs as I talked.

Perkins squinted at me. "Why? They're the best bet we have of capturing this guy."

Early stopped shaking and popped to his feet, spinning like a marionette, wooden and inhuman. His blank eyes fixed on us. Wherever my friend was, he no longer controlled the driver's seat.

"Ohhhhh..." Perkins breathed. The police captain and I put ourselves in front of Sorya, and we backed away from Early while moving down the hill. "Could he take control of any of you, any zombie, if he had hair or skin samples?"

Early hefted a cordless, rechargeable electric nail gun in one hand and a handsaw in the other. Flashes of every horror movie I'd ever seen ran through my head. Freddy. Jason. *Texas Chainsaw Massacre*. All of them.

I didn't have time to think of anything else.

Early bashed his way down the hill in big, honking steps, and we took off to get away from him. Sorya was fast, but I was faster. Without a care about her sensitivities, I scooped her up, threw her over my shoulder in a firefighter's carry, and bounded for safety. Perkins found cover and took six steady shots at Early.

"Keep shooting!" I screamed over my shoulder.

Four more shots.

"Why'd you stop?" I screamed again.

"Because they didn't do any good!" Perkins scrambled to catch up, his gun holstered and arms pumping.

"What do you mean?" asked Sorya, but it came out more like, "Wwwwaaaaatttttddoooooyooooomeeeaannn," as her chin bounced against my back.

"He took three and didn't slow down is what I mean," said Perkins. "No more questions! Run." He looked over his shoulder. "Change of plans. Zig!"

"Zigging!" Zig we did. We zigged. We zagged. We see-sawed all over the place, but Early followed anyway. We ran to the edge of the park, and slid down the hill, stumbling on rocks. Though Perkins exercised religiously, the flat-out run took a toll. He drew to the side and blew chunks all over a tree as Early drew closer.

"New tactic," I said, nudging Perkins to a copse of fir trees. He wiped his mouth with his sleeve and sank to the ground while I dumped Sorya, not gracefully. "Sorry, honey."

She waved me off, rolled to her side, and gulped air.

"Hide here," I told her. She huddled up next to a wide swath of bushes. "Perkins, keep to the tree line and keep your gun out. If we can get Thomas out in the open, we don't have to worry about Early. Early's the marionette. Thomas is the puppet master. Shoot Thomas, and you stop Early. Got it?"

He nodded and crawled into position.

I ran into the clearing.

"Early, you mother-luckin' piece of poop! Thomas, you fake player, wannabe, get your ass out here where I can see you, you vile piece of crap. You're hiding behind your brother, you coward! What's your excuse for taking over a zombie you didn't make? Can't get one up yourself? Flagging a little, dear? Lacking the potency you once had?"

Heavy breathing to my right.

I moved to give Perkins a clean shot. "Still upset about your daddy? Get over it. It was what? Over a hundred years ago? I mean, I understand holding a grudge, but this is unbelievable. It's not like your hands are so clean. Look what you've been doing to these poor people you've killed! What's with taking their eyes, you freak?"

The swamp-gurgling laugh rose in the air, and the light dimmed around us. I shivered in the preternatural gloom.

"The eyes are in the name of science, Waylon." The witch doctor chuckled, his evil laugh echoing through the trees. "I'm unraveling a problem an associate is paying me to solve. Getting back at my brother is a bonus. But you are right. I'm not innocent. This is an opportunity to even an old score."

"A bonus? This is all a game to you?" My voice rose a few octaves. "Who are you working for?"

Perkins took a shot at a shadow in front of me and to my right.

I skipped to the left and then the right, doing my best nimble elf impression as Early flew in out of nowhere. I was barefoot to boot. Lucky for me, the possessed zombie stereotype held. Early moved like the proverbial Tin Man. He tried to shoot me with the air-compressed nail gun from a distance, but the nail puffed out and tumbled away, flathead over shank. The attack startled me though, and I tripped, landing on my keister and rolling to a stop.

Early rushed forward, slammed the nail gun to my foot, and drove a nail through my right pinkie toe into the dirt. I tore my foot away and left the appendage in the grass, the nail sticking up from the mangled flesh like a sword in a mini-stone.

Early scrambled to his feet, tackled me, and pinned me to the ground with his body. My mind snapped. I froze, blinking, seeing red, as my brain went staticky. I flashed back to the first time Early restrained my body, when my soul collapsed back into it, squelching back inside like an overstuffed sausage, too big for the body it had just left. It was as if it expanded in a kind of barely remembered glory, and now, it was jammed in the wrong way 'round. Explosions battered my ears, and the wet grass, slick with blood, stuck to my fingers. Screams of the dead and dying rang in my ears, the cry of a bugle, and the beat of a drum.

The Battle of Shiloh. My private Hell.

I surged upward, throwing Early to the ground several feet away, where he landed with an audible smack. A harrowing chortle rose in the air, followed by a woman's scream.

"Sorya!"

I ran at full speed back to Sorya's hiding spot. Perkins followed, yelling something I couldn't hear. He grabbed my sleeve, but I shook him off and plowed on.

"Sorya! Where are you? Sorya!" In the dim light, I fell to my knees searching for her with my hands, stretching out as far as I could reach, feeling for her, hoping she'd rolled somewhere safe, but all I found was a shoe and a sock. I stuffed the sock in the shoe and carried them with me.

"Perkins!" My whole body quaked with fear. "She's not here!" I ran toward him, holding out Sorya's footwear, my feet barely keeping under me, my arms all elbows and jerking at all angles. I slipped, fell, and crawled the last few feet to Perkins, who crouched down near the spot where I'd lost my toe. "She's not there." I grabbed his pant leg with my free hand. "She's not there."

"Early's not here either," he said.

"I don't understand."

Perkins helped me to my feet. "Thomas kidnapped Sorya, then called Early to him. He played us perfectly, running us in both directions, and we missed him completely."

His words made little sense at first. I dropped the shoe and staggered around the space, looking left and right, hoping to find evidence of what had happened, sinking again to my knees to touch the earth, feeling for a clue, any clue, in the dirt and grass. My vision blurred, and I lost feeling in my arms and legs as terror took over. I collapsed to the ground and rocked like a child, arms around my knees, whimpering.

"We'll get her back, Waylon." Perkins placed a warm hand on my shoulder. "This is my fault."

"No, no, no. It's mine."

"We can argue later. I called a canine unit. Give me that shoe and sock.

We'll get the best search and rescue team in here, and we won't stop until Sorya is safe. Call Eddie. Don't bring him here, but call him. Let's see what the team thinks and if they know anything else."

"Clipper can move satellites," I choked out. "He moved a satellite..."

Perkins bent to hold on to me. "Well, damn it to hell, he can move them again if it helps Sorya." He stood and got busy, radio crackling, barking orders, using code words I didn't understand. Sirens blared in the distance in a matter of seconds.

"There's one other thing you have to know, Captain," I said, pulling out the flashlight on my phone, my mind clearing enough to think. I illuminated the soil and grass in the area.

Sure enough, it wasn't there.

"What's that?"

"Thomas has my toe."

"Oh, crap on a cracker." He got back on the radio. "Sorya Sang. Dr. Sorya Sang. Yes, the medical examiner..."

My short-circuited brain had focused on one word and one word only.

Sorya.

10

I moved like a sloth on Ambien. My fingers hovered over the phone's keypad, frozen in place. Gravity eventually took over, my fingers dropped, and I dialed Eddie's number.

"Waylon?" Eddie said.

I couldn't speak. I squeaked, maybe, but it didn't fall into a sound category I knew.

"Jenkins? What's happening?" Eddie's voice assumed a tone of command. He knew panicked silence from bored silence from my-mouth-is-full silence, but I don't think it had anything to do with being a zombie. That was all him, his character, his empathy, and his natural leadership skills honed by training.

"Ah...uh...uh..."

"We're on the way. Everest! Clipper! Gear up! Waylon, I'm tracking your phone. Stay there."

"Nn...No...Don't," I stammered, my voice weak.

"What's wrong? I'm putting you on speaker. Everest and Clipper are here. Oh, and Peter joined."

"Waylon." Everest's baritone flowed through the phone and wrapped me in a hug. He just had that way. "You need to tell us what's happening. We can't help you otherwise."

"Sorya...is..." The words jammed in my throat. "I...I lost..."

"Put Sorya on, Waylon," said Eddie, smooth, orderly, in charge. "Let me talk to her. We'll straighten out whatever is wrong."

I burst into zombie tears, which means I dry sobbed, heaving, spewing loud moans of agony, shock, and humiliation. "She's gone! He got her! We ran, but he took control of Early, and Perkins and I couldn't get away, and we hid Sorya in a bush, but Early had a nail gun, and he tricked us, got my toe, and kidnapped Sorya!" I screamed the last part.

All I heard was the *click-clack* of Clipper's keyboard.

Eddie spoke in a voice reserved for hostage negotiations, softer than before but no less direct. "Waylon, start from the beginning. Who's got Sorya? Thomas?"

I gulped. "Yes."

"Thomas kidnapped Sorya?"

"Yes."

"How long ago?"

Sirens. Flashing lights. Dogs barking. I blinked and shook my head. Was it happening again? Where were the Union soldiers? The rifles? The bayonets? Why wasn't I bleeding?

"Waylon."

No, this wasn't Shiloh. I focused on Eddie. "I'm here." I pulled the phone away from my ear and checked the time. "Maybe ten minutes ago. Fifteen?"

"Okay. You mentioned Captain Perkins. Is he with you?"

"Yes. He summoned back-up. Canines, search and rescue. A lot of people. Ambulances."

"Excellent. You're doing great, Waylon. Focus on my voice." He continued. "What did you mean when you said, 'He took control of Early'?"

The words tumbled out of my mouth. "Thomas made a poppet with Early's skin or blood or hair and used it to control him. Sam tried to fight it. He did, but Thomas's magic is strong, and he overpowered him. He, Sam, I mean, chased Perkins, Sorya, and me with a nail gun from the treehouse, and it was all we could do to stay ahead of him."

Everest exhaled a long breath as if he'd been holding it the whole time I spoke.

"Sorya hid under a bush. Perkins and I tried to draw Early and Thomas away from her, but we failed. Thomas used Early to distract us and took Sorya himself. By the time we realized what was happening, she was gone."

"Why did you say Thomas has your toe?"

"I meant that literally. The nail gun ripped my toe off, and I left it behind. When I went back to get it, the toe and the nail had vanished."

Clipper broke the silence. "Which means he could make a poppet out of you, too."

"Damn," said Everest. "He could have bits and parts of any of us. We don't know how long he's been following our team."

We all considered the horrifying thought of being controlled by that bastard.

Eddie's voice stayed gentle but held an edge of worry that hadn't been there before. "Anything else to tell us, Waylon?"

"Yes. Thomas is torturing Early because the first zombie Early ever made came back and killed Thomas's father, but this whole revenge thing is a side job, an added benefit. The murders, the eyes… It's an assignment from a paying client."

"Who?" asked Everest.

My mind finally snapped into gear. "We've circled it the whole time, but it never came into focus. Remember my squiggles on the legal pad?"

"The Rorschach test?" said Everest.

"Yeah, exactly. It was right there. We suggested retinal scans instead of fingerprints because our eyes don't change when we switch bodies. We're still identifiable. Someone is trying to solve that conundrum. Someone wants to make us truly invisible."

I sensed Eddie's grimace through the phone. "Only one person we know of who'd want to do that."

Peter said it first. "Quint Addington."

I nodded. "Bingo."

Eddie barked orders. "Waylon, go home. We'll meet you there. Get out of the way and let Perkins do his job. Only humans on site now. We'll send Peter. He'll be our eyes and ears."

"I'll need to tell Amalia." I also needed to tell Mrs. Ross. My stomach sunk at the thought of telling them that Quint Addington had returned.

I hung up with Eddie and dragged myself to my feet, searching for Perkins in the swirling mass of lights, police, crime tape, and radio crackle. I approached a cop I didn't know. "Captain Perkins?" I queried.

He pointed me in the right direction.

Perkins stood at attention with his back to me as a grim man of possibly Thai origin in a police uniform interrogated him. The stranger jabbed a thick index finger in the air to punctuate his questions, one after another, so Perkins barely had time to take a breath.

A police officer with a clipboard and a cup of coffee walked by me. I hailed her with a raised hand and nodded toward Perkins. "Who's that with the captain?"

She watched the scene before us and winced. "Commander Brolin. Glad I'm not Perkins."

She hurried along before I could ask more, so I did a quick search on my phone. Brolin reported directly to the Chief at North Point Station, making him Perkins's boss.

Commander Brolin wasn't tall, but he was barrel-chested with broad shoulders, and looked as if he never smiled. I decided not to interrupt and texted Perkins that I was leaving. Perkins touched his pocket when his phone buzzed but didn't otherwise react. It occurred to me that Brolin might want to speak to me as well, and I decided to leave before that could become a thing.

I hiked up the hill, retrieved my shoes, and climbed into my car before anyone realized they wanted to talk to me. I made it by thaaaattt much. As I locked my door and started my car, two cops charged toward me. I "la-la-la'd" my way right past them and zipped on by, running a red light to get away. They'd find me at home and probably slap me with a ticket for the red light, but it was better than hanging around. I couldn't risk Thomas magicking me in a public place. At home, I'd have other zombies around to tie me down or lock me up if Thomas made me dance like Ginger to his Fred Astaire.

I concentrated on driving, counting road signs and mile markers to keep myself present, trying not to imagine what Sorya might be living through. If Thomas hurt her, I'd turn him into a zombie myself. I'd lock him up in a small, dark box and never let him out. He'd exist in that oubliette, and then, when I was good and ready, I'd destroy his body on a deserted mountaintop and let him linger there for eternity.

The thought brought me up short. What was wrong with me? When had I become so cold? So violent and inhumane?

I pushed those questions away for another time. Or for never. I wasn't sure I wanted to examine that part of me. Instead, I drove home.

I came in through the back door, shoving my key fob in my pocket. "Mrs. Ross?"

My personal assistant floated into existence. "You've been gone awhile."

"It's been…" I tried for snark but ended with a sob.

"What's wrong? What is it?" Mrs. Ross hovered in front of me, hands clasped as I collapsed on the couch.

The entire story poured out, a stream of words that must have made sense because she didn't interrupt. She paced, if you can call whizzing back and forth at increasing speeds pacing. Her feet never touched the ground, and she eventually moved fast enough that light streamed behind her.

"Mrs. Ross! You're about to go supernova."

She whipped a quarter turn. "He has Sorya captive?"

"Yes."

Her ferocity infused me, and I surged to my feet, strode to my back sliding glass door, and stared at my trees. Although guilt was practically my middle name right then, I didn't have time for self-reproach. I had to get Sorya back, and soon, which meant shoving that crap aside and thinking clearly.

"Let's review what we know, Mrs. Ross."

She tipped her head and motioned for me to proceed, returning to her normal translucence.

"First thing. Sorya isn't a zombie, so he can't make a poppet of her."

"Correct."

"Second. He's got Early, so why would he need Sorya?"

Mrs. Ross opened her mouth to answer but never got a word out because the front door opened, and Eddie and the team strode in. I forgot I gave Eddie a key for emergencies. It said something about Mrs. Ross's preoccupation that she didn't hear them coming. We both flinched in surprise.

"Who the hell are you?" Eddie stared at the semi-transparent Mrs. Ross.

"You look like a fucking ghost," Peter said, dumping bags on the ground.

"Language," Mrs. Ross replied.

"Mrs. Ross is my executive assistant," I said. "Don't ask personal questions, Peter, it's rude."

Everest proffered a monster hand. "Nice to meet you, ma'am."

I'd never seen my executive assistant shake hands, but since she could answer doors, it seemed possible. She reached out and tried, but her hand passed through Everest's palm like it wasn't there.

"She *is* a ghost, Everest," Eddie chided.

"No, that wouldn't have happened before," I said. "Mrs. Ross, you could solidify before."

She sighed. "It's the *thing*," she said, jerking her chin toward the painting. "I have a theory."

A whirring sound brought my attention to new computer equipment sitting on my dining room table. Clipper, who I hadn't seen come in, was setting it up, plugging things in and muttering to the electronics like they were wayward children. His eyes flicked to Mrs. Ross, took her in, and filed her away somewhere in his brain.

"Uh, hi, Clip. Didn't see you there."

"Er."

"I'm sorry? What did you say?"

"ClippER. Not Clip. Clipper. Like the ship."

"Like the ship! Not the thing that holds papers together." I'd always wondered, and now it finally made sense. He'd been in the Navy. Or the Marines. I snapped my fingers. Navy Seal.

"Obviously," Clipper said.

"Yes. Yes, it is." I gave myself a mental shake and tried again. "So, whatcha got there?" I reached out to touch the jet-black monitor.

"This is a NASA computer. Touch it, and you'll have to find a new hand," Clipper said.

I quirked my head at him. He'd said two sentences in a row. Weird.

"And I can't sew one back on right now, and Early's not...available," said Mrs. Ross, stumbling on that last part.

"She sews?" Peter asked.

"Mrs. *Ross*." Eddie emphasized her name while he elbowed Peter. "Mrs. Ross, you dimwit."

"No waaaaaaay."

Mrs. Ross sniffed.

"Can we get back to finding Sorya?" I asked, my hands on my hips.

"Yeah, sorry," said Eddie. "We talked to Perkins. The dogs picked up her scent, and between that and Clipper's technomagic, we think we found her." He pointed to a red dot blinking in a mass of green and yellow, taking care not to touch the pristine screen.

It made more sense as I concentrated on it. It was a heat map of the park. The greens and blues represented the cooler grassy areas, but the walkways, still warm from the day's sun, glowed yellow. The red dot was one of two, although only Sorya's blinked.

"Why aren't there more people?" I asked.

Clipper answered. "The police cordoned it off."

"Why isn't Thomas's dot blinking?"

"Because I don't want it to," said Clipper.

"If we know where she is, why don't the police go in and get her?"

Eddie shifted his footing, standing back from the screen, drawing my eye. "They're holding back. The captain fears Thomas will hurt her, maybe even kill her."

Everest's normally booming voice sounded small but hard. "The best thing to do is draw Thomas out. Going in after her without separating them will make him retreat and move her farther away. We've got to get him to leave her behind, so we can go in and extract her."

"How are we going to do that?"

"Give him something he wants," said Eddie.

"Like what?" I asked.

"You," said Clipper. "We think he'd like you very much."

11

The door swung open, and Amalia blew in.

"Oh, for Heaven's sake, everyone's bursting into my house like they own it. I'm changing the locks." I gestured for Amalia to enter. "Come on in." I turned to Clipper. "Of course, the answer is yes. I'll trade myself for Sorya any day."

Amalia shoved her way in, breezing by Everest like he weighed a buck fifty of grisly sinew, not two hundred pounds of solid muscle. "What's going on? Who has Sorya?" She suddenly caught sight of Mrs. Ross floating in full ghostliness and gaped for a count of three. She turned to me and then back to Mrs. Ross, slowly nodding. "Ohhhh, that explains so much."

"I'm Mrs. Betsy Ross," said Mrs. Ross, "Waylon's executive assistant."

"I knew he had to have one. You keep a low profile."

Mrs. Ross gestured to her translucent state. "Comes with the territory."

Amalia glared at me. "I can't believe your assistant is a ghost, and you never told me."

"Not my secret to tell. I don't out People of No Color," I said. "Let's get back to the issue at hand. Amalia, let me bring you up-to-date." I summarized the situation with Sorya, Early, and even Reborn.

Amalia dropped into the wingback chair, hand to her mouth.

"You okay?" I asked.

"No, I'm not." She shook her head and said, "This sucks monkey balls."

"That's one way to put it."

"The worst is that you're vulnerable to Thomas's control. He has your toe, you knucklehead! How could you let this happen?" She let off a string of expletives in Spanish that I had trouble translating, but I understood the overall meaning.

"Who else could be the bait?" Peter asked.

"Send me."

We stared at Amalia like a troop of Boy Scouts ogling their first stripper.

"What?" said Peter.

"Send me," repeated Amalia, a little louder. "I'm human. He can't control me."

"Why would hc want you?" I askcd.

The look she threw me wasn't kind, and even Clipper cleared his throat.

Peter smacked the back of my head. "Look at her, man!"

Everest smacked Peter on the back of his head, significantly harder. "Don't gawk at her, Peter."

Peter rubbed his skull. "I mean, what man wouldn't want her? She's literally a beauty queen."

"Sit down before I tape your mouth shut," said Eddie, nudging the smaller man into a chair and glaring at him. Peter tried to say something, but Everest leaned down and whispered something in his ear that silenced him. I caught the word "fist."

Amalia ignored Peter. "He'll see me as a way to get to Waylon."

Mrs. Ross drifted closer. "I'll go with her."

"You can do that?" asked Clipper. "Travel, I mean?"

"Yes, Waylon and I have a way."

Clipper stared at my assistant. "Fascinating."

"Thanks, Spock." I turned to Mrs. Ross. "How's that going to help? I mean, not to make light of your offer or anything, but I don't understand."

"He can't touch me or catch me. I can shift back and forth between her and your team. I'll be your eyes and ears so you can keep your distance, but Amalia won't be alone. All she needs to do is keep the *you-know-what* in her pocket."

I stepped closer to her, my voice low. "We'll have to cut a second piece, Mrs. Ross. I'm not sure you can survive that."

"I can, Waylon. To rescue Sorya and Early, I have to."

"What's the 'you-know-what'?" asked Peter, hands on his hips. "And it better not be wrinkly or putrid."

"Get your mind out of the gutter," I said, walking to the picture of George Washington. I took it off the wall and opened the safe behind it. When I looked at Mrs. Ross one more time to make sure, she nodded.

I extracted both the flag and the piece I'd cut earlier.

A hush fell over the room.

"Is that…?" asked Clipper. He stopped and tried again. I'd never seen him so rattled. "Is that the *actual*…?"

"Yes," said Mrs. Ross.

"My God," he said.

"You cut a piece off of *this*?" said Eddie. "This flag? This?" His mouth dropped. "This is an heirloom! It is a priceless piece of history. It belongs in a museum."

"It belongs to me," said Mrs. Ross. "I made it."

"We fought for it," said Eddie. "What it represents, anyway."

Mrs. Ross touched the flag and replied, her voice quiet, "And I honor that. You're patriots. But, when it comes to this flag, I get to decide."

Clipper motioned for Everest to help him move the computer equipment so we could lay the flag on the dining room table. I'd never seen Clipper discard electronics so readily before.

"It's in incredible shape. How has it not disintegrated?" asked Everest.

"It belongs to me," Mrs. Ross repeated. "It's mine, and it is me."

"Yes, but how…?"

"Stop," I said to him. "It's magic. We don't know."

The flag lay on the table. The zombie team considered it in awe. Eddie lifted his hand to his forehead in a reverential salute, and the team followed.

Once again, I glanced at Mrs. Ross.

"Do it," she said.

I got the scissors and a towel from the kitchen, shifted the flag so I faced the exact point of the other cut, and snipped a rectangle of the same size, anticipating what would happen. Eddie, Everest, Clipper, Peter, and Amalia did not. They gasped as thick, red blood seeped from the wound, and Mrs. Ross doubled over, gasping in pain.

Eddie placed his hand on my forearm. "This can't be a good idea. Not with this kind of reaction. Please, stop."

"Keep going, Waylon," Mrs. Ross commanded. "Finish it."

Amalia and the men watched in horror as I cut the last of it and staunched the blood with a towel from the kitchen.

Mrs. Ross caught her breath. "It's okay. I'm better now."

"You're thinner," I said. "More translucent."

Mrs. Ross whirled on me. "Did I ask you to comment on my personal appearance?"

I wrinkled my nose in confusion. "Uh, no?"

"Do I comment on your personal appearance?"

"All the time."

She raised her eyebrows at me. "That's different. Let's practice."

"Practice what?" I asked.

"Amalia," Mrs. Ross said, "please take one section of the flag."

Amalia pinched one square between her index finger and thumb and grimaced like she'd picked up a New York subway rat by the tail.

Mrs. Ross motioned toward the newly cut piece, still wet at the edges. "Waylon, that one is for you."

I took hold of it but got the willies, a whole body chill.

"Now, Waylon, go to your office. Eddie, go with him."

The two of us followed her directions. Eddie flapped a hand at me. "So, what exactly are we doing here?"

"Waiting for Mrs. Ross to appear, I think." Mrs. Ross appeared next to me with an audible crack, a massive burst of air displacement that made me jump and scream. "Don't do that!" I said. "Can't you be quieter?"

"Well, la di da, aren't you picky? It's my first time. I'm sure your first time wasn't perfect."

I ignored the innuendo. "Try it again, please?"

"Yes, one moment." Mrs. Ross winked out of existence and a minute later winked back in, this time with less noise.

Eddie clapped once. "Well done!"

She flashed a triumphant grin.

"Where are your feet?" I asked.

She looked down. "Damn."

We practiced until Mrs. Ross could move between two places with little noise and her body intact most of the time, but by then, she'd faded to almost nothing. I gestured for her to stop. "You look tired. Keep both pieces of the flag with you and rest." She didn't sass me and simply left, proof of her exhaustion.

Eddie and I walked back to the living room. "I didn't know ghosts could get tired," he said.

"Until two hours ago, you didn't know ghosts existed," Everest said.

"Well, not like Mrs. Ross," Eddie admitted.

"There's no one like Mrs. Ross," I said. "At least, I've not met anyone else like her."

"Fascinating," Clipper said again. "Extraordinary."

I squinted at him. He'd said more today than I'd heard him speak in months. "You're weirding me out. Go man your station. Check for anomalies or something."

Peter sat at one end of the couch and Amalia at the other, but Peter's eyes never left Amalia's face as she absently ate grapes and doodled in a notebook. Everest growled so deep that the dogs across the street barked before he plopped himself between them.

Peter looked away.

Good boy.

"Peter, get yourself something to eat. I think we have some bread and cheese in the kitchen," I said. "You and Amalia need to keep your strength up."

While Peter obediently fetched himself a sandwich, the rest of us mapped out the rest of the plan.

Amalia as bait.

Mrs. Ross as go-between.

Eddie and team as strike unit.

My job? Stay out of the way.

"Where are the police on this?" I asked Clipper. "I hate going around Captain Perkins."

Everest answered. "Commander Brolin took over. He's a mite upset about the FBI's inquiries. Seems Perkins didn't inform him."

"Enough." Eddie's voice brokered no argument. "It's time we move. It's a crappy plan, but it's our crappy plan, and Sorya's running out of time. Amalia, wear a jacket and make sure it has a hood."

12

Peter and I could see and hear everything through a series of monitors that gave me access to multiple angles. We'd parked at the crest of the street across from the playground, and Clipper had set us up with what we needed to observe from our hiding spot in the car. How he did it, I didn't know and didn't ask.

Perkins leaned on the hood of a cruiser scanning a map, munching a protein bar someone had shoved in his face. He wore a rain slicker and had trouble keeping the map in place as the wind picked up. He had a thick five o'clock shadow, and the circles under his eyes were so deep you could swim in them. Ford Explorer headlights lit the area ahead of the oncoming dusk, but someone had called in a GloBug, a super cool outdoor diffuser balloon light with its own power source.

"Commander! There's a woman on the hill!"

Commander Brolin startled at the officer's words and barked back as he donned a windbreaker. He swiped at a leaf that blew in his face. "How did she get there? Don't we have this entire area cordoned off?"

"Yes, sir! Officers are monitoring the perimeter, but she somehow got up there."

"Well, get her down! What's she doing?" A branch rolled by his feet, knocked down by a wind gust. He gestured for the officers to move under the raised tailgate of a Chevy Tahoe for protection from the elements.

The young officer wiped the lenses of his binoculars and peered through them, aiming at Amalia as she circled the maple, peering at the construction. "She's, ah, looking at a treehouse, Commander."

Brolin glared at the newbie, his stiff stance communicating his exasperation. "Go. Get. Her. Down."

"Yes, sir!" The officer scampered up the hill, his partner following.

Perkins scanned the area with narrowed eyes, hand to his forehead to deflect the rain. He turned toward our hiding spot, and while I didn't think he could see us, I ducked down anyway.

With the help of Everest, Eddie, and Clipper, Amalia had slipped past the police cordon, a flag square in her pocket. I had the other one, but I stayed on the neighboring hill, far enough that Thomas's magic couldn't get to me.

We hoped.

Peter touched my shoulder. "I'm moving in. Stay here. Whatever you do, don't run in to save the day. He's got your flesh. He can turn you. Promise me you won't be stupid."

I nodded.

Peter was a punk, but he seemed sincere. He shook his head and sighed. "Don't be a hero, Waylon."

"Yeah. No hero stuff."

Peter shot me one last look and slithered, ah, walked, away.

I stared at one of the monitors. Brolin's officers charged up the hill like they had muskets aimed at the British. But then a genuine ghost of the American Revolution popped up out of nowhere and frightened the poor kids out of their knickers. Mrs. Ross indulged herself and screeched, moaning and waving her arms. Mitzi would have appreciated her performance.

The two baby officers took off running. They flailed down the hill screaming, and I lost them for a moment, but then switched my view to observe them reaching the police staging area. The wind messed with the audio, but I heard them shouting about the ghost. They got into Perkins's squad car, locked the doors, and refused to come out.

Luckily, Clipper had hacked into the squad car's video monitor so I could see and hear what happened next.

"What the actual hell?" asked Brolin. He rapped on the car windows, motioning for the officer in the passenger seat to roll down the window. The poor kid did as he was told, his thin mustache quivering.

"Torres, explain," Brolin demanded.

"*Fantasma*! Ghost! Whatever's up there is not natural. *Es un espectro*."

"Bullshit. Jackson, you want to try a better story?"

The rookie's freckles popped against his paled face and ginger hair. "Uh, no, sir. I have nothing to add. Sorry, sir."

I switched to another view and observed Perkins scanning the area again, hands on his hips, blinking into the wind, but a small smile lifted the corners of his mouth. He pulled his hood over his ears and held his hands to his forehead to shield his face from the rain. He surveyed the park and hill with knowing eyes.

I turned my attention back to Amalia at the top of the hill. Mrs. Ross now floated next to her, and the two opened their arms wide. Black clouds gathered overhead.

"Let Sorya go, Thomas. No one has to get hurt. Let her go, and we'll no longer hunt you. The team will let you live in peace," Amalia said to the empty space, addressing Thomas wherever he'd hidden. She'd lifted her voice to be heard against the rain and wind.

A laugh echoed across the hill. "Who are you, beautiful? And what, exactly, are you, you stunning ghost? I've never seen a specter such as you."

"I'm a friend of Sorya's," said Amalia. Her voice wobbled, but she stayed strong.

I was proud of her.

"Are the zombies afraid to show themselves?" Thomas's voice shifted, and I prayed the team tracked his movements.

"They're smart, organized, and prudent. You don't stand a chance," Mrs. Ross said.

"Ah, they know I have Waylon's toe. Prudent means scared."

"We want the toe back, too," Mrs. Ross added.

"Sentient! Verbal! Oh, you *are* a treasure! You aren't really a ghost, you know. You're something more. Something so much more. I must have you." Mrs. Ross's back was to me, but her face must have shown surprise. "You don't know what you are, do you? I can tell you. Come with me. I'll explain everything."

I couldn't take it any longer. I got out of the car, closed the door, and locked it.

The unfinished treehouse sat abandoned, surrounded by scattered tools and discarded toys. Lightning flashed, illuminating the branches in stark relief against the sky, and my discomfort grew. I didn't like that I couldn't see Thomas, and I didn't like that I could sense him encroaching on two people I cared about. My skin crawled like fire ants had taken up residence in my flesh. I ducked and waddled between cars to cross the street into the park, then dropped to my hands and knees.

Frozen like a scared rabbit, I waited for a cop to demand my identification or zombie magic to snare me. Why did the zombie cross the road? To rescue the beauty queen and the ghost, of course.

When nothing happened, I crawled to the edge of the hill opposite Amalia and Mrs. Ross, a narrow section of field separating us. I lay on my stomach to watch from this vantage point. A replacement Joy Lucky sign sagged in the rain.

A slim penlight lit the ground next to me on the right. "Figured you'd be up here."

"I figured you'd figure it," I said to Perkins, who'd belly-slithered next to me, despite the rain and thunder.

"Surprised you used Amalia as bait."

"She volunteered, and we were short on options."

"So Mrs. Ross is a ghost?"

The downpour plastered my hair to my head, and I pushed it back out of my eyes. "You've missed some things."

"Seems like Thomas thinks she's a special ghost," he said.

"She's always been a special ghost to me."

"Have you told her this?" A gust of wind blew by, and Perkins reached up to hold his hood in place.

"Are we having therapy right now?" I asked.

"You have to tell special people they're special, or you lose them."

"This *is* therapy, then."

"Tell Mrs. Ross. Tell Sorya and Amalia. After this is all over. Okay?"

I turned my head to the right. Perkins wiped the rain from his face. He blinked several times, his eyes distant as if remembering someone he'd lost.

"Okay," I said, my voice quiet. "I will."

He gave me a terse nod. "Good. What's the play?" he asked, sounding more like himself.

"Get Thomas out in the open. The boys move in."

"The cops are ready, too. They're on a loose perimeter so as not to scare him, and to capture him if he rabbits. Does Amalia have an earpiece?"

"Better. She has wraith radio."

"What?"

I tugged on my piece of the flag, and the flag tugged back. "She'll be here in a minute."

Amalia and Mrs. Ross retreated several steps but kept Thomas talking. Mrs. Ross's outline wavered in the wind, which continued to intensify. Lightning roiled across the darkened sky, and thunder boomed, cracking the night. The park lights automatically turned on, and the area lit up bright as day.

I spied foliage rustling on the edge of the park, signaling the zombie team's movements. They'd inched closer. I told Perkins what I'd seen.

"Tell Amalia to run down the hill as fast as possible," Perkins said to me. "The zombies have the mid-ground. The police have the front. We'll take up the far rear. We've got him pinioned."

I tugged again.

Mrs. Ross snapped into the space on my left, making Perkins jump.

"What?" she demanded. "I don't want to leave her."

"Where did she go, pretty girl?" Thomas crooned to Amalia, stepping out onto the grass. I could see him plainly, despite the downpour, but the lightning flashes interfered with my vision, blinding me for seconds at a time.

"Tell Amalia to run down the hill to the police," I said.

Mrs. Ross vanished and appeared next to Amalia.

"Who have you been talking to, my ghost?" He raised his voice, the wind threatening to drown it out, but we still heard him. "Don't anyone get fresh now," he said, holding up a poppet. "Don't start thinking. One wrong move, and the toe gets it."

Thomas moved closer.

Red medical tape, the kind they used after you gave blood, criss-crossed the fabric doll, holding my toe in place. It looked like a poppet suicide bomber. Thomas held a long, thin pin in his other hand. I couldn't hear what he said next because thunder boomed overhead. I didn't need to hear it. If he stuck my toe with that pin, I would lose control and hurt the ones I loved. I reversed crawled, frantic to create distance between me and the madman holding my toe hostage.

"Give me that," said Mrs. Ross as she winked into existence next to me. She grabbed my section of the flag before I could stop her. She instantly popped back and snatched the flag from Amalia's pocket. I blinked rapidly, trying to keep track of Mrs. Ross's movements, and prayed the wind wouldn't blow the flag sections away.

As Mrs. Ross took possession of both pieces, she became more solid, but she slipped between physical spaces faster than before. Between her speed and the weather, I didn't see her move.

Neither did Thomas.

When Suicide Poppet Waylon jumped from his hand into hers and disappeared, he screamed, "No!" and tried to grab it back but got nothing but air. Snarling, he lunged for Amalia.

That's when Perkins and I sprinted for him, and the zombie team pounced.

Perkins shouted into his radio, telling the cops to go.

Eddie and company had Thomas flat on the ground before the police arrived. Perkins slid in the mud but managed to cuff Thomas and lift him to his feet. Everest gave me a nod, and then the zombie team melted away. I grasped Amalia's hand, pulling her toward the car. We crouched behind an SUV, hiding from the police, who were now swarming the scene. The weather helped conceal us.

We watched as Brolin directed search and rescue to find Sorya. They found her immediately, shackled, bruised, and soaked. Sorya emerged from the deeper end of the field, and I yearned to go to her, but I relied on Perkins to explain my absence.

"Where's the girl?" asked Commander Brolin, rain sluicing down his slicker.

"Gone," said Perkins. They screamed to hear one another over the strengthening rain and thunder.

"Why were you up here? What happened?" We couldn't hear the rest.

"I figured he might make a run for it up here. I circled around." Perkins pointed to where he and I had hidden and said something else we didn't make out.

Brolin looked around, counting police officers. "Where are the officers we'd stationed up here? We surrounded the area."

I hadn't seen any officers.

Oh. No.

"Perkins!" I yelled, but of course, he couldn't hear me.

Three officers fell, one, two, three. Early was a crack shot. The fourth and fifth bullets missed, but only because of the wind.

Officers hit the deck, crawling to their fallen comrades, trying to roll to safety, but the muddy park stretched out flat and open, minimal coverage provided by the treehouse and other equipment. They needed to get down the hill and out of sight.

Three more shots. Screams for help. Another officer wounded. Early must have had the guns and rifles from the officers he'd already disabled. I prayed he hadn't killed them all.

"Run!" I pushed Amalia away toward the car across the street and took off back toward the park.

"Early!" I screamed, skidding on the wet grass. "Stop this! This isn't who you are!"

Between the wind and Thomas's control, there was no way he could hear me, but I couldn't help myself.

Early shot the officer restraining Thomas in the arm, and the poor woman let go, bleeding from her bicep. Thomas got to his feet just before I tackled him, knocking him back down to the ground with an audible grunt. I ground his face into the muck, and my heart leapt at his cry of pain. "You reckless, sonofabitchbastard!" I smacked the side of his head, and he grunted. "You've killed so many people and took my friend. Why? Why?"

As I prepared to hit him again, he shifted under me, and we rolled together, each scrambling for leverage. I had body weight and use of my hands, so you'd think I'd have the clear advantage, but when he spat in my eye and started chanting, I panicked.

I sprang to my feet and fled, leaping into the tree, jumping to the second story. The structure swayed side-to-side in the wind, and I slipped, my feet skating out from under me. I grabbed the handrail, my wet hands barely holding on.

Thomas, his hands still cuffed, screamed at me from the ground. "Early told me why you kept him alive. Hoping to die, Waylon? Really? Why? Immortality is for gods."

A sudden squall rose, and the supporting beams, the ones I knew wouldn't hold without the proper accommodations, cracked. I jumped up and down as hard as possible, jerking laterally to give them a little help.

"Well, one thing is for sure," I shrieked down at him. "You're no god."

I dropped the house on the witch.

13

The main tree didn't make it, which made me horribly sad, but several fresh shoots sprouted around the stump. I staked the largest, laid a fence around it, and placed a plaque in Samuel Early's honor at its base. If I knocked down another Welcome to Pee-Wees Park with Joy Lucky's face on it to make way for the plaque, more's the better. We'd need to tend the little tree for a while, but I hoped it would grow well.

The park's construction ceased temporarily as they removed the remnants of the treehouse, reseeded the damaged lawn, and repaired the lavatory building. Early's stray bullets hit the facilities, cracked a toilet, and busted a water main. I wrote another big check and handed it to Ebony personally.

Sam Early, my long-time companion and friend, ran away after Thomas's death. We recovered the poppet and destroyed it. Without Thomas's magic to fuel it, Early regained his senses, but he fled once he realized what he'd done. I hoped he would return, but after everything he went through, I couldn't be sure. I missed him.

With Zed still on walkabout and Early in the wind, our team was down by two.

The police honored their fallen officers, and I attended several miserable funerals.

I'd limped home with my mangled toe in an evidence bag Perkins had slipped me. With practice and both pieces of the flag together in the main part in the safe, Mrs. Ross became solid enough to sew on my toe.

"You'll need a new one. This one is in awful shape," she said.

"I don't have another one, and until Sorya returns to work, I don't think I can get another." Sorya and I talked every day but hadn't seen each other yet. She'd taken a leave of absence from work, partially her idea, but mostly the administration's.

"We could have taken one from Thomas."

I shivered. "No, thanks. I wouldn't want any part of that man."

She considered me for a second. "No, I don't think you would."

I watched her put the finishing touches on my sad, little toe. "Mrs. Ross."

"What?" She quirked her head at me.

"I don't know what kind of 'special' ghost you are, but you are always special to me."

She flicked her eyes at me. "What's wrong with you? Lose your toe, lose your mind?" She tugged at her finishing knot. "I want a raise."

"A raise! I don't pay you anything."

"Exactly."

"What do you want? You can't use money."

She sniffed. "I want outings."

"Outings?"

"I want to take a flag square and do things. I want to see places outside of this house."

"You want me to take you on trips?"

"Did I mumble?"

"No, but you mean like dates?"

"Not dates. *Outings*." She tucked the needle into the thread spool and dropped it into her sewing box.

"Where do you want to go first?"

"Disneyland."

I stared at her open-mouthed. "Why there?"

"I want to see my friend again."

I looked at her, suspicious. "Which friend?" I yanked my foot from her grasp and shoved it into my sock.

"George."

"George?" Then it hit me. "George Washington? That's the Hall of Presidents. That's in Florida. Disney*world*, not Disney*land*."

"Oh! We get to go on a plane! Even better."

"I think you fail to see the complications. A trip to Florida is not something I can whip up out of thin air. I mean, think about it. It's obviously out of the question." I rose from the couch and dismissed the thought with a sharp flick of my hand.

"What's out of the question?" Amalia sauntered in, a mango smoothie in hand, a regular California girl.

"Wait. Amalia, I want to tell you something."

She sipped her smoothie, pushing the straw around to get every drop, making a horrible squeaking noise that hurt my ears. I braced against the sound, stifling a shiver. She opened the top and hunted for a chunk of mango. "What?" she said.

"I want you to know you're special to me."

"Uhmmm. That's nice." She continued to poke in her smoothie. Spying a hunk, she speared it with her straw and sucked it off the end. Happy with her find, she finally looked up. "What's out of the question?"

I threw my hand in exasperation toward Mrs. Ross. "She wants to go to Disneyworld! In Florida!"

Amalia's eyes grew wide. She dug her phone out of her pocket and jabbed at the screen with her thumb. "Cool! I've always wanted to go to Florida! It's almost the end of the semester, and then we can go. I'll tell my dad. He'll be happy to transfer some money."

"Wait! No, we can't *go*. Why can't we stay here and drive to Disneyland?" Disneyland seemed like a plausible option all of a sudden though unfathomable five minutes ago. But a trip on a plane? No way. Not happening. Ever. Over my dead body.

Bad choice of words.

Just no.

"Because Disneyland doesn't have the Hall of Presidents, as you so kindly explained." Mrs. Ross smacked her hands together. "Tell me when we're going. I'll be ready. Not like I have to pack or anything."

"I'll consider it. I'm not promising." I left the room, both women staring daggers as I passed. I would *not* be bullied into a trip to Florida. I hated Florida. They had bugs there. Also,

nasty attack birds with gangly legs, noodle necks, and beady eyes. It's true. Flamingos. Ask anyone who lives in Florida. Tough as nails, hyperactive, dinosaur throwbacks, with sharp, pointy beaks. Never trust an animal that stands on one leg.

Needing to escape the women in my life, I drove to The Industries to check in with the zombie team. I hadn't spoken to them since Thomas's death, except for a few texts. No one knew of their involvement. They were more like ghosts than my actual ghost.

The zombies had reported that the retinal technology worked great, but since I hadn't been there to set up my scan, the stone-faced guards still required my pass. They accepted it, handed it back to me, and I turned to face front, waiting for them to lift the gate.

Tap. Tap. Tap.

The closest guard tapped my window.

"Yes?"

"No joke for us today?" she asked.

And just like that, my day improved.

"Knock knock," I said.

They didn't say anything.

"Oh, that's how it's going to be? I get it. Okay. Who's there?" I filled in their part. They wanted their joke but couldn't pretend to enjoy it.

No answer, of course.

I continued. "Ice cream."

I waited a beat.

"Ice scream if you don't let me in."

I winked at them, and the gate lifted.

The building bustled, as usual, people rushing to and fro, laptops in hand, notebooks and pens clutched to their chests as they gibbered about the next meeting. I gave them all polite nods.

The Dead Zone buzzed with the activity of lifeless men. Clipper pecked at his computer while conferring with Eddie. Peter paced, animated, and involved in his phone conversation, barely acknowledging me when I entered. Everest studied papers spread out on the table, his eyes and forehead tense with unusually serious concentration.

"What's going on?"

Everest spared a strained smile for me. "With Doc Early gone, we've had to scramble to figure out what to do with Reborn. The FDA and DEA are on our backs, and our lead scientist is AWOL, so we're screwed. We haven't found investors, and it's causing regulatory trouble, so Oliver's cutting it off."

It figured. My bright, beautiful idea never got off the ground. Born by accident and nurtured by necessity and hope, Reborn Luxury Cosmetics seemed like an answer to our prayers, a way to make money legally and continue our research into true death. It also fulfilled my dream of marketing my face cream.

Everest motioned for me to sit. "We're determining what Early left behind. The science trail is tough to figure out without another scientist, so we're making copies of everything before Oliver officially tells us the news."

"Wait, he hasn't told you yet?"

"No. Clipper's been keeping an eye on Oliver's email and is monitoring his phone. In the meantime, we're getting all the data before Oliver locks us out."

"Smart." I grabbed a pile of papers and flipped through them. "What's Peter doing?"

"Calling in some favors, I think. I don't know exactly."

"Once we get the boot from Oliver, what's next?"

"Don't know. Waiting for Eddie to tell us the plan." He motioned for me to return the documents, and I handed them to him. The big man grasped the papers on the table, rolled them into a cylinder, added the papers I had just returned to him, and placed them all into a canister.

Clipper's hand shot into the air, his other hand on his headset. "Ten minutes!" he announced.

Everest handed me a stack of folders. "Place these on the desks, quickly. Anywhere, make it look like we've been working on them. Spread them out. Add some pens. Here." He handed me a random assortment of writing implements.

I distributed them across the desks, making them messy, then sprinted down the hall and retrieved some old coffee-stained napkins from a break room. Adding them to the desks earned a thumbs up from Everest.

Clipper stared at his computer, rotating his index finger in a hurry-up motion. Eddie hung over him, doing the same. Clipper raised his hand again. "Five," he said.

"Hurry, hurry," whispered Eddie. "Waylon, we need three more minutes. Stall him."

I nodded and left, walking down the hallway toward Oliver's office. His voice got closer, and I intentionally stumbled, tripping as he came around the corner so we both fell to the ground. As I tried to gain my feet, gosh darn it if I didn't slip again and take down his assistant, Todd Something, poor guy. The three of us lay there in a tangle of arms and legs.

"Oh, ow! Oh, Oliver, I didn't see you. Are you okay? Tom?"

"It's Todd." He held a clipboard and wore a bowtie, which I liked very much.

"Oh, Todd. Right. So sorry. Those new shoes you're wearing are soooo slippery. It helps if you scuff them a bit. Take them out on the sidewalk for a few blocks. Here, Oliver, let me help you up."

"No. No!" He pushed me off. "I've got it. Thanks, though, Waylon. I'm sure it was an accident."

"Of course, it was an accident," I said, making my most offended face, hand to my heart. "Do you think I would knock you down on purpose? How could you think that? I'm a cosmetologist, not a wrestler. By the way, I've got some beard oil to recommend to you. You can use it damp or dry, and the scent is fab-u-lous. The women, oh, or maybe the men? Honey, what do I know? Will. Just. Love. It. I guarantee. Not too oily and so moisturizing. I can get you a sample."

"I don't think that's necessary. Thanks for the thought. I have some products I like."

"Really? What are they? I must know. Anyone with a beard like yours has secrets. Tell me. Cedarwood? Eucalyptus? If I could smell it…" I leaned in, and Oliver jerked back.

"Something my father gave me, and I've stuck with it. I think it has grapeseed in it? Maybe castor oil? Something pine? I don't know. I'll show it to you one day. Now, if you'll excuse me, I really must be going." He tried to brush past me, but he leaned hard on his ankle and winced.

"Oh, no. Let me get you an ice pack. Here, step into this huddle room, right here. I'll go fetch an ice pack from the kitchen." I herded them into a small meeting room and pushed him into a chair. "Stay right there."

"I'm fine, Waylon. Let me up."

I wagged a finger at him. "It's for your own good, I assure you. I could never live with myself if I hurt you. Please." I pointed at him. "Stay put."

The kitchen wasn't far away, but it didn't have an ice pack. I searched the whole freezer. Wasn't there a rule about this? I grabbed a package of organic mac and cheese and scampered back.

"No ice pack!" I announced as I skidded into the conference room.

Damn. He'd left. I ran to the Dead Zone and got there just as he limped in.

Everyone scattered about, normal people working, going about their day. Eddie gave me the tiniest of nods.

Whew. I threw the mac on the table. Someone would be upset about their lunch, but I couldn't worry about it now.

"Gentlemen," Oliver intoned.

"Yes?" we said in unison.

"I'm afraid I have some bad news, and my philosophy is to rip off the bandage. I don't like to beat around the bush or lollygag. It isn't my style to go on and on before telling it like it is. I feel the best way to tell someone something is to get on with it. You know, leap into the breach, pay the piper. Face the music."

We all stared at him.

Oliver stroked his beard and took a deep breath. "I know this will be hard to hear, but sometimes you've got to take your medicine."

We continued to stare.

Todd said, "Let's just tell them, sir." He tapped a pen on his clipboard.

Oliver stroked his gorgeous beard again. I truly wanted to know what he used on it. I bet a pricey brand from London, not that I had anything against that. The British did well with beards. Actually, it was the Scots. They knew facial hair.

"We're canceling the Reborn Luxury Cosmetics line, effective immediately, and you're, unfortunately, terminated. You'll receive two weeks' pay and a letter of recommendation."

He waited for a reaction. He didn't get one.

"Reborn was an offshoot of our wound care research, and with Dr. Early gone and the problems the project is giving us on the regulatory front, we can't justify fighting to keep the project going. We thank you for your service to the company. Now, if you would like to talk to our placement advisor, Todd will be happy to arrange that. We know transitions like this are difficult."

Silence.

He nodded. "I'm sure you're still absorbing this. I'm sorry I have to deliver such bad news." He scanned the team's faces until he got to mine. "Uh, Waylon, since you were a consultant, you're not entitled to anything, as I'm sure you understand."

"Yup. No problem," I said.

"Oh?" He seemed confused but relieved. "Okay. Ooookay. Good. That's good."

The zombie team sat there, unfazed. Maybe Everest raised an eyebrow.

Oliver narrowed his eyes, skeptical of their silence. "Gentlemen, how are you feeling about this?" he asked in a low, soothing voice.

"We're good, sir. We see your position. We'll clear out in under an hour," said Eddie.

"It was nice working with you." Everest held out his hand for a shake. Oliver took it with suspicion.

“Here’s your computer.” Clipper handed the machine to Todd. “It’s company property.”

“You guys are sure? You don’t want to see a counselor?” Oliver asked.

“No, we’re fine,” said Eddie.

Oliver suddenly noticed Peter. “Peter! I didn’t see you. You aren’t terminated. You’ve been with this company for too many years, and your skills are useful elsewhere. I’m sorry, I didn’t mean to include you in this group. We’re transferring you to a new position in management. It’s a promotion, actually.”

“That’s great, Oliver. Glad to hear it. Thank you,” said Peter. He’d known this already, thanks to Clipper’s spying, but he still played the part, holding both hands to his chest in a gesture of gratitude and relief.

“Todd will give you your next assignment. We’re hoping you’ll enjoy it. It’s in finance. They need someone with your discipline.”

Peter controlled his smile. “Finance will be perfect. Thank you.”

“Okay then. Thank you for your time with The Industries. Please see human resources on your way out for exit interviews. It has been a pleasure getting to know you.” Oliver shook hands with each of us and motioned for Peter to follow him out the door.

“Hey,” said Todd, pausing before he walked out of the room to look at the mac and cheese on the table. “Is this yours, Waylon?”

I nodded, a slow up and down, and crossed my fingers behind my back.

“I eat the same brand. Funny. Do you shop at that gluten-free, corn-free, whole food co-op near the power yoga studio? The one with the meditation goat in the back?”

“Uh, sometimes?”

“Small world. Isn’t their beet juice divine?”

“Haven’t had it yet.”

“You must. It totally cleanses you.”

“Good to know. Thanks for the tip.”

“I didn’t know we had so much in common. Good luck.” He hurried out.

“Thanks,” I said to the empty doorway, sagged into a chair, and put my hand over my mouth to keep back the laughter.

14

I pulled into a visitor spot at the police station and parked. Before I stepped out, I dialed Mitzi, who hadn't returned my message.

"Mitzi?" I asked when the phone connected.

"Waylon. You've been on my mind. Thank you for calling back."

Feeling terrible with the way we'd left things, I started in right away. "I'm so sorry I didn't tell you the bad news immediately—"

"No, it's me that should apologize. You didn't want to tell me bad news over the phone, nor in front of people. I lost my composure because of the tragic news. I knew Travis for a long time. It hit me hard."

"Of course, it did," I replied, breathing freely for the first time since she stalked out on me.

"Captain Perkins called. They got the guy. That makes it a little easier."

"Yes, he's gone now, permanently."

"I heard."

"Can't say I'm sorry he's dead, although perhaps you wanted a trial? Observe justice being delivered?"

Mitzi sighed. "No, he got what he deserved, although it was pretty ironic that the treehouse fell on him."

I coughed. "Yes, yes, it was. A total coincidence."

"I know! I mean, of everything there, *your* project killed him?" She sounded genuinely baffled.

I laughed. "Divine intervention, maybe?"

"I believe," Mitzi said in a fervent voice. "It's all in The Plan."

I didn't know about that. I couldn't believe "The Plan" called for Travis being killed in the first place, or for me to become a zombie, but it was a nice idea that The Plan existed. I hoped so, and that it included me.

A smile snuck into her voice. "And, well, I'm the worst person in the world today...but thank you for taking care of the poster."

"They used a terrible photograph. I did her a service."

"Yes," she intoned, holding back her laughter. "A courtesy."

"A good deed," I added. "Out of total benevolence."

We burst out in hysterics and hung up, friends again. I sat back and reveled in the relief.

Then, I exited my car and went to find someone less lighthearted.

As soon as I entered his office, Captain Perkins scowled at me across his desk and pointed a pen at my nose. "No more of these antics, Waylon. I'm serious. I almost lost my job."

I sat in a chair opposite him and crossed my arms. "I have no idea what you want me to do differently. You dragged me into this. I begged you, *begged* you not to bring me in, but did you listen? No. You said it was all 'woo-woo' stuff and you needed me, and then, when it all goes belly up, it's my fault? That's not the way this works."

Perkins sighed. "Yeah, you're right."

"What did Commander Brolin say?"

"I should have called in for backup sooner, which is correct. He also was a touch perturbed that I didn't tell him about the FBI sniffing about."

"What happened with that?"

"I don't know. They stopped asking about the murders and went away. No reason given."

I had a mental image of Peter on the phone calling in favors, but let it pass. "You didn't call in back-up because of the weirdness. You didn't know how to explain it to people."

Perkins grimaced. "Turns out there's an entrenched community of sasquatches in Muir Woods. Did you know that?"

It took a few moments to take that one in. "No. I did not."

"Mermaids in San Francisco Bay."

"No way!"

"Seems there's a lot more out there than I knew. Brolin didn't bat an eye when I told him about zombies."

"When did you tell him? Because he didn't seem to know when I was there."

"Afterwards. He got suspicious about Sorya's lucky rescue and the treehouse."

"The treehouse wasn't supernatural. I jumped on it."

"Still, he's not stupid. He suspected other players in the mix. I stopped lying to save myself and hoped he'd believe the truth."

"What's he going to do now?"

He cast me a sly grin. "You'll see."

"What do you mean?"

A sharp rap on the door interrupted me.

A familiar head peeked in. "Captain?"

"Sorya!"

My sorta girlfriend entered the door, fluttering her fingers at us. "Waylon! I'm so glad you're here too. Captain, I stopped by to tell you I need to come back to work. I can't stand sitting around anymore, but it seems when you get kidnapped, they insist you take a certain amount of time off and go through all this therapy. Do you have any pull with the city? Either of you?" She said all of this without taking a breath.

I stood and wrapped her in my arms. "Sorya, have I told you how special you are to me?"

She pushed me away. "Yeah, yeah. That's nice, Waylon. Can you get me back to work?"

Perkins smirked when I glanced at him. "I tried, okay?" I said. "Mrs. Ross and Amalia couldn't care less either."

"They'll know you said it," he replied.

"Said what?" asked Sorya.

Before I could reply, four zombies barged into the room.

"Zed!" I exclaimed, thrilled to see the Aussie. Clipper, Everest, and Eddie lined up beside him.

"Hey, mate." Zed fist-bumped me.

"You feeling better?" I asked.

"A bit. Better to be with friends, you know?"

I nodded. "Yes, I do. Glad you're back."

"Me too."

"Captain, this is Zed, another member of the team," I said.

"A zombie?" asked Perkins.

"Yup," I answered. "Zed, this is Dr. Sorya Sang. She's the medical examiner, and my girlfriend." I held my breath, hoping she didn't mind me introducing her that way.

Zed stepped back and gave me a once-over. "Good on ya, Waylon. Nice to meet you, Dr. Sang."

She blushed, a bit of pink to her cheeks at my words. "Sorya, please," but she looked delighted, which made me happy.

Eddie rapped the top of Perkin's desk and eyed the captain with an unyielding stare. "Now that the pleasantries are over with, why are we here?"

"Because I wanted you to be," said a deep voice. "And what I want, I get." A brawny man in uniform entered the room, and I recognized him immediately. Perkins rose to his feet.

The man motioned at all of us. "Perkins, introduce us, please."

"Zombie team, please meet Commander Knox Brolin, my superior. Commander, this is the team. I won't introduce them by rank because I don't actually know their ranks, but they are all military men with distinguished backgrounds."

Everest, Clipper, and Zed eyed the commander, their faces blank. Eddie let out an uncharacteristic huff of displeasure.

"Perkins," said Eddie. "You gave a lot away in that introduction." Though his voice remained neutral, his meaning was not. The implied threat startled me. Always dangerous, Eddie now had an edge to him that spoke of too much disappointment in command and a belief that he and his men could only depend on each other.

Eddie and company were a leaderless crack military team held together by honor and honor only. It frightened me. It might be too thin a thread to hang by.

The commander, to his credit, sensed his tenuous position and kept his hands visible while he took a chair. This put Eddie and the team at the advantage while showing he didn't fear them. Stupid for self-preservation, maybe, but deliberate.

Eddie flicked his eyes to the team. Everest, Clipper, and Zed spread around the room, wordlessly taking positions to surround Commander Brolin. I pulled Sorya to the side, and we hugged the wall out of the way.

Perkins approached Eddie carefully. "He already figured out there was another team in place at the park. I told him the truth."

"Why?" asked Eddie, his eyes on Brolin.

"Because I'm his commanding officer," said Brolin.

"Not good enough."

"I have a job offer for you."

Eddie scoffed.

"It's a legit offer."

This time Everest harrumphed.

"You want us to be a secret kill squad," said Zed.

"No, that's not it at all," said Brolin.

"Then what?" asked Eddie. "You have two minutes."

"We want to set up a new department. Classified, yes, but legit. We have more cases involving supernatural stuff, and we need people to help. That's where you come in."

"Why would we do this?" asked Eddie.

"Because we'll also give you funding and lab space to do your research. If your Dr. Early comes back, and he's in shape to help, he can join. If not, we'll assign some of our scientists to the project. You'll be a part of the LAPD. LAPD Zombie Operations Office."

"ZOO?" asked Zed, incredulous.

Brolin shrugged and grinned. "We had fun with it."

Everest broke out into a contagious belly laugh. Even Clipper joined. Sorya doubled over, and Perkins sank back into his chair, amused but relieved he'd avoided a fistfight in his office. Brolin grinned.

Eddie crossed his arms.

"We want quarters with cold rooms. We don't need food, but we need ample funding, suitable lab space, and we want to interview your scientists. The average lab monkey can't handle the research we need."

"They're experts in forensics."

"Not enough. We also need everyone to sign nondisclosure agreements, and they must be rock solid. We have serious rules about killing, and this is non-negotiable."

"We're the police. We have serious rules about killing too." He pointed at Eddie. "Also, we won't issue you sidearms."

Clipper rolled his eyes, but Brolin didn't see. Like he needed a gun to end someone.

Eddie let the statement pass. "Clipper needs the highest-level technology, no questions asked. When he asks for tech, he gets it. Period."

"Done," said Brolin.

"Where are you getting the money?" Eddie asked.

"Why does it matter?" Brolin asked.

"Because it does," said Everest.

"It's legal. We have discretionary funding. This is what we're using it for."

Everest grunted something, and Eddie nodded. "We'll want our accountant to review it."

"You have an accountant?"

"Yes."

Brolin sighed. "Fine. It's tax dollars at work."

Peter would get a look at the police coffers. Cool.

Eddie cocked his head. "Who do we report to?"

"Me," said Brolin, pointing to his chest. "Directly."

"We want Perkins when needed and Waylon as a consultant, too."

"Perkins, of course. What's a cosmetologist offer?"

"Nothing," I said as fast as possible. "Absolutely nothing."

"You'd be surprised," said Eddie, like I'd never spoken.

Perkins nodded in agreement.

"Hey! Standing here."

They ignored me.

"I think we can work something out, but we won't start immediately," said Eddie, leaning back, finally, resting his weight on a coat closet door.

"Why?" asked Brolin.

"We left our last position at The Industries," Eddie said, too casually, I thought. I wondered what he was hiding.

"So? People leave companies all the time."

"The team needs some R&R."

"Okay, I understand. Perkins needs to take some time too. Take your holidays and get in touch with me as soon as you return." Brolin shook hands with each member of the team, nodded at me and Sorya, and left.

"What did you guys do?" I asked.

"Nothing, really," said Eddie.

"Everest?" The man couldn't lie.

"The Industries might have a small computer virus problem, is all."

"Clipper?" I asked the tech wizard.

He gave me one long, slow blink.

Everest answered. "They should have known better than to connect the computer he returned to them without scanning it first. They plugged it into the main server."

"Lying low might be a good idea," said Eddie.

"I'm being forced to take some of my vacation," Perkins muttered. "I've got three months backed up."

"They're forcing me to stay away from work, too!" Sorya grumbled. "Stupid kidnapping rules."

"Well…" I said.

"What?" said Sorya.

"How do you guys feel about Florida?"

POSE & CONS

1

The flamingos attacked in standard "V" formation.

As soon as our zombie feet hit the sidewalk, the birds rounded the corner of our Orlando hotel, their spaghetti necks stretched tautly. Sharp, lethal beaks readied to pierce flesh as their war cry filled the air.

"What the hell is this, Waylon?" yelled Everest, the largest of our team, currently dressed for the climate in a hot pink tank top paired with board shorts, straw hat, and flip-flops. The others were similarly dressed, although they wore sneakers.

"Run!" I commanded.

Everest, Eddie, Clipper, Zed, and I—all the zombies present—took off. Everest lost his flip-flops in two steps and ran barefoot. The reigning Miss Mango, Amalia Flores stayed behind with Sorya Sang, MD, and Captain Jacob Perkins. A ghost did, too, but no one could see her.

"Enemy left! Enemy left!" Eddie announced, and sure enough, another hit squad of pink bombers flanked us from the man-made pond across the street.

"Can these fuckers fly?" Clipper asked as we sprinted, parting humans in front of us like Moses parted the Red Sea, an entire battalion of shrimp-eaters in pursuit.

"A team broke off and is circling us on the right," reported Zed, who smiled. I think he liked the action. He'd been hanging disembodied around a Central American jungle for a while so being chased by zombie-sensing flamingos was a nice change of pace.

"In here!" I yelled, pointing to a marina entrance on our right. We veered and made it through the rotating doors just in time. One flamingo tried to follow but got caught between spins, and even we had to look away. Women and men alike cringed. Children cried.

The flamingos peered into the entrance as one, yellow eyes and black-tipped beaks bared, creeping everyone out.

"I've never seen this behavior before," said the marina manager. Her nametag said, 'Sue.'

"Sue," I said. "These birds can eat poisonous blue-green algae. Flamingos are some of the toughest birds in the world. Never," I said, pointing at the flock. "Never underestimate them."

She took two steps away from me and muttered, "I'll keep that in mind, but now I have to call Fish and Wildlife and close the rotating door. Look at that mess. Ewww."

The wildlife authorities rounded up the birds, which snaked their heads around the keepers' legs to hiss at our backs as we returned to our hotel.

"I didn't believe you, Waylon," said Eddie, "but the proof is right there." We traversed the sidewalk, passing tourist shops selling shell necklaces, an ornate water fountain, spas, a sandwich shop, and a number of eateries boasting fish specials.

"I warned you," I said. "Flamingoes have zombie radar. They're the cadaver dogs of the bird world, except more vicious."

"How did you discover this?" asked Everest, picking up his discarded flip-flops in one smooth, ultra-cool dip of his arm. We'd arrived back at our hotel, where we'd started.

I grimaced. "The hard way."

"One day, I want to hear that story."

"One day is not today."

"Where did you guys go? What happened?" Amalia asked. Our resident beauty queen flipped her long dark hair and turned her big brown eyes, superweapons of truth, on us. The simple toss of her mane caused one poor man in his mid-twenties to plow into another man of the same age, and the two dropped to the sidewalk like coconuts from a tree. We were used to it and ignored them.

After all our little group had seen, attack flamingos and addled men didn't faze us.

"Flamingos," said Eddie, like this explanation made complete sense. "Let's go inside." He ushered Amalia in before her tiny shorts and tank top caused another accident. Captain Jacob Perkins, the local Calabasas, California police captain, followed last. He scowled, despite the beautiful scenery and the promise of a wonderful vacation visiting Disney World. He didn't enjoy being off the job, but his commander had forced him to take some time. Sorya Sang, our medical examiner and my girlfriend, had also been ordered to take a vacation. We'd all wound up down here in the Sunshine State because my personal assistant, Mrs. Betsy Ross, wanted to see her old friend George Washington in the Hall of Presidents.

The Great Orlandian Hotel boasted the largest lobby of all the Disney properties. Rembrandts graced the east and west walls, and a grand piano sat positioned direct center. The entire room could have swallowed most ballrooms, and the stunning octagonal glass ceiling and apricot marble flooring radiated the grandeur of a Versailles palace.

"Peter is checking us in, but look at this, Waylon." Amalia pointed to an easel in front of the registration desk. "It's the big Disney float parade this week! I didn't know. That's so exciting." She clapped her hands and bounced on her toes like a five-year-old. "They do a float parade around the entire Magic Kingdom, enacting classic scenes from their movies. They only do it once every five years, and we'll be here to see it! Isn't that amazing?"

I wrapped an arm around Sorya. "Sure. I guess that's why it's so crowded this weekend."

Perkins elbowed me in my other side. "And why the hotels are so expensive? I mean, they're always pricey, but this is outrageous."

"Oh, get over it. You've got the money. Plus, didn't the department give you a vacation bonus or something?"

He huffed. "It was a 'get the hell out of our hair' bribe."

I nodded. "Same thing. So, relax and enjoy."

"How can I enjoy it when—" Perkins got cut off when a herd of people rushed the front doors and staff had to intervene, herding them to the side. Security entered from the street and cordoned off the area.

One security officer swept by us, holding a radio to his mouth. "Why didn't she enter from the back?" he asked. I didn't hear the answer.

I strained my neck to see who he was talking about and about died (again) when my old friend Mitzi waltzed in the door, a Fendi bag swinging from one arm.

"Uh, Amalia?"

"Yes?"

"Does that poster say something about Mitzi?"

"No."

Sorya provided the information. "*It* doesn't, but the notice *above it* says Mitzi is this year's Parade Queen."

"Waylon! Waylon, is that you?"

"Mitzi, darling! I just saw the sign. You're the Parade Queen?"

Several burly men surrounded us in a menacing circle, but Mitzi disregarded them, hugged me, and kissed my cheek. "Oh my gosh, the gang's all here! Hello, Michael," she said, greeting Everest. "And Amalia! Wow. This is so wonderful. A vacation with friends, not just work. We'll hang out by the pool together."

"We'd love that," Everest said, kissing Mitzi's hand.

"Only with sunscreen, my love." I wagged my finger at her. "Luckily, I brought some of my special mixture."

She pressed her hands together in a prayer position. "Thank goodness you are here, Waylon. You are heaven-sent. Will you do my makeup before the parade? I was so worried about it with the heat, but now that you're here, I don't have to be concerned."

"Of course, and don't forget a hat. I'll shop for one for you if you don't have a suitable one."

She pouted, lower lip out, eyelashes fluttering. "But if I wear a hat, people won't be able to see my face."

"We'll have to discuss this with the parade organizers then. Perhaps a parasol. Must protect your skin."

"Oh, Waylon, thank you!" She threw her arms around my neck in another hug. I smiled and hugged her back. How could you not?

Mitzi pointed with one manicured finger to her security staff. "This man is a friend, as are these people. They are to have complete access to me, understand?"

The neckless men nodded, and I hoped they remembered. I could survive broken parts, but where would we find a fresh cadaver to replace missing ones? One grunted at me, and I shook my head. It might be hopeless. I didn't think these guys could count to ten. For now, they stepped back so they could keep an eye on their charge but far enough that they couldn't hear what we were saying.

Peter rejoined us. "We're all set. Why, hello, Mitzi."

Mitzi glanced at him. "Have we met?"

"On the cruise ship, with Michael and Waylon."

"Oh, I don't recall." She sniffed and turned from Peter to Everest. Peter glowered. Zed studied the ground and coughed. Everest, however, practically glowed with happiness. Eddie, standing behind him, smirked for a millisecond. I'd given up keeping track of Clipper.

"I'm here," said a voice in my ear.

I jumped with my hand to my heart, a total artifact of my past condition being alive, and jolted around to see Clipper with a huge smile, the first I'd ever seen on the guy. He'd surprised me and loved it, and my ire rose in a pounding rush. Before I could contemplate my actions, I pulled my fist back and hammered him in the mouth, hard enough to snap his head back, and I followed through with an uppercut to his jaw that popped his neck up with a crack. It felt great.

Our group went silent. I tilted my head, hands upraised, daring him to come at me.

Mitzi's security rushed forward and inserted himself between Mitzi and us.

Clipper stared at me for a moment, rubbing his jaw, held out his right hand, and said, "I deserved that. Nicely done."

We shook and turned back to the group.

Eddie, Everest, Zed, and Peter gave us each a nod. Perkins shrugged. Mitzi, Sorya, and Amalia crossed their arms in utter disgust.

Amalia spoke first. "Are you guys going to whip them out and measure them? Would that settle things?"

I'd win hands down. My penis had won acclaim, awards even, at least when it had been attached to its former porn star owner.

Mitzi fumed. "I fail to see what is so funny. Waylon, that was an unconscionable loss of control. If you lost the use of your hand, how would you apply my makeup for the parade?"

I sobered up. "You are right, dear heart. I wasn't thinking, but rest assured, my hand is fine. I didn't hit him that hard. Look, his mouth isn't even bleeding."

"It's true, Mitzi," said Clipper, moving forward to look her in the eye, all business. The security goons almost didn't let him, but Mitzi nodded her assent. Clipper swiveled his head so she could inspect both cheeks. "Waylon and I were practically play-fighting. I'm fine. Not even a bruise."

My star client leaned in, studying Clipper's face, and saw what anyone would see on a zombie—nothing. "It sounded so awful. I heard a pop and thought you'd fractured something, but you're okay, and there's no mark.

It's like nothing happened." She nudged him on the shoulder. "Are you sure you've got blood running through those veins?"

Clipper bowed over her hand and kissed the back of it. "I'm sorry we worried you."

She waggled a finger at us, then beckoned her guards. "Come on, boys," she said to her security squad. "Let's get out of here. Waylon, Amalia, we'll see you later. Toodles." She did a little finger-wave and whooshed away in a light cloud of Chanel No. 5. I approved. A classic.

"That was exciting," said Peter. "We've got the whole band back together. Now, let's get the rooms sorted. I've got the keys here." He handed them out. Zed, Eddie, Everest, and Clipper bunked together. Peter buddied up with Perkins. as did Amalia and Sorya. I got one for myself, which I loved because I could turn the air conditioning to freezing and rest well at night. The colder, the better.

For the millionth time, I wondered where Dr. Samuel Early was. After turning me into a zombie during the Civil War, Doc Early became my closest friend, or at least my confidant, and had eaten a bit of my flesh every month for years to slow down his aging process. He did it to live long enough to find a way to kill me for good once we discovered zombies couldn't die. We'd tried it all. I'd even jumped into a volcano once.

Total vaporization, but luckily, we'd discussed how to test if I'd really passed on. If I'd truly "left," we assumed I wouldn't be hunting for a corporeal form.

I didn't truly die, so I hung around waiting for Early to get his act together and make with the magic and snap, crackle, pop; as soon as he summoned me and provided a body, I was on two feet. We went along like this for decades. Testing, failing, and finally, he turned to scientific research to see if he could solve the problem of zombie true death. Recently, after he was mortally wounded and in a moment of debatable judgment, I'd turned Early into a zombie, using his ritual.

Oddly, we'd never talked about whether he'd want to become a zombie, and I'd made an on-the-spot decision. It took some soul-searching afterward, but he'd made peace with it, and he seemed okay.

Until a bad magic user, an actual witch doctor, came back a few weeks ago, killed a bunch of people, messed with Early's mind, and made the good doctor do evil things. Until I'd dropped a treehouse on the witch, that is. With the witch dead, Early came to his senses, realized everything he'd done while under the witch doctor's control, and ran away. We hadn't heard from him since.

Eddie pounded my back twice. "Stop thinking about Early."

"I wasn't," I said, my voice tinged with sadness.

"Yes, you were. You've got that look. Early will come back when he's good and ready."

"You think? I left a note on the kitchen table telling him we're here in Orlando, you know, just in case he comes home and we're not there. I don't want him to think we abandoned him."

Eddie chucked my shoulder. "He'll appreciate that. Don't worry, Waylon. Every bird comes home to roost, eventually. Zed did. Early will too."

"We had to go get Zed."

"But then he did a walkabout, remember? And when he was ready, he came back. Early will make his peace and return."

Damn, I hoped so.

A security guard behind me cursed, and I turned to see him talking rapidly into his wrist. I followed his gaze to see what caused such alarm.

A busty blonde on sky-high red heels tottered into view wearing a tight white skirt and a red and pink polka-dotted crop top. She jangled a couple of bangle bracelets while carrying an oversized bag. A bellboy rolled an overburdened luggage rack with a squeaky wheel behind her.

"Isn't that . . .?" asked Amalia.

"Yup," I said.

"Do you think Mitzi knows?"

"Absolutely not."

Sonya sidled next to me. "She's gonna have a cow."

I flicked my eyes to her. "I'm not going to be the one to tell her."

Amalia elbowed my ribs. "There's no way she isn't going to find out."

"Is that Joy Lucky?" asked Everest in his big, booming voice.

"Shhhh!" Amalia, Sonya, and I said at the same time.

Everest hunched down, which was as effective as a sasquatch hiding in the grass. He whispered. "Is that Joy Lucky?"

I huffed a big breath. "Yes, Everest."

"Isn't she the one who bad mouths Mitzi? Got in her way with the playground?"

"The very one, big guy."

Everest's face fell. He looked like someone kicked his puppy. "Mitzi is going to be sad."

"Let's get out of here before Joy sees us," I said, slloooowly turning so as not to draw attention. Movement attracts a predator's eyes.

"Waylon Jenkins! Is that you?"

"Aw crap."

Peter, Everest, and the zombie gang shoved their card keys in their pockets and left, sneaking off like thieves. Amalia and Sorya suddenly became engaged in an urgent conversation and scuttled away. Cowards. I faced Joy Lucky by myself.

"Hi, Joy."

"What a co-inky-dink seeing you down here," she said, all air kisses and cinnamon breath, although I smelled vodka when she got closer, not that I was judging. I wished I could drink.

"What are you doing here, Joy?"

"Why the same thing you are, I would think! Taking part in the float parade! Had to be a part of the biggest Disney event of the year."

"Especially because Mitzi is the hostess?"

"Is she?" Joy's eyelashes fluttered. Cheapies. The corners popped up and she kept rubbing them. Sticky glue and a thick, heavy, non-transparent lash line are not a good look. It was a shame because she had beautiful eyes.

"You know she is. You follow her everywhere."

"She's the best. I want to be the best. How else will I learn?"

Ugh. My stomach clenched as I chastised myself. Maybe I'd been too harsh on her. I couldn't blame her for wanting to be like Mitzi. Everyone wanted to be like the one-name-only star. I vowed to start over.

I moved in a little closer. "Joy, let me help you with those lashes. I've got some extra wispies in my kit."

Her eyes widened, and she pumped a fist, her giant bag banging into her leg. "Would you? That would be great. These are terrible."

"Where's your room?"

"Main building, club level, of course. My suite faces the park. Oh, this is just great. Thank you, Waylon!"

I signaled to Sorya and Amalia that I'd be back, and they both frowned at me, but I waved to show it was okay. I promised to be the better person, ah, zombie. The bigger human. I grabbed my roller bag, shouldered my backpack, and followed Joy through the lobby to the elevators. Amalia caught up with me and grabbed me by the elbow.

"What are you doing cavorting with Mitzi's sworn enemy?" She practically hissed.

"I think I've misjudged Joy. She's following Mitzi because she sees Mitzi as a role model. Every actress in Hollywood wants to be like Mitzi. How can I blame her?"

"Don't fall for her innocent act now."

I released the roller bag and rubbed the back of my neck. "Maybe she's not as bad as we've assumed."

"She's a cat with her claws out. Be careful." Amalia shook her finger at me, and I could almost envision her in ten years with kids. "You know what my mom used to say."

I smiled. "No, I don't. I never met your mother."

"It's all fun and games until someone loses an eye."

I jumped back. "No one is losing an eye!"

"It's a *metaphor*. It means it all seems innocent until someone really gets hurt, and this someone will be Mitzi."

"I'm going to help mend fences, Amalia. Set things right."

"You keep telling yourself that."

"Waylon, are you coming?" Joy Lucky called to me from the elevators, where she waited with an empty elevator, her foot in the door to claim it. People tried to get past her, and she shooed them away. An impatient security guard looked like he was about to confront her, schooling his face into a friendly mask as he took a step toward her.

I motioned to him that I got it, extended the handle on my roller bag, hurried up, and hoped I wasn't making a huge mistake.

2

The bellhop followed with Joy's groaning cart. As soon as he left, I put my bags down and took a look around. Joy's room was fancy-schmancy with a lock she programmed to her fingerprint. She read the instructions on how to do it in front of me, completed the task with a huge grin, and let me in. I bet all the suites had such cool technology.

As soon as we were alone, I knew I'd made a grievous miscalculation.

Before I blinked, she wrapped her arms around my neck and snuggled her head into my chest. She lifted her mouth to my neck and planted tiny kisses along the length of it, right down to my collar bone.

I got a full-body chill. If my loins had been working, they'd have shriveled up. My loyalty to Mitzi and Sorya made this nauseating.

"I think there's been a misunderstanding," I said as she buffed her ample bosom on my chest.

"Oh, no, there hasn't," she said, her voice breathy in a sexy way. "I want to give you Joy." She giggled and winked at me, pawing at my shirt.

Hell to the ick, no.

I gently took her wrists, one in each hand, pushed her away, and stepped back at the same time. "Joy, that's not my intention here at all. I'm here to help you with your lashes. You have stunning blue eyes. You need lashes to highlight them, and the ones you're wearing aren't doing you any favors. I can teach you how to put them on correctly and give you a nice pair you can wear again and again."

She fell backward on the chaise lounge, a lovely mint green number that accented the décor in the suite. In the manner of an old black and white movie goddess, she threw the back of her hand to her forehead and with all the drama she could muster, yelled, "I can't believe you shoved me, Waylon! You have a reputation for being such a gentleman! Get out! Out! Before I call security. Look what you've done. You've bruised my wrists."

Oh, my gods.

"You came on to me, Joy, and you know it. I tried to help you. Don't pretend something happened that didn't." I opened the door, held it with my foot, and spun my roller bag out into the hallway, my backpack on one shoulder. Joy fake cried in the background, and I didn't have time for it. I'd been stupid.

"What are you doing, Waylon?"

My most famous client stood in the hallway, looking lovely even in the poor fluorescent lighting. She held a hand delicately to her mouth, her security trailing behind her. She dropped her designer purse to the floor in surprise at seeing me.

"Mitzi?"

"Yes. I have a Victorian suite here. I love the Magic Kingdom view. Who's crying in there?" She peeked around me and stiffened. "Joy Lucky!"

"It's not what you think, Mitzi. I tried to help her with her lashes, and now she's making a big deal out of nothing. I didn't touch her."

"Of course, you didn't. We all know you're gay. You hear that, you stupid cow! Your big boobs mean nothing to him! But, Waylon? How could you help her after all she's done to me?" She faced me, unshed tears in her eyes. I let go of my roller bag to hug her, but she backed away as Joy's door closed.

"I didn't know she'd be here until I ran into her in the lobby. She told me she follows you because she admires you. I thought if I talked to her, we could make peace. I thought maybe I'd misjudged her."

Mitzi sniffed. "Well, Waylon. Maybe I've misjudged you."

I slumped in relief. "Yes, thank you for understanding."

"I understand everything. I thought I could trust you. Perhaps that's where I judged wrong." She flicked a spot of lint off her shoulder and pivoted away.

"Come on! I'm in your corner, always." I called to her, but she was already walking away, and one of her security guys gave me the finger.

Great. I'd been in Orlando for an hour and already screwed up. It didn't help when Joy opened her door, flashed me an evil, self-satisfied grin, and then closed it in my face again.

I stomped to my room, unlocked it with a regular old key card—no fingerprint for me—and unpacked. I threw my shoes against the wall in frustration.

After the initial satisfying *thunk*, I hurried to them, murmured apologies, and immediately lined all my footwear in the closet in color-coded order.

I hung my nice shirts and slacks in the closet, placed my folded undies in the dresser's top drawer, and my T-shirts in the second drawer. Socks went in the third drawer and bathing suits in the bottom. By the time I finished, I had a measure of control. I cranked the AC and hibernated.

After half an hour, I felt ready to face people again. Amalia left a message on my phone saying she and Sorya were at the pool. The hotel had several, but I assumed she meant the main pool in the rear, near the beach.

This pool put every other pool I'd ever seen to shame. A mammoth one-hundred-and-eighty-foot slide at one end plus a small one for littler folk, the calm swimming area stretched forever along a serene, waterfall-like setting with natural rock and zero-depth entry. I walked the length, observing the many sunbathers and running children, and wondered how I would find them. As I passed, I caught snatches of conversation. I let them float by until I heard one that caught my ear coming from a cabana.

"It's all a matter of talent, you see. I'm not usually this mean-spirited, but why is she here? Wasn't it enough that she ruined my plans for the playground? I don't understand."

Ah. Mitzi. I couldn't see her around the cabana wall, though, and she couldn't see me.

A different voice said, "I know, but Waylon meant well. You know how he is. No one has a softer heart. He thought he could steer her in a better direction."

Amalia.

"He adores you, Mitzi. You have to know that."

That was Sorya.

"They're still working on launching Reborn Cosmetics, and when they do, Waylon has mentioned to me that he wants you to be 'The Face' of the company."

Perkins and I'd indeed told him that.

"Oh, Jacob! That's wonderful! I can't imagine anything more exciting than being part of a company launch, and for a product like Waylon's Rescue Remedy? Fabulous! Do you know if they are going to call it that? It's the perfect name."

"Yes," said Perkins. "You named it, Mitzi, and it's splendid."

"I'll give Waylon the name of my agent, and we'll work out a contract."

I grinned. When it came to money, Mitzi was all business.

I moseyed around the corner. "Hey, guys, glad I found you."

"Oh, Waylon, I'm so sorry. I judged you too harshly," said Mitzi. She stood to give me a kiss on the cheek, and I bent to accept it. "It was silly of me to get so upset. I swear that woman's only job is to ruffle my feathers. I don't know why I let her."

"We'll just let her be for now, won't we?" I asked. "Let's enjoy the beautiful weather and relax."

Mitzi took her seat, reclining on one lounge chair, stretched out in all her glory, her long, gorgeous legs on display. Amalia and Sorya shared a double-wide rattan chair, Everest stretched out on a recliner, and Perkins took the last chaise lounge, smiling up at me as he put his hat over his eyes. The luxury red and tan cabana covered the entire area, providing enough shade for everyone although not enough seating. With a sigh, I snagged a long pool float in Nassau blue and stretched out on it.

"Where are the others, Jacob?" I used Perkins's first name because Mitzi had used it.

He scowled at me. She could use his first name, but I couldn't. "Alligator farm nearby," he replied. "They wanted to see it."

"Seriously?" Sorya asked. "They came all the way here, and the first thing they want to see is an alligator farm?"

"Boys will be boys," said Amalia with a flick of her manicured fingers, and Mitzi reached out a fist for a bump, which they blew up.

"Geez, ladies, how disparaging," I said.

"Just speaking truth, Waylon," said Amalia.

Sorya made a little "Amen" sound.

With a wink, I reverted to his last name. "Why didn't you go, Perkins?"

"I would rather stay with you lovely ladies," he said.

"I asked the nice *Captain* to stay with us so my security squad could take a break," said Mitzi, reaching one graceful arm out to pat his hand. "It's nice to have a real lawman around."

Perkins lifted his hat and nodded at her, serious. "I should tell you,

Mitzi, I have no official authority here, but you aren't in danger. The resort is used to having celebrities and placed extra security around this area for you. They know how to deal with paparazzi and stalkers."

"I feel safe around you, Jacob."

I would have barfed if I could have. All the cooing and flirting made me sick, or, if I was being honest, made me jealous. I didn't want to look at it too closely. Truthfully, Perkins was the best bodyguard she could have. Dog loyal and tenacious as a bear with a honey jar, he'd never let anyone lay a finger on her.

"Perkins," I said, clearing my throat, "Can I chat with you a minute?"

He stared past me for a second and said, "Sure. I could use a short walk." He stood, all cop, all the time, immediately proven when a thin, tan Indian man tried to walk by on Everest's left and found himself stopped with a hand to his chest.

"No, you don't, sir," said Perkins, using his right hand to pluck a tiny camera out of the man's Hawaiian shirt top-left pocket. "Saw you a mile away, you dope."

Two of the resort's security guards moved in smoothly to back up the captain. Perkins was an L.A. police officer. He could smell paparazzi a mile away.

"Meh!" said the little guy. He stomped his foot and lost a sandal. "I'm even a crappy pap. I just wanted a picture of Mitzi. I suck at everything."

"Oh, come on. I bet you don't suck at everything," said Perkins, which surprised me. He's usually the kind of guy to agree with that type of statement. The sunshine must have been getting to him, shining a light on the deep sarcasm in his soul.

The guy's mustache twitched, and he ran a hand through his stringy dark thinning hair. He retrieved his missing sandal and kneeled to put it back on. "No, I do. My wife divorced me and took my kid. I got kicked out of my apartment, and my cat ran away. Now I sleep on a friend's sofa listening to his daughter's guinea pig squeal all night."

"What did you do before taking photographs of celebrities?"

"I was a newspaper photographer, and I didn't suck at that; in fact, I was good at it, but all the papers centralized, and no one needs photojournalists anymore."

"Give me your card. You gotta card?" asked Perkins.

The Indian guy nodded and produced a moist, crinkled card from his back pocket.

Perkins read it. "Stanley Argawal. Photojournalist. Specialist in Indian wedding photography. Wait? Indian weddings?"

"It's aspirational. I hope to get into the biz," said Stanley, a gleam in his eye. "Good money there."

The security guard took firm hold of Stanley's elbow. "Time to go, sir."

"Maybe you'll let me get a photo?" Stanley called over his shoulder as they led him away. "Help a guy out?"

"Can't promise, Stanley, but we'll see," Perkins called back. As Mitzi walked off to take a dip in the pool's cool water, Perkins poked my float with his foot. "Is Indian wedding photography a specialty?"

"Oh, yes. Indian weddings are extravaganzas. Gorgeous! Magnificent colors and they happen over multiple days. I once did the makeup for a wedding party, and I—"

"Never mind."

"You don't want to know? Why did you ask then?"

"I do want to know, but luck is not on our side. Look." He jerked his chin toward a side door from the hotel to the pool area.

I followed his gaze and breathed out a sigh of annoyance. "Aw, crap. You mean luck is literally against us."

The bane of my existence sashayed across the pool deck from a door near a drink stand, opposite where I'd entered. She carried a large multicolored beach bag and a towel. She wore a bathing suit and a sarong. She spotted us easily. It took mere minutes for her to arrive at our cabana. As superb as Perkins was at stopping small Indian photographers, he sucked at stopping angry B-list actresses. She wagged a finger at Perkins and me. "You drove off the one paparazzo that got through the security. Figures. The one chance to get a proper photo taken, and you had to go and ruin it."

I looked up at her, still angry about our last interaction. "Joy, go somewhere else. There's miles of beach and pool here. Find another place to haunt."

Joy shook out her towel and draped it over her shoulder. "I have a right to be here."

"Why here? Why not some other hotel? City? State? Planet?" I asked, wishing I had sunglasses so I didn't have to look at her. Her Cheshire-cat grin grew wider by the second. She leaned down to speak directly to me.

"Because I know something you don't know."

"What? You're not left-handed?"

She shook her head. "You never learned to toe the line. That's your downfall."

"That doesn't make sense. You're spouting nonsense."

"Forget it. I'm going to have a word with the queen bee." Joy Lucky marched past us, her beach towel fluttering in her wake.

Mitzi saw her coming and stood, eyes blazing, hands on her hips, and ready.

I could practically hear the theme song to *The Good, the Bad, and The Ugly*.

Mitzi wore a classy, backless black halter one-piece suit and a brilliant aquamarine skirt. Joy wore a fuchsia bikini with a layered crisscross over the breast area and a high hip bottom peeking out beneath the flaming apricot skirt. Fire and ice were ready to rumble on the pool deck.

I stood and hurried over to stop whatever was going to happen, but Everest pulled me back with a firm yank. "You don't want to be in the middle of this. No way, no how this is going to go well."

"I'm already in the middle," I grumbled, but Perkins nodded his agreement with Everest, so the three of us stood back to observe.

"What is it with you?" Mitzi asked Joy. "Showing up at every event I attend, shadowing me? Weaseling your way into the Pee-Wees & Playgrounds marketing campaign? You even stalked me at Chibo's Vegan Eatery when I had a lunch meeting!"

"Chibo's is supposed to be very good," Perkins whispered.

"I didn't stalk you." Joy snapped. "I happened to be there and overheard your conversation. You're totally wrong for the part." Joy checked her nails. "I eat at Chibo's, too, you know. Their 'Vegan Steak Sandwich with Happy Pear Salsa' is divine."

"Ewww," I said.

"I'm supposed to believe you were there by coincidence?" Mitzi asked, fuming.

"Believe what you want."

Mitzi stepped forward. "Why didn't you get your disgusting lunch and move on then? Why interfere with my meeting? Why shove your double D's in his face and tell him how you were right to play Jenny?"

Joy stepped closer too. "Because I saw who you were meeting with and took my shot, you bitch! That's what *young, talented* actresses do."

"Did she say young?" I asked Perkins.

"Uh-huh, she sure did."

"Oh, snap."

"What is your damage?" Mitzi yelled.

A crowd had gathered, mobile phones out. No way to hide this fight. Suddenly I felt sorry for Stanley. He should have been able to get a picture since everyone else was getting one for free.

"Why are you so high and mighty?" screeched Joy in return, and she reached out and grabbed at Mitzi's sarong. Instead of slipping off, it ripped.

Mitzi made a fatal error.

She went for the hair.

She shoved one hand into Joy's sprayed blond mane and tugged, pulling Joy toward her and to the ground. Joy shrieked in pain and struck out with her fists, managing to grasp a halter strap and yank it off so Mitzi was now topless. Mitzi struggled to get her hand free from Joy's shellacked hair while holding her top up with her other hand.

I, having had enough, darted over to get in between them as the crowd chanted, "Girl fight! Girl fight!"

Mitzi relinquished her hold on Joy's hair after one last yank, and Joy scrambled to her feet.

I slid between them, one hand out on each side, palms forward. "Ladies, enough!"

And got slapped in the face—KPOW!—by Mitzi and on the back of my neck—KBLAM!—by Joy, as the two women tried to get to each other. I crumpled like a tissue.

Perkins pulled Joy away as security finally arrived, and Amalia and Sorya wrangled Mitzi back to the cabana. I stumbled away to a margarita mix machine, and the nice man handed me two bags of ice, which I didn't need for bruising but felt nice all the same as I held them to both sides of my head.

"Waylon?"

"Yeah?"

Perkins approached, putting Stanley's camera away. "I took a pic of the fight for Stanley since everyone else got one for free anyway."

"I thought you hate paparazzi."

"I do, but Stanley seemed down on his luck, and since everyone else got one, it wasn't fair that he didn't."

I stared at him. "Florida's changed you." I called to Sorya. "Florida's broken Captain Perkins. He's acting weird."

She laughed and settled down in her chair with a book, unperturbed by the actresses' scuffle.

No one took me seriously.

3

Mitzi needed a spa day after the kerfluffle with Joy, which I supported a hundred percent. I overhead a hotel team member saying a higher-up authorized the full works, so I expected Mitzi to be pampered up to her eyeballs. I didn't know what was happening with Joy, and I didn't care as long as she wasn't in my way.

Perkins, Peter, Sorya, and Amalia wanted cocktails, not food, and seemed happy to subsist on olives and cherries. Sorya joined us with a margarita, and Amalia slipped in beside her with a Tequila Sunrise. Peter and Perkins ambled up with draft beers a second later. Zed, Eddie, and Clipper joined us when they returned from the alligator farm.

The returning zombie team hung on every word as Perkins regaled them with a reprise of the altercation between the two ladies. Everest and I interjected here and there to ensure he got the details right. When we finished, it was my turn to ask questions.

"Why are you guys so beat up?"

"What do you mean?" Eddie asked, too nonchalantly.

"You look like you've taken a dip in the swamp," Amalia said.

"We can neither confirm nor deny anything like that happened," Eddie said.

"So?" said Sorya, sipping her drink. "What happened? You smell terrible."

Sighing, Eddie tried to explain. "We wanted to see alligators."

Sorya rolled her index finger in a 'keep going' motion.

Zed interrupted. "The show was cool, but the alligators didn't do much, you know? It's hot. And they just wanted to be left alone."

I put my head in my hands. "What did you do?"

"It was boring, mate, not like the crocs back home." Zed the Australian proffered his hands in supplication.

I didn't know what I was supposed to understand, but I was certain I wouldn't like it.

"I may have," Zed continued, "when the staff and guards weren't looking, jumped in with them, just to wrassle a bit."

Finally, Clipper said something. "Because you are as stupid as they come."

"I have to pretend I don't know you. I should leave now," Perkins said. "You broke a hundred different laws."

Zed punched Clipper's shoulder, and Clipper punched him back until Eddie issued a sharp command, "Stop!"

The two men ceased their childish behavior instantaneously. Commands from a superior officer still resonated with the zombies.

Eddie drew in a controlled breath. "Zed made the mistake of getting in the show arena with the alligators, which forced us to overpower the guards."

"Which we did easily," Zed said, only a touch defensively.

"Of course, we did, numbnuts, but that isn't the point," said Clipper.

Eddie pinched the bridge of his nose. "We had to jump a fence, an electrocuted fence no less, got caught on camera and waded through the swamp to get back. We've been here a day. A DAY, and we're Florida's most wanted."

"I had to hack into their systems and wipe their camera files," said Clipper.

Eddie wiped his fingers down the corners of his mouth. "We've lost military discipline, something I am going to rectify as soon as possible. The Los Angeles police force expects professionalism. Zed, Clipper, Everest, tomorrow at 0500, meet me at the pool entrance. We're going from there to the beach for drills."

"But, we don't have to exercise—" Zed started.

Eddie shut him down with a look. "It's about discipline, something you need more of if you are going to function within this team."

That shut Zed up. He had nowhere else to go and knew it. He'd been on walkabout already and returned to his team because being alone sucked. He sat up straight and clasped his hands in front of him, cowed. He met his commander's eyes and whipped out a sharp, "Yes, sir."

Eddie nodded his approval. "Peter, please join us. We need someone to time our sprints."

Peter just lifted his beer in acknowledgment.

That got me thinking.

"How did Peter get over the electric fence and through the swamp?" I asked. "He's not a zombie."

"We aren't talking about that," said Peter, fast.

"Oh, yes, we are." Amalia leaned back with a small smile, twirling the little umbrella that came with her drink.

"Well, Amalia," said Zed with a malicious grin, his embarrassment at having been chastised by Eddie quickly dissipating with his zeal to tell the tale, "it's not the thing you fling, but the fling itself."

"You tossed him?" Amalia exclaimed, now sitting straight up.

Peter leaned in. "Really, do we have to get into it?"

Amalia ignored him. "Tossed him? Like Gimli at Helm's Deep?"

"Just like." Zed's eyes gleamed. "Tossed him over the fence, and Clipper and Eddie caught him, then he rode on my back."

"This was supposed to be between us," said Peter.

Perkins rapped the table twice. "I can't believe I missed this."

"Remember who's timing you big boys tomorrow." Peter got up to get another beer.

"We need to move on," Sorya said. "Let's plan tomorrow, stick together, and do something fun. No alligators. No actresses, and no drama."

"I agree," said Amalia.

"I agree, too," said Mrs. Ross, who appeared out of nowhere, making everyone jump, including the bartender, who rubbed his eyes in disbelief. Yeah, that's right, buddy. You thought this was the most magical place on earth before? I'll meet your magic and raise you one actual walking and talking ghost. Take that to your "Imagineers."

Everest, like the giant child he could be, said, "I want to go on Space Mountain! You go through a wormhole."

Peter piped up, almost at the same time, "Pirates of the Caribbean has always been a fantasy of mine."

Amalia raised her hand. "Under the Sea!"

Sorya held her palm out in a 'stop' motion. "Those three things are literally at opposite ends of the park from each other. Here," she drew a map from her back pocket and unfolded it on the table. "Look."

While the group argued over where to head to first, Mrs. Ross whispered to me, "Waylon, you promised."

I dropped my voice so only she could hear. "I know, and we will. I keep my promises." I turned back to the larger group. "People, whatever else we do, we have to go to the Hall of Presidents."

The bartender approached our merry band. "Uh, hate to interrupt, but you're going to have to order more if you want to hold this table. We've got others waiting." He stared at Mrs. Ross. She put a little extra oomph into her appearance, touching my arm where I'd tucked the flag piece into my pocket, and solidified, indistinguishable from a real person. The bartender frowned nevertheless.

I gave him my credit card. "Three vodka martinis, please. Bleu cheese olives, Grey Goose. A large platter of nachos. Another margarita and another tequila sunrise, and a 'shroom burger with fries."

The bartender nodded, but slowly. I kind of up and down that said, 'I'm a second away from calling the police.'

"Don't worry, Adam? Is that your name?" I read his nametag. "I tip well. Promise."

Amalia smiled at him and placed a hand on his arm. "He does, really. He's my uncle, and this is my extended family. We're just a bunch of silly gooses, don't mind us. Can I walk to the bar with you, Adam?"

Adam's face lit up like the sun came out on a rainy day. Amalia walked to the bar with him, chatted him up, and our useless drinks and food arrived in record time. Our humans did the best they could to put a dent in it.

A young couple with twins sat at the table next to us. The twins tugged at their parents' clothes, jabbering on about Mickey and Donald. Just watching made me want to take a nap.

"Hi," I said to the parents.

The mom waved a weary finger wiggle. The dad sunk in his seat and closed his eyes.

"The bartender just delivered these two vodka martinis. We don't need any more alcohol, and the two of you look like you could use them," I said.

The dad lifted his head and opened one eye.

"Really, it's our pleasure." Sorya picked them up and handed them to the young parents, who continued to look at us askance. "I'm trying to get this bunch of yahoos to cut back, so you'd be doing me a favor." She smiled. "Trust me, I'm a doctor."

The parents might not be Dr. Who fans, but that joke made me all warm and tingly inside. This was why I loved her.

And that thought made me go cold and scared. Loving her hadn't been on the agenda, and I didn't know if I could do it for real. She deserved more than a zombie. She deserved a life with a man who could grow old with her, give her children if she wanted, or at least love her properly. Eat with her, sleep with her, kiss her, make love to her. Create a life. The best I could hope for was to make a half-life.

I pushed the thoughts and bad feelings away for the moment, but I'd have to come back to them.

The parents acquiesced and accepted the drinks with grateful smiles, convinced by Sorya, the ice-cold glasses, appetizing olives, and their complete and total exhaustion.

Kid One pointed to a sign. "Pancakes! Pancakes with ears. Pleeease, Mommy?" The breakfast favorite came in the shape of the mouse's head. Eleven dollars for two, with syrup.

Kid Two begged for a souvenir cup and chicken nuggets. The cup, by itself, cost ten dollars.

Not having children: priceless. It's not that I didn't like kids. It's just when I was born, kids that age would have been milking cows.

I brought my attention back to my table. The rest of the gang had ceased arguing about how we should spend our time and came up with a plan. We'd stay together, go up Main Street, head left to Liberty Square to see the Hall of Presidents, then continue to Adventureland. We'd do Space Mountain, the Speedway, and any other rides in that area the next day. We could do Fantasyland, too, or save it for the following day.

"This is a vacation," said Everest. "We need to relax. We're supposed to be getting some R&R."

Perkins glanced at his watch. "I'll be right back."

"Where's he going?" asked Eddie.

"Don't know." I had a sneaking suspicion a certain Indian photographer was getting his camera back. Mitzi would be mad Perkins helped him, but like Everest said, this was vacation. What happened in Florida, stayed in Florida. Besides, I had checked my phone, and pictures of Mitzi and Joy fighting on the pool deck had already made it onto the Internet. Perkins couldn't give Stanley anything that wasn't already out there. I put my phone on do not disturb, determined to focus on the people with me and not worry about what was going on back in Los Angeles. A new scandal happened every week there. Scratch that; every day.

We spent the rest of the evening chatting and laughing. Everest told us a story about how, during a training exercise, Clipper once snuck behind the 'enemy' team's tech defenses and programmed their phones to ring every hour. The commander collected them and shut them off, chastising his team for having phones on them at all, but Clipper 'woke' the phones and kept them ringing. Finally, their commander ordered the men to destroy their phones by running over them with a truck, really angering everyone. Once the equipment was in pieces, Clipper and Everest snuck behind enemy lines, planted new phones in their camp, and set them to ring at 0300.

By eleven o'clock, we'd finished our drinks and were all relaxed and happy. Everyone smiled and joked with one another. Amalia and Sorya shared a plate of mozzarella sticks, chatting about Amalia's classes. It was the nicest time I could remember.

I did a quick check to see what other photos of Mitzi had hit the gossip sites.

"Perkins!"

"What?" Perkins had been talking with Everest, and he spun around at the sound of my voice. The rest of our group turned to us, watchful.

"What is this?" I shoved my phone in his face. He studied it and bit the inside of his cheek.

"Well?" I demanded.

He contained a laugh. "I see Stanley made a deal fast."

"I thought you took pictures of Mitzi!"

"I would never do that to Mitzi." He put a hand to his heart.

"Let me see, Waylon," Amalia said. "Hey, look at you!"

Everyone collected around my phone and then pulled out their own devices to stare at the close-up image of me getting smacked on both sides of my head by Mitzi and Joy. My nose bent one way and my jaw the other as my eyes bugged out like a gecko. A montage of me sitting forlornly at the margarita machine holding ice packs to my head followed with random people gawking in the background. The caption read, "Hollywood Makeup Artist Waylon Jenkins Really 'Sees' Stars." The first line read, "Waylon Jenkins, celebrated cosmetologist and make-up artist to Hollywood's greatest actors, should know better than to get in between two women, but that didn't stop him from trying. Looks like he might need some of his own under-eye concealer to hide the bruises."

I didn't have the heart to read on. "Perkins, this is a *national* magazine."

"You may make the cover of the print edition," he replied, tipping his beer to finish the last swallow. "Congratulations. My work is done here. G'night all."

That's when I realized my phone showed thirty-five missed messages and seventy-eight emails.

"Good night," replied Amalia. She pecked me on the cheek and jogged away. The zombie team peeled off as well.

Sorya was the only one left. She kissed me on the lips. "It's not bad, Waylon. It's endearing, and it takes the heat off Mitzi."

"That's true." I listened to the first message, then the next. I had expected all of them to be requests for comment from the entertainment magazines and TV shows, and most of them were, but some requested appointments for new clients. Others came from current clients checking to make sure I was okay and teasing me a little. Maybe there really was no such thing as bad press.

4

Bam! Bam! Bam!

The pounding made my door rattle on its hinges.

"Waylon Jenkins! This is the police. We need to speak with you."

Police? Why were the police at my door?

I shook myself from my zombie rest and raised my voice so they could hear. "I'm coming." My first thought went to Amalia. "What's wrong? Is Amalia okay?" My second went to Sorya. "Oh, no. Is it Sorya?" I rushed to open the door.

"May we come in?" they asked.

"Of course. Why are you here?" I opened it wide, not knowing what else to do.

The two stern officers, both with stars on the upper left of their shirts, didn't answer my question but did enter my room. One was a handsome, brown-eyed, dark-skinned man with a neatly trimmed beard and mustache. The woman, light-skinned but I was betting on some Seminole in her background by her cheekbones, wore her hair in a painfully tight bun.

I wore jeans and a Goofy t-shirt I'd picked up in the gift shop yesterday. Not needing pajamas, I'd rested like that overnight, but the lack of awkwardness didn't stop me from going from calm to fretful at warp speed. As a zombie and a cosmetologist, fretful was practically my middle name in regular times. Now, after everything I'd been through, it was a miracle I didn't have a seizure with the police hammering my door first thing in the morning.

"What's going on?" I asked again, trying to keep my foot from tapping with anxiety.

"We'd like to ask you some questions, Mr. Jenkins. Hope you don't mind?" asked the male officer. His bald head gleamed in the sunlight from the windows.

I didn't have time to answer because the man continued speaking. Even if I had the chance, I wasn't sure I could have, anyway. My mind buzzed with static as I counted down from one hundred in sevens to get it under control.

"I'm Captain David Waters, Commander of Sector Six. I represent the Orange County Sheriff's office. You may want to sit down, Mr. Jenkins." He gestured toward a chair. I couldn't help but notice his carefully manicured nails, and I stared at them.

I didn't answer.

He raised his eyebrows at me and motioned to the chair a second time. "Please, the chair. This is Deputy Kim Jackman."

Deputy Jackman held a pen and paper, poised to take notes.

When I'd hit seventy-two on my countdown, I spoke. "Nice to meet you but, again, why are you here?" My voice trembled.

He pointed to the chair.

This time I took it, and he sat in one next to me. Deputy Jackman stayed standing.

"I take it you haven't gone downstairs yet this morning?"

"No." I glanced at the clock on the side table. "It's only seven a.m. What's this about? Did something bad happen?"

"You had an altercation with Mitzi and Joy Lucky yesterday?"

I'd lost count somewhere around fifty-eight, but the static had retreated. Unfortunately, a deep, sinking feeling replaced it. "I didn't have an altercation. I intervened when things between them got heated, but no real harm was done. I don't understand. Is Mitzi okay?"

"Why do you ask about Mitzi?"

Captain Waters raised an eyebrow. The deputy scribbled in her notebook.

"She's my client."

"Not Joy?" He studied me with deep, brown, penetrating eyes.

"No. Joy was never my client."

"Interesting," Deputy Jackman said, her first words since their arrival.

"Why? Lots of celebrities aren't my clients. There are a ton of make-up artists in Hollywood—I'm hardly the only one." I let out a breath I hadn't known I'd been holding.

Waters crossed his arms. "But you are the only one staying in this hotel this week."

"What does that have to do with the price of eggs?" I squirmed in my seat. "I'm not saying anything else until you tell me what's going on."

Captain Waters looked me straight in the eye and said, "I'm afraid I have some shocking news, Mr. Jenkins. Ms. Lucky was found dead in the pool this morning."

The deep, sinking feeling sunk lower. "That's not possible, sir. Ms. Lucky was alive and well yesterday. There must be some mistake." I rubbed my thighs and bobbed a knee going over the catfight in my head. How could this have happened?

"There is no mistake, Mr. Jenkins."

I gnawed a cuticle, rolling this news over in my mind, unsure what to say or how to act. I hadn't liked Joy, no, but I most certainly hadn't wanted her dead. Did she die accidentally? Die by suicide? No, that couldn't be right. She thought way too much of herself for that. "Did she fall in?"

"We don't know."

"Did she drown?"

Jackman raised an eyebrow. "You know a lot about drowning, Mr. Jenkins?"

"More than I would like. My girlfriend is a medical examiner in Calabasas, California. She's here with me, in fact, as is the local police captain, Jacob Perkins."

"You keep interesting company," she said.

"Does the resort have video cameras in that area? Who found her? What time?"

The deputy grimaced. "You ask a lot of questions for a cosmetologist."

"What can you tell me about these photos?" Captain Waters pulled out his phone to reveal the pictures of me in the middle of the Joy/Mitzi fight and the one with the ice packs.

"Mitzi and Joy had a little actress spat yesterday. I stepped in to stop it and paid for it with a whack to the noggin. I'm fine this morning, as you can see. It was nothing." Thank goodness zombies don't bruise.

"Bet it made you mad." He put his phone away. "Pictures sold to the rags. Pretty embarrassing."

I shrugged, the sinking feeling settling, frustration taking its place. I met his gaze for the first time. "No, not really. I got a couple of new clients out of it."

His eyes opened wide, and the deputy stopped scribbling to stare at me, eyes hard and cold.

Waters cocked his head. "You benefitted from it?"

"I wouldn't say that. I'm just doing my best to let the humiliation not get to me. Now, if you will excuse me, I need to call my friends and let them know what happened."

Deputy Jackman stepped closer to me, hand on her duty belt.

"I do not excuse you, Mr. Jenkins," said Captain Waters. "In fact, we're not done at all. You said your police captain friend is here as well as your medical examiner? We're meeting on the second floor in the Tallahassee meeting room. I've turned it into my new headquarters. You like coffee, Mr. Jenkins?"

"No, I don't drink it."

Waters opened his arms wide. "Well, I like it black and bitter, and they make a good brew here at this resort. Deputy Jackman will escort you downstairs while we collect Dr. Sang, Captain Perkins, and that lovely Miss Mango, Amalia Flores." He smiled at me. He knew a lot more than he'd been letting on. "You know, one of the things I'm most interested in is how Stanley Argawal got pictures of you *after* hotel security escorted him off the premises. Did you do that?"

I said nothing. I'd already accidentally raised their suspicions about me.

"As I said," Waters continued. "I have questions."

"I have plans today."

He shook his head in mock dismay. "I'm afraid you'll have to rearrange them. Murder is so inconvenient."

Great, I'd gotten a comedian. I stood to my full height and gestured to the door.

"I need to shower first," I said. Of course, I needed to do no such damned thing, but I wanted a few minutes to get it together. My insides squirmed like worms on the line, but I wasn't under arrest, so what did that mean? Who did they think murdered Joy if not me? Or was I the only suspect?

"I'll wait outside your door," said Deputy Jackman. "You have ten minutes."

"I require fifteen," I grumbled. "I have an intense moisturizing regimen."

She shook her head but didn't argue.

As soon as the door closed behind her, I grabbed my phone and headed into the bathroom. I texted Sorya first. Unfortunately, having thick thumbs made me a terrible texter.

Sorya, the poliixe ae hr re Mitzi.

I know Waylon. I don't understand how this could have happened!

R U ok? Amalia?

We are ok. You?

Yes. Mtttg dwonstirs. 2 floor

Meet you there. Love you.

Ok. Gud.

Next, I texted Eddie.

Eddde, Joy is ded.

I heard. Clipper protocol. Over and out.

I flushed the toilet because that's what the deputy would expect, then ran the hot water in the shower, jumping in to wash my hair, because why not? It felt good, and I liked the honeysuckle soap, and I needed a moment to breathe.

I let the hot water sluice down my back and exhaled a sigh of relief that the bad news wasn't about Amalia or Sorya. Selfish, I knew, but the fear faded as I repeated to myself, "They're okay. They're okay."

I assumed Clipper protocol meant they'd get back to me when Clipper dug up something helpful. My head settled into a semblance of calm again. Unhappy and stunned, but calm. I further gathered myself by moisturizing my face, neck, and arms, making sure my skin looked supple and as human as possible.

I dressed in a blue short-sleeved button-down shirt, khaki shorts, and sockless loafers. Then I texted Mitzi.

Are you ok? DnT worry, darlig.

She didn't answer. I wondered how they were treating her. If they thought I might have done it, they might consider her a prime suspect since she'd literally fought with Joy at the pool yesterday. Bad publicity did exist, after all. I shoved my phone and a few other essentials in my pocket and opened the door.

The deputy was swiping right and left on her phone but looked up when I entered the room.

"I'm ready, Deputy."

"About time," said Jackman. She pocketed her phone. Her beautiful skin glowed, highlighting those amazing cheekbones.

"What do you use on your face?" I asked. "It's lovely."

She flashed me an aggravated look as we walked down the hall to the elevator. "Would you ask that of Captain Waters?"

"Actually, his perfectly manicured hands caught my eye. I hope to ask him if he uses a particular cuticle cream, but men sometimes don't like to talk openly about grooming habits."

A small, inadvertent chuckle escaped before she clamped her lips together and regained her tight control. "Okay, fair enough. My grandmother swore by rosehip oil, so that's what I use, plus a sweetgrass lotion when my hands get chapped. I even use it on my lips."

The elevator arrived, and we stepped in. Deputy Jackman pushed the button for our floor.

As the door closed, I examined the back of my hands. "I've used rosehip oil but never sweetgrass lotion. I'll have to try that." We descended to the second floor, and the door opened. "Thank you for sharing your secrets."

She gave me a brisk nod, but I sensed a bit less animosity. It's hard to hate someone once you share beauty tips.

We entered a large rectangular ballroom with twelve round tables, covered by white tablecloths, each seating eight. Chandeliers dotted the ceiling, and a side rectangular table held drinks. Heavy navy-blue velvet drapes lined the walls, hanging from ornate gold valances. Coffee scented the air.

"Mr. Jenkins, thank you for joining us," said Captain Waters. He stood in front of one of the round tables, a carafe before him as well as papers, pen, his phone, and several cups. For the second time since meeting him, he gestured to a chair. This time I took it without hesitation. Why argue? I had questions I wanted answered too. Jackman took up a position behind her boss.

"Where is everyone else?" I asked. "My friends?"

"They are talking to other deputies. They'll be along shortly. Can I offer you some breakfast? The hotel has offered anything from their menu."

"No, thank you."

"No coffee and no food?"

"Not now, thank you."

"You are a man of controlled appetites, Mr. Jenkins." He took a sip of his coffee. "What are you doing in Florida?"

My pocket twitched. "Vacationing."

"You came with an odd group of friends."

My pocket twitched again. I reached in and extracted my phone, placing it in my lap. "Why do you say that?"

Twitch. Twitch.

Waters held his coffee cup but didn't drink. He stared at me over the rim.

I wriggled in my seat. What did she want? I touched the flag to assure Mrs. Ross I felt her presence.

"Are you uncomfortable, Mr. Jenkins?" asked Captain Waters, finally swigging his coffee. He drained it and poured himself another cup from the carafe on the table.

"No, not at all."

"You keep shifting in your chair."

"I usually go for a walk in the morning," I lied. "I'm used to getting exercise." The flag calmed under my hand just as my phone played *La Bamba* by Ritchie Valens. "May I get that? It's my ward."

"Your ward? You mean Amalia? Tell me more about that. How did she come to be your ward?" Waters leaned back in his chair, awaiting my answer. His casual posture didn't fool me. His keen eyes held too much suspicion.

The music stopped.

"Amalia isn't technically my ward, but her father expects me to take care of her while she's in school in Los Angeles.

La Bamba blared out again. I pulled it out and waved it in the air, impatient. "I need to answer the phone."

"Then please do."

I answered, turning slightly away from the captain. "Amalia, I'm with the police in the Tallahassee room on the second floor."

"Okay, I'm coming to join you."

"That's not necessary," I said.

"You don't understand," she said. "They're bringing me there too."

I disconnected and stared at Captain Waters. "What does Amalia have to do with this?" He'd activated my protective streak, and my annoyance rose.

"I told you I was talking to her."

"Yes, but you didn't say you'd be dragging her here. Why couldn't she answer a few questions in her room? Why go this extra step? What's the deal?" I squeezed my hand into a fist and pounded it on the table.

"Let's just get through this interview, shall we?" He stood, walked to the drinks table, and poured a glass of water, which he put in front of me on his return. His smile didn't reach his eyes. I didn't touch the water, but I did take a deep breath to calm down.

He continued his interrogation. "How is it that you are friends with the police captain in Calabasas?"

I thought about how to answer that question. I couldn't tell him that Perkins and I first met in the Los Angeles Pet Memorial Park when I'd helped a movie star bury a dog named Hugo, or that years later, he'd suspected me of murder and harvesting limbs. In fact, I was hard-pressed to determine when we'd 'officially' met.

Oh, wait. How could I forget?

"We met in Paramount Ranch when I found Jason Teague's body while taking a walk."

Deputy Jackman's eyes widened. "I remember that case."

Waters shrugged. "Everyone remembers that case. It was on the national news."

"No, boss. I read the details they didn't release to the public. Teague's penis was missing. Someone removed his dick post-mortem."

Waters placed his coffee mug on the table carefully. "I beg your pardon?"

The deputy continued, warming to her topic. "Yeah, it turned out Teague was actually a porn star in his past life with a ding-a-ling so big it was called The Colossal. Legend says he turned the phrase, 'What a dick,' into a compliment."

Captain Waters swallowed and rolled his index finger in a "go-on" motion.

I looked anywhere but at the deputy.

"The point is someone wanted The Colossal. I mean, who would want that?"

Betsy Ross's flag jiggled with laughter. I slapped my pocket.

Captain Waters eyed me. "Ants in your pants?"

"Flag in my pocket."

"What?"

"Never mind."

"And you," Jackman turned to me with slitted eyes, "You're Chet Manning. You're the co-star in the stagecoach scene—you lead a double life, make-up boy." She crossed her arms and propped herself against the wall.

Waters studied me and drummed his fingers on the table. "Did you cut off Jason Teague's manhood while pretending to be an actor named Chet Manning?"

"What? This is absurd! I didn't cut off his willy!" Early removed it. Mrs. Ross attached it. Technicalities. "I admit I'm Chet Manning. It was a side gig, and I did it under a stage name. So what? People do that all the time." I gave him a half-smile. "At least in Los Angeles."

Waters rolled his eyes. Deputy Jackman gave me a blank stare.

I took a breath and continued. "After filming the stagecoach scene, I went for a walk on the ranch, in the same area, to clear my head. A lot had happened the day before, and I had gotten a boatload of unwanted attention. I stumbled across Jason's body. I called the police, naturally, and that is how I met Perkins."

Officially.

"Is this how you met Dr. Sang?" asked Waters.

"Yes."

"And now you are all friends who vacation together." This wasn't a question, so I didn't answer.

Besides, Miss Mango's chatter took any opportunity I had to respond. She prattled at the young male officer with her. "Mitzi is a beautiful woman inside and out, and there is no way she did this, so you better stop asking questions about her because that's just dumb. Hi, Uncle Waylon, these people are digging for things that just aren't there simply because Joy Lucky was horrid, and Mitzi is nice."

Waters had gotten to his feet as Amalia arrived, but now, he looked down at me. "*Uncle* Waylon?"

"Figure of speech."

"Is she your ward or your niece? Your story keeps changing."

"She's neither. She's a young woman for whom I am responsible, and she uses the term 'Uncle' as a term of affection and found family."

"Uhm." His look of distaste told me what he really thought. What a filthy mind our Captain Waters had.

Amalia snagged a mug from a side table along with creamer and sugar and held it out expectantly. The officer who'd accompanied her grabbed a carafe and filled it without a blink, which made Waters cough. Loud.

The young man realized what he'd done and stepped back. "I'll go check with the crime lab, sir?"

"Good idea."

Amalia flashed him a smile. "Bye, Gene."

He stopped and smiled shyly back. "Bye, Amalia. Great meeting you."

Waters cleared his throat, and Gene fled.

Amalia pulled out a chair next to me and sunk into it, crossing her legs. "No need to be rude, Captain," she said.

"That young man has a job to do, Miss Flores, and flirting isn't part of his duties."

"He wasn't flirting. He escorted me here with professionalism and kindness." She sipped her coffee and stared him in the eye.

Waters sighed and sat down, placing his head in his hands. "Why couldn't you people have stayed in California?"

"I ask that every time Floridians come to my state, Captain." Perkins entered the room with a small smile, hand outstretched. His "escort" trailed behind him, shoulders to his ears. The poor kid couldn't match Perkin's air of authority. "Believe me, I feel your pain. Want to swap murder stories?"

5

Waters stood, accepted Perkins's hand, pumped it once, and offered him coffee. Perkins thanked him and sat down at our table. Waters walked to the door and spoke to a waiter, who delivered more coffee and additional creamer and sugar, which we didn't need since Waters didn't use it. Once everyone settled, Waters got to the point.

"What are you doing here, Captain Perkins?"

"Call me Jacob."

"What are you doing here, Captain *Jacob* Perkins?"

Perkins didn't smile *per se,* but whatever goodwill he'd had faltered. "Hum. Okay, *David,* I'm vacationing. I'm on holiday. Paid time off. Pick a word."

"Enforced PTO after not informing your commander about some details in a case he felt he deserved to know about, correct?" Captain Waters didn't look at any notes.

Perkins stilled. Amalia tapped her long fingernails on the side of her mug. I settled for gripping the sides of my chair.

Waters continued. "And this all happened after closing a serial murder case that drew the attention of the FBI and involved the kidnapping of Dr. Sorya Sang, who is also here." Waters raised his hands in mock wonderment. "And can you believe it? At some point, the reports say, a mysterious woman who looked *remarkably* like this young lady right here showed up on the top of the playground hill, but no one knows who she is." He pointed to Amalia, who didn't acknowledge him but did keep drumming her fingers.

Perkins spoke, keeping his voice low and steady. "Where did you get this information?"

Waters leaned forward, elbows on the table. "I know people who know people."

"Commander Brolin did not give this to you."

Waters quirked his lips into a sly smile. "I didn't say he did."

I reminded myself to tell Clipper and Eddie about this. Who was Waters's source?

"What's your point, Captain Waters?" I asked. "Joy died. I'm sorry she's gone, but we don't know how she died or what happened, and you haven't given us any details. None of us liked her much, but we didn't have anything to do with her death. We're happy to tell you what we know, but you seem to know far more about us than you have any right to. So, what's the deal?"

Waters scoffed. "I think you more than didn't like her, Mr. Jenkins. I think you were already violent toward her, and I have a witness."

"What are you talking about?"

"In point of fact, someone heard you outside of Joy's room yesterday." He checked his notes. "She pushed you out of her room sobbing that you bruised her wrists."

What the ever-lovin' hell?

Waters leaned forward, a Cheshire grin on his face. "Here's what I think happened. I think you and Mitzi killed her, maybe with the assistance of Dr. Sang, or at least with the knowledge you've gained being her boyfriend, in order to remove a serious rival to Mitzi's career."

Amalia slammed both hands on the table. "Murdered? That's ridiculous!"

Perkins shushed her. "Don't say a word, Amalia."

"Oh? Are you a part of this, too, Captain Perkins?" asked Waters.

"No, and there is no 'this,' here, and you know it. While I'm normally all about police cooperation, you've jumped to conclusions without evidence. This is a snow job and witness intimidation. We're done here. Waylon, Amalia, let's go. They can't keep us here."

Amalia and I stood and followed Perkins's lead, although I wanted to strangle Captain Waters. Amalia shook with rage and gave Jackman a stare that should have frozen the deputy in place. The woman sniffed and jotted in her notebook, unaffected. Guess she was used to that sort of thing.

Captain Waters spoke to our backs. "Don't leave the area, folks. I'm not done with you, and if you do leave, I'm calling Commander Brolin and having you arrested the moment you step off the airplane at home."

"You can't do that," said Perkins, turning to face him. "You have no evidence. You're all bluster."

Waters flashed us a crooked smile and poured himself yet another coffee. "Maybe."

Amalia and I both patted our pockets as our portions of the flag jerked.

Captain Waters's mug tipped ever so slightly, and the scalding coffee spilled over his hand and into his lap. "Dammit!" he yelled as he jumped to his feet.

Jackman hurried to hand her captain a cloth napkin while we walked out the door, along with one self-satisfied, ticked-off revolutionary mother of a ghost.

We stalked to the elevator, quietly seething.

Perkins hit the button for the lobby but motioned for us to stay silent. We walked through the main area and out the front to a lovely patio before he let us speak. He made sure no one was within hearing distance. Other than a few angry glances from a couple of wayward flamingoes, no one paid us any attention.

I spoke first. "I didn't like Joy, but I didn't want her murdered, and I will never believe Mitzi did either."

Perkins nodded. "None of us think she was involved, Waylon. By the way, where's Sorya?"

"She said she'd meet us downstairs. Let me text her."

Sorya, Whre r u? We r outside patio

Come later. ME wanted me to look at body.

Relly? Police not nice to us.

?? ME is cool. Mateo Vasquez, MD.

"She says the medical examiner wanted her to look at the body, which is good news because we can get all the details this way. Name is Mateo Vasquez."

Perkins craned his neck to look at the text. "I wonder why the medical examiner wanted Sorya to visit him? I wouldn't think Captain Waters would allow it, given how suspicious he is."

"Maybe he's more enlightened than Waters, or Waters doesn't know,"

Amalia said, then she giggled. "Captain Waters sounds like Captain America's sidekick."

I laughed, but Perkins pretended he didn't hear. "Anyway, it's good for us," he said, agreeing with my original assessment.

I rubbed my eyes. It had been a long morning. "Did you notice they didn't mention anyone from the zombie team being with us? We checked in at the same time, came in on the same flight, but they didn't put us together."

"Maybe Clipper did some magic," Amalia said. "I'm grabbing a pastry."

"Get me one?" asked Perkins, handing her a ten-dollar bill.

"Sure," she said.

I sat there wishing I could have a pastry but settled for texting Eddie.

Updtes on Clpper protocol?

I got the three moving dots indicating he was texting back. Then they stopped. They started again. What the hell was he doing? How long was this text?

A couple roller-skated by, each holding a Minnie Mouse balloon, crossing paths with a family of five, two girls and a boy. The little girls wore yellow ball gowns like Belle, and the boy sported floofy blue Alladin pants.

Amalia came back with two pineapple pastries.

Finally, Eddie's text arrived. *Meet at Plaza Ice Cream Parlor.*

"Eddie wants to meet at the Plaza Ice Cream Parlor. Where's that?"

Amalia smiled ear-to-ear, and the flag in my pocket wiggled. "Why, in the Magic Kingdom, naturally. Let's grab the shuttle. Everyone got their phones? You need your MagicMobile pass."

"Yup. Got it." Perkins and Amalia waved their phones in the air to acknowledge as well. "Let me grab sunscreen." I didn't want to chance re-entering the hotel, so I ran into a store and bought a new bottle. I made my companions put it on, too, and while they applied liberal layers at my insistence, I texted Sorya, letting her know where we would be. Prepped and ready, we got on the shuttle.

Sounds and color assailed my senses as we entered the theme park. From the toot-toot of the railroad to the bright green topiaries, the "May the Memories Begin," signs, the crush of people jabbering all at once, the band music playing in the square, and Cinderella's blue and white castle in the distance, I didn't know where to look first. We walked down Main Street USA until we found the ice cream shop on our left and the castle right in front of us. Folks around us took selfies and begged costumed actors to pose. A dad tried to eat a hot dog while holding three large bags of purchases.

Since Amalia and I were together, Mrs. Ross could witness everything, her presence a slight pressure over my left shoulder. Her excitement registered as a tiny *whump, whump* beat at the edge of my hearing, and I smiled at her enthusiasm. This was what I imagined taking an eight-year-old to the park must be like, without the bathroom breaks and the constant need for snacks.

Eddie stood ramrod-straight, waiting for us patiently. Zed sat at a table, leaning back, hands behind his head, one foot up on a chair as an enormous ice cream sundae melted in front of him. Everest sat at the same table, dwarfing the small white chair. He noticed Zed's foot and slapped it off the seat. Clipper sat nearby, nose in a tablet, while Peter sat beside him, munching on a cone with two scoops.

"Hey, sweets," Zed called, addressing Amalia. "Gotcha a waffle sundae, but you better eat it fast. This heat is killer."

Amalia skipped with a coo of delight and dove into the sundae with gusto. Boy, that chocolate sauce looked delicious.

"What flavors did you get, Peter?" I asked.

"Vanilla and vanilla with a chocolate swirl."

"You've got to be kidding me."

He scrunched his eyebrows together. "No. Why?"

"That much vanilla in one cone is a crime against humanity. No chocolate? No strawberry? Peach? Raspberry? Oreo? Cookie Dough? Caramel? Hot fudge? Something?"

"What do you care? You can't eat it."

"I agree with Waylon," said Clipper, not looking up from his typing. "It's a travesty."

"Thank you, Clipper," I said.

Perkins reached for his wallet and looked at the menu. With a sigh, he placed the wallet back in his pocket. He motioned toward the menu. "A sundae is almost fifteen dollars. Highway robbery." He turned to Eddie. "Okay, spill. What do you know?"

"Every resort has cameras out the wazoo. We thought it would be a simple matter of accessing the camera feeds and seeing what happened."

"I'm guessing that didn't work?" asked Perkins.

"There's nada, nothing, zero," said Eddie. "Either someone covered their tracks, or we had a really odd fluke in the technology."

Perkins rubbed the back of his neck, “Are you saying someone killed her?”

“Oh, it’s murder all right,” said Sorya, coming up behind us. “Blunt force trauma to the back of the head, but that didn’t kill her. She struggled with her assailant, and then she drowned.”

6

Mateo and I agree this is a homicide. Joy Lucky was hit on the head, here," Sorya indicated the upper back right of her own skull, "then the assailant pushed her into the water. Joy's fingernails were torn to the quick, and she had bruising around the neck."

"*Mateo*?" I asked. Since when were Sorya and this medical examiner on a first-name basis, and why was Sorya blushing?

Perkins held up a finger to get Sorya's attention. "But you still didn't explain if she drowned or died before hitting the water."

"She drowned."

"She had water in her lungs?" I asked.

Sorya shook her head. "That's not the way it works. The epiglottis closes, and water doesn't go into the lungs."

"Wait," I said, rubbing the bridge of my nose. "Every TV show ever has gotten it wrong?"

"Sorry, Waylon." She leaned down to kiss my cheek, making me feel better about this *Mateo* guy. "Joy's lungs swelled up with gasses. When Mateo did the standard Y incision, all you could see was lungs, lungs, lungs. They practically touched. When we pushed the heart aside, we saw right ventricle dilation. Classic signs of drowning."

"Poor Joy," said Everest.

"Poor Joy is right," said Sorya. "Drowning is a terrible way to go. You starve for air and are aware of it, panicking. I wouldn't wish it on anyone."

Everest tapped the table with a meaty finger. "Who would want to do this to Joy? No one liked her that much, but hitting her on the head and holding her underwater until she drowned?"

"That's personal," said Zed.

"I agree," said Eddie. "That's a crime of passion, not some random dude looking for money. Someone wanted Joy dead and lured her out there."

"Keep in mind they'd have to hold here there for at least a minute, maybe a minute and a half. That's a long time," said Sorya.

Everest recoiled. "That's cold. Real cold. Brass balls to do that."

Perkins grimaced. "The word you're looking for is evil."

The manager of the ice cream store stepped out the door. "Excuse me, folks, but are you finished with your ice cream? You've been here a long time, and other guests would like to occupy these seats." He walked closer. "Plus, if you don't mind me saying so, your conversation is morbid, and we don't do that in the happiest place on Earth." He chirped all of this with a jaunty smile.

I looked around and realized we'd scared everyone away. It looked like we'd sprayed bug repellant in a five-foot circular radius. Moms and dads with strollers and couples in love hovered around the periphery like mosquitos afraid to get zapped.

"Maybe we should move on." Amalia smiled at the crowd.

"Hey, isn't that Miss Mango?" someone shouted in English with a Hispanic accent. "Miss Mango! I saw you win the pageant on TV. You were so beautiful. That *dress*."

The reigning Miss Mango stood gracefully and shifted into catwalk position, one foot forward, elbow on hip.

"Chin up," I whispered.

Despite wearing almost no makeup and her hair up in a high pony, that girl had it going on. She signed autographs and posed for photos and selfies with adoring fans, giving Eddie and his team time to slip away.

Eddie texted me *Clipper protocol, phase 2,* and that was all.

Amalia made it up to the store manager by telling everyone how divine the hot fudge waffle cone sundae was, and suddenly, everyone was ordering it. The manager gave her a double thumbs-up.

"Well, hello, helllllo!" A lovely young woman with loose, tousled, absolutely adorable brown waves and a smile as wide as the Rio Grande approached us, along with an equally endearing young man with tidy, short hair and rimless glasses. They wore matching red, blue, and green checked vests over white short-sleeved shirts with blue ties and gold buttons bearing Mickey Mouse's face. They each wore gold name tags. Hers said "Courtney," and his said, "Cameron."

Courtney and Cameron also sported large gold buttons that said, "VIP Tour Guide." Wasn't that special? Courtney offered her hand to Amalia and to me. "I'm Courtney, and we heard we had a VIP here today!"

"How did you hear that so fast?" I asked.

"Oh!" said Cameron, also offering his hand, which I took, regretting it immediately when he pumped it wildly three times. "Sam, here," he said, pointing to the manager once he released me from bondage, "let us know right away."

I turned to Sam and mouthed, "Traitor."

He shrugged, and his ears blushed red at the tips. "Sorry."

Cameron smacked my shoulder lightly. "Oh, don't be grumpy," he said. "He had to—it's in his contract."

"Now, Miss Mango, we are so glad to have you in the park today. Anything you want, we are here to assist you. And who are you, exactly?" Courtney turned to me, smile intact, but her sparkling eyes pinned me to the ground.

Geez, what kind of training did they give these kids?

"I'm her chaperone and cosmetologist."

"Her what?" asked Cameron.

"Cosmetologist and chaperone. You don't think an international pageant winner travels completely on her own, do you?"

She sucked in a hard breath like she'd been caught breaking the law.

"Of course not," replied Courtney, recovering quickly. "Your name, please?"

"Waylon Jenkins."

Courtney stumbled, threw out a hand, and caught Cameron's shoulder. "Mitzi's 'Waylon Jenkins'?"

"The very same."

Courtney and Cameron exchanged glances, their smiles faltering for a second before they flickered back to megawatt life.

"Please come with us."

I frowned. "Why?"

"Just come with us, sir. We don't let our smiles turn upside down here in the park." She couldn't have been more upbeat, but the way she took my elbow communicated urgency. Cameron offered a jaunty elbow to Amalia and led us away.

"Hey, wait a minute. You want us to come?" asked Sorya as she and Perkins ran to catch up. They had to hustle because the creeper twins dragged us along like we needed to catch a train.

"I think we'll be okay," I said over my shoulder. "I can't imagine this is more than a lipstick emergency. You guys enjoy the park and then go back to the hotel and find our friends. I'll take care of Mitzi. She's probably a little stressed with the parade and whatnot."

Cameron pulled to a stop, blinking like a metronome. "Oh, she's stressed, alright. That's where we're taking you. She's looking for you."

"Where is she?"

"Sitting in a private booth at Club 33."

I whistled. "Whew, ritzy."

Amalia poked my side. "What is that?"

"An exclusive Disney club. I've heard of it but never seen it."

Courtney hustled us along, cheeks frozen in a crazed smile. "Well, you're in for a treat. You'll get to see it now."

Club 33 had a storied history. I expected luxury and I wasn't disappointed. Gleaming glass and equally shiny hardwood paired with plush carpeting and fine china. Solicitous wait staff trained to provide what you wanted before you knew you needed it moved silently with pleasant smiles through the space. I promised Amalia I'd buy her a pair of rose gold Mickey Mouse ears with a subtly embossed Club 33 logo, and she kissed me on the cheek and followed another handler to meet some "super VIPs." Whatever that meant.

Courtney and Cameron led us through the restaurant until we arrived at a back table far from the other guests. Mitzi sat hunched over her phone, scrolling quickly. Every once in a while, she'd pause, read something and clench a fist. I cleared my throat to get her attention. The "C" twins backed into a corner and stood by, out of hearing range.

"Oh, Waylon, I'm so glad to see you." Mitzi's eyes filled with tears. She wore ratty pink shorts, a white tank top with a pink bra under it, and a messy bun. The bra strap kept slipping down her shoulder. I had never seen her so disheveled.

"Captain Waters thinks I murdered Joy!" Mitzi hiccupped. "Can you believe it? Me! I can't even kill a spider. Was she my favorite person? No. Did I like her? No. But kill her? Drown her? Look her in the eye while she struggled and hold her underwater? That's what they told me happened! How terrible for her, and to think I did it? That's insane."

I slid into the booth next to her and put my arm around her shoulders.

"Of course, it's insane. No one who knows you believes you could do that."

"Really?" she says. "Then explain this." She entered her password into her phone and scrolled through until she found what she wanted. She handed it to me. The front page of a Hollywood gossip rag.

Ditzy Mitzy's Killer Looks?

"That's one headline, and they couldn't even spell your name right," I said, poo-poohing it.

"Then, there's this," she snapped, reaching over to swipe to another.

"Mitz Put the Hitz on Joy!"

"Okay, so there's two. Maybe you'll get a police procedural series when we go back to California."

"Stop dismissing this, Waylon. It's serious. This is my career we're talking about. Look at what my agent sent." She extracted the phone from my hands and pulled up an email.

Mitzi,

The press is having a field day, and 'you-know-who' is threatening to pull your contract for Our Nation's Talent. Do you have any idea what the parade people want to do? Do they still want you on the float? No one is returning my calls.

I turned to Cameron and Courtney and waved them over. "Do you still want her on the float?"

The two looked at each other and communicated telepathically or through a mind-meld of some sort or cyborgs talking sub-sonically. Maybe blinks or clicks—I couldn't tell.

"One second," said Courtney, and she stepped out to contact the mothership.

"Waylon, who would want to kill Joy?" Mitzi asked.

"That's the trick of it, love. Waters can't find anyone else who would benefit from Joy's death, and drowning is a very personal type of murder. Sorya explained it's violent and slow. Torturous even."

Courtney returned, all smiles. "Good news. We still want you to be the star of the parade, Mitzi."

Mitzi smiled back. "Oh, that is such good news."

Courtney kept smiling. "With one caveat."

"What?" I asked, suspicious.

"We'd like Miss Mango to appear with you. We feel it would be a sign of goodwill to show that another celebrity has faith in your innocence."

Amalia arrived a millisecond later.

"I'll be proud to stand by Mitzi!" said Amalia. "Although I think it's ridiculous it is my honor and pleasure. Also, let me get you my agent's number. The VIPs I just discussed this with asked me to give it to you."

Mitzi blinked fast at this news but swallowed her discomfiture. I knew what she must have been thinking. It wasn't that she didn't want Amalia with her; she resented the lack of trust. "I am happy to fulfill my contract to be Queen of the Parade and to have Miss Mango at my side," she said, but her smile was forced.

You go, girl, I thought. Remind them there's a contract involved. This is business, after all.

Courtney smiled her eerie grin again. "Yes, a contract with a morality clause, Mitzi. Shall we begin your fittings, ladies?"

7

I placed a hand on Courtney's shoulder to stop her for a moment. "Before you go, Courtney, was Joy Lucky involved in the parade? She implied she was."

"No, she wasn't. We hadn't hired her for any reason."

Mitzi tapped a taloned finger to her lower lip. "Are you sure? Not a last-minute replacement?"

Courtney tilted her head in thought. "No. I'm sure I would have been told. Cameron, do you know?"

Cameron shook his head. "I hadn't heard of anything either."

"Okay, thank you."

As Mitzi and Amalia departed with Courtney, Cameron turned to me. "You may eat anything you like at the buffet, on the house. I assure you it is an amazing selection. We're famous for our lobster, of course. Never-ending shrimp and Caesar salad! Try the pineapple sherbet; it's to die for. We have it specially brought in from a small-batch supplier outside of town. The hostess will take care of your bill."

"That's very generous. Thank you," I said.

"Enjoy your day in the park."

Forgoing the food, I went to check on Amalia's ears. The lady behind the counter showed me how much they cost.

My mouth dropped open. "Are you serious? I'll have to take out a second mortgage."

Geez, I thought. *Amalia's getting paid for the parade. She should buy* <u>*me*</u> *the ears.*

"They're quite exclusive, sir. I'm certain your girlfriend will love them."

"I'm buying them for my ward."

"Of course. Your ward. I'm sure she will love them." The lady winked. "Maybe she'll wear them for you during special times."

It took me a long second to get the insinuation, but once I did, I swallowed convulsively, totally squigged out. "Just ring them up, please."

"As you wish, sir. Ride'em, cowboy." She put them in a bag, and I paid.

Humiliated, I grabbed the bag and left as fast as my feet would carry me. I re-entered the park, leaving the enclave of hushed sophistication back into the colorful, loud mayhem. As overwhelmed as I was, I almost didn't recognize the man in uniform as he came toward me.

"Mr. Jenkins, how lucky I am to find you here."

Luck, schmuck. This man could access all the Disney cameras, and he knew where I was.

"Captain Waters. I don't believe luck had anything to do with it."

"Where are you headed? Maybe I could show you a shortcut."

My pocket beat a rhythm. I touched it to let Mrs. Ross know I understood.

People gave the policeman a wide berth. "I was considering Liberty Square."

"Ah, the Hall of Presidents. A classic. Everyone wants to see Honest Abe." Waters gestured for me to follow, and we walked around a phone case kiosk.

"I'm more interested in George Washington." I'd been around during Abe's presidency. He was honest, and he did the right thing. Thank God the North won. Lots of blood, though. Typhus, gangrene, and soldiers freezing to death. People forget that part.

"Fascinating. Were you a history buff in school?" Waters pressed casually, doing a good job sounding interested.

"I've always liked history."

The cop walked with his hands behind his back, moseying along. "How did you get from history to cosmetology?"

"Something that interested me as well. Special effects makeup, skincare, the change a woman, or a man for that matter, undergoes when they look their best."

"Where did you go to school?"

"I studied with private makeup artists."

"Ah. I didn't know you could do that."

"I'm licensed in California. Why are you digging for personal information, Captain?"

"There's not a lot of info out there about you, Mr. Jenkins."

"I'm a private person, Captain Waters. Would you like to tell me about where you grew up and what made you want to become a cop?"

He halted in the middle of the walkway, forcing tourists to move around him.

I stopped as well but several steps ahead and looked back.

He answered my question. "My family and schooling aren't relevant to the case."

"I'm sort of thinking it is. I'd like to know how you know so much about my friends and me, so understanding your biography is entirely relevant. Nevertheless, I think I made my point. I have a more pressing question for you. Do you know why Joy was here in Florida, Captain? Because I do not. I thought it had something to do with the parade, but the parade folks say that's not true."

Waters stooped to pick up a piece of trash and dump it in a can. He acknowledged me with a bob of his head. "I wondered when you would bring that up."

"Why?" I asked.

"Because it is an excellent question. According to her agent, Ms. Lucky came here to meet a boyfriend."

Now I halted, and he kept walking. "Her boyfriend? Roger Something-or-other. He's here?" I called to him.

I hurried to close the gap between us.

Waters answered me as I reached his side. "No, that's her sugar daddy. He's still in California. It seems she recently took up with a new boyfriend. Her agent didn't know his name, only that he rained money on Joy, and she was besotted."

"Any description?"

Waters crossed his arms. "Wealthy, that's it."

I rubbed my face with my hands, still holding the bag with Amalia's Mickey ears. "That doesn't give us anything to go on."

"Just the money angle. Incidentally, how much did a visit to Club 33 set you back?" asked Waters. He kept his voice mild, but the accusation was there.

"Huh? I didn't pay for anything."

"Don't bullshit me," he sneered. "I know what the membership costs."

"You know more than I do then because I don't."

"I'm watching you, Mr. Jenkins. You're young, mysterious, and loaded, plus you're connected to both Mitzi and Joy. I'll figure you out, and when I do, I'll put you in prison. Have a good day." He stalked away.

The flag in my pocket pulsed. "Yeah, I know. He's such a people person."

My phone buzzed, and I checked my messages. There was a new one from Eddie asking me to meet him in Joy's room.

I patted the flag. "Sorry, Mrs. Ross. The Hall of Presidents will have to wait." I got an electric shock as an answer. "Hey! Active murder investigation here."

I double-checked my phone to make sure my MagicMobile pass worked and left the park. The shuttle dropped me near the hotel, and I hurried through, head down, not wanting to talk to anyone.

No sentries guarded the entrance to Joy's room, and it wasn't marked with crime tape either. I supposed the hotel didn't want to mar the hallway with unpleasant reminders of murder.

As soon as I got within three paces of the room, the door opened, and Everest ushered me in. "Quickly, Waylon."

I slipped in, and he pulled the door shut. "Are we allowed to be in here?" I looked around at the suite. "Didn't the detectives search already?" They would have already gone through her things. I couldn't imagine what would be left.

Eddie stood in the center of the room, scanning it with his eagle eyes. Someone in the bedroom opened and closed drawers.

"To answer your question, Waylon, no, we aren't allowed in here, but I'm hoping we can find a clue the police couldn't. We didn't know Joy well, but according to Captain Waters, all they found here was the normal stuff you'd expect a traveler to carry. Clothes, toiletries, a plane ticket confirmed to have been purchased only a few days ago, and that's it. I have to believe there is more."

"How do you know this?"

"Clipper."

"Ah."

"They haven't removed her belongings yet." I stated it as fact because I noticed her perfume bottle on the dresser and a pair of sandals in the corner.

"Correct. They'll be coming later today to gather it all. We have an hour, tops. You're the closest thing we have to a woman in this room, Waylon. Where would you hide something important?"

I decided to take his statement as a compliment, so I put on my imaginary diva couture hat and Kate Spade heels and examined the space. I circled the main room. A long sofa with a glass coffee table. Disney character coasters and an illustrated Disney Park guide rested on the table in neat, square angles. She'd never touched them.

The green chair with a small side table holding the TV remote. The gargantuan flat-screen hung on the wall.

All normal. Sterile, in fact.

"Not in here."

In the bedroom, I found a toe-tapping Peter. "Move, Peter. This is a job for a cosmetologist."

"Gladly," he said, stretching his back. "There's nothing here. She probably kept any information on her phone or computer, and the cops have that already."

"Begone." I swept him away with a wave of my hand.

A huge bedroom lay before me, with a California king, numerous throw pillows, and side lamps for ambiance.

Where would I keep something if I was a movie star goddess wannabee?

Not the side tables next to the bed. Too obvious.

Not under the mattress. Too cliché.

Clothes in the closet. She'd unpacked them, but the police had undoubtedly gone through those.

I pointed to the closet. "Did you look in there?"

Peter nodded. "Yeah," he said. "I also searched the dresser drawers. Nada."

Everest entered and stretched out on the bed. It was the first time he looked like he had a bed for his size.

I spun in a circle, index finger to my lips, considering this conundrum like I would evaluate a pageant contestant's strengths and weaknesses. Evens and odds. Good points and bad ones. Jeans, two wide-sleeved floral tops, a short skirt. A dress bag.

Why would she need a dress bag?

I checked it. A simple black cocktail hung inside. Tasteful, too. Guess a girl couldn't go wrong having a little black dress with her, but it told me she expected to be taken somewhere nice. and probably someone else had purchased it. Joy preferred gaudy.

Maybe she expected to go to Club 33? Waters and his whole 'boyfriend with money' thing?

Sure enough, black stilettos sat neatly on the floor below the dress bag, which meant somewhere there'd be accessories.

"Where's her jewelry?" I asked.

Everest spoke from his prone position. "Haven't seen any. Maybe she's one of those girls who travels with it all on."

I shook my head. "She wore a swimsuit yesterday, and I don't remember her wearing any bling."

Eddie whipped out his phone. "Jewelry?" he asked into the receiver.

I couldn't hear the answer.

"Clipper says she wore a thin gold chain to the pool with a tiny pendant that said, 'sisters forever.' Plus, a cheap drugstore watch."

"Gurl's got an LBD here, so you know she had bling," I responded with a snap of my right hand.

Peter's eyes bugged out. "She had a what, what, what?

Everest still lay on the bed, eyes half-closed. "Joy has a little black dress, meaning she planned to go out on a date or at least somewhere fancy, so Waylon assumes she has appropriate jewelry to accompany the dress."

I doffed my pretend couture fascinator. "Thank you, Everest. It's nice to have someone who understands simple English."

He flashed me a quick salute.

I wandered to the bathroom, which had a spa tub, a stand-up shower with jets, and a separate loo. The Estee Lauder foundation and blush in her makeup bag made me happy, but I tsked at the HD finishing powder. If not applied correctly, high-def makeup shows cakey under camera flash. I would have warned her away from it for everyday use. Her Elf brushes were perfectly fine and a good deal for a drugstore brand. I used them myself, and if you're going to use an eyebrow product, you couldn't do better than Bobbi. However, the state of her lipstick was atrocious, and why would anyone with baby blues wear blue liner? What incompetent poser had been advising her?

"Waylon . . . ." Eddie drew me away from her cosmetics. I hadn't even examined her cleansing products, but I moved on before I became depressed by the oily skin products she'd used on her combination skin.

Get back on task.

It had to be the bathroom.

Hmmm.

I dialed my phone. "Sorya?"

All I heard was screaming.

"Sorya!"

"Standing in line for Space Mountain, Waylon." She sounded happy.

"Okay, hate to interrupt you for a *murder investigation*, but was Joy menstruating?"

"Currently? Mateo did not mention that, no."

Mateo. Pfft.

"Do you want me to check with him?" she asked. "I can as soon as I get off the ride."

"No, it's okay. Carry on."

"Okay. We're almost there. Can't wait to get on this ride. Even Perkins is having fun."

"Take a picture. That I have to see."

"I'll try!"

I hung up and stared at the floor at the side of the toilet. A massive box of heavy flow maxi pads, a smaller box of liners, plus a big box of plus-sized tampons, and another box of mid-sized tampons.

Even if Aunt Flo was visiting, this seemed extreme. She had enough here to fill a small suitcase, and no one travels with all of this stuff when you can buy what you need at any convenience store.

I dragged the boxes to the sink counter and studied them. They were all open, so I reached into the box of liners to see what was there.

"What are you doing? I know you have an affinity for feminine wiles, but this is beyond the pale, Waylon." Peter hugged the doorframe.

"Move, Peter," said Eddie.

Peter skittered to the side to lean against the shower.

"What did you find, Waylon?" Eddie asked, face placid as if he encountered a male zombie searching a box of women's menstrual products every day.

Everest joined us, opened the tampons, and peered inside. "Whatcha got?"

"Don't know yet," I said. "Hold on." I fished inside the box, touching soft cotton, sticky tape, crackling plastic, and stiff cardboard. Nothing out of the ordinary until I got stuck by something sharp. I pulled that pad out and laid it on the counter.

Two gold earring backings poked out of the cotton padding. The earrings had been pushed through the pantyliner's cotton and secured on the backside. It was clever, really. I pulled off the fatbacks. I secured first one earring post, then the other, and displayed them face up on the cotton.

"Diamond Victorian style yellow gold drop earrings," I said, studying them. I hefted one in my hand and then held it to the light. "This hangs about two inches, with pavé set diamonds, inset with five oval emeralds. I'm guessing six carats just in this one earring. Stunning." I hadn't seen the likes of them before.

Peter whistled. "I can see why she wouldn't wear those around a pool." He whipped out his phone and snapped a few pics.

"You are correct," I said. "These aren't what you would call 'casual' earrings. Let's see what else we can find."

"You think there's more?" asked Eddie.

"Earrings like this always have a matching necklace."

Sure enough, there it hid, in the middle of the maxi pad box. A pendant the same shape and style as the earrings but twice as large, with double the diamonds and a large central emerald on a thick Omega yellow gold chain. We found the bracelet in the plus-sized tampons, a cuff with the pattern of the earrings and pendant worked into the gold. It was my favorite of the set. Peter photographed these as well.

Everest finally spoke up. "Joy had expensive jewelry and hid it well. That's all we got here. There's nothing nefarious about hiding pricey items. I'd do it, too, if I were her."

Eddie drummed his fingers on the bathroom door. "We need to get out of here. We've used up too much time. Peter, Everest, get gone."

"What about you, Waylon, and the goods?" Everest asked.

Peter was already in the bedroom and moving fast.

"I'll take care of it," Eddie replied. He jerked his head. "Out."

Everest slipped out of the room like smoke.

"Waylon, we've got to leave as well."

"I have one more thing."

"What is it?"

"There has to be . . . Ah, there it is." I dug around in the last box and found tampons laying on the top, horizontally, which is not how they're packaged, so I removed them and found what I was looking for, slipped on a single tampon. Underneath, I discovered newspaper cuttings and printouts.

I put the articles on the counter. "Eddie, look at these headlines. She's been tracking us. *Reborn Never Born*, that's harsh, and *Mitzi Parade Queen in Disney,* and even *Deputy Medical Examiner Stepping in While Dr. Sang Takes Time to Heal.* This is nuts."

"Who are you talking to, Mr. Jenkins?"

I slipped the last tampon deep in my pocket and whirled around to find Deputy Jackman standing behind me, two officers behind her, and no Eddie in sight.

8

The holding cell looked exactly like the ones I'd seen on television. Sparse, metallic, uncomfortable, and windowless. It sucked the life right out of you. Ten minutes in, and my cellmate had wrinkles. He'd be a raisin within twenty-four hours. I didn't have to worry about the physical effects, but that in and of itself was a problem. The police would eventually notice I didn't eat, pee, or drink. Staying in their Bates Motel raised serious zombie concealment issues.

After Deputy Jackman discovered me in Joy's hotel room either "stealing or planting evidence," she arrested me, proving her sense of humor had taken a vacation when she'd pulled her hair into that tight bun. I tried explaining before ending up here, but she refused to have any of it.

"Deputy, I thought I'd search Joy's room for any clues. I'm as concerned as you are. The headlines point to my client, Mitzi, and we need to clear her name by finding the actual killer. And for some odd reason, your police captain suspects me, and he thinks I'm Joy's wealthy boyfriend, which isn't true either."

"Or maybe, Mr. Jenkins," she said as she turned me around to slap handcuffs on me, "You are indeed the real killer, and you're planting evidence to throw us off track?"

"What? No! I found this expensive jewelry hidden in her feminine hygiene products, plus those newspaper clippings. Captain Waters told me she had a flashy new boyfriend spending money on her. He must have given her those baubles, but what I don't understand is why is she tracking Mitzi, Sorya, and me? Probably Captain Perkins, too."

"All excellent questions," Jackman responded, guiding me to her car on a perp walk through the hotel. I heard the cameras flashing and got a thumbs up from Stanley. "We'll talk about them at the station. You have the right to remain silent."

I huffed, but as I got to the doors, I caught a quick glance of Clipper, who flashed me a peace sign. No way would I have seen Clipper if he hadn't wanted me to, so that made me relax. Clipper was on top of the situation.

Now I sat in the holding cell hoping he would get on it fast because my cellmate, Will by his uniform's nametag, had recently lost his job as head security guard at an alligator show on a nearby farm. It seemed some yahoos got into an alligator exhibit, and he couldn't figure out how it had happened because some clever shmuck wiped the security feed. His buddies tried to cheer him up, and he'd gotten drunk, decided to take a ride in a purloined golf cart, and hit a wild alligator on a nationally ranked course. At least he hadn't gotten bitten, but he'd still been arrested for theft, drunk and disorderly, animal abuse, and whatever they called "messing up golf course grass in Florida."

"They framed me, man," Will said. "You gotta believe me." He scooted next to me, and my sense of smell mutinied.

"I'm sorry, Will," I said, shifting away. "That sounds terrible."

He scooted right back, threw an arm over my shoulders. I almost keeled over at the stench. "See, homie, I don't understand it. Why weren't those guys hurt by the fence? It's an *electric* fence! What happened to the feed? The only thing I can figure is my boss set me up. But why go to such lengths? He could have said, 'Will, you're not working out. I gotta let you go,' and I wouldn't have liked it, but this crypto shit? What's the point? It's like secret agent man stuff. I think they were testing the security, ninja spy style, found a hole, and used me as the fall guy." He poked me in the arm. "Someone was out to get me."

"What's your last name, Will?"

"Waldeck, why?"

"No reason. I'm sorry, buddy. That's a bad bit of luck right there."

Will slid away from me and leaned against the concrete wall. "Yeah, then I had to make it worse. I'll never work again. I've got a mortgage, you know? I can't even make bail. Did you know they can hold us here for up to thirty-three days without charging us?"

I startled. "Thirty-three days? Are you kidding? In California, it's forty-eight hours."

"Florida, man." He held his head in his hands. "Fucking Florida."

I agreed. I wished I'd never come to this state, and the flag in my pocket jumped. "Sorry," I muttered. I actually owed Mrs. Ross one. The police had gathered all the jewelry as evidence, but I kept the very last tampon I'd found and the knick-knack that came with it. I'd crammed it in the same pocket with the flag, crowding Mrs. Ross, so to speak. When the officers searched me, they found the flag but missed my purloined menstrual product.

"What's this, Waylon?" one officer asked as he patted me down. He extracted the flag from my pocket, not realizing the treasure he held. He shook it out and stuffed it back into my pocket.

"It's just an old snot rag."

The officer grimaced. "I'm going to wash my hands."

"Wise," I responded, nodding in a slow up and down. "Very wise."

They'd thrown me in this cell and left me alone since. No phone call, but I didn't worry about it. Clipper had seen me.

The guards brought some food, and I gave mine to Will while I tried to piece together what was happening.

Joy followed us to Orlando for reasons unknown, falsely claiming to be part of the parade.

She'd recently acquired a rich boyfriend, who showered her with diamonds and emeralds that she took great lengths to hide.

She'd been hideously murdered after a confrontation with Mitzi.

Will's statement that he'd been set up made me think. What if we weren't looking deep enough? What if meeting at the pool wasn't accidental? What if Joy sought Mitzi out and forced a confrontation?

But it made no sense. Joy wouldn't have planned her own murder, so what was the point of staging a fight?

An obvious shift change indicated day turning to night. Will and I couldn't tell because the overhead fluorescent lights stayed on. He dozed, and I rested. So far, we'd avoided the toilet discussion. Quiet minutes passed.

Then, the light fixtures flickered, and I smiled.

I heard a banging from down the hall and a muffled *thwump*. My roomie woke and mumbled, "What's happening?"

"Nothing, dude. Go back to sleep."

"Can't. I'm awake now."

The lights turned to an emergency amber glow. I stood in the middle of the cell, loose and ready. Two dark shapes moved with purpose down the hallway, opened my cell door, and I moved with them. They closed the door on poor Will, but I whispered, "I won't forget about you. Don't worry."

"You're jailbreaking? Fuckin-A."

One man tugged my sleeve with a single, sharp jerk. The efficient move told me it was Eddie.

"Gotta go," I said. "I got your back."

We slipped out a side door into a dark van, and that was it. Clipper protocol achieved.

9

Thanks for getting me out," I said. We'd congregated in the main room of a bungalow decorated in blue and tan wicker B&B chic. It screamed rental. "We've got to help Will."

Eddie crossed his arms. "Why?"

I pointed at Zed. "Because when some mysterious men decided to go gallivanting around the alligator farm, jump the fence, bother the animals, and erase the evidence, guess who got fired?"

Eddie dropped his face into his hands. "Will?" he said, wincing.

I pointed at him next. "Bingo. Granted, he made it worse by getting drunk and driving a stolen golf cart onto a pristine fairway, hitting a wild alligator."

Clipper raised his head from his computer to look at me like a meerkat on patrol.

I waved him off. "Don't worry. The alligator is a mascot of sorts named Chubby, and he's fine. No animals were harmed in the making of this personal disaster. Point is, Will Waldeck wouldn't be in this mess if it weren't for you, so you owe him."

Peter scrunched up his nose to hide the snicker. "Will Waldeck? That's his real name?"

"Shut the fuck up," I said, pointing at him now. "Don't make fun of him."

Clipper gazed at me with new admiration. "First, he punches me, and now he tells Peter to go fuck himself. Our Waylon is growing up."

"You shut up, too," I said. "You made this man's life a disaster. He has a mortgage to pay and now an arrest record. You're going to go all 'Clipper protocol' and fix this."

Eddie straightened his shoulders. "You're right, Waylon. What do you suggest?"

"First, we pay the man's bail."

"How much is it?" Zed bounced a ball against a wall in a most irritating manner.

"Twenty-five thousand dollars."

Zed burst out laughing. "We don't have access to that type of money."

"I do," I said. "Stop bouncing that ball."

"No, you don't," said Clipper. "Your accounts are frozen thanks to your arrest."

"Then, it's up to you and your magic, Clipper. What can you do?"

"I can't get him out of jail, and it wouldn't help him in the long haul. I'll handle the video with the golf cart."

I tapped my fingers on the side of my chair. "That's something."

Everest stood from where he sprawled on a sofa, caught Zed's ball midair, and crushed it with one meaty hand. I sent him a grateful salute, and he sunk back down on his couch and tapped his chin. "We'll investigate the jewelry too. If we can determine who designed it, maybe we can find the buyer. It's custom stuff. No one walked into their local mall and purchased it."

Eddie ignored Zed's pleading look.

"Right," I said, thinking. "It's definitely custom. By the way, where are Sorya and Perkins? How are Mitzi and Amalia?"

"Doing fine. Sorya and Perkins are enjoying the parks. They went to Animal Kingdom. With you in jail and then breaking out, the cops stopped looking at Mitzi. She and Amalia are prepping for the parade. Dress fittings tomorrow."

"Great. I'm glad they're out of the murder drama. I need a phone."

Eddie narrowed his eyes at me. "Why?"

I shot him a baleful stare. "I just need one."

The team hesitated a beat, but with a nod from Eddie, Clipper threw me a burner. I considered who I should contact first while I showered and dressed, grateful the team had picked up extra clothes. A Mickey T-shirt and gray cargo pants would make me practically invisible in Orlando.

I'd prepped dozens upon dozens of actresses for awards shows, doing skin prep and makeup, and knew every stylist in the business worth their grain of salt. Most people don't know, but actresses usually wear borrowed gowns, shoes, and jewelry on the red carpet. They don't keep those ensembles in their closets.

I pondered it all night while the other zombies rested and Peter slept.

I placed a call in the morning, which led to other calls, which finally led to someone in Orlando I'd been assured was discreet.

I gathered the team in the bungalow's main room. "I need special effects makeup, including scar wax, cotton balls, Pros-Aide adhesive, petroleum jelly, and contact lenses."

Eddie stopped reading the morning paper to prop his head on his fist. "Why, Waylon?" he asked.

"I'm going to turn Clipper into someone named 'Simon Fishman,' and he's going to make a deal for me."

"No, I'm not," Clipper said, his face a thundercloud.

"You have to. Who else is going to do it? Everest? I think not. Eddie? Zed? No, you're the only one who can play Simon Fishman from Fishman and Sons Gemstones in New York. I'm going to tell you what to do."

10

I gave "Simon Fishman" the tampon, and he visited my contact's contact's contact. Afterward, he left in a taxi, which then dropped him at a bail bondsman. Within two hours, Will Waldeck walked free with the phone number of a good attorney. The attorney had already been paid for the first fifty hours on Will's case, and she assured me additional payment was unlikely given that the police couldn't find the video of either the alligator farm escapade or Chubby's cart fiasco.

With that behind me, I turned my attention to the murder. If we didn't clear my name, again, I'd be hiding for a long, long time. Why did everyone always think the zombie did it? I paced the bungalow, thinking.

"You're going to wear the carpet to threads," said Eddie, keeping his voice mild. He and the other men itched to get out too, but we'd agreed to keep our heads down while we puzzled things out.

"They're still looking for me?" I asked, knowing the answer.

Clipper gave a rare, feral grin. "Oh yes. They can't figure out how the break-in happened, which is ticking them off. Will's interrogation led to nothing, and they had to let him go when the bail money came through. I've got a feed into the captain's office if you want to listen."

I strode over to him. "Captain Waters's office?"

"Yes. Oh, lookee here. Captain Perkins just strolled in."

Eddie, Zed, Everest, Peter, and I crowded around Clipper's computer. Clipper tensed his shoulders because he hated having people at his back. I didn't say anything but stepped to the side. I didn't want to aggravate him. That man could ghost better than Casper.

Waters greeted Perkins with the whole courtesy thing on high. "Something to drink, Jacob? Coffee, tea, lemonade?"

"We're on first name terms now?" Perkins asked, wary, taking a seat. "And yes, thanks. I'll take a lemonade."

Waters handed him a can of something with a lemon slice on it and shrugged. "I think we got off on the wrong foot. I'd like to try again." He turned to an old Mr. Coffee on top of a minifridge in the corner of his office. He checked the pot's temperature with his index finger, grimaced, but dispensed a cup of black sludge into a "World's Greatest Dad," mug.

Hmm.

Waters sat in his rolling chair and took a sip, then placed the mug on his desk and leaned back, his hands laced over his head. "Your boy jumped ship, Jacob. He's the subject of a manhunt."

Perkins nodded. "Yeah, that's not how I would have liked this to go."

Waters sipped again, then said, "How would you feel if someone escaped from your holding cell?"

Now Perkins swigged his drink. "A point of fact, someone did escape on my watch, and you seem to know about it. Quint Addington. Then he showed up in Central America as 'Señor Cinco,' because he thinks playing on his first name is clever."

"Playing on his first name?" Captain Waters stared at the ceiling. "Oh. Quint means five. Got it."

"Yeah, but authorities lost him there too. Disappeared again. We've never found him, and he's dangerous. Waylon isn't, but I get how you feel."

Captain Waters surged forward in his chair so that he leaned on the desk, forearms flat. "Then help me find him. If he's innocent, why did he run? And who helped him? Who has tech advanced enough that it knocked out ours, opened our jail, and sprung him in under two minutes?"

Perkins met him with his own steely gaze. "David, I'm a lawman, like you, and I'll do what I can to uphold the law, but I think you've lost the big picture."

Waters dropped back in his chair and picked up his mug. "What do you mean?"

"Mitzi didn't kill Joy. You know how much strength it takes to hold down a thrashing woman. What kind of mindset that requires." Perkin held his arms out to his sides. "No way does Mitzi have it."

"Agreed. That's why I think Waylon did it."

Perkins held up a finger to stop him from continuing. "Waylon doesn't have the temperament either. He's a makeup artist and cosmetologist, not a hardened criminal, not a murderer. But someone wants you to think he is. Or, someone wasn't trying to kill Joy at all."

"What do you mean?" asked Waters.

"Think about it. What if murdering Joy wasn't the plan? What if the plan started much more mundanely? What if the original plan is this: Joy starts a fight with Mitzi, who gets some bad press? Mitzi gets kicked out of the parade, and then Joy just happens to be here to take her place on the float?"

"Okay, sure, but who killed Joy?"

"There's a boyfriend out there, right? Someone she'd come to see?"

"I didn't tell you that."

"You told Waylon, and he told me. In the park, remember?"

Waters nodded. "Go on."

"The point is, there's another player in this game, and we don't know who he is or what he wants. Who's the wealthy boyfriend?"

Captain Waters studied Captain Perkins for a full minute. I timed it. Perkins didn't so much as twitch.

Waters sighed. "I liked Waylon for it, but we haven't been able to locate the boyfriend, so I'll play along."

"What about the jewelry Waylon found?"

"Or planted," Waters huffed.

"Let's go with found."

"Millions of dollars. Special order. A custom job by a special designer."

The team and I nodded as one. So, Waters had gotten at least that far.

"Will that help you track down the buyer?"

Now Waters laughed out loud. "The designer won't tell us, and since he's in Central America, we don't have jurisdiction."

"Cell phone records?" Perkins asked.

Waters held up a sheaf of papers. "We're combing through it."

"Can I see? Maybe I can recognize some of the names?"

Waters sighed and stood, walking to the big window of his office, which looked out on a parking lot. He stood still as if considering his options, then turned. "Tell you what, Jacob. You help me find Waylon, and I'll get you those cell phone records."

Perkins stood and held out his hand. "Deal."

"Duuude," said Everest. "Captain Perkins is going to sell you out."

I shifted on my feet, uncomfortable. "I don't think so. He wouldn't do that. He's angling to get a look at those records."

"Maybe, maybe not." Eddie tapped his upper lip. "Either way, we have to respect that Perkins is exactly what he said, a lawman, and he's probably not happy we got you out."

"If you hadn't, they'd have realized I'm not a normal human."

"This puts Perkins in a pickle," said Zed, with a surprising amount of empathy.

Eddie stood in front of the window and looked out at the yard. "It does," he said. "For his sake, we stay out of his way and make sure he doesn't get any 'leads' on Waylon so he can tell Waters he hasn't found him and mean it."

"But I want to see Sorya, Mitzi, and Amalia. I can't hide here all the time," I said.

"You're a fugitive, Waylon," Everest said. "And we can't break you out twice."

The big man had a point, but I had a counter. "I'm a master of special effects makeup—no one will notice me."

Peter sat at a small table, his hands deep in a bag of greasy chips. "I could pick you out in a crowd no matter how good your makeup."

"No, you couldn't."

"Uh-huh. No problem."

"How?"

"It's just the whole Waylon-ness. The 'you-ness.' You're so *you*. You stand out like a turkey in a flock of chickens." Peter stood and wiped chip crumbs onto the rug. "Even if you were covered head-to-toe, I'd know it was you."

Everest placed a quieting hand on Peter's shoulder and handed him a sleeve of cookies. "Here, eat these. You're much nicer to be around when your mouth is full."

Peter looked up at the big guy. "Hey, thanks!" he said, wiping his mouth with a kitchen towel.

"Have at it. Finish the whole thing." Everest sat in front of the smaller man, eclipsing him. I couldn't see Peter and his big, crunching mouth at all, and I preferred it.

Eddie rolled his eyes but said to me, "It's not safe for you to be out there. Don't go out. I'll try to bring Sorya here. Mitzi and Amalia are too public, but maybe Sorya, if she isn't being watched." He scratched his forehead. "Remember, though, that the Happiest Place on Earth is also Big Brother central. Cameras everywhere."

"Promise you'll try, though?" I grumbled. I knew I was being a baby, but I hadn't done anything wrong, and all I wanted to do was go to Disney with my girlfriend and my ghost seamstress. Was that too much to ask?

Eddie gave me a long-suffering look. "I'll try, Waylon. Try."

11

I'd promised I wouldn't leave, so I didn't, although I did sit on the back porch. Everest assured me no one could see me from the street, but I wore a hat and sunglasses all the same. The big guy and I played checkers; he beat me twice. After that, I paced the bungalow and finally baked cinnamon-streusel apple muffins for Peter.

That's how bored I was.

Eddie, Zed, and Clipper had run out to contact Mitzi, Amalia, and Sorya and let them know I was safe, if worried and trapped. When they returned, I accosted them for information. "Did you see them? How are they? What did they say?"

Eddie motioned for me to hang on a moment while he locked the door behind them. "We saw them. They're all fine. Mitzi and Amalia are rehearsing for the big parade."

"Rehearsing?" I asked. "What do they have to rehearse? They stand there and wave."

"Something about the size of the float. I don't know; that wasn't my main concern."

Argh. I hated missing all the fun.

Clipper booted up his computer and a new cell phone. "We caught Sorya alone in an electronic dead zone in the hotel. I gave her this phone number," he pointed to the new burner, "for emergency use."

"Smart," said Everest. I didn't know how he could be so calm and content trapped in this tiny house. He watched movies, checked on me, shushed Peter if needed. All with the equanimity of a house cat on a windowsill.

Zed kicked off his shoes. "Perkins got a hold of Sorya after looking at the cell phone records. He couldn't identify anything in particular, but there are calls made to someone with the initial 'V.' Possibly the boyfriend."

"Did you catch anything else from Waters? From the video in his office?" I asked Clipper.

He shrugged. "Video feed is compromised."

"They found it?" asked Everest.

"No. Some yahoo billing himself as an electronics specialist knocked out all their electronics, ours included." Clipper shook his head in disgust. "Some expert."

Zed laid back on the couch until Everest tapped Zed's large feet. Zed sighed, removed his feet from the upholstery, and sat up straight. "We have an initial and that's the main thing. Clipper has something to go on.

Peter joined us, his mouth full of apple-streusel. "Who was the last person Joy spoke to?" Muffin sprayed all over the place. I turned my back. Just because I'd made them didn't mean I had to watch him devour them.

"Chew and swallow, Peter, please," Eddie ordered.

"Her sister," Eddie answered Peter's question. "She spoke to her sister last."

I remembered something. "'Sisters forever.' Joy's necklace at the pool. I'm assuming the police have spoken to her?"

"Yes, but Perkins didn't provide any details to Sorya. Clipper, see if Perkins knows what the sister told the police."

Clipper palmed the burner phone and shot off a text.

Zed stretched and placed his feet on the coffee table, glanced at Everest, then immediately removed them. "Mother hen," he grumbled. Then, he continued. "Sorya may learn more at dinner tonight."

"What dinner?" I leaned forward.

Eddie smacked Zed on the back of the head. "Sorya's having dinner with Mateo tonight. I'm sure it's collegial."

I jolted to my feet. "She's going on a *date*?"

Zed shook his head and held out a hand palm up in a "stop" symbol. "Don't get overwrought, mate. Not a date. A friendly, academic dinner where they'll discuss areas of mutual interest."

I glared at him. "So much better. Thank you."

Eddie scowled at Zed for spilling the beans. He tried to assuage me. “She’s going to pump him for information, Waylon. Don’t get jealous.”

“I’m not.” I crossed my arms across my chest. “I’m fine. Fine. It’s all fine.”

“What did you expect, Waylon?” Peter gestured outside. “It’s beautiful, sunny Florida, and Sorya is by herself on holiday. This is her time to live it up. It’s not like you can give her a wild night of pony rides.”

Everest shoved another muffin at Peter. “Shut up.”

“What?” asked Peter. “Am I the only one not afraid to tell the truth? A zombie isn’t long-term dating material. You don’t age, and she does; besides, your dick fell off not so long ago, remember? She’s a normal, red-blooded woman. Mateo’s a hunk. You can’t blame her for playing the field.”

My anger rose. I turned to face him, ready to object, but stopped. He was right. Sorya deserved better than me.

Eddie tapped my shoulder. “It’s okay, Waylon. There’s more you can do—”

Clipper cut him off, holding up the phone. “According to Perkins, the sister said she never met the boyfriend in person, but he traveled a lot and had a slight British accent.”

Things started clicking in my brain. The “V” in Joy’s phone might stand for a Roman numeral, not the letter. The British accent. The Central American jewelry designer. Maybe this wasn’t about Joy or Mitzi and more about the zombie team and me. About revenge.

“Patience,” said Eddie. “It’s more than we had this morning.”

I didn’t have patience. Absolutely none. Patience had left the building long ago. I needed to see Sorya with a desperation I hadn’t felt before. Mateo’s arrival made me realize I’d skated on the surface of living, always waiting for Dr. Samuel Early to find a way to kill me. I’d lived a mindless existence focused on what I’d lost.

Then Sorya had come along, and the zombie team, and Amalia, and I’d discovered living again. Sorya brought me back. If she wanted out of our relationship, I’d survive, but I had to tell her how I felt. I had to speak to her, even if she wanted to end it. I wouldn’t blame her if she did. I loved her enough to want her to be happy, no matter the personal cost. The handsome doctor might be what she needed, and if so, I’d back off, grateful for the time we had.

But I’d fight for her. I refused to sit here and watch her drift away. And if I was right, danger crouched just around the corner.

I checked to make sure I had Mrs. Ross's flag in my pocket and left the team brainstorming how to find Joy's boyfriend, the motive for her murder, and what to do about the manhunt for yours truly. Thinking only went so far with this bunch. Built for action, the zombie team would move soon, and I didn't want to be there when they came looking for me because they'd try to stop me from doing what I needed to do.

I located the supplies Peter had bought earlier to turn Clipper into "Simon Fishman from New York." I quickly created a new nose and chin, carefully sculpting them to fit my face. Happy with the outcome, I slipped into cargo pants and a blue T-shirt from Everest's wardrobe, which fit my height, but not my girth. I also borrowed a belt, threw on my hat and sunglasses, and exited through the master bedroom's sliding glass doors to the back deck. I hopped the fence and walked to the main road. I lucked out right away, finding a refrigerated truck waiting open in front of an ice cream parlor.

"Heading back to the city?" asked the ice cream proprietor to the driver.

"Yup, last haul of the day. Those Disney execs sure like your pineapple sherbet."

The proprietor crossed his fingers. "And hopefully, they will continue to do so. They're sending my kid to college. Make sure to get it to Club 33 ASAP. It's best served ice cold."

The driver tipped his hat. "I gotcha, hoss."

I jumped into the cold car and hid behind one of the giant white refrigerators. The driver placed the sherbet inside another one, closed the door, and drove away with me inside.

I couldn't suppress a giggle. I'd snuck away from the zombie team right under their noses. That was, well . . . cold.

12

Getting from the truck into the park required creativity. Cameras covered every inch. My altered face helped avoid the facial recognition programs, but my essential "Waylon-ness" could give me away. I'd spent a lot of time around actors and took a cue from their approach to characterization by altering my walk. I put a tiny rock in one shoe, causing me to limp. I counted on the gait change to trick anyone watching.

If anything, people avoided me, giving the "injured" man extra space. That suited me fine.

I needed to think logically. The parade was this afternoon. If Mitzi and Amalia were here, they'd be working on the last-minute preparations. If I could find them, they'd help me find Sorya. I could do this. When the driver wasn't looking, I walked back to the truck, pulled a tray of sherbet out from inside one container, and held it on my shoulder like a waiter. "Hey, man. Can you help me?" I asked the nearest Disney employee, who smiled fanatically while ticking off boxes on a clipboard. "I'm looking for the parade staging area. They're expecting this special sherbet."

"Is that the pineapple?" he asked, eyes wide.

I nodded.

"Oooooh. Spectacular. They rarely let us have that. I hope I get some."

"I'll bring you some on the way out."

He clapped me on the shoulder with a huge grin.

"Really? You're the best. The food cart is that way."

I walked in the direction he'd indicated, maintaining the limp, hoping I'd figure it out from there. I dropped into line behind other employees and noticed a man carrying a huge number of bags, including several long garment bags holding what had to be gowns. I dropped the sherbet on the food tray to a chorus of *ooohs* and *aahs*.

"Here, let me help." I offered the gown carrier. "I was just on my way in." The overwhelmed guy muttered his thanks, and I used the bags to hide my face from the guard arguing with a florist holding an enormous bouquet of roses.

The guard huffed an exasperated breath. "Get the damn flowers out of my face. The float flowers were delivered three days ago."

"These are a personal bouquet for Mitzi from the higher-ups," said the florist, keeping his voice low so as not to attract attention.

"I don't care. Where's your ID? And why are you dripping water on my shoe?"

The florist had a towel draped over his arm. He bent, dabbed at the guard's shoes, begging. "Look, here's the card addressed to her and my credentials. I'll get fired if I don't get these to her. Give me a break, please?"

"Oh, for crying out loud, go in," said the guard. "She's in the back with the main float."

Well, that was handy-dandy information.

I helped the ball gown guy get his stuff to costuming, hanging the bags properly on the higher clothes racks so they wouldn't bunch at the bottom. I'd done this before, and my precision earned me a handshake.

I snagged a nametag and spare headset from the costuming department's temp reception desk on my way out. Striding with purpose, my hand to my right ear, I gestured with my left hand and whispered urgently into the headphones. No one gave me a second glance, assuming yet another float crisis they wanted nothing to do with.

I headed for the back to find Mitzi and Amalia. I spotted them, got closer, and raised my hand to get their attention. They spoke to a woman in a suit, but Amalia stared past her and peered at me through narrowed eyes. I smiled at first but frowned as a mustachioed gentleman in black jeans, a black t-shirt, a baseball cap, and sunglasses approached them from the side. Was he security? The bulge in his jacket hinted at a gun. Mental alarm bells clamored for me to put two and two together.

I stared, thinking, thinking, until he got near enough to catch a whiff of his unmistakable cologne. Bubbling with panic, I started forward, but a hand grabbed me, pulled me into an alcove, held me against the wall, and suffocated me with flowers. Rose thorns pricked my forehead and chin, and a gun poked my side.

"You didn't think you could hide from me, did you?" a voice hissed in my ear. "I see through your disguise." A hand snuck between me and the bouquet, touched my cheek, and scrambled around on my face. Before I could stop it, nails scraped at the edges of my fake nose, peeled it off, and dropped it on the ground. I yelped at the intrusion but kept still as the gun pushed into my abdomen.

"Don't move, or my colleague will shoot Amalia."

"You mean Santiago Aguilar. He always did wear too much cologne."

Quint dropped the flowers so I could see him. I'd been expecting him. I'd had a lot of thinking time in the bungalow and the cold truck, and I'd put the pieces together.

Like Santiago Aguilar, Quint wore black pants and a black shirt, his utterly forgettable face now more memorable with its ferocious, hideous grin.

"He's useful," Quint said. "Now come along like a nice zombie." He pointed to his wristwatch. "I have an open channel to Santiago. If you don't do what I say, when I say, he'll kill Amalia." He draped the towel over his arm to hold me close and hide the weapon.

"I don't remember a downloadable kill switch app," I replied, trying to sound cool. I smiled at the innocent folks hustling by. I didn't want to cause a scene and get someone shot. We moved as one unit, nodding and grinning like proper Disney employees.

"Newest thing," Quint quipped in my ear. "Move faster, or I'll shove you in the flower truck and shoot you in the head."

"What's the point of all this? You got away. Sure, your little drug operation took a hit, but so what? There was no need to come back."

Quint ushered me through a plain door, and we walked down steps into the utilidors, the underground tunnels which park employees and cast members used to get around without being seen. He pulled me along the plain corridors, smiling at the cleaning crews coming through with their trash cans, nodding at actors hurrying along with their costumes half-on. "You destroyed everything," he said, his hand tight on my elbow, gun still in my side. "My zombie military plan is shot to hell, you killed my witch doctor, and when you interrupted the shipments at the pageant, the cartels didn't want to do business anymore."

I had never been more proud. Or scared.

"Shit happens," I said.

"Shit doesn't happen to me," Quint said through bared teeth. "It is time to get rid of you, your zombie friends, and Amalia. I'm sick of all of you."

"Nice villain speech," I said. "Should I call you 'V'? 'V' for the Roman numeral five? You lured Joy here and pretended to be her boyfriend, you miserable piece of shit." My pocket pulsed twice. "One for no, two for yes," I said out loud.

"What?" Quint pulled me harder, making me move faster.

"Are they safe?" I asked. "Did they get away?"

"Amalia and Mitzi will die on the float, never knowing where your body lies. I'm going to bury you in pieces in different corners of the world. I'll chop you up and feed you to pigs."

My pocket pulsed twice again.

"Excellent," I said.

"Didn't you hear a thing I said?" Quint demanded as he maneuvered us to the side of the corridor so we could pass a stack of bins being loaded on a small truck with a forklift in the middle of the hallway. The truck beeped its intention to back up, and I yanked my arm out of Quint's grasp. He lunged at me, and I grabbed his shirt, pulling him into the truck's path, and flattened myself against the wall. Quint's head met the back of the forklift with a resounding thump. The driver leaped out of his seat to see what happened, and I grabbed the topmost items in the bins and fled.

Blood spurted from the wound on Quint's head, and well-meaning people surrounded him. I prayed he wouldn't shoot anyone and snuck into a bathroom. I kicked off my shoe, removed the rock, put it back on, and donned my newly purloined costume bottoms, minus the head. I made my way to the first exit I saw, leaving the crash scene behind me.

"You!" yelled a voice I knew.

I halted in my tracks, my back to him.

"You know better," chastised Cameron in his absurdly cheery manner. "Put that head on before you go up top. I'll help you out. Where's your guide?"

I smashed the costume head on mine and shrugged.

Cameron sighed. "I'll lead you then. Can't have you tripping over any little kids now, can we? Tigger is one of their favorites."

13

Up and out we went, emerging in Tomorrowland, home of Space Mountain. A flying car ride spun in circles, signs advertised a Space Ranger show, and carefree kids exited the Speedway with their nauseous parents. Cameron smiled, naturally, and I waved my big Tigger arm. We stopped multiple times to take photos with families.

"Stop being so antsy, Tigger," Cameron whispered to me. "This is your job, remember? Now, pose and hug!"

I bent and hugged children, one after the other, snot getting all over my fur while the heat built up inside the costume to the point of melting. How I could get away and back to the float prep area?

A distracted father approached, holding an enormous cotton candy, a giant soda pop, and a stuffed Dumbo. Beside him walked a tired little girl. She perked up when she saw Tigger and wrapped her tiny arms around my leg. I jigged gently up and down and patted her back.

"More!" she cried. "Tiggers are bouncy, trouncy, flouncy, pouncy, schmouncy, douncy, fun, fun, fun, fun, fun, fun!"

I gave her points for creativity and bounced.

She crossed her little arms and stomped a foot. "You're not bouncy enough."

"Bounce, Tigger," Cameron said through his teeth.

I bounced higher, putting extra oomph in my knees. I hadn't been trained for this.

A gaggle of kids gathered around me, all singing. "Tiggers are wonderful things! Their tops are made out of rubber! Their bottoms are made out of springs!"

The distracted dad scowled and jerked his chin at me. "Oi, Tigger! Go on then, bounce!

Oh, I bounced all right. I bounced right out of there. I jumped on both feet and jumped, jumped, jumped, looking for a way out. The children laughed and followed my pied piper of a Tigger, a chain of happy, singing kids bouncing along behind me.

Cameron beamed from ear to ear and skipped beside me. "Great job, Tigger. Excellent effort!"

I bounced in a circle until I spotted a Kanga. I hopped right on over, hooked that poor schlep, and made her go with me. I hugged Kanga and pointed and made a huge deal of finding my friend from the Hundred Acre Wood until the kids asked where Roo was.

Silently, I backed away and bumped into someone.

A voice I recognized said, "Watch it, you overgrown tiger."

Another familiar voice said, "Shut up, Peter."

"What?" grumbled Peter, pushing me out of his way. "Stupid costume freaks can't see where they're going. How are we supposed to find "you know who" in this crowd? Why did he run away, anyway? We should leave him to his fate."

Everest clamped a hand over Peter's mouth and spoke in Peter's ear, using a crowd-friendly code. "The ladies got away from Señor Smelly Cologne by the skin of their teeth, Peter, and only because our friend, 'the flag lady' warned them, but we don't know where the makeup artist is. And that means Señor Five is here, and he may have the cosmetologist in a hidden location. Now, shut up, and use that brain of yours."

I waved my big paw at Everest and Peter.

"Hey Tigger," said Everest, giving me a high five. "Good to see you. TTFN!"

I shook my head and held up my paw again, bouncing after them.

Peter gave me a high five. "Yeah, yeah, hi to you, too, Tigger."

So much for my overall "Waylon-ness" making me easy to recognize.

I cuffed Peter upside the head with my giant Tigger paw. Given the thickness of the paw, it seemed like a playful jostle. Everest and Peter shoved me out of the way and moved on. I started to run after them, but the loudspeaker's announcement stopped me cold.

"Ladies and Gentlemen: Please gather on the parade route!"

Cameron grabbed my elbow. "Come on, Tigger! Let's lead the way!" And off we went, me bouncing along the posted route to watch the Float Parade, fretting about Santiago's next move, if Quint had recovered enough to wreak his revenge, and if Mitzi and Amalia were on the main float.

Scratch the last part.

They'd be on the float.

Mitzi was a professional, and if the show must go on, the show would go on. A little appearance by Santiago Aguilar wouldn't stop her or Amalia, especially since they'd notified Eddie and the team. With the zombie team in the park and the cameras on them, an attack seemed unlikely now.

I hopped on down toward the castle and stopped at the Prince Charming carousel, basically upper center in the park. The crowds gathered behind well-positioned barriers decorated with sparkly lights so the floats could pass through with ease. Parents lifted their children onto their shoulders so they could see better, and a swell of anticipation filled the air. Despite my worry, I couldn't help but be carried away too. Cameron also caught the fever, stopped paying attention to me, and I deliberately lost him in the crowd.

The first float paid homage to silent movies with a Charlie Chaplin lookalike twirling an umbrella. The second represented scenes from old Western movies with names of classic films printed around the bottom of the float. The gunslinger actors shot each other and fell as the float traveled by, recreating dramatic standoffs between the sheriffs and the villains.

The third was a clever representation of the original Mickey Mouse in black and white on the bow of a riverboat. The floats kept on coming, a celebration of cinema and Disney ingenuity. Flowers rained down on the crowd as princesses threw kisses to their adoring fans.

Finally, the last float arrived. Mitzi and Amalia adorned the top, waving like queens. The announcer introduced them, although Mitzi needed no introduction. Amalia beamed with happiness, and Mitzi soaked in the adoration like the star she was. I was thrilled to see them and glad Santiago hadn't ruined their experience.

As the float passed, I followed, bouncing toward Liberty Square and Frontierland. Children trailed behind me singing, "The Wonderful Things About Tiggers!" I gave them a thumbs up and kept on bouncing away.

The float parade continued along the route unhampered, and I wondered if Quint had been injured seriously enough to be sidelined. If so, maybe Santiago had left.

As we entered Liberty Square, a familiar face caught my eye. Bold as brass, Santiago stood in the doorway to the Hall of Presidents holding a woman's arm.

Sorya. The sight of her struck my heart.

I dropped any pretense of being Tigger and walked over to them. We stood before the pillared building with the flag and clock and the embossed 1787 on the roof's gable.

"Waylon?" Santiago asked in a steely voice.

I nodded.

"Inside," he said. He kept hold of Sorya's arm and gave me a genteel bow.

Sorya's eyes shot daggers at him, but he didn't notice. He had a knife pressed to her side. I wondered where he'd hidden his gun and decided it didn't matter. Knives were deadly too.

He whispered "Code 101" to the cast member stationed at the front entrance, placed a "Closed for maintenance" sign in front of the doors and opened the door to the Hall of Presidents. I bumbled through the entryway in my costume, much to the chagrin of the children and adults waiting in the queue. He closed the door behind me, and I removed the costume head, so I stood there all furry Tigger body and legs.

We stood in the atrium. The blue and gold carpeting, white walls, and presidential seal made it look like the oval office. Portraits of presidents lined the circular walls.

The flag in my pocket wiggled in excitement.

"Not now," I whispered. "This isn't the time."

"You look ridiculous," Santiago said. He dragged Sorya into the animatronics auditorium and positioned himself behind the last row of chairs at the top. The presentation played every twenty-five minutes. The blue curtain parted, and a film started with the paintings of the Revolutionary War.

"I'm not the one chasing people to another country to exact some kind of stupid revenge," I said over the sound of the movie. "*That's* ridiculous."

"I just want my jewelry back," Santiago said, raising his voice so he could be heard. "We gave it to Joy for safekeeping. Where is it?"

"That was your jewelry?" I scoffed. "You sad sack. The police have it. Once Quint murdered Joy, they took it as evidence."

Santiago pressed the knife into Sorya's side harder, and she stiffened. "He said you got to it."

"I did," I said. "But the cops found me with it. Didn't he tell you they arrested me?"

"You gotsch away though, Waylon," said Quint, who entered from the auditorium door near the stage. Quint's swollen face made it hard to understand him, and when he grimaced, he was missing two teeth.

The movie's narrator described George Washington's address to the nation when he'd stepped down. Mrs. Ross's flag shook with happiness at his name.

The curtain lifted, and Abe Lincoln rose from his chair, intoning "Four score and seven years ago. . . ."

"What happened to your face and teeth, Quint? You don't look so good. And you're limping. That must have been some hit." I said this last part with some satisfaction.

"They gotsch most of the schtuff but not the wing," Quint said, climbing the ramp, slowly, toward our position.

"The what?" asked Sorya.

"The ring," said Santiago. "At least tell me where to find the ring."

"Oh! Right. A ring. The police have a necklace, bracelet, earrings, but they don't have a ring. You would expect one, wouldn't you? A whole set? Geez, I don't know," I said, shrugging. "I don't have one either."

Quint leaned on the double doors.

The room grew dark, and the announcer continued the presentation.

Santiago's face flushed, and his mustache quivered with anger. Quint just looked tired. I almost felt sorry for them until Quint pulled out his gun and pointed it at Sorya.

"Tell me where the wing is."

"I have no idea. It's the truth."

"What did you do wif it?" Quint wiped drool with his wrist but kept the gun steady.

"I'll tell you, but you have to let Sorya come over here first."

Quint gestured for Sorya to join me.

She walked over to me, head high, practically vibrating with fury.

"Now I hash botsh of you," Quint said. "Whersh the wing?"

The film continued. The drums of World War Two pounded around us. President John F. Kennedy asked what we could do for our country.

"I found it on a tampon and gave it to a man named Mr. Fishman, who sold it to a purveyor of fine jewels here in Orlando."

President Reagan tells Mr. Gorbachev to "tear down this wall."
"Whosh Mr. Fishman?" Quint asked.

"A man from New York who knows his diamonds and emeralds."

The curtain rises, and all the presidents of the United States of America appear on the stage. The narrator begins to name the presidents. Chester A. Arthur, the twenty-first president, moved his arm in a most realistic way.

"Whosh did he shell it to?" Quint moved closer, menacing despite his injury.

I told him.

"What did Mr. Fishman do with the money?"

"Bailed out an alligator farm employee."

Santiago started at me. "What the actual fuck? You're serious."

"The guy hit Chubby with a golf cart."

Santiago marched away from us, down the ramp's incline and into Quint's face. "What are we going to do now, Quint? We have no money." He threw his arms out to the side with clenched fists and raged. "We sunk everything in that jewelry. We should have gone to Europe, but no. No! You had to get your revenge on Waylon and his team first."

"Shut up, Shantiago," said Quint, like he was speaking to a toddler. They both ignored the incredible presentation behind them.

"I will not 'shut up,' you bombastic ass. Set Waylon up for murder, you said. Ruin his career, expose this weirdo military team, bring Mitzi down, and then we'll make our way to Europe to regroup." Santiago, ordinarily cool and calculated, ran his hands through his hair. It stood up on end.

"Shantiago, you're embarrassing yourself."

With them facing each other, I pulled Sorya's wrist, and we backed up to exit the exhibit. The narrator continued introducing presidents—George had not yet spoken.

Quint yelled, "Hey!" and got off a shot, but it ricocheted off the Tigger head I carried in my hand, knocked off an ear, and we burst outside.

"Run!" I said, but I didn't have to tell Sorya twice.

14

"Hey, Waylon! Why are you wearing half a Tigger costume?" came a voice behind me. I recognized the voice but didn't acknowledge its owner. He'd said my name, and now I caught attention from onlookers.

"Keep running," I said. "Let's catch the float."

Stanley Argawal scampered behind us, breathing hard. "Waylon, I didn't know you worked at the park. You know it is against the rules to be above ground without your head, right?"

I jammed the head back on.

"What happened to Tigger's ear?"

"Stanley," panted Sorya. "Keep running or get out of here."

"Oooh! Is something afoot? Another fight? Can I get pictures? I only got regular old float photos, nothing interesting. Those pics of Waylon between Mitzi and Joy made me more money than I earned all last year."

"Bounce, Tigger! Bounce!" screamed a couple of tiny humans next to me, their sticky fingers pawing at my fur.

"Tigger can't bounce now, kids," said Sorya. "He promised Mitzi he'd meet her at her float."

One of the kids gave her the beady eye and pointed. "Tiggers bounce. That's what they do bestest."

"Yeah," said his mom. "And in the happiest place on Earth, kids make the rules."

So I bounced. I bounced really, really fast and away from them all, but I bounced.

Let those rugrats keep up.

The children did fine; the parents struggled. They caught up eventually but panted so hard they had to bend over and place their hands on their knees to catch their collective breath. The kids gathered around me, and I shooed them off.

They burst into tears and pouted. Their parents pulled them back from "mean Tigger."

The parade had rounded the corner toward the Liberty Square Riverboat Dock, where it stopped so the main float could, it turned out, actually float. Mitzi and Amalia's float was designed to go on the water and travel around the river, which I hadn't expected. From Amalia's face, she hadn't either.

Workers hustled around the bottom of the float, prepping it for entry into the water. Someone at the top chatted with Mitzi and Amalia, who gestured with concern. I heard the word "weight," "heavy," and "not swimming in this dress," and I wished I could lend my support. I shared Amalia's concerns.

But I had my own problems, namely Quint approaching from the southeast.

And then more concerns from the northwest. A flock of flamingos attacked from the island in the middle of the river.

And they had learned from the last bunch.

The flamingos modified their approach, communicating and coordinating via hivemind. They broke into two teams to flank me, once again in precise formation, attempting to pinion me from the left, their beady eyes aflame.

From the right, Quint pointed his gun at me.

The flamingos tightened their assault position.

Stanley focused his lens aperture.

Kids drew close, fascinated by the Borg birds.

With all my strength, I pushed Sorya out of the way and then swung children behind me, arms outstretched, facing Quint, guarding them with my body. They could survive the flamingo brigade but not a hail of bullets.

I took a deep breath. Whatever came next, life as I knew it was over.

But none of it was necessary.

Eddie and Everest appeared out of nowhere and disarmed and zip-tied Quint in the time it takes to say Tom Sawyer Island. They handed him to Zed and Clipper, who whisked him off. The children and parents burst into applause, thinking it was a show.

The flamingos didn't attack either. Instead, they besieged the float with their steely beaks and crazy feet. Someone erected an emergency ladder, and Mitzi and Amalia climbed down. Flamingos screeched around them, and people ran in every direction, but the flamingos ignored the women, beating at the foot of the float. The kids behind me hooted with laughter.

I counted five zombies. Me. Eddie. Everest. Clipper. Zed. Everyone accounted for. Yet flamingos attacked?

I pointed to a stunned Cinderella and Prince Charming, corralled the children toward them, and then loped to a men's room, ditched the costume, and sprinted back outside. I gestured for Everest and Eddie to come with me to the float, but they took one look at the flamingos and shook their heads. Blowing out a frustrated breath, I mouthed, "Really?" and hurried there myself. I took a flamingo beak to the scalp but managed to slip under the skirt.

Two men wrestled underneath, both crouched low.

Santiago.

And Early.

"I knew you'd come back," I said.

"Shut up and help me." He punched Santiago in the gut, and the villain screamed. "He's scrappy."

I crawled over, grabbed Santiago's foot, and yanked, dropping him on his butt. Early elbowed him in the jaw like a professional wrestler, and Santiago passed out cold.

"I am so sick of these madmen," Early said, sitting back but still hunched over. He kicked a flamingo's head. "What's with the pinko commie birds?"

I backhanded another one, and it squawked, withdrawing. "Zombie detectors. Don't know why."

"They've been chasing me all over Orlando."

"They're mean, alright. Did you know they eat blue-green algae?"

"No!"

"Yes. Never underestimate these suckers."

"Bastards."

Finally, a human head popped under the float's skirt. "Hello! Aren't you two cute, hiding under here, Sirs, we got the flamingos under control.

No idea why they did that. They've always been peaceful before." He saw Santiago. "Oh, dear. We'll get an ambulance for him."

"Yeah, thanks. Is Captain Waters here?" I asked.

"Uh, yeah, how did you know?"

"Lucky guess."

We dragged Santiago out and waited for the "alpha team," Disney's code for their medical crew, to arrive. Sorya checked him out while we waited and said he'd be fine. He'd regained consciousness and moaned something about an airborne assault. The paramedics reassured him he'd fainted from the heat and must have hit his head when he fell. How quickly people dismissed murderous flamingos.

Sorya did a double-take when she saw Early, then gave him a short hug, whispering something in his ear.

Everest's mouth dropped when he saw who I had brought with me. "Early! Haven't seen you in a while."

"Nice to see you, Everest," said Early, shaking the big guy's hand.

"Where you been?" asked Eddie, his arms crossed, not offering a hand yet. "How's your psyche?"

Zed and Clipper joined us. "Perkins is coming," Zed said. "Waters, too." He brought his hand to his heart when he saw my companion. "Early? Is that you? What the hell? Where did you come from, mate?"

"He was under the float," I said.

"The whole time?" Zed asked.

Clipper smacked him on the arm. "No, numbskull."

"The last two hours or so," Early replied.

"So, where have you been the rest of the time?" asked Perkins, who'd joined the crowd in time to hear the last bit. "And is your head on straight?"

"That's what I want to know," said Eddie.

Early held up his hands, palms out. "I'm doing better. Been working my own op and getting a little help."

Clipper raised one eyebrow. "Your own op? Do I vomit now?"

"You can't vomit at all," I reminded him.

Amalia sauntered up in a pair of tiny shorts and a crop top.

"You changed fast," I said.

She jerked a thumb behind her. "Changed over there. They have tunnels everywhere. They wanted to mop up the mess fast." She, too, started when she saw Early.

"Sam! Are you back?" She stared hard at him, and the flag in my pocket jiggled hard. Amalia's square must have jerked as well.

"Let's scoot out of the way so we don't make more of a scene." I held up a finger to my favorite Indian photographer, and he nodded. "We're being photographed. Nothing we can do to stop it, but if we move aside, we can minimize the lingering hubbub."

"Damn, I hate photographs," whispered Eddie.

"I know, but everyone's got a camera these days."

We moved down the walk and found a quieter section on the grass near the lavatories, a closed seasonal restaurant, and a non-working *Fast-Pass* kiosk.

As soon as we did, Amalia and I removed our flag squares and held them together. Mrs. Ross materialized out of nowhere, as substantial as any living, breathing person. She pointed at Early and shook her finger. "It's about damn time you showed up," she said.

"Okay, okay," Early said. "I bolted, but I got some help, and I've been chasing Quint on my own."

"Who helped you?" asked Eddie.

"I did."

We turned toward the voice, and the entire zombie team said, "Fuuuucccck."

Mrs. Ross disappeared.

I just stared.

I'd know that beard anywhere. And Captain Waters stood next to him. "Oliver? Oliver Bramwell? You're Captain Waters's source?"

Bramwell stepped forward. "Yes."

"Which alphabet agency do you belong to?" asked Everest, "And why didn't you tell us?" Everest and Zed stood side-by-side, forming a muscular wall of indignant zombittude.

Bramwell gave a half-smile. "CIA and I couldn't. I didn't get involved until Quint disappeared and the zombie program fell off the map. I had strict orders to observe the zombie unit only. Your messages got through, Captain Smith."

Eddie's stare could have frozen a Great Lake. "I don't go by rank or last name anymore, Agent Bramwell, if that is your real name. Perhaps I shall simply call you Agent Son-of-a-Bitch for not helping us when the *boker*, the witch doctor, was killing and dumping men in the river, kidnapping Sorya, and torturing Early."

Sorya also looked at Bramwell with a glint in her eye. Clipper didn't shift next to Zed and Everest, but he stood loose and ready, like a mongoose facing a snake. I stepped three paces away from Bramwell and Waters, guiding Sorya and Amalia to follow. Perkins followed.

Bramwell seemed surprised by the hostility. "I kept an eye on things, and you handled the whole situation well."

Peter ran up, out of breath. "Guys, I figured something out. Oliver Bramwell is . . . ." He looked around and noticed Oliver and the stand-off. "CIA. But, I see you know this. Early? Is that you?"

"In the flesh, so to speak."

"You throw in with Bramwell?"

"He helped, yeah."

Peter, the oily pain-in-the-ass, got in Bramwell's face, and I wanted to cheer. "If you helped Early, I'm willing to hear you out, but that's the only reason. You knew we faced a killer who took human lives, and you did nothing. Nothing."

Bramwell stroked his beard. "How did you figure it out?"

"Are you really that dumb?" Peter cocked his head. "You gave me that new position in Finance, remember? I did what I do best. Followed the money. You weren't all that clever at hiding it. Seriously? Only two shell accounts? Puullease. Child's play."

Oliver blinked a few times, still stroking his beard.

I shook my head. "Oh, come on, Bramwell. You know what they say. Who's the best agency at finding someone out of the CIA, the FBI, or the KGB?"

"Who?" asked Amalia, being helpful.

"The IRS. The money people find everything."

Oliver rocked back on his heels and glared at Peter.

"How did he help you, Early?" I asked.

"When I ran from you, I was in a bad way. I needed some things from my office so I could escape. I meant to leave forever, but I ran into Oliver. Long story short, he revealed who he was and got me some counseling. It . . . helped."

"You wouldn't have needed it if he had helped in the first place," I said. "Why didn't you come to us?"

Early studied the grass and kicked a rock with his toe. "I couldn't. After everything I did. How I hurt people. I felt guilty."

"How did you get here?" Sorya asked.

"Oliver asked me to track Quint. The CIA believed he was making his way to South America, but that didn't sit right with me."

"What did you do to pick up his trail?" Amalia didn't look at Oliver either. By silent agreement, we gave him a pass, but he wasn't a part of the team.

"I asked Oliver to look for names that meant 'five.'" Early grinned and gave a little chuckle. "I tracked down a Monsieur Cinque and an Englishman going by Mr. Penta then, lo and behold, Oliver found Facebook chatter about the exquisite diamond and emerald earrings seen on Joy Lucky by her mysterious boyfriend V. How very vendetta of him. Joy's sister went on and on about how her sister had made bank with this new guy."

Clipper nodded. "And you thought, no way is this a coincidence."

"On the nose," said Early.

Eddie considered this and nodded. "Smart."

"It brought me here, and one thing led to another, and I hit pay dirt. I didn't expect to see you guys. "

"Paid Time Off," said Sorya, with a frown and note of disgust.

"Vacation," said Perkins, as if this explained everything.

Maybe it did because Early bobbed his head in understanding and said, "Ah. Yes. Of course."

Waters, who'd remained silent during Early's explanation, ran his hands over his face and turned toward his informant. "Who killed Joy Lucky?"

"Quint," I said. "Hold on, I can prove it." I left the group, returned to the main walkway, and scanned the crowd until I found who I was looking for. He'd waited for me. "Stanley, hey, can you help me for a second?"

He practically bounced over like Tigger. "Anything for you, Waylon. You're my cash cow. You should see my new photos!"

I sighed inwardly. "Don't ruin my career, Stanley, please."

"Oh, no, all very tasteful. I promise."

I studied his bell-bottom jeans and lime green Nepalese style cotton shirt. It was awful and stylishly retro simultaneously. Maybe I could make this work. I focused on what I needed. "Can you email Amalia and me a copy of that picture you took of me at the margarita machine? The one of me holding an ice pack to my head?"

"You got it." His eyes widened. "Will it help with the murder investigation?"

"I don't know, but it may."

He held his hand to his heart. "This is so exciting. I'm telling you, my life has become so much better since you came to town. You are my good luck charm."

"That's great. Can you send it now, please?" I gave him my email address.

"Sure thing. I have it on my phone." A few swipes and clicks, and he said, "There. You both should have it."

"Thanks."

He smiled from ear to ear. "And now I have your email address. We can be pen pals! You can recommend me for Indian weddings."

"Just don't sell any photos that embarrass me. My rep is your rep now. And also, don't take any of my friends. They don't want the attention."

Stanley cast a worried glance at my ward. "Amalia? You and Mitzi are fair game, right? You're public figures."

Amalia nodded. "Just not the guys."

I tapped his chest. "What she says."

He nodded and gave me a thumbs up. "You got it, boss."

Amalia opened her phone and retrieved the picture. I borrowed the phone, walked back to the team and its carbuncle, Oliver Bramwell, and showed the photograph to Captain Waters. "Look closely."

He enlarged the pictured and studied it. "It's you with an ice pack, and you look confused."

"Don't focus on me. Look in the background."

Perkins sidled next to him and studied it as well. He pointed to a man in profile. "There's Quint."

"He came back to the scene of the crime," Waters said.

"He wanted to see what would happen, and Santiago wanted to get into Joy's room before you, but he miscalculated, forgetting that Joy had a suite," I said.

Waters snapped his fingers. "The new fingerprint locks."

I pointed at him. "Exactly."

Peter laughed. "Well, boo boo ka choo for him."

That made me laugh. "I know. Foiled by technology. I mean, what's a man gotta do to frame someone for murder, retrieve priceless jewels from feminine hygiene boxes, and slip out of town?"

"The devil's always in the details," said Perkins.

Amalia scratched her head. "Who was he trying to frame?"

"Me," I replied. "We made him angry by harshing his vibe with the drug dealers and killing his witch doctor."

"Don't try to sound cool, Uncle Waylon," said Amalia, shuddering. "You saying 'harshing his vibe' is not okay."

Sorya chuckled, and I elbowed her, frowning. "Don't encourage her," I whispered.

"She's right," she whispered back.

I wrapped my arm around her shoulders and pulled her close. I liked having her by my side.

"Don't date Mateo," I said, keeping my voice low.

She turned to me, startled. "Why on Earth would I do that?"

I released the tension I'd been carrying. For all my "whatever Sorya wants" inner monologues, I'd have been devastated if she left. I leaned down and kissed the top of her head.

Amalia snapped in front of our faces. "Hey, we're still here, you two. You can do lovey-dovey stuff later."

I smile, relaxed now. "Yes, Your Highness."

She rolled her eyes, but Eddie smiled and gave me a thumbs up.

Waters left to clean up the paperwork and call Deputy Jackman to fill her in. The magic Disney broom had already erased all evidence of a float/flamingo mishap.

The rest of us had a day of vacation to fill.

"So? What do we do?" I asked.

My pocket jerked forward, and Everest raised an eyebrow. "Is that a flag in your pocket, or are you just glad to see me?"

15

Mrs. Ross materialized and led the charge.

"Come on, everyone, let's go see George," I said and followed, Sorya next to me, Amalia behind with Perkins. The zombie team filed along, Eddie bringing up the rear, still keeping a close eye on things. He jerked his head at Everest and Zed, and the two stayed outside the Hall, surreptitiously guarding the entrance. I'd expected someone to notice the "Closed for maintenance" sign, but no, it stood sentry just where Santiago had placed it. Clipper hung out inside the foyer while Eddie escorted us into the presentation. Several tourists followed.

Peter sat with us. Perkins's knee bobbed up and down next to me. Sorya sat on my other side. I reached out, and she put her hand on top of mine.

I bumped Perkins's shoulder. "Stop that knee thing. It's driving me crazy," I said. "I'm trying to relax here."

"Can't help it. I'm on edge."

"Why? It's over. Quint got arrested. Santiago's in the hospital. We're good." As I said this, my tummy tightened. What was I missing?

A rustle of cloth captured my attention. The zombie squad guarded the main entrance, so who caused the noise?

Perkins looked over his shoulder. "Waylon, there's another exit in the back."

"Who's coming in?"

"Disney cops."

I dropped my chin to my chest. For Heaven's sake, when would this be over?

A discreet security officer tapped my shoulder. "Would you come with me, sir?"

The room turned dark, and the presentation started. I extracted the flag from my pocket and handed it to Perkins. "Give this to Amalia, please. I owe Mrs. Ross."

"What is this about?" I asked as we walked to the door. Another guard boxed me in on the other side, taking a discreet hold of my elbow.

"Shhhhh!" said a tourist on the aisle.

We walked into the brightly lit atrium. Clipper eyed the security guards as we exited. "Waylon?"

"Not sure," I replied.

He followed us until Zed and Everest took over, and Clipper stayed behind. The security guards saw the two big zombies but only because they made sure they were noticed. If they wanted to stay hidden, they would have.

"Who're the goons?" asked Security Guard Number One. He had two different colored eyes, one brown and one blue, like a Husky dog I once knew. The other man was Black, his shirt straining to hold his muscles. He moved like a weightlifter, tight and blocky, but I bet he couldn't touch his toes.

"Them?" I said, jerking my thumb behind me where Zed and Everest trailed us. "Oh, they're my stalkers. Guess they're cosmetologist groupies. The big one on the left always says you can never go wrong with more mascara."

Everest choked behind me. It sounded something like, "Bastard," but I could have been wrong.

Guard Number Two, the muscled one, shoulder bumped me with a growl, and Zed clipped the man's right shoe. Cause and effect.

The security personnel escorted me down the sidewalk, past topiaries and pretzel stands. "You going to tell me what this is about?" I asked.

Husky pointed and said, "They want to ask you a few questions."

Courtney and Cameron waited for me at the entrance of a plain building painted light blue, out of the way of the main traffic. Their crossed arms and pursed lips looked wrong on their normally cheery faces.

"What's up, kids?" I asked. "Turns those frowns upside down."

On command, Courtney flashed a brilliant smile, all white teeth and perky cheekbones. "You purloined a beloved character costume and flaunted the rules pertaining to wearing said costume."

"Purloined?"

She pulled her shoulders back and lifted her chin, her smile more of a grimace. "Pilfered, looted, stole. Choose your word."

"I choose borrowed. Cameron was there."

Cameron's face flushed bright red. "I didn't know who you were. I never saw your face. You abducted Tigger, despoiled him and his characterization. You should be ashamed of yourself."

"Hey! I bounced with the best of them. I bounced, I flounced, I pounced, and I made sure the kids had fun, fun, fun, fun, fun. I was a wonderful Tigger even if I was *not* the only one, which is something you should think about before you accuse me of despoiling anything."

"Whatever do you mean?" asked Cameron, thoroughly insulted.

I turned up my nose in righteous indignation, pulled out my ace, and shook my finger in his face. "The song clearly says, *'But the most wonderful thing about Tiggers iiiiiiiiiis I'm the only one!'*"

"So?"

"You had three Tiggers bouncing around the park today," I waved my arm across his field of vision to emphasize my point. "So *clearly* there is *more* than one." I crossed my arms. Take that, Cameron.

Cameron and Courtney turned to one another with wide eyes. Cameron's lower lip wiggled. It trembled. Courtney's eyes brimmed, and she gripped her clipboard tightly.

"Uh, Waylon," Everest leaned in close, "I think you're making them cry."

"Whatcha have to go and do that for? They're just kids." Zed stage whispered.

"I'm pointing out that a discrepancy exists between the song and the characterization in the park, that's all." I flapped a hand. "What? I didn't drown Winnie-the-Pooh."

Husky and Muscles's mouths dropped open. "You're a meanie," said Husky.

"Oh, for goodness's sake. I didn't mean to hurt anyone's delicate sensibilities."

The guards lost interest in me and went to the wonder twins' sides to reassure them that little children everywhere wouldn't be scarred by the sight of three simultaneous Tiggers.

"You should have gone easier on them," Everest scolded.

I watched them walk away. "This is ridikkerous." I ran onto the main path and yelled at their departing backs. "Hey, I'm sorry! Don't think twice about it. The Tiggers spread out, so no one saw more than one Tigger at a time. It's totally okay."

Cameron acknowledged with a small wave.

"TTFN!" I yelled.

Finally, Courtney turned and gave me a thumbs up.

Stanley tapped my shoulder, and I yelped.

"Where'd you come from?"

Stanley ignored my question. "You want to see what's already up on *Celebrity Today?*"

"You sold photos that fast?"

The slight man bounced from foot-to-foot in excitement. "Digital's a taskmaster, an endless hungry beast. Twenty-four-seven. And with Venmo, I get paid right away."

I covered my eyes with my hand. "Dear God. What do you have?"

Stanley handed me his phone. I removed my hand from my face and looked at it, deeply apprehensive.

There I was, clad in half a Tigger costume and bouncing after the float under the headline "*Waylon Jenkins Earns His Stripes*." The first line read: *Waylon Jenkins, super cosmetologist and make-up artist to the stars, goes to great lengths to help his clients, even dressing up in a costume to follow Mitzi in the Disney Float Parade, just in case a lash falls out of place.*

"Hey, that's not bad," I said.

"No, it's good," said Stanley, chucking me on the shoulder. I wondered when we'd gotten to that phase of our friendship. He must have wondered, too, because he backed up a step. "I can be helpful, see? Positive press, like I told you."

"Yeah, that's great. Thanks, Stanley."

Stanley's phone beeped, and he scrolled down. "Cool. Another deposit."

"What did you sell?"

He tapped his screen and looked at the photo. He quickly backed away. "Got to go, Waylon. See you around."

"What did you do?" I caught up, tugged on his arm, and grabbed his phone. The screen had gone blank. "Open it."

Stanley scrunched up his face and eyed the pavement.

"Stanley!"

"Fine." He thrust the phone at me. "Just remember, I don't make the headlines."

I gazed at the picture in a rag called *"Hollywood Plus."* It was me with Cameron and Courtney. My arms were outstretched as I leaned forward, my mouth open in an astonished "O." The guards stood between the twins and me. The caption read: *"Waylon Jenkins Ruins the Fun for Everyone."* It went on: *Meanie Waylon Jenkins made two young Disney World cast members cry when he yelled at them in the middle of the park as they tried to explain simple and reasonable rules about costume use. Jenkins made the most wonderful place on Earth the saddest. What a monster.*

Well, wasn't that a kick in my colossal . . . borrowed part.

I handed Stanley his phone, and he pocketed it.

"We're still on for the Indian weddings, right?" he said. "You'll put in a good word?"

"Sure. You find one, I'll recommend you," I said, sinking onto a bench. I was done. Cooked. Burnt. Toast. No matter what I did, it didn't come out right, so I was going to sit right there and do nothing. I emptied my mind and enjoyed several minutes of Zen until Amalia found me and everyone else followed, including Sorya, who sat next to me on the bench.

"The show is over, Uncle Waylon," Amalia said.

"Did you enjoy it?"

"It was pretty cool. I liked Lincoln." She pumped a fist. "Badass to fight a civil war and free the slaves. Abe rocked."

Of course, she thought that. He was everyone's favorite, and I despised slavery, but I had mixed feelings about that time in history. I'd acquired a severe allergy to dying during the Civil War's Battle of Shiloh. Also enjoying food and other Earthy pleasures.

"What did Mrs. Ross think?"

"Meh," Amalia said.

"Meh? That's the whole reason we came!"

"Let's get back to the hotel, and we can talk some more." Amelia offered me a hand and hauled me to my feet. I, in turn, helped Sorya.

Eddie joined the conversation. "We'll get our stuff from the bungalow and meet you later. We're clear with the cops. We've got one more night and half a day before the plane back. Let's enjoy it."

I nodded and pulled Sorya to me, placing my arm around her. She smiled up at me and nodded. “Fine, but no park,” she said. “Let’s relax at the hotel.”

I squeezed her tight. “Excellent thought.”

16

Zed had to ruin it. He challenged Peter to a game of darts.

Sorya and I lounged in the small bar off the pool. She sipped a glass of riesling, and I gazed at her lovely face. We chatted about her return to work and a movie I hoped to be asked to work on. Until a reluctant hotel manager approached.

"Sir. Mr. Jenkins?"

"Yes?"

"I recognized you from *Celebrity Today* and *Hollywood Plus*. I hope you don't mind me intruding."

"Which photos did you see in that online rag?"

He smiled wide. "All of them and I bought the print versions. You're a star!"

"Even with the nasty headlines?"

He brushed that away with a flick of his hand. "No one reads anything. We just look at the pictures."

"See? No such thing as bad publicity," Sorya said, patting my hand. "You should check your email."

"I guess," I replied, still shocked at the whole thing. I'd avoided my messages and emails again.

"Anyway," the manager cleared his throat, "could you come with me to the game room and ask your friends to tone it down? They're disturbing the other guests, especially with their creative use of profanity."

Sorya rubbed her temples, and I ran my hands through my hair. "What did they say?"

The manager pulled a notepad from his pocket and read it in a monotone voice. "Eyewitnesses said that the skinny guy yelled, 'I'm going to drag you outside and leave you for the fuckin' flamingos,' to which the Australian gentleman said, 'Bugger off, you dickhead,' and it went south from there." He replaced the notebook with a decisive click of his pen. "It's supposed to be a family area, sir. Children are present."

I sighed. "Any of our other friends in there?"

"Not that I know of."

"Okay."

Sorya and I got up from our comfy couch and walked to the game room. Five feet away from the door, I could hear them arguing.

"Scared you'll piss your knickers, Peter? Just give it a go already!"

"I'm lining up my shot, asshole. Get ahold of yourself. I'm juuuussst about ready."

"Come on already, Peter. One . . . two . . . ."

We walked in, and it was just the two of them. They'd driven the other guests away. They stood side-by-side, arms and legs spread. Someone had shoved a pool table out of the way. They looked like gunslingers facing bank robbers in the old West.

I raised my voice. "Hey! You two! Cut it out. Your behavior is a—"

Peter turned towards me, surprised to see me, and his arm lowered . . .

I saw it coming . . .

. . . the dart shot forward . . .

Nothing I could do . . .

Amalia's words echoed in my head. *It's all fun and games until someone—*

Blam!

—loses an eye.

I fell backward onto a couch and sunk to the floor.

I ripped out the dart and handed it to Zed while viscous fluid ran down my shirt. I glared at Peter with one good eye, and he backed away. "I'm sorry, I didn't see you," he said, lifting his shoulders in apology.

"Well, I see you, but now with no depth perception."

Zed dialed his phone with his free hand, his face a mask of panic. "Eddie's gonna be so mad."

Sorya was on her phone as well. "Let's go."

"Where?"

"Just follow me," Sorya said and handed me her sunglasses.

A taxi ride later, we arrived at the morgue, and Sorya sweet-talked hunky Dr. Mateo into letting us see Joy's body. He retrieved it from cold storage for us. Joy's body lay in repose on a standard stainless-steel table. Sinks and hoses lined the walls, a scale hung from the ceiling, and red-lined bio trash cans stood next to the table.

Sorya went to work with slick expertise. She donned gloves and grabbed a scalpel.

I stopped her with a hand on her upper arm. She paused, confused. "I need to say something, Sorya."

I touched Joy's cold, stiff hand. "I'm sorry, Joy. You have the most beautiful eyes. Thank you for giving me one." I said a small prayer and nodded to Sorya to continue.

Sorya did what she had to. While she worked, I handled my own eye removal and then popped Joy's in.

Flashbacks of Joy's life zinged through my brain, and the strength of her memories forced me to lean against the mortuary table.

Suddenly, I became her.

My stomach ached with hunger from the extreme poverty of my childhood. I curled up on a thin mattress next to my skinny sister, promising I'd make it better someday. My head whipped back with a punch to the face, but I still used my looks to make money. I bore other things that made my body sing with rage and pain.

Joy's secrets, which never should have been shared.

Jealousy and admiration for Mitzi and my determination to succeed in Hollywood. Quint offering a well-deserved lifeline. Simple money, a just reward, and finally appreciation from a handsome man.

Which changed into suspicion that Quint had tricked me, yet another man in a long line of them using me for their ends.

Fear at the sight of his cold eyes.

I gagged as she held her last breath, panicking with her desperation.

I clawed for air, my chest heaving in and out.

"Waylon! What is it?" Sorya grabbed my shoulders, shaking me.

"She struggled. Dying by drowning . . . ." I stared at Sorya and shuddered. I couldn't stop shaking. "You're right. It's a horrible way to die."

"Yes, it is."

She guided me to a chair, and I sunk into it.

Sorya closed the white body bag around Joy's head. I talked while she worked. "She was a complex person. She made some bad choices, and it led her down a destructive path, but she admired Mitzi as much as she despised her. I can't help feeling if someone had gotten to her earlier, helped her a little bit, it would have turned out differently."

Sorya hugged me. "Let's tell Mitzi. Maybe we can do something to remember her and honor the good parts of her legacy."

"I'd like that."

I didn't know what Eddie said to Peter and Zed, but they wouldn't meet my eyes when they apologized the next morning. They sat separated in the hotel lobby. Eddie snapped something about discipline and control, and Clipper kept things sharp and tight. Everest rode herd on Peter. No one acted out in front of Eddie. I suspected he threatened to take literal body parts.

Mateo came to say farewell to Sorya, but he also had a message for me. He cornered me as we were getting in the taxis, leaned close so his stupid, sexy, minty breath wafted past my nose when he said, "Take good care of her, my friend, or I'll fly up there, knock your teeth out and make sweet, sweet love to her until she forgets all about you. You give me an opening, one opening, and she's mine."

I narrowed my eyes at him. "See that mountain of a man over there? The big Black guy who looks easy-going, but isn't?"

He nodded, deflating a little at the sight of Everest.

"And the tousled-haired Australian next to him?" Zed heard me and flashed his teeth.

"Uh. Yes?"

"They're my friends. Come anywhere near Sorya and they'll beat you to a pulp. And the dude with the computer? He's smarter than you by a hundred-to-one. You make a plane reservation, even under a fake name, and he'll see you coming. And the skinny, smarmy one wearing a suit even though it's ninety-five degrees? Those two together can make you disappear. They'll make your body vanish, sell your house, erase your birth certificate, give your life savings to charity, and if you have a dog, a cat, a fish, or a houseplant, they'll find it a good home. No one will remember you. Not even your mother."

Clipper gave Mateo a dead-eyed stare, and Peter snapped the medical examiner's photo.

Mateo blanched.

"So, stay the hell away. This is your one and only warning."

Then I walked away and didn't look back.

The plane took off and we reached altitude. Sorya tapped me on the shoulder. "What did you say to Mateo before we left?"

I shrugged, pulling the airline magazine from the back pocket of the seat in front of me. "Do these things have crossword puzzles?"

She punched me on the arm. "I mean it. What did you say? He turned pale."

With a sigh, I turned to her. "I told him you were my girl, and he'd better stay away."

"Of course, I'm your girl." She blushed a little, not much, just a little highlight on her cheekbones.

"You know, Sorya," I lowered my voice to make sure we couldn't be heard. "I've been thinking about something Zed told me."

"What?"

"While we are dealing with my, err . . . " I glanced down at my crotch, "ah…colossal problem, it occurred to me that . . ." I looked both ways and lowered my voice even more. "It occurred to me my tongue has never fallen off."

She lifted her eyes to meet mine, her mouth a big "O," then she lifted the armrest between us and snuggled up next to me. "Oh, Waylon. I can't wait to get home."

The End

ACKNOWLEDGMENTS

Thank you to Joseph Felo, D.O., Chief Medical Examiner, Cuyahoga County, Ohio for helping me get my medical details right. Any errors are mine, and mine alone, and probably because I wrote something without consulting him first. I'd also like to thank Harry Wingo, faculty member at the College of Information & Cyberspace, National Defense University, for his help with a military practice . Again, all errors are mine. Last, I'd like to acknowledge Officer Thomas Syto for answering questions about police procedure.

ABOUT THE AUTHOR

J.D. Blackrose wrote The Summoner's Mark urban fantasy trilogy for Bell Bridge Books, consisting of *Demon Kissed, Fae Crossed,* and *Hell Bound.* She's published *The Soul Wars, The Devil's Been Busy,* and *Zombie Cosmetologist* novellas through Falstaff Books.

She's published short stories such as "Don't Fool an Earth Witch," in *Mother's Revenge,* "The Book Burning," in *Curiosities,* and "Poisoned by Sugar," in *Witches, Warriors, and Wise Women.* Her short story, "The Ghost Train," was published by *Third Flatiron* in their Spring 2019 Anthology and Best of 2019 Anthology. "Welcome, Death," appeared in the *Jewish Book of Horror* in Fall, 2020 as did "The Space Ark," in the *HOZ Journal of Speculative Fiction.*

Under the name Joelle M. Reizes, she co-wrote a children's Hannukah story entitled, "Courageous Candles." She blogs, reviews books, and does author interviews on www.slipperywords.com.

FRIENDS OF FALSTAFF

Thank You to All our Falstaff Books Patrons, who get extra digital content each month! To be featured here and see what other great rcwards wc offcr, go to www.patrcon.com/falstaffbooks.

PATRONS

Dino Hicks
John Hooks
John Kilgallon
Larissa Lichty
Travis & Casey Schilling
Staci-Leigh Santore
Sheryl R. Hayes
Scott Norris
Samuel Montgomery-Blinn
Junkle

Lightning Source UK Ltd.
Milton Keynes UK
UKHW011952300522
403757UK00009B/237/J

9 781645 541592